An Unexpected Wish

A Lady's Wish Series by Eileen Richards

An Unexpected Wish

An Honorable Wish

AN UNEXPECTED WISH

Eileen Richards

LYRICAL PRESS
Kensington Publishing Corp.
www.kensingtonbooks.com

LYRICAL PRESS BOOKS are published by

Kensington Publishing Corp.
119 West 40th Street
New York, NY 10018

All Kensington titles, imprints, and distributed lines are available at special quantity discounts for bulk purchases for sales promotion, premiums, fund-raising, educational, or institutional use.

Special book excerpts or customized printings can also be created to fit specific needs. For details, write or phone the office of the Kensington Sales Manager: Kensington Publishing Corp., 119 West 40th Street, New York, NY 10018. Attn. Sales Department. Phone: 1-800-221-2647.

Lyrical Press logo Reg. U.S. Pat. & TM Off.

First Electronic Edition: October 2015
eISBN-13: 978-1-60183-443-0
eISBN-10: 1-60183-443-8

First Print Edition: October 2015
ISBN-13: 978-1-60183-444-7
ISBN-10: 1-60183-444-6

Printed in the United States of America

For my mom, who taught me to never give up on my dreams, and for Rick, who shows me every single day what love really is. Love you more, babe.

Acknowledgments

While writing a book may be a lonely business, the journey to publication is not. It's hard, bumpy, and filled with potholes, but not lonely. Thank God!

For my dear friends who read this book so many times you were ready to kill me, thank you. Erica Monroe, Darla Kraft, Reagan Phillips, and Irene Thomas: You guys put up with me more than you had to. I'm sorry I didn't listen more. You are the best friends a writer could ever have.

For my RWA Chapter-mates: Carolina Romance Writers rock! Thank you for giving me that once-a-month crazy-writer fix that I need so much.

My kids: You know who you are. Thanks for the encouragement and love. For giving me the time to write and not letting me feel guilty about it. And just for the record, Son, it's not smut, it's romance. There's a difference.

Any mistakes found in this book, historical, grammatical or otherwise, are mine. Sorry. I have to give a shout-out to Martin, my editor, who really tried to catch them all. Thank you for believing in me and in this series. I still find myself wondering why. Finally, for Jessica, my agent, thanks for agreeing to take this journey with me. Here's hoping the roads get smoother as we go.

I know I'm forgetting so many who have encouraged me, pushed me, and shoved a drink in my hand through the rejections. Thank you. All of you make the journey a great ride. It wouldn't be the same without you.

Chapter One

"Thereby decree the word *spinster* be stricken from all manner of speech." Anne Townsend waved her makeshift wand from her perch at the top of the Fairy Steps. She cleared her voice in her most royal manner. "Furthermore, the word shall be stricken from every document in my fair kingdom!" The small village of Beetham shimmered in the gold cast of the late autumn sun, completely unaffected by her pronouncement.

Typical. She threw the stick down the uneven stones she'd just climbed.

Plain, practical, boring Anne
Was too plain to catch a man.
If she caught the eye of one,
To her sister he would run.

The truth of the hurtful childhood taunt stared back at her every blasted day. She was plain. She'd never attracted any man she deemed suitable. It wasn't as if she was being picky. He just had to be reasonably wealthy, reasonably handsome, reasonably witty, and not stupid.

Therein lay the difficulty. No man had met all the requirements. If he was handsome, he was either poor or witless. If he wasn't handsome, he had funds and was as old as the Fairy Steps.

It was of little matter. A modern woman made the best of things. Modern women didn't settle for some old shriveled-up man. And she would be a modern woman if it killed her.

Five years ago, the lure of magic in the Fairy Steps had stirred her romantic heart. A wish could fix anything: poverty, loneliness, and love. God, what a ninny she'd been.

The only thing that fixed poverty and loneliness was money.

Daily her sisters, Sophia and Juliet, whined about their lack of funds. They argued over hair ribbons. They complained about their old, unfashionable dresses. Her sisters had no inkling of the trouble they were in.

They needed fuel for the approaching winter, food for larder, and coins to pay the two servants Anne couldn't do without. It took blunt. Blunt was what she needed more than anything.

If the confounded fairy showed up today, Anne wouldn't hesitate. She'd wish for the ready. Pots of it.

Anne closed her eyes and embraced the rare moment of peace. No arguing, whining, bickering, nagging, tormenting, or complaining. Just beautiful, glorious silence.

A cold gust of wind blew the tendrils of hair from her face and chased a shiver up her spine. Dried leaves rattled behind her as they skated across the rock. A twig snapped behind her.

Her eyes flew open. She wasn't alone.

Anne's heart pounded so hard she could hear it thumping in her ears. Hair lifted on the back of her neck. Anger warred with fear. Anger won.

She picked up a good-sized limb from the ground and gripped it with both hands. "Show yourself, coward."

"Speak your heart's desire, my lady." An odd, otherworldly voice filled the air. The breeze kicked up again.

Anne tightened her grip on the tree limb. She threw her shoulders back and stood taller. She wasn't going down without a fight.

"You climbed the steps properly and earned a wish, you have." The voice cackled.

She lowered her arm. Blast, this was nothing but a prank. Probably some child bribed by Sophia. She'd box the child's ears and send him on his way. She'd deal with her sister when she got home. "The joke is over. Come on out."

"'Tis a magical place you've found, as well you know for the many times you've climbed these steps." The crackling voice sounded old, not childlike.

"Enough!" Anne was sick to death of being the whipping boy.

A wizened, bent old woman with a twisted cane shuffled out of the trees at the foot of the stairs. "Always you must see to believe."

"You must think me dicked in the nob, madam. There are no

fairies." Anne threw the limb into the bushes behind her. "Be gone now, and tell my sister Sophia to try harder next time."

"How hasty and untrusting you young people are. Make your wish, child."

Anne studied the old lady. She looked like one of the Gypsies who came around at harvest time. How much coin had she bilked out of Sophia for this prank? "Fine. I wish you to be gone."

The old woman cackled. "I should take you up on that, but your heart speaks differently. It speaks of struggle and loneliness."

What did this woman know of her life? "I'm sick of this game. Good day, ma'am." Anne turned toward the path.

"Wish for anything, my lady. Wish grandly." A gleeful, wicked light gleamed in the old woman's eyes. She lifted her cane and jabbed it toward Anne. "Little wishes are for little souls. They are not for the likes of you. Now wish. You are wasting my time."

Well, rats, she might as well wish for something. It would shut the woman up, everyone would have their fun, and Anne could go home.

"Perhaps a prince? Grand properties? Great beauty?" the old woman teased.

Anne dropped her hands and glared at the old hag. "You are bamming me."

"Anything is possible, miss." The old lady cackled. "You'll never know, if you don't believe."

Anne had the old woman now. She'd make the wish so impossible, so farfetched, that it couldn't be fulfilled. No fairy magic could conjure love. Everyone knew that. The mad woman would look like a fool. "Very well. I wish for a handsome man so rich that he will be able to provide a Season in Town for my sisters. He must also be passionately in love with me."

"Done!" the old lady crowed.

"You cannot be serious!" Anne turned to glower down at the old lady who had just taken the fun out of the game, but found no one there. "Well, rats, where did she go?"

Dried leaves danced where the old bat had stood. Maniacal laughter echoed in the wind. The old witch probably knew the game was up.

"How foolish do they think I am?" Perfect. Now she was talking to herself. Her sisters were going to drive her crazy. "Wishes, indeed."

"Were you granted a wish? Or are you the fairy?" A deep male voice, filled with laughter, echoed up the stone steps.

So much for peace and tranquility. Suddenly the Fairy Steps were the most popular place in Beetham.

With a huff, Anne leaned over the edge of the steps. Her mouth fell open. At the foot of the steps, seated on a large black horse, was the most handsome man she'd ever seen. Gorgeous, dark wavy hair curled around his high collar. Blue eyes danced with laughter. A navy blue coat had been tailored just right to fit his broad shoulders. Tight-fitting buckskin breeches outlined muscular legs. *Thank you, Providence, for buckskins*, thought Anne.

She swallowed to ease the dryness in her throat. "Excuse me, sir, did you pass an old lady on your way up the path?"

He smiled and those crinkles appeared around his blue-blue eyes. Anne fought the urge to swoon. Seriously? No man made her swoon. She looked down at his face again and fought the urge to gape.

"Depends. Are you the wisher or the fairy?" The elegant tone of his voice echoed a bit against all that stone.

Anne was done with being the ball for the bat. It was outside of enough. She crossed her arms over her chest. "Sir, if you didn't pass her, then just say so."

His smile fell and he shook his head. "An unbeliever."

"There is nothing wrong with being sensible."

"You are right, of course. Perhaps the fairy will grant you a wish for some fun in your life."

Good Lord, Anne hoped the fairy didn't hear that statement. She'd probably take it on as a challenge. Sophia was forever accusing Anne of extracting all the fun out of life. "Who are you?"

She cursed her propensity to speak before thinking. His face grew hard at her rudeness. Anne pulled her shawl tighter around her shoulders. Her embarrassment aside, no one came to Beetham without a reason for being here. It was ten days from London and so far off the main road, it rarely showed up on a map of the area.

"Nathaniel Matthews, at your service, ma'am." He touched his hat.

Oh no, he definitely had a reason. Anne's heart tripped in her chest. Her stomach clenched. He wasn't here for pleasure. He was here to stop the engagement.

"You're Lady Danford's grandson."

"Yes, ma'am. She is my maternal grandmother."

His tone hit her like the cold November wind blowing off the steps. She shivered and wrapped her shawl a bit tighter around her.

"Why are you at the Fairy Steps?" She narrowed her eyes at him. "You're lost."

He had the grace to blush. "It's been a while since I've been here."

What man couldn't find his way home? Men were supposed to be good at directions. It was probably more likely he was too busy to call on his grandmother. Did he not know how lucky he was to have her? "Take the path back to the lane. The Lodge is down farther, to the right."

His dark eyes flashed. "Thank you, Miss—You didn't tell me your name." His tone, saber sharp, cut through her skin to the fear she buried deep. This was not a man to cross.

"Anne Townsend." She dipped a curtsy.

"Thank you, Miss Townsend." He tipped his hat again. "Perhaps we shall see each other again?"

"I'm sure we will, sir." He reined in his horse and turned toward the lane. Anne watched him disappear into the woods. *Blast.* As if things couldn't get any worse, she'd just angered the one man who could make or break the match that would save her family. She just couldn't keep her mouth shut.

Nathaniel followed Miss Townsend's directions and arrived at the Lodge in short order. His brain had a natural aversion to coming here. Too many bad memories.

The dark gray stone house looked like the set of a bad play filled with ghosts and tragedy. He could vouch for the tragedy. It was tragedy that brought him here the first time.

Too many images filled his head. The sound of a gun being fired. Pity on the face of the man who'd ruined his father so completely that a gunshot wound to the head was the only answer. The fear and uncertainty of what would happen to him and his brother. There was nothing he could have done to stop those events. He hated that he couldn't avoid the memories, couldn't move past them.

Lady Danford, his grandmother on his mother's side, had brought Nathaniel and Tony to the Lodge. Yet even her kindness couldn't remove the pain of those awful years. Her husband had been knighted and had left her a comfortable sum when he passed. With no other heir, the house would one day be Nathaniel's.

As much as he loved his grandmother, he hated what the house represented: his father's weak mind and foolish decisions. Decisions that would have left Nathaniel and his brother to fend for themselves if not for their grandmother. Decisions made trying to keep up with the *ton*. Decisions that left Nathaniel no choice but to sell the house in Sussex to pay his father's debts.

Nathaniel wouldn't be staying long.

"Sir, we were about to send a search party for you!" the footman said as he approached.

"Has the carriage arrived with my trunks?" Nathaniel dismounted and handed over the reins to the worried footman.

"Yes, sir," the footman said as he led the horse away.

Damn, his ability to get lost was well known and once again affirmed by the servants. Nathaniel pulled down on his jacket and girded himself to enter the house. Though much of it had been completely redone, it hadn't wiped away the images in his head. Like a hammer to his skull, they hit him hard as he entered.

He shoved the bad memories deep as he found his grandmother in her overdone, floral drawing room. Dust motes danced in the late afternoon sunlight that was streaming into the room. "I see you are holding court as usual, Grandmother."

"There you are. I thought I was going to have to send someone after you." Lady Danford's tone was sharp, but her smile was warm. She reached out a hand to him.

Nathaniel clasped it and raised it to his lips. Her skin was cool and papery. "I thought you at death's door from the sound of your letter."

"You're gone for nearly a year and treat me to impudence." She sat back in her chair and pulled her coverlet about her legs. "Come kiss me and tell me why you have stayed away so long."

He pressed a kiss to her papery cheek. "Beetham doesn't have a port."

Lady Danford laughed. "I've missed you, Son."

He studied her for a long moment. The years had taken their toll. He'd lost his parents, but she'd gained two grandsons to care for. He took a seat near her and crossed his legs. It was time to get to the point of his visit; the only reason he'd come back to Beetham.

"I take it I was summoned because my brother, Tony, is in some sort of trouble." Nathaniel leaned back in his chair, his hands folding and unfolding. "I've paid his gambling debts from Cambridge."

"He's a young man. You remember what that's like, don't you?" She smoothed the coverlet over her legs.

Nathaniel winced. "I'm not that old."

"Good heavens, your own father had more of a life than you do." Her voice was sharp.

"Don't compare me to him," Nathaniel said rather sharply. *Damn.* Lady Danford watched him closely. "Forgive me, ma'am," he muttered.

"Still haven't let that go?" She shook her head. "Nathaniel, Son—"

He stood and paced to the window, staring out. "We aren't discussing this." The last thing he wanted was a discussion of his cowardly father.

"Our past always comes back to haunt us in one way or another." Lady Danford's voice was soft but firm. "At least until we deal with it and move on."

Nathaniel let the comment pass. It was a reoccurring argument. "Has Tony been giving you any trouble during his visit?"

"No more than usual." Lady Danford picked up her embroidery. "He's infatuated with one of the local young ladies."

"Next week it will be some other girl." Tony changed women like most changed stockings. Nathaniel could hardly keep up. "You brought me this far from London because he's involved with a local girl?"

"He's driving me to distraction," Lady Danford huffed. "He's spouting that god-awful poetry he writes. All that education to write bad poetry."

"A quality education," Nathaniel quipped.

"You had the same, and you didn't turn out that way," she grumbled.

Thanks to his father's propensity for gambling away every shilling they possessed, Nathaniel had been head of the family at sixteen. He had been forced to grow up fast and figure out how to rebuild the family fortunes. It left little time for poetry. "Who is the young lady?"

"Sophia Townsend. She is the prettiest girl in the county, until she opens her mouth."

Nathaniel's bark of laughter filled the room. "So I take it you don't approve."

"The girl is a twit."

He fought the urge to chuckle further. "Townsend? Would she be related to Miss Anne Townsend?"

"Anne is her older sister." Lady Danford eyed him speculatively. "How do you know Anne?"

"I happened upon her on my way here," he said casually. He didn't need another person making note of his inability to get from one place to another without getting lost.

"She gave you directions to get home, didn't she?" Lady Danford cackled.

Nathaniel felt the heat rise in his face again. Hell, this was worse than when he was a child. "I did *not* get lost."

His grandmother rolled her eyes. "Where did you find her, then?"

"At the Fairy Steps." He flicked a string off his sleeve. Truth be told, he'd wanted to find the steps first, hoping for a moment of peace before going to the Lodge and facing his demons.

"She must be hiding from her sisters again."

Good to know he wasn't the only one who hid from his family. "What's wrong with this chit that Tony is interested in, if her own sister hides from her?"

"I'll let you decide when you meet her." Lady Danford motioned for a footman. "Bring tea and wake Tony. A good dousing of cold water should do the trick."

"He's still abed?" Tony had obviously been spending too much time with gentlemen. "Things will be different when I get him to Town."

"And you call Tony a dreamer." Lady Danford's tone was acerbic. "He'll be out every night with the rest of the young bucks."

Nathaniel sighed heavily. Tony's spending habits were eating into the cushion Nathaniel had worked hard to build with his investments in the textile business. If Tony wasn't going to contribute, he'd have to marry well. "What are this girl's connections?"

"Her half brother inherited the title, but doesn't support his sisters." Lady Danford had a white-knuckled grip on her cane. "I have no patience for such a lack of responsibility."

Nathaniel had no doubt she would use her cane on this missing brother if she could. "Who is he?" He'd been so distracted by his meeting with Miss Townsend that he hadn't connected her to *that* Townsend family. Surely she wasn't related to—

"He's a baronet. Sir John Townsend. The family is very old."

Nathaniel set down his teacup with a rattle. Hell, it couldn't be. All the way up here?

"Mind the china, Son. I have no desire to replace it."

What did he do to deserve the continuing irritation that was Sir John Townsend? Or his relations? Sir Walter, the elder Townsend, might as well have put the gun in his father's hand after winning everything Nathaniel's family had. Sir Walter had died before Nathaniel could confront him with what he'd done. Now Sir John was bent on continuing down the same path as his father. Nathaniel couldn't allow that to happen. He couldn't let another man suffer what he'd seen his father suffer at the hands of Sir Walter, not that Sir John seemed to be experiencing the same success his father had.

And Tony's marriage would join the Townsend family to their own. Over his dead body.

"Are you sure he's not providing for his sisters?" Nathaniel didn't know why he felt the need to try to salvage something of Townsend's reputation. The man couldn't be so bad as to not take care of his own family. But perhaps Townsend was following in his father's ruthless footsteps.

"I'm unsure of the particulars, but Anne brought her sisters to Beetham five years ago with nothing but the clothes on their backs," Lady Danford said. "God knows what would have happened if I'd turned them away. They lease the old gamekeeper's cottage on the estate."

His jaw tightened and hatred chewed at his stomach. "I only hope that it's not too late to stop the engagement."

"Had she a dowry, it would be a good match." Lady Danford sipped her tea thoughtfully.

"Not to that family." Nathaniel stood and paced the room. He flexed his hands, itching to punch something.

Lady Danford carefully set her teacup down. "I thought you let that go, Son." She watched him closely, her face soft with understanding.

"Justice must be served." His voice was hard.

"What justice? Your father took the cowardly way out. He killed himself." Lady Danford's tone was cold, emotionless.

"Townsend forced him to when he lost everything. For that there must be justice."

"Oh, Nathaniel, what have you done?"

Nathaniel winced at the disappointment in her tone. The past ate at him like acid on skin. "I've given Sir John a taste of his own medicine. He is determined to repeat his father's mistakes" He stared out through the window at the garden. Devoid of leaves, it was as desolate as he.

A wrinkled hand tugged at his arm. "This is beneath you, Son."

"I had to stop Sir John before he ruined another man." Before he caused a good friend to shoot himself to escape his problems and left his family destitute. Nathaniel's hands tightened into fists. "I'll take Tony back to Town with me. Distance will cure any emotion he feels for this young lady."

Lady Danford sighed. "You can't stay longer?"

He winced. "I only came because you implied an emergency. Besides, you'll be in Town in a few months for the Season."

"I've not decided yet." Lady Danford shot him a meaningful look.

He looked back at her, startled by this sudden revelation. The London Season was Lady Danford's favorite time. He always looked forward to having his grandmother at the town house in London. "You won't miss a Season in London. You thrive on the gossip."

"I'm getting too old and stiff for the long carriage ride, dear."

Nathaniel watched his grandmother. She moved slowly. Her face was etched with deepening lines. Her shoulders had a slight stoop. He'd never thought of his grandmother as old until today. Panic clogged his throat and he had to clear it before he could speak. "Are you sick?"

Lady Danford laughed. "I'm just old, not sick."

At that moment, Tony burst into the room. "Nathaniel! You're here? Why?"

"Good to see you, as well. I'd say you look a bit worse for wear." Nathaniel took in his brother's wrinkled linen and lack of a coat. His hair was a mop of uncombed curls. At least he had shaved. "Didn't bring your valet?"

"Still the stick, I see. I'm sorry I'm not up to your usual standards." Tony slumped into a nearby chair and grinned. "Still, I make this look good."

"I was hoping university was going to make you realize your place in the world," he said dryly. "What have you been doing here at Beetham?"

"He didn't get in until almost dawn," Lady Danford grumbled. "Woke the staff trying to get into the house."

"What is there to do at that hour in Beetham?" Nathaniel said.

"Shared a pint with the locals." Tony ran his fingers through the tangle of his hair. "I repeat, what brings you here, dear brother? I know you didn't come all this way just to see me."

There was a bitterness in his tone that Nathaniel didn't understand. "I'm not allowed to visit our grandmother?" Nathaniel raised an eyebrow.

"You never leave London." Tony glared at his grandmother. "I suspect you told him about Sophia."

"Yes, she did."

Tony slouched lower in the chair. "I think I may have found my future wife. I've a mind to paint a picture of her."

"Paint? You?"

"It has to be better than the poetry," said Lady Danford.

Tony frowned. "It's not that bad."

Nathaniel laughed. "Why did you stop writing?" Tony had a tendency to flit from interest to interest, never staying too long. Currently he was supposed to be studying law.

"I couldn't get anyone to publish it. But Sophia inspires me. Such a beauty."

"Let's be honest here. Tony, your poetry is awful." Lady Danford waved the maid over with the tea tray. "You need a focus for your life."

Tony raised his chin defiantly. "I have a focus. Sophia and my art."

Nathaniel sighed. Once again it was up to him to be the responsible one, the voice of reason. "And do you propose to support this woman with your art? Have you given any thought to her connections or fortune?"

"I don't care what her connections are, nor that she lacks a fortune," Tony said. "It's not as if we need the money."

"The lack of fortune is a material issue," Nathaniel pointed out. "With your spending habits, we'll be in the workhouse in no time."

"I take it back. You're a bigger snob than you are a stick," Tony said. "You'll have to increase my allowance after we marry. And provide the younger sister with a Season. I suppose the eldest is firmly on the shelf. You'll probably have to provide for her as well."

Nathaniel cocked an eyebrow at his brother. The man had it all planned. Except it was the vision of a boy, not a man. "Why would I do that?"

Tony looked puzzled that he should ask. "It would only be right given they have no other protection."

"While it's honorable that you wish to take care of these young women, do you think it wise to marry someone of such reduced circumstances?" Nathaniel fought to keep the edge of impatience out of his voice. His brother was acting like a child. "We were left nothing by our father. He had no entailed property. You must consider what income a bride will bring to the marriage."

"You speak of dynastic marriage," Tony said. "I would rather marry for love than live such a cold existence."

"Poverty is a cold existence. Your young lady may not be suited for it. Unless you marry a fortune, there are few choices."

"We aren't poor."

"Nor are we wealthy, though your brother's investments and careful management have improved our circumstances," Lady Danford said. "It's time you did your part as well."

"And doing my part is marrying someone for her fortune? Someone I don't love?" Tony slammed his fist into the side of his chair. "That never made anyone in this family very happy."

"Enough!" Lady Danford pulled herself up slowly from her chair with the aid of her cane. "Don't assume that my marriage or that of your parents was less than it was. I loved my husband."

Nathaniel studied the stubborn look on his brother's face. "Tony, if you are serious about marrying this girl, then you have some decisions of your own to make. As of your birthday, your allowance will cease. Find a way to support your new family. Take your place with me in London. Practice law as you were trained to do."

"Gentlemen do not work." Tony jumped to his feet. "Nathaniel, be reasonable. Four months' notice is not enough time."

"All of us must attain adulthood at some point, Brother. Even you." Nathaniel sipped his tea, ignoring the growing color in his brother's face. "I suggest you think long and hard as to whether you can afford this young woman."

"Grandmother—" Tony whined.

Lady Danford paused at the door. "Tony, I must agree with Nathaniel on this. The next move is yours." The door closed behind her with a sharp bang.

Tony stared at the closed door. "She's in a fine temper."

Nathaniel shrugged. "With good reason, I think." He had to know where they stood. "Have you proposed to Miss Sophia?"

"Not yet," Tony mumbled.

Good. It would be a bit easier to extricate Tony if he hadn't proposed. "But her family is expecting you to?"

"Of course." Tony looked up. "This is madness. Why can't I marry for love?"

"You can—just make sure she brings money to the marriage."

Tony groaned and collapsed back in his chair. "I hate this."

Anger bloomed as Nathaniel witnessed his brother's petulant behavior. "You do realize who her father was, don't you?"

Tony raised his head, his eyes cold. "I'm not an idiot. I don't hold the children accountable for their parents' mistakes."

"Unlike me?" Nathaniel held his brother's gaze for a long time, waiting for confirmation. While Nathaniel had borne the brunt of the stigma and cleanup after his father's suicide, Tony had been protected from it all. He'd only been nine at the time, too young to remember the worst of it.

"I didn't mean that." Tony stood and started pacing in front of the fireplace. "I thought you'd be more supportive, especially given the nightmare that was our parents' marriage."

Nathaniel sighed. "If her relations were anyone else, I might consider, but not this family."

"It was a long time ago, Nathaniel." Tony sat across from him. "Do you really blame Sophia and her sisters for their father's sins?"

Nathaniel studied his brother for a moment. How much should he tell him? He fought the urge to protect him, but decided against it. It was time for Tony to deal with the consequences of his choices. "Have you met Sir John, the brother?"

Tony shook his head.

At least he wasn't moving in those circles—yet. "I caught him cheating at cards at White's."

"Does Grandmother know?"

"No one does." Nor would they, if he had anything to do with it. "You certainly can pick them, Tony."

"I had no idea!" Tony plopped back into his chair and draped one leg over the arm. "I still think you should meet the family. It will at least prove that the sins of the father have nothing to do with the children."

Nathaniel sighed. "If you insist." He had no doubt that the girls would be charming. He already liked Anne Townsend. Hell, even Sir John was charming when he wanted to be, but good manners did not imply scrupulous behavior. In his experience, good manners served more as a veneer for the unscrupulous to hide behind.

Anne walked briskly toward home as the wind picked up. She pulled her shawl around her and quickened her pace. The old lady she'd spotted at the steps must be from Beetham. Or perhaps the Gypsies were back in the village, though they usually went south before now. It'd be easy enough to find out. Beetham was a thriving community of gossips. Someone would know who the old lady was.

She should be focusing on Nathaniel Matthews. Not because he was handsome as sin, but because of why he was here.

To keep his brother from marrying Sophia.

Instead, she was worrying about some old lady and fairies. But there were no fairies.

The air came alive with sound, causing Anne to jump. She looked around her to see Cecil Worth, the vicar, leaning against a tree, watching the path back to the cottage. She quickly stepped back out of his line of sight. Maybe he wouldn't see her. Please God, don't let him see her.

"Miss Townsend!"

Lovely. Could this day get any worse? "Mr. Worth." She dipped a curtsy. "What brings you out this far?"

"I was hoping to find you, Miss Townsend. Miss Sophia said you walk this way most days." He doffed his hat and bowed prettily. He was dressed in a blue coat that stretched across his girth.

"You came to see me? For what reason?" In the three years he had been the vicar of St. Michael's, he'd never even noticed her before.

"Do I need a reason to visit a young lady?" He chuckled as he replaced his hat with a flourish. "My dear Miss Townsend, I have shocked you."

"Sir, I—uh." Shock was an understatement. While the man never missed a chance to speak with the lovely Sophia, he wasted no time on plain Anne Townsend. Being plain and poor had a dampening effect on most men's ardor.

He moved closer to her and smiled. "I imagine you have come to expect only sermons from me."

She took a step back, not liking the strange heat in his pale gray eyes or his scent. The man had apparently bathed in perfume. "You are the vicar, sir. Why would I expect anything else?"

He clutched dramatically at his chest. "Ah, you wound me, Miss Townsend."

Anne forced a laugh at his comical expression. "Then I offer my apologies."

"Apology accepted." He offered her his arm.

Anne took it and fell into step beside him. "How is your mother, Mr. Worth?"

"She is quite well. I will tell her you asked after her."

Mrs. Worth would probably give him a severe tongue-lashing for walking with Anne. Anne and her sisters were not rich enough for her precious son, despite having a baronet as a father.

"I wanted to speak with you privately before I spoke to my mother." He paused, looking down at her hand on his arm. "Such a small hand for the burdens you carry."

"Burdens?" Anne desperately needed him to get to the point. She had the beginning of a headache brought on by his cologne.

"You've taken care of your sisters for years, all on your own. Such a strength of character." He stroked his hand over hers, caressing her skin.

Anne snatched her hand away and put some distance between them. She suddenly didn't like that she was in these woods alone with Cecil Worth. She glanced around, hoping that perhaps someone else would also be walking in the woods this afternoon. But they were quite alone. Too alone. A frisson of fear coursed down her spine.

A twitter sounded in the trees around her. Was it the old lady? Please let it be the old lady. Anyone to keep her from being alone with the creepy vicar.

Mr. Worth shot her a pitying look that caused her temper to heat. "Have you heard from your brother?"

"My brother? No. I suppose he is still in London."

"Being so connected to a baronet, I can't imagine why you would abandon the position it offers you and your sisters. I imagine he worries about you all. Three young women quite unprotected."

John, worry about them? As if that would happen. Anger bubbled up and out of Anne's mouth before she could stop it. "Thank you for your concern, but this is none of your business."

"I only meant that it would be better for you if you had stayed with your brother."

"You've no idea what you're talking about." Anne started down the path toward the cottage.

"And to settle for being the companion of an elderly lady." Cecil Worth's voice echoed through the empty woods.

Anne turned and glared at him. "Lady Danford has been very generous. I feel privileged to be of assistance to her."

"Still, your brother . . ." He let the thought trail off.

Enough was enough. "Mr. Worth, my half brother's title doesn't put food on the table or provide heat for winter, and, for that matter, neither does he."

"I can see you still harbor anger toward him. As the vicar, I must urge you to forgive. He is your brother. Perhaps you may yet reconcile."

"I harbor no hope of our brother seeking reconciliation." It would be a cold day before she let John enter their life again. She glared at Mr. Worth and noted the odd expression on his face. He looked like a fish. She stepped farther away from him as he beamed at her, his gray eyes half-lidded and a crooked smile on his over-full lips.

She fought the urge to grimace. "I beg you to not discuss the matter further. Thank you for accompanying me. It looks to rain soon. I'd best hurry home. Good day, sir."

"But Miss Townsend—"

She ignored his cry and kept moving. Presumptuous man. How dare he cast judgment upon her and her sisters? They had no say in the decision. Leaning against a tree, she closed her eyes and still she could see his cloying, besotted face. "Fairy wishes indeed. Absurd."

Anne entered the cottage from the back. She hung up her pelisse and removed her bonnet. If, by some bizarre chance, she had been granted the wish she hadn't spoken, she needed to find a way to undo it before something even more horrid and humiliating happened. Lady Danford's grandson and Mr. Worth were quite enough.

"Anne, you will never guess!" Sophia rushed into the kitchen, but stopped short at the sight of her sister. "What's wrong with you? You're as pale as a corpse! An unkempt corpse."

"You've never seen a corpse, Sophia, unkempt or otherwise. Why do you ask?" She closed her eyes and tried to relax the scowl from her face.

"Your hair is tumbled, you are out of breath, and your expression is twisted more than usual." Sophia glided farther into the room, looking perfect, as usual.

"Thank you, Sophia, for reminding me." The comment flew out of her mouth before she could stop it. "If you have something to tell me, please do so."

"We are invited to Lady Danford's for supper and cards. But that isn't the best news. The best news is that Tony's brother is here!"

Anne bustled to the cabinet and placed cups out for tea. Just what she needed—another evening of men fawning over her sister. "Must we go?" She scooped tea into the pot.

"Of course we must go." Sophia plopped down into one of the kitchen chairs. "I will need a new gown."

Juliet huffed as she walked into the kitchen. "You had the last two new gowns, Sophia. I think it's Anne's turn." Seeing Anne laboring alone to set the table for tea, while Sophia sat like a princess, Juliet tsked and plated the cake.

"Anne doesn't need anything new. It's not like she'll attract notice." Sophia toyed with one of her dark, glossy curls.

Anne paused, the lid of the teapot suspended in her hand, and tossed aloft a prayer for patience. On the best days, Sophia was trying. Having Mr. Matthews in the village would only make her even more intolerable.

"Really, Sophia. You don't need to be cruel." Juliet plunked the cake on the table and glared at her sister.

"Thank you, Juliet." Anne poured hot water over the tea leaves and then returned the kettle to the stove. Sophia was working herself up into a fine temper.

"Well, I hope there will be some new people at the party." Sophia waved her hand dismissively. "I want to consider my options before accepting Tony. Did you see the invitations, Anne?"

"I thought you already had an understanding with Mr. Matthews," Anne said carefully. Her plans depended on Mr. Matthews coming up to scratch. If he didn't, she was going to have to come up with another way to buy the fuel they needed for winter. That meant borrowing money from Lady Danford. There was no other way.

"Not yet," Sophia said. "I do wish we could go to London for a Season. Then I could have the chance to marry a titled gentleman."

"Don't reach beyond your grasp. We have little to offer such a man," Anne said sharply.

"We? You do not, but I have had no end of offers, even without a fortune. Why wouldn't a titled gentleman want a pure, beautiful bride? Besides, the further I reach, the better I shall be able to take care of my sisters," Sophia said confidently.

Too confidently, in Anne's opinion. She rolled her eyes. This plan to marry off Sophia was getting more complex as the day went on.

"You have had no end of offers from the local gentry, Sophia," Juliet snapped. "I thought you liked Tony."

"I *do* like Tony," Sophia said. "I just want to make sure he's the right one. Anne, if you would only contact our brother, I'm sure he would invite us to London. I don't know why you hate him so. What has he ever done to you?"

Anne clenched her teeth to keep the bitter truth behind them. Her sisters would never know the extent of their half brother's perfidy, if she had anything to do with it. "We've not heard from him in five years," she reminded them. She took a seat at the table across from Juliet and poured the tea. "We must go on without him."

"But we can't be seen by Lady Danford's guests in these old rags," Sophia whined.

"Since we will be meeting some of them for the first time, they won't know these are our old dresses." Anne passed a cup of tea to Juliet.

Sophia huffed. "Why must we be so poor? Our father was a baronet!"

"Be thankful that our mother left us a little to live on," said Anne. That was something John couldn't take from them no matter how he tried.

"Sophia, some things we must accept," Juliet said, and pushed her old spectacles back on her face. "Besides, no one notices your dress."

"Well, it isn't fair." Sophia pushed away her cup. "I think I'll go see if I can make over a dress. I'll take the lace off of your dress, Anne.

And the flounce."

"As you wish." Anne waited until she heard Sophia's steps on the wooden stairs. "You don't have to defend me, Juliet."

"She can be so hateful," Juliet said. "As if her beauty entitles her to act like that."

"Sophia will save this family if she marries well. She can be a bit overbearing, but she knows her duty."

Juliet crossed her arms. "I don't have to like it."

Anne laughed. "Perhaps marriage will soften her up a bit."

"That's doubtful, isn't it? I don't want her to marry Tony. She's not good enough for him."

"I see." Anne laughed at the blush that rose on her sister's cheeks. "I'd wondered if you admired him."

"Don't be ridiculous."

So that was how it was. Juliet was suffering through her first infatuation. Better that she learn now that Sophia would capture everyone's attention. No matter what.

"Take care, Juliet. He has eyes for Sophia." Anne patted Juliet's hand.

"It doesn't matter. He sees me as a child, not a grown woman of eighteen," Juliet complained as she stood to clear the dishes.

"There will be other men like Mr. Matthews. I'm sure you'll have your pick of gentlemen in the coming years. You're every bit as pretty as Sophia, though I doubt she agrees."

Chapter Two

Nathaniel scrubbed his face with his hand as if he could chase away the tiredness caused by a sleepless night. After ten days on the road, he should have been exhausted, but his thoughts wouldn't let him rest.

He couldn't stop thinking about Anne Townsend. Every time he closed his eyes, she glared at him as her things were hauled off to pay her brother's debt. She cried. She accused.

He had enough guilt while awake. He didn't need it while he was sleeping.

He was now in hell, sitting where his father sat, behind the desk in the library, where his father put the gun to his head and started the nightmare that ended Nathaniel's childhood. Weak sunlight filtered through the windows where he dragged the curtains open. Anything to brighten the room up and remove the taint it had for him.

The household accounts for the Lodge lay open in front of him. He flipped through the pages, noting Miss Townsend's precise hand as she detailed each entry. Precise and controlled, much like the lady herself.

What was her place here at the Lodge? His grandmother had stated that Miss Townsend was her companion, yet the ledgers bore different proof. Lady Danford had always insisted that the household wasn't large enough for a housekeeper. She enjoyed handling the household accounts and managing the servants. Was Miss Townsend now acting as housekeeper?

Nathaniel didn't know how he felt about a Townsend having access to the household accounts. Yes, he reviewed them quarterly, even from London, but it was easy to steal if one had access and opportunity.

He hated to admit it, but Miss Townsend was taking prodigious care of his grandmother. She was modest and polite. No woman could be this perfect. There had to be a chink in her armor somewhere.

He rubbed at the pain in his stomach. He wasn't cut out for this revenge business. When he'd set out to ruin Sir John, he had no idea that Townsend had sisters. Nor did he expect to like any member of the Townsend family. He liked Anne Townsend a great deal.

A shadow fell in the doorway and a feminine voice said, "I'm sorry, sir. I didn't know anyone would be in here."

As if his thoughts had caused her to materialize, Anne Townsend entered the room and stood before the desk with her hands folded serenely in front of her. The dark green of her dress accentuated the creaminess of her skin. Lace clung to the bodice and sleeves, and a tight bun attempted, with mixed success, to control her dark hair. She was the picture of innocent womanhood. She had even left the door open for propriety. God, he hoped looks were deceiving, or he was in trouble.

Nathaniel stood and cleared his throat. "Miss Townsend. Grandmother said you'd be expected this morning. I was just going over the ledgers," he said as she approached. He motioned to one of the big leather chairs in front of the desk.

She shook her head at his offer of a chair, instead choosing to lean over the desk to look at the ledger. "Is there a problem?"

The scent of lemon filled Nathaniel's head. He could see the fragile bones of her hand as it rested on the desk for support. He cleared his throat again. "I usually check the ledgers for Grandmother. Just want to make sure things are in order."

She stepped back as if he had slapped her. But then her expression grew more serene. It was irritating as hell. "The ledgers were sent to you just last month, sir. Did you not receive them?"

He fought the urge to squirm. "I did not have the time to review them before leaving for Beetham."

"I see."

He needed a different tack. "How long have you been handling the accounts, Miss Townsend?"

She stared down her nose at him, her green eyes hard and cold as stone. "Your grandmother first asked me to record the receipts into the ledgers for her about a year ago. Her eyesight is failing, as you know."

Nathaniel set down his quill. "You only record the receipts, then?"

She rubbed her hands on her folded arms. So she wasn't so calm after all. "I might have assisted in some of the decisions made on the estate, but not without Lady Danford's approbation."

He flipped through the pages of the ledger. "The Lodge made money this year. I'm surprised your brother doesn't take advantage of your skills for his own estate."

"My half brother neither wants nor needs my assistance."

Nathaniel watched as she closed her eyes and calmed herself with a deep breath. The serene mask was back in place. "Does your brother spend all of his time in London?"

She shrugged. "He prefers it to the estate."

"I saw him the last time I was in Town. At the club." He watched her face closely, waiting for a reaction. Needing to squash that calm façade she so carefully maintained.

She frowned back at him. "You know my brother?"

Nathaniel set his quill down. He had an uncontrollable urge to prick her anger, to see that serene mask slip. She had to be hiding something. She was a Townsend. "I'm surprised that you choose to live so far away from him. Most young ladies would prefer Town to Beetham."

Her eyes shifted to the ledgers and then back to him. She was silent for a few seconds before replying. "Is there a problem with the accounts, sir? If not, then I need to see Lady Danford."

"Why aren't you living under the protection of your brother? Three young women, alone and vulnerable, can lead to all sorts of problems."

"I don't see how that is a concern of yours." Her eyes flared and her voice was as sharp as the letter opener he toyed with on the desk. Temper put bright slashes of pink across her cheeks.

"Forgive me, Miss Townsend. It just seems strange to me that you'd choose to live so far away from your own brother."

Her green eyes were hard.

"When did you last see your brother?" Nathaniel prodded.

Anne looked away toward the window. He wasn't sure that she would answer, but she turned back and met his eyes.

"His business doesn't allow him to be so far away from Town. I do write regularly."

"Does he reply?" He kept his voice soft. He wanted her to trust him, to reveal something.

She looked down at her feet. "He sends the girls treats from Town now and then, though it has been a while since we've last heard from him."

She was lying. He knew it. "Miss Townsend, how long has it been since Sir John contacted you?"

She dropped her arms to her sides and looked into his eyes. "If there's nothing else, sir, I should see to Lady Danford."

She refused to tell him, damn her. Nathaniel studied her closely. "You take special care of the lady, don't you?"

Anne Townsend genuinely smiled for the first time during their conversation. It transformed her face from almost plain to beautiful. Guilt bubbled up in Nathaniel's stomach.

"Lady Danford has been so kind to us. It's my pleasure to see to her comfort," Anne said.

Nathaniel snorted. "Only if you don't cross her. She can be quite acerbic."

"I agree. If you will excuse me, sir."

She is lying about her brother, Nathaniel thought as he watched her leave the room, closing the door behind her. Repaying Sir John for trying to cheat at cards had just become more complicated.

Anne stood on the other side of the door, deep in thought over the strange conversation she had just had with Mr. Matthews. He knew her brother. Fairly well, if his comments were any indication. And Nathaniel Matthews didn't like Sir John any more than she did.

Mr. Matthews also knew she was lying about the gifts and cards. She had said it to avoid the pity that usually came with the truth. She could take just about anything but pity. Anne made her way to the kitchen, needing a cup of tea.

"Now, what has put that frown on your pretty face, Miss Townsend?" Mrs. Fellows, the cook, asked as she waddled in from the pantry.

"Nothing," Anne said simply.

"She just came from the library with Mr. Matthews," the maid explained, following Anne into the kitchen.

"I'll not have you gossiping, Mabel," Mrs. Fellows said sharply.

"But the door was open, ma'am," the girl complained.

Mrs. Fellows shoved a tea tray in Mabel's hands. "Enough. Go and take Master Nathaniel his tea."

"Yes, ma'am," The girl scrambled to obey.

Mrs. Fellows poured a cup of tea and placed a biscuit on a plate. "Come sit down, Miss Anne, and rest yourself. Her ladyship will be needing you shortly, and you are looking a bit peaked."

Anne took her seat at the table and helped herself to the biscuit. She bit into it and smiled. "Ginger biscuits, my favorite."

"They are Mr. Matthews's favorite as well. I thought I'd make them for him since he's finally come home." Mrs. Fellows added one to her own plate.

Anne finished her biscuit and eyed another. "I don't remember him ever visiting in the last five years."

"He hates it here. So many bad memories of his father. The man died in the library." Mrs. Fellows poured another cup of tea and pushed it toward Anne.

Anne added sugar and stirred. "Good God, I had no idea. What happened?"

"His father gambled the entire estate away, except for what was entailed to Mr. Matthews. They think he did it while in mourning for his beloved wife. Left behind those two boys with nothing."

"Until Lady Danford came," Anne whispered.

Mrs. Fellows pushed the plate of biscuits at Anne. "They say Mr. Matthews was the one to discover his father."

Anne felt the blood drain from her face. As bad as things were in her life, she had never had to live through discovering a parent bleeding on the floor. "He killed himself?"

"No one says. No one would, now would they?" Mrs. Fellows sipped her own tea. "Mr. Matthews has done well for himself, though. He's not like his father in that respect, nor his grandfather. I imagine the old man is turning in his grave watching his grandson in trade, even if it's only investments."

"In trade? I thought he was a gentleman." Anne sipped her tea.

"He is, but he's been rebuilding the family fortunes the only way he can. The man is a genius with numbers, much like his grandmother. Mr. Matthews took advantage of the large number of factories built in Lancaster."

At least they had family to go to. She didn't have such contacts. "That explains why she and Mr. Matthews are so close."

"There aren't many people besides her ladyship who can pull Master Nathaniel away from Town."

"He's here to separate Tony from Sophia. He won't allow his brother to marry into our family."

"Could be. I'm not saying Miss Sophia isn't a fine young lady, but I suspect Master Nathaniel would want his brother to marry a young lady of substance, if you see what I mean." Mrs. Fellows poured another cup of tea. "He's worked hard to rebuild the family fortunes from the ground up. He'd want to make sure his brother is cautious in his choices."

Anne played with her teacup. The consequences of the engagement not happening were just too scary to think about. Sophia would have the man she wanted.

The craggy face of the old lady from the Fairy Steps popped into Anne's head. Could it be possible that Mrs. Fellows had seen the woman in the village? "I ran across an elderly lady by the Fairy Steps yesterday. I was wondering if you knew her."

Mrs. Fellows leaned her double chin on her pudgy fist. "Goodness, not many of the old dears in the village walk that far. What did she look like?"

"Swarthy skin, no teeth, very short. She walked with a cane. She looked like one of the Gypsies. Are there any in the area?"

"Lord, no. They've been gone since the harvest."

Anne set her teacup down with a rattle. She'd hoped the old crone would have at least been seen in the village. Mrs. Fellows knew everyone, as she'd been raised in this area.

Just then a footman came into the kitchen. "Her ladyship is settled in the parlor, Miss Matthews."

Anne smiled. "Thank you."

"I'll have Mabel make you both a fresh pot. It's a cold day and her ladyship will be feeling it in her bones today," said Mrs. Fellows.

"Thank you."

Anne made her way to the cozy sitting room Lady Danford preferred in winter. She tried to push the worry about Sophia and Tony to the back of her mind, but the cold winter weather kept the reason she needed her sister to marry Tony Matthews foremost in her thoughts. "Good afternoon, your ladyship."

"Anne, there you are. Can you fetch me my wool shawl? I sent the maid but she is taking forever. I can't abide this chill." Lady Danford sat before the fire, her feet resting on a stool, her workbasket on the floor beside the chair.

Anne gathered the shawl from the maid. "Thank you, Mabel. Please set the tea tray there by that chair." She wrapped the shawl around the dear lady's shoulders. "There, that should help."

Lady Danford patted her hand in return. "Thank you, child."

"Your hands are like ice. What have you been doing today?" Anne scooped up Lady Danford's hands and held them between her own.

"I walked into the village to call on Mrs. Norris. She's been so sick."

"You should have taken the carriage. It was too cold to walk today." Anne picked up a poker and stirred the fire. "Is that better?"

"I saw Mrs. Worth."

"How is Mrs. Worth today? I can't imagine she was happy to see you." Mrs. Worth and Lady Danford disliked each other intensely.

"She has some crazy notion that woodcock son of hers is courting you. She wanted me to put a stop to it. I informed her that you had more sense than that." Lady Danford's lips trembled as she tried to resist laughing.

Anne took her seat in a nearby chair with her workbasket. "Mr. Worth happened upon me on my way home from my walk yesterday. I thought it rather odd. He hasn't shown interest in all the years we've lived here." She profoundly hoped it had nothing to do with the old, strange, cane-wielding woman and fairy wishes.

"He's an odd one. Can't string a sentence together in company," Lady Danford said. "I suspect his mother writes his sermons."

Anne covered her mouth to stifle a giggle. "Surely he writes his own sermons."

"If you like him, Anne, I'll have to question your sense. Tell me you aren't considering it."

"It would be an equitable match, and beggars can't be choosers." Anne picked up her darning and wrinkled her nose. "It's doubtful I'll have another offer."

"I'd rather see you an old maid than have you subjected to that woman's harping for the rest of her days," Lady Danford said. "I know you, Anne. You won't tolerate her meddling. And that son of hers doesn't have the backbone to stand up to her."

Anne fought a shudder. "He's not that bad. Don't worry, I have no plans to settle as yet, especially with Mr. Worth."

"Someone might turn up who will catch your eye, my dear."

It was an old discussion. One Anne grew weary of. "Perhaps some nice farmer will want me. You know how I love the country."

"You're the daughter of a baronet, Anne. I'd be remiss in my duties to your mother if I allowed you to marry a farmer."

"I'm not allowed to marry a farmer. The vicar is too stupid. What will you have me do?" Anne teased. Lady Danford was determined to see her married, and Anne was determined not to settle.

"Go climb those steps you love so much. Maybe a fairy will have better luck than I." Lady Danford closed her eyes. "Lord save me from very picky spinsters."

Anne chuckled. "You'd miss me if I married. I'd not be here to challenge you."

Lady Danford lifted her head and shot Anne a look. "Challenge? I thought you were being impertinent."

Anne grinned and returned to her handwork. "I was, but only because you'd walk all over me if I didn't."

"Right you are, girl."

"What's so amusing?" Mr. Matthews's baritone voice rumbled into the room ahead of him.

Lady Danford sat up abruptly and announced, "The vicar is courting our Anne and I won't allow it."

Anne's face heated. "It is of little consequence. I have as little grace for his sermons, as he has little grace for us," she said softly. "Too many rules. Not enough mercy."

"Heavens, those long sermons. The man can talk for hours about nothing," Lady Danford said. "He probably puts God Himself to sleep."

Mr. Matthews moved to take a seat near his grandmother's chair. "I would think Miss Townsend would be honored by a marriage proposal from the vicar. He doesn't have warts, does he?"

"He has invisible warts." Lady Danford sniffed.

"For shame, my lady, calling his mother a wart," Anne said in a low voice.

Lady Danford laughed. "Anne, dear, she's not invisible. She's glued to his side like a barnacle on a pier."

"Then we shall pity the woman who marries Mr. Worth. She will have to be a saint," said Anne.

"A wealthy saint, at that." Lady Danford wiped her eyes. "As long as it's not you, my dear. Pour Nathaniel some tea, please."

"Yes, ma'am." Anne moved to do as requested, careful not to bang the china. Her hand brushed Nathaniel's fingers as she handed him his cup. She glanced down at him to find him watching her with an odd look in those blue eyes. She quickly returned to her handwork.

"So the vicar is calling upon you?" Nathaniel said, returning to the topic and setting his cup down with a rattle. "Why didn't you say something?"

Anne and Lady Danford both jumped at the abruptness of his tone. Anne quickly looked down as Lady Danford gave her a speculative look.

"Anne, dear, you can do so much better," Lady Danford continued. "Besides, I couldn't call on you if you married Mr. Worth. You know I don't get along with that harpy of a mother."

Anne laughed quietly. "You have nothing to fear, my lady. I doubt it will come to anything."

"Why is that? Surely the man is good enough for a baronet's daughter," Nathaniel said accusingly.

Anne glared at him. "If I loved him, I'd marry him."

"Love has gotten too many a couple into trouble," Nathaniel griped. "It's best to arrange these things based on mutual respect and money."

"Ah, you prefer arranged marriages then." Anne smirked. "Why am I not surprised?" She returned to her handwork, dismissing him. Lady Danford was watching the exchange with interest and Anne fought the urge to groan. The woman could weasel secrets from the prime minister himself.

"What is that supposed to mean?"

"You probably prefer the business arrangement of a dynastic marriage. So old-fashioned." Anne looked down at her work. "Those marriages rarely make anyone happy."

"Happiness in marriage is a matter of chance." Nathaniel picked up his teacup. "I would assume someone as practical as you appear to be wouldn't put much stock in romance."

"I speak of respect and love. Where there are both, there is peace and harmony in the home." Anne pushed on. "Surely that is something a man such as yourself would want as well."

"And you've seen couples united in this type of marriage?"

"Well. Not yet," Anne admitted. "But that doesn't mean it doesn't exist."

Mr. Matthews crossed his legs. Arrogance oozed from his pores like sweat. "I agree with you on respect, but love? More peace and harmony were gained in a financially sound marriage than one based on love. You can't dine on love, Miss Townsend."

Anne glared at him as she yanked a thread through the fabric with so much force it broke. She tossed her work beside her chair. "Spoken like a typical male. Your sex in general seems to fear love for some reason. Why is that, do you think? Control, perhaps?"

"Common sense, mostly, Miss Townsend." Nathaniel rose from his seat to pace the room. "Most men understand that being unable to support their family is the worst sort of sin."

"Are you suggesting that Mr. Worth is just toying with me for some reason?" Anne stood up, her hands balled into fists. "The man is a gentleman. You do know what that is, don't you, Mr. Matthews?"

"Enough, both of you," Lady Danford said. "Nathaniel, quit baiting the girl. You never know when to quit."

Anne returned to her work, trying to hide the tremor in her hands. "Mr. Matthews knows exactly what he's doing, ma'am." She would bet her last shilling on it.

Nathaniel Matthews clutched his chest and collapsed into his chair. "You wound me, Miss Townsend."

"I think you are incapable of being hurt by words." She rethreaded her needle and attacked the fabric with it.

"Men feel pain, Miss Townsend. They just hide it well. Unlike women, who thrive on emotional manipulation."

"Perhaps you've hidden your emotions so well, you have ceased to experience them." Silence filled the room. Anne met Mr. Matthews's eyes, the space between them like a wide canyon. She'd carried things too far. Again. She refused to apologize, despite the sick feeling near her heart.

"Enough, both of you," Lady Danford said. "I won't have my two favorite people bickering."

"I'm sorry, Grandmother." Nathaniel picked up his teacup. He drank in silence.

"My apologies, my lady," Anne said, her voice low.

"Anne, dear, will you go and see when luncheon will be ready?" asked Lady Danford.

"Of course. Excuse me." Anne passed Mr. Matthews on her way to the door. He avoided looking at her.

Once in the hall she leaned against the closed door, hoping to overhear some part of the conversation. Were they discussing Sophia and Tony? Given her behavior, it wouldn't surprise her if Mr. Matthews grabbed his brother by the cravat and forced him back to London. Matthews was not going to provide his blessing. No, Anne had taken care of that with her temper. And without one of the Townsend sisters marrying well, there was no way they could survive the winter on their own.

Too bad Mr. Worth didn't have a fortune.

Nathaniel watched Anne leave the drawing room. He turned and caught his grandmother staring at him, looking quite pleased with herself. "What?"

"What was that about?" Lady Danford demanded.

Nathaniel looked at his nails to keep from looking the old lady in the eye. She could spot a lie like no one else. "Just a friendly debate."

Lady Danford snorted. "Not very friendly, I'd say. You were baiting her. Why?"

He finally did meet his grandmother's eyes. "I thought you were against the match between Tony and Miss Townsend's sister."

"Only because they are both immature. I thought you liked Anne Townsend."

"What's not to like? She takes good care of you as your companion. Though I imagine her stubbornness would prevent her from accepting charity."

Lady Danford laughed. "Anne Townsend rivals you, dear, in stubbornness. Still, she is devoted to me."

Nathanial had one question that still needed answering. "Not many young ladies would travel across England on their own with two younger sisters in tow. I am curious why she came here."

"I only know that her brother tossed them out with barely the clothes on their backs. Anne and her sisters arrived with little money and a few trunks." Lady Danford shot him a strange look. "There is a dark side to arranged marriages."

"As we have seen," he replied curtly. His own parents' marriage had been awful. They argued incessantly, and once the two boys were born their parents lived separate lives. "It must have been after her father died."

"Yes. Her brother had no patience for providing a Season for his sisters." Lady Danford frowned. "I had thought perhaps it was the cost. When Anne's mother was alive, there was economy in the home. Sir Walter gambled, but still managed to provide for the family. The son was indulged. The girls were just an expense."

"What happened to her mother?"

Lady Danford looked at her hands and was silent for a long time. "I was such a fool in those days. Bent on making matches, seeing couples happy where I was unhappy. I made a horrible mistake in introducing Mary, Anne's mother, to Sir Walter Townsend."

Surprised, Nathaniel asked, "How so?"

"I never met a more selfish, conceited man. Sir Walter cared nothing for the heartache he caused his wife. He even rejected Anne as she wasn't as pretty as the younger two."

"Miss Townsend told me she was responsible for the household for a time."

"I believe she was fifteen when her mother died. She stepped in and took care of everything: her sisters and the estate. The servants grew so loyal to her, I believe they all left when her brother forced his sisters to leave the household."

Nathaniel set his cup down hard. "What kind of man leaves his sisters alone in the world without protection?"

Lady Danford studied her grandson and a slow smile twisted one corner of her mouth. "You are showing a rather keen interest in Anne's affairs."

"Do not get any ideas."

Lady Danford chuckled. "I warn you, she might be a dainty little thing, but Anne has a backbone of tempered steel. She'll not tolerate your meddling in what she considers her affairs."

He'd already had a taste of that lesson. He was looking forward to crossing paths, and swords, with Anne Townsend in the future. He hated to admit it, but he liked her. She took remarkable care of his grandmother, which he appreciated. She made the dear lady laugh, which was something he never did. Anne Townsend required further study. Yes, an in-depth study indeed.

Chapter Three

The next afternoon, Anne placed an apple cake on the small wooden worktable in the cottage kitchen. She breathed in the scent of cinnamon and apples. She sent a mental thank-you to Mrs. Fellows for the generous gift of apples from the Lodge's orchard. She would also make jam with Hannah, their maid of all work, later. She loved baking. Had they stayed with John, she'd never have had the opportunity to learn to cook.

"What is that glorious smell?" Juliet bounded into the kitchen, her glossy dark hair dancing around her face. "Please say I can have some."

"No, you may not," Sophia said as she entered the kitchen behind her sister. "We are expecting guests. I just dusted the parlor." She tossed down the rag with a martyred flourish. "I don't understand why Hannah can't dust."

"Hannah can't do everything." Anne gently placed the cake on a plate. "Juliet, pass me those herbs, please."

Juliet passed the basket to Anne. "Do I have to listen to Mr. Matthews spout his pathetic poetry about Sophia's eyes?"

Anne stifled a laugh. "It's not that bad. I need to go up to the Lodge."

"I'll be sick if I have to sit and watch him make cow eyes at her again," Juliet said.

"Anne, you have to be here! Tony's brother is coming specifically to meet the family." Sophia tsked at her sister. "You are covered in flour."

"I've already met Mr. Matthews's brother." And it wasn't something she wanted to repeat. Anne brushed out her dress. "Lady Danford needs me. Juliet will be here."

"*You* will be here, Anne. I insist." Sophia took Anne's arm and tugged her toward the stairs. "I've laid out your green dress. Change out of that old thing."

"Surely having tea with the man's brother isn't worth changing for," Anne argued. It was one of the few nice day dresses she owned.

"I can't believe we are having this conversation. You are the one pushing me to marry well," Sophia said with a toss of her head.

"I'm not pushing you—"

"You most certainly are!" Sophia said. "Please change. And do something about your hair. It's worse than usual, if that's possible."

Anne gritted her teeth and waited for her temper to cool before trusting herself to speak. Lord, Sophia was a trial. She needed a comeuppance, but not today. "Very well, the green dress."

"You needn't act as if the green dress were an elegant ball gown. Only Sophia gets new dresses. How can we make a good impression if the two of us look like we dressed from the rag bag?" said Juliet as she toyed with the cake.

Sophia sniffed. "If I'm to marry well, then I must dress well. I don't see why you're complaining. Once I'm married, you'll have new dresses."

"Juliet, leave the cake alone," Anne said. "Sophia, there's no need to crow at your sister."

"I'm the one making the sacrifice and saving the family," Sophia cried. "I get so sick of listening to her complain."

"Poor Sophia, so deprived. I'm sick of you!" Juliet stomped up the stairs.

Anne winced as a door slammed. "Sophia, that wasn't helpful."

Sophia huffed and pulled a face. "This wouldn't have happened if we'd stayed with our brother."

Anne couldn't win. She sighed, her shoulders slumped. "Go prepare for your visitors. We can discuss this later."

There would be no running away to the Fairy Steps today. Not with Mr. Matthews and his brother coming to call. She pressed a hand to her forehead. The visit from hell, and no way to escape.

Anne made her way to her small room and quickly brushed the flour from her hair and slipped into the green dress. She tucked a lace fichu into the low neckline and glanced at herself in the small looking glass. It would have to do.

She made her way back to the kitchen to prepare the tea tray.

Sophia's attitude grew worse every day. She complained about having to marry Tony Matthews, but sang a different tune when he was around. If their circumstances weren't so dire, Anne would let her drop the whole thing.

She placed the kettle on to boil and turned to look out the kitchen window. Winter was just around the corner. How Anne wished her mother were alive. She didn't know how much more she could take. She might have to throw her pride away and ask her brother for help after all.

"The cake looks nice, miss," Hannah said as she entered the kitchen. "Fine job you've done."

"Thank you." Anne sat at the table and played with the herbs she'd placed around the cake "What news from town?"

"Everyone is talking about the handsome young man who is visiting Lady Danford," Hannah said as she tied on her apron.

Anne made a face. "Mr. Matthews's brother."

"So you've met the young man? What's he like?"

"Arrogant," Anne said shortly.

Hannah laughed. "Aren't they all?"

"True. This man more than most."

"Perhaps this will speed up the engagement," Hannah said.

"I doubt it. Although if they don't marry we won't have to listen to Tony Matthews's poetry anymore." Anne groaned. "It's dreadful." She cut the cake into thin slices and readied the tea service with their best cups and saucers. This visit had to go well. She needed Tony Matthews to propose to Sophia.

"Anne! Anne, you'll never guess! Our brother is here!" Sophia danced into the kitchen. "At last! Isn't it exciting?"

A teacup crashed onto the table as it slipped from Anne's hand. "Here? In Beetham?"

"No, here, in the parlor! Oh, do you think he'll take us all back to London with him?" Sophia capered like a child.

"Calm yourself, Sophia." Anne smoothed her skirts down, patted her hair, and tried vainly to calm her racing heart. What could he want? She knew better than to hope he'd had a change of heart. He lacked a heart to change. "Please join Juliet upstairs while I see to him."

"But, Anne, I want to see him now. It's been ages." Sophia locked her jaw.

"Do as I ask for once, please?" Anne growled.

"But Anne—" Sophia whined.

"Now." Anne stared her sister into submission. Sophia turned and stomped up the stairs.

Releasing the breath she had been holding, Anne turned to Hannah and asked her to fetch her husband, Thomas.

"He walked into town, miss. Do you expect trouble?"

"I don't know. To say that my brother and I didn't part well is an understatement." Her stomach lurched.

"I'll fetch him right now, miss." Hannah grabbed her wrap and hurried out the kitchen door.

Anne pinched her cheeks for color. The last time she had seen Sir John he was in the process of throwing his half sisters into a carriage along with all their belongings. Anne could remember watching him turn his back before the carriage rolled away, leaving her to explain his actions to her younger sisters. They had cried for hours. She took a deep breath and entered the parlor.

"John, how kind of you to call." She smiled tightly.

John rose from his chair. "Anne, you've changed so much, I'd hardly know you."

She ignored his comment and stood by the fire. The years of his profligate behavior had aged him. Only three years her senior, his face was florid and he had a bit of a paunch. "What brings you so far from London?"

"Always the civil one." He immediately sat back down and fidgeted with his gloves. "Can't a man visit his sisters?"

"Half sisters. Abandoned half sisters."

He cleared his throat. "Anne, sit down so we can talk."

She sat down near the fireplace. "What is there to discuss? Why you threw us out?"

John studied her with narrowed eyes. "Perhaps I was hasty."

"Hasty in throwing us out immediately after Father's death, with no funds, no connections? Imagine that." Anne laughed harshly.

"Grief can make a man do daft things."

Anne raised one eyebrow at him. "I heard you were to be married. How is your wife, John? Did you bring her with you?"

"Her father refused the match," he mumbled, and pulled at a thread on his waistcoat. "I'm in need of funds, Anne."

She blinked at him, beyond astounded. "Funds? Look around you, Brother. Does it look like we have money?"

"You always jump to conclusions."

Anne almost denied it, but let the comment pass. He had a point. "Very well then, do go on."

"I was hoping to sell your mother's jewels. I remember a ruby necklace that would fetch a good price."

Anne laughed bitterly. He had come all this way not for them, but for jewelry. "I don't have any of Mother's jewels. If I did, I would have sold them long ago. I thought Father had them."

"I've searched everywhere. They aren't at the manor. I need those jewels, Anne." He became stern, as if he could demand she hand over what was never his.

"I'm sorry, but I haven't seen them since my mother's death. How much trouble are you in?"

"A great deal of trouble." He stood and paced back and forth in the small space. "Those jewels must be here." He crowded her in, blocking her exit.

"I assure you, they are not." Anne stiffened. She felt like she had as a child, when he tormented her. "Step away."

"Where are they, Anne?" he yelled. His eyes were shiny and wild as they darted around the room. "I must have them." His breath smelled of old ale.

"I can hardly give you what I do not have." She fought to keep the tremor from her voice. Her hand found the poker hidden beside her chair.

"Don't lie to me!" He raised his hand to slap her as she swung the poker around and blocked him, cracking it against his down-swinging wrist. He yelped and stepped back as she stood and stabbed the sooty end firmly against his waistcoat, pushing him back. "You will not lay a hand on me. Never again."

He rubbed his wrist and pulled an aggrieved, confused face. "Damn, that hurt, Anne. I wouldn't have struck you. I just lost my temper for a moment."

She merely waited, poker at the ready.

"What of Sophie and Juliet? Perhaps they would like a trip to London? They must be tired of Beetham. It's dreadfully dull here," he said.

Anne lowered the poker as her shoulders slumped. "And how would you provide for them, John, when you come demanding that I provide for you? Will you see to it that they marry suitable gentlemen, or just marry them off to the highest bidder?"

"I hear Sophie is practically engaged to a gentleman already." He laughed softly. "You're such a little hypocrite. She is marrying to save you and Juliet."

"Sophia can wed anyone she wants and she knows it. I'm doing no less than what our mother would do in seeking connections that will ensure Sophia's happiness."

"Is the man rich?"

Anne stared at him. "He makes her happy."

"It is my place to negotiate with this man. You had no right to do it without me."

Anne raised one eyebrow. "Sophia is of age. This is none of your affair."

"But Juliet isn't. That makes me Juliet's guardian. You don't want me to make things difficult here, do you?"

"How dare you come here!" She tightened her hold on the poker, fighting the urge to hit him.

"Have we come at a bad time?" a deep voice suddenly asked at the door.

With Tony hovering behind him trying to see what was going on, Nathaniel Matthews kept his eyes focused on Anne Townsend. Her cheeks were flushed and she fairly vibrated with anger as she clutched the fireplace poker so tightly that her knuckles were white. He smiled gently at her. "We knocked at the door." He glanced across the room. "Sir John."

"Matthews. What are you doing here?" Sir John sneered. His face went from flushed to pale and back again. "Shouldn't you be in Town, minding your own business?"

Nathaniel's jaw tightened at the condescending tone. He turned to Miss Townsend. "Perhaps we should return at a more convenient time."

"Please come in." She glared at her brother. "Sir John was just leaving."

"Trust me, Anne, this discussion is not over," Townsend barked as he gathered up his hat and gloves.

"Good day, John." Anne's jaw was thrust forward and sparks seemed to fly from her eyes.

Nathaniel and Tony moved away from the doorway to let Townsend pass, but Nathaniel kept his eyes on Anne. She closed her eyes for a moment, then seemed to relax, and placed the poker back beside the fireplace.

The serene mask was back. "If you will excuse me, I will fetch my sisters."

Nathaniel looked around the small parlor. The furnishings were worn, the rug and curtains faded. The nicer pieces were from the Lodge, courtesy of his grandmother.

"You are already judging them," Tony said. "Why can't you just accept people for who they are? The rest doesn't matter."

"Success is determined by money and connections," Nathaniel replied sotto voce. "You know this as well as I."

"Is that your definition of success, Mr. Matthews?" Anne came into the room carrying a tea tray, accompanied by two other young women.

Tony quickly took the tray from her and set it on a nearby table.

Anne turned to Nathaniel. "May I present my two younger sisters, Mr. Matthews. Miss Sophia Townsend and Miss Juliet Townsend."

Nathaniel bowed. "I'm pleased to make your acquaintance." He could see why Tony was so enamored with Miss Sophia. She was quite beautiful with her porcelain skin and dark hair. The youngest Miss Townsend wasn't as pretty as her sister yet, but showed promise, even with her spectacles. Neither, however, had the character that Anne Townsend had. He looked at his brother and frowned. The man was staring at Miss Anne Townsend with the oddest expression on his face, totally ignoring Miss Sophia.

"Shall I pour tea?" Anne asked.

"I thought we'd walk to town, Miss Townsend," Tony said quickly. "There won't be many fine days to come."

Miss Sophia stood and tried to take Anthony's arm. "Tony, what a splendid idea! I had a thought to go look at ribbons for when we are next at the Lodge."

"Sophia, I thought you might walk with my brother so as to get to know him better. I could escort Miss Townsend and Miss Juliet." Tony smiled at Anne.

Tony's eyes were not leaving Miss Townsend's face and she was getting flustered from the attention. Nathaniel glanced at Miss Sophia.

This did not bode well for Tony. Nathaniel suspected Sophia had a temper similar to her sister's.

"I think a walk is a splendid idea, but I insist on escorting Miss Townsend. We met briefly yesterday as I was arriving," Nathaniel said. Tony glared at his brother. What the hell was wrong with him? Did he think to fight over who would walk the eldest Miss Townsend? Nathaniel glanced at the overt pout on Miss Sophia's face.

"I think a walk to town would be refreshing," Juliet stated to no one in particular. "We won't have to listen to poetry if we walk to town."

"Juliet!" Anne whispered.

Nathaniel choked back a laugh. "Shall we go then?"

"I suppose," Anne said cautiously. She looked down at the tea and cake. "If you'll excuse us, we'll just fetch our coats."

Damn. He'd forgotten she'd prepared tea. The tea and cake would be wasted, something Anne Townsend could ill afford, but the small parlor with its sagging couch only exacerbated the odd pull he felt whenever he was near Anne. He needed to put space between them, lessen the effect until he could figure it out.

Not to mention he had to apologize for his earlier behavior or his grandmother would kill him. He'd prefer to not do that in front of an audience.

"You should have taken tea first, Nathaniel," Tony whispered angrily. "Anne went to all this trouble."

"Leave it," Nathaniel said.

The girls whispered furiously on the stairs before a sharp shush stopped the noise as they descended the stairs. Nathaniel offered Anne his arm. She glared at him, but accepted. He led her out of the cottage and into the lane. Tony and Anne's two sisters followed. Nathaniel urged her up the lane toward the village so that they would have some space from the others.

"Is this a race, Mr. Matthews?" Anne's voice was frosty as she released his arm.

"Miss Townsend, you were in some distress when we arrived." He kept his voice low, his head angled down so not to be overheard.

"Not at all."

He raised an eyebrow at the coolness of her tone. Interesting. She stared straight ahead with her arms swinging by her side, her chin up.

"I had no idea when we met yesterday at the Fairy Steps that there existed a connection between my brother and your sister." He glanced back at the threesome behind them. Miss Sophia continued to pout and Tony kept his eyes on Anne. "Though it looks as if they've had a tiff."

Anne glanced back at the couple. "I'm sure they will make amends. They've been living out of each other's pockets since Tony arrived."

"Tony mentioned that he might wish to marry your sister. He asked what I thought of the matter." He had Anne's attention now. "I believe him too young to marry at this time."

She said nothing for a long moment and Nathaniel wondered if he'd heard her. The composed mask that he so disliked was back.

"They are young, but many other couples have married at the same age," Anne finally said.

"Tony, as second son, has no inheritance. He will need to marry well."

"I see." If possible, her spine stiffened more.

Nathaniel watched her face. "I've advised him to think carefully about the matter. As his allowance will stop now that he's finished university, he'll need to think about a living of his own."

"That shouldn't prevent him from marrying whom he loves," Anne defended. "Surely you wish your brother to be happy."

"It's very difficult to be happy with little money," Nathaniel said quietly.

"Of which I am well aware." She wrapped her arms tightly around her and waited for her sisters to join them.

"I meant no insult," he offered. He had this uncontrollable urge to comfort her.

"I'm sure you didn't, Mr. Matthews." She stared back at her sisters as they approached with Tony. "We have few connections and no money. You only spoke the truth."

Nathaniel frowned. "I didn't mean to imply—"

Anne met his gaze, her green eyes hard. "Of course you did. Your message is quite clear."

"That's not what I meant. They cannot live on love. He has no more money than she."

A bitter smile played on her full lips. "Let's not fool ourselves, sir. Your message was received." She turned back to her sisters as they approached. "Sophia, I'm afraid I must leave you. There are things I need to see to."

"Anne, we were going into the village," Sophia cried.

"Miss Townsend, it won't be the same if you don't join us," Tony added.

"I'll walk back with you, Anne," Juliet said.

"You should stay with Sophia," Anne said quickly. She didn't need Tony and Sophia wandering off alone. God forbid that Nathaniel Matthews think she was trying to force them into a marriage.

"I'll accompany Miss Anne. I need to return to the Lodge anyway," Nathaniel said, putting an end to the discussion. He bowed to the two sisters and offered Anne his arm once more. She hesitated but took it.

As soon as they rounded a curve in the road, however, Anne dropped his arm. Nathaniel had to widen his pace to keep up with her as she stomped down the path toward the cottage. Her back stiff as a rod, she swung her arms at her sides to aid her speed. She moved fast for someone of her stature.

She abruptly stopped and turned to face him, forcing him to step to the side to avoid colliding with her. "It appears you know my brother a great deal better than you led me to believe."

Nathaniel stumbled over some stones in the path. "As I told you, we belong to the same club."

She snorted. "There is more to it than that."

Nathaniel hesitated. Telling her the truth would only make her dislike him more, as he'd caused her brother's current situation. "Do you see your brother often?"

"We've not seen him for five years, not since he packed us off. Yet suddenly he's here at the same time as you." Her voice dripped with suspicion. "Coincidence?"

"I'm sure it's mere chance, Miss Townsend."

"Chance? I'm not an idiot. What are you about, Mr. Matthews, besides ruining my sister's chance for happiness?" She blew an errant hair out of her face.

"I'm sorry. I swear his presence here came as a complete surprise." He softened his tone. "Why do you fear your brother, Miss Townsend?"

Anne's eyes widened and she looked away. "We didn't part on good terms."

Nathaniel wanted to take her hand, fold her in his arms and protect her. She'd probably hit him with a poker if he did. "I suggest you keep your distance from him, Miss Townsend. Trouble seems to follow Sir John."

"I can handle my brother."

"Miss Townsend, men do things when they are desperate."

She eyed him suspiciously. "How do you know he is desperate?"

He hedged. "It is hardly my place to say."

"I see. Mind your own business, Mr. Matthews, and I will mind mine."

Nathaniel's eyebrows rose at her frosty tone. "Of course, Miss Townsend."

"If you will excuse me . . ." She stalked toward the cottage.

"I thought we would walk to the Lodge together." He frowned after her, watching the way her rounded hips swayed, even while she stiffly tried to seem several inches taller than she was.

"I'm afraid I can't at this time," she said as she reached the cottage, opened the door, and slammed it behind her.

Once out of her sight, Nathaniel allowed himself to smile. She truly hissed like an angry kitten. A pretty, frightened, brave little kitten. He liked Anne Townsend. Hell, he admired her. She was a fighter.

Nathaniel turned toward the Lodge as a stranger dressed in a shabby brown coat and hat rounded the corner. The unkempt fellow spoke no greeting, but kept his head down and his face turned away. Nathaniel moved on but then stepped off the road into the trees to watch as the man stopped in front of the cottage and just stood there. Then, to Nathaniel's horror, the man stepped inside the garden gate.

Nathaniel walked quickly back, and raised his voice as he approached. "May I help you?"

The man jerked his head up, revealing a long, thin, scarred face. Gray bristles edged his chin. The man turned away quickly and shuffled past the cottage toward the main road. What the hell was a vagrant doing staring at the cottage? First Sir John and now a stranger. This stretched the limits of coincidence.

Anne closed her eyes. She was exhausted and tired of fighting. She whipped her bonnet off her head.

Nathaniel Matthews, with his high-handed arrogance, tried every shred of her patience and there wasn't much left.

Sophia would *not* be marrying Tony.

If they married without Mr. Matthews's approval, without his financial support, then she would have one more mouth to feed.

She closed her eyes against the stinging tears. She had hung so much hope on this marriage. Well, it was time to plan how they would cope this winter. She hated taking charity, but she'd set her pride aside once again, for her sisters' sake.

Then there was John. What was she supposed to do with him? He wanted money and they had none. Perhaps it was better that Sophia didn't marry Tony. There was no reason for Tony and Sophia to start their lives together with Sir John's troubles hanging over their heads. Tony was kind enough to want to help.

A knock sounded on the door and she jumped. She turned and opened the door to find Mr. Cecil Worth standing there, hat in hand. She was beginning to think God hated her. "Mr. Worth."

"Miss Townsend. I hoped you were home." He played nervously with his hat.

Oh dear God, he wants to visit? Anne didn't think she could take any of his pontification now. She forced a cheerful smile. "You've caught me just as I was leaving, sir." She stepped outside and closed the door behind her.

"Perhaps I can accompany you? Are you for the village, perhaps? I saw your sisters with Mr. Matthews, heading in that direction."

"Actually, I must call at the Lodge." She started walking and almost groaned aloud as he fell into step beside her. "How is your mother?"

"How thoughtful of you to ask, Miss Townsend. Mother is well. She sends her regards."

Doubtful, Anne thought. The woman despised her. "Thank you. Please pass my regards to her as well."

"You are kindness itself, Miss Townsend," he gushed. "I wanted to speak with you about your sisters."

"My sisters? Is there a problem?"

"Just that gossip has reached me that relates to Miss Sophia. I hear she is to be engaged to Lady Danford's grandson."

"They like each other, sir, but there is no understanding," Anne clarified. God would forgive her for lying to a vicar. She hoped.

"I wanted to warn you before that could occur."

Anne stopped and faced him. "What do you mean?"

He fiddled with his waistcoat. "His brother is in trade. One must be careful of the connections one makes."

Anne furrowed her brow. "I'm not sure I understand your meaning. Mr. Matthews is a gentleman."

"Yes, but given your own lineage, it would be beneath her to marry Mr. Matthews."

"Ah, you mean as the daughter of a baronet." Titles didn't put food on the table or buy fuel. She had learned to place little importance on her heritage.

Mr. Worth nodded and hustled to keep pace with her as she launched herself forward once again.

"You are too good, sir." Anne quickened her pace, nearly forcing him to break stride. First Mr. Matthews and now Mr. Worth, spouting the importance of connections. "Frankly, I don't see an issue with Mr. Tony Matthews. He is a gentleman."

"Yes, well—" He waved his arm vaguely.

"As are you, Mr. Worth. What difference is there between you and him?"

"I . . . uh . . . I take your meaning, ma'am."

Anne smiled as they reached the park in front of the old house. "Thank you for your escort, sir." She dipped a curtsy and rushed toward the door.

"Will we see you on Sunday, Miss Townsend?" Worth shouted.

"Yes, sir. Good day." Anne knocked on the door of the great house, praying the footman would open it quickly. He did, and she rushed inside to the kitchen. She shed her coat and hat as she pondered how strange people were acting today.

"Are you well, miss?" Mabel ventured.

"Yes, thank you."

"Should I let Lady Danford know you are here?"

"No. Thank you, Mabel."

Anne waited until Mabel left the kitchen and then made her way to the library. The door was closed, so she knocked softly before entering. She didn't want to encounter Nathaniel Matthews again.

The silence in the dark library wove a spell around her and Anne felt herself relax for the first time all day. She opened the desk drawer where the key was kept. It wasn't there. Nathaniel must have moved it.

The world was against her. She quickly searched the desk for the key, locating it underneath a mat. She pulled the ledger and stack of receipts from the desk drawer. She picked up the quill, opened the ledger, and went to work.

It took hours. As the room grew dark, she lit a candle and stoked the fire as the room grew colder. She verified each entry in the ledger, going back three months, looking for the error Nathaniel had spoken of, but found none. She looked at the entries again.

She closed the ledger and the files.

"Damn his black heart."

She tucked the ledgers away and locked the drawer. She replaced the key beneath the mat and blew out the candle. The glow of sunset warned her she needed to get back to the cottage. She opened the library door and peeked out into the hall to make sure she could escape unnoticed.

"Miss Townsend? I didn't know you were here."

She jumped and whirled around. Nathaniel Matthews stood in the gloom of the hall.

"How dare you?" She stomped toward him. She had never wanted to strike someone so badly.

"Pardon?"

"You led me to believe there was an issue with the ledgers," she snarled. A footman stuck his head into the hallway. "Why would you do this?"

"Leave us," Nathaniel commanded. He took Anne's arm and tugged her back into the library, closing the door behind them.

She glared at him. "I want the door open."

He reclined in a casual, dominant pose that she read clearly. "Simply put, because of your brother."

"I am not my brother."

"I had to be sure. My grandmother means a great deal to me."

She couldn't fault him for looking after his grandmother. She did the same and she wasn't even related to the lady. "If I were a man, I would call you out."

He smirked but didn't laugh outright. Instead he stood tall and then bowed in her direction. "Please accept my apology, Miss Townsend. I should have trusted my grandmother's opinion of you."

She turned to go.

He was at the door instantly to open it for her. "Won't you forgive me?" His low voice rumbled across her senses, leaving her muddled for a moment.

"P-please move aside, sir." The scent of his soap filled her head. She blinked up at him. He was so tall; she barely reached his shoulder. She should feel afraid, but didn't for some reason.

He cradled her hand in his. "Grandmother won't like it if we fight," he murmured as he slowly kissed each knuckle and turned her brain to mush.

This wouldn't do. She tried to pull her hand away from his. Preferably before she said or did something truly foolish, like kiss his hand in return. How could she be so angry with him and still stand there in the shadows waiting for . . . what? "You treated me like a servant."

"I apologized."

He was so arrogant. She yanked her hand from his. "If you'll excuse me—"

His eyes dropped to her mouth and lingered a moment. "I'll accompany you home."

"That really isn't necessary." She darted away from him in the dark hallway.

"I saw a strange man on the land earlier today, studying your cottage," Nathaniel said, following her into the kitchen. "An older man with gray hair and a long scar on his face. Have you seen him?"

Anne turned to face him with her coat and bonnet in hand. "No. Did he say anything?"

"No."

"Perhaps he was looking for Mr. Jenkins."

"Mr. Jenkins hasn't lived in that cottage for five years." Nathaniel took the coat from her hand and assisted her as she put it on. Anne tied on her bonnet.

"Perhaps he was just a tinker," she said. She walked to the kitchen door. Nathaniel was already there to open it for her. "Really, Mr. Matthews. It isn't necessary to accompany me."

"Might as well give in, Miss Townsend. I will walk you home. And I prefer to use the front door. And so should you." He took her hand and led her through the hall again. He gathered his own coat and hat and then opened the front door for her. "After you."

Anne stomped outside. "This doesn't change my opinion of you."

"Nor would I expect it to."

When she tried her usual tactic of dashing ahead, he commandeered her arm and tucked it into his own in order to force a slower pace. After a tug or two, she acquiesced. It was less than a quarter mile to the cottage. The sky melted from fuchsia to purple as they walked, the beauty around her soothing her temper. Crazy thoughts whirled in her head, like how good it had felt when his mouth pressed against her hand. His lips had been warm. Just before they left the library, he'd stared at her mouth. Would he have kissed her?

They covered the short distance quickly and were at the gate of the cottage before she knew it.

"Good evening, Miss Townsend." He startled her when he leaned in and planted a chaste kiss on her cheek. His mouth was cool, but his breath warm.

Her cheek tingled from the contact. She staggered inside and closed the door. Anne pressed a hand to her cheek. How had he known she was thinking about him kissing her?

Anne pulled on her apron while she walked to the parlor to collect the tea tray from earlier. A whole pot of tea wasted. The cake was stale now as well.

"There you are," Sophia said, coming down the stairs. "We were wondering where you were. It's nearly dark."

"I went up to the Lodge. I had some work to do." She carried the tray into the kitchen and set it on the wood table. "Did you have a nice walk with Mr. Matthews?"

"All Tony could talk about was you. He watched you as you walked with his brother. He paid no attention to me whatsoever until after you left."

Juliet skipped into the kitchen. "Anne, you're back."

Sophia sneered. "Congratulations on stating the obvious. Now tell Anne how Tony stared at her."

"He did seem focused on you, Anne. I thought it rather strange after his previous performances. Not one cow eye for Sophia. Rather refreshing, I think."

Anne put away the cake and poured out the tea as Hannah prepared supper. She didn't want to think about Tony and his silly cow eyes, or Mr. Worth and his effusive speech. What was it with the three of them? She was a spinster, usually invisible when her sisters were around.

"Oh, Anne, he spoke of writing poetry to you!" Sophia cried. "It's supposed to be about me."

"Do you hear yourself, Sophia?" Juliet said. "Honestly."

"Dear God, I hope he was joking."

Juliet snickered. "Me too. No more poetry, please."

"What did you do to him?" demanded Sophia.

"Nothing," Anne said. Good heavens, she had forgotten about that blasted wish. She'd been so busy dodging Mr. Matthews and Mr. Worth, it had slipped her mind. She ran the events of the day through her mind: Tony's strange attention, Mr. Matthews's persistence. Cecil Worth's unwelcome attentions. Nathaniel might be excused, as he had just met her and could be simply addlepated. But Tony and Mr. Worth had known her for some time and never expressed interest before.

"Anne, are you quite well? You've gone pale," Juliet asked tenderly.

"I'm fine," Anne answered automatically. No matter how hard she tried to dismiss it, she now suffered the attentions of three men, whereas she had never suffered the attention of one before. Not one. And the only change she could think of was the encounter with that bizarre old woman at the Fairy Steps. And that damned wish.

"Oh, my Lord in heaven!" Anne collapsed into a kitchen chair. It wouldn't be Mr. Matthews who ruined Sophia's chances with Tony. It would be her.

"Anne, are you paying attention to me?" Sophia demanded. "What did you say to Tony?"

"I said nothing." Anne rubbed her eyes.

"Perhaps Tony is finally seeing what a shrew you are, Sophia," Juliet suggested sweetly.

"What?" Sophia screeched. "I'm sacrificing my life for you, ingrate! You should remember that!"

"Lord, Sophia, haven't you nursed that one enough? I'm so sick of hearing about your great sacrifice for the good of all," Juliet snapped. "If you don't like Tony, let him be. No one is forcing you to marry him."

Anne groaned. Her head was starting to pound. "Must you two argue?"

Sophia sat down beside her. "What were you and Mr. Matthews discussing today during our walk?"

"He's against his brother marrying at this time," Anne said. "He says Tony is too young."

"What?" Sophia cried.

"Tony needs to marry well. We are too poor. Not to mention our connection with Sir John," Anne said as gently as she could. The last thing she wanted was a hysterical Sophia.

"Of course, being estranged from our brother hurts my chances of a good match," Sophia accused.

"What do you mean?" Juliet asked. "What does John have to do with any of this?"

"John is a baronet. Our connection to him would give us more prospects, not to mention a trip to London for the Season," Sophia answered. "If Anne weren't so angry with him, we wouldn't be in this dreadful place."

"Don't blame me for this, Sophia," said Anne. "John threw us out."

Sophia plopped down into a chair with a pout. "And just what did you do to John to make him send us away like that?"

"What did I do to John? Oh, let me see, no more than you and Juliet. I ate, drank, required housing and clothes. Dreadfully selfish of us, don't you think?" Anne regretted the harsh words the moment they left her lips. "I'm sorry, Sophia, but you harbor a false idea of our half brother. He has blown through what was left of Father's assets. He is penniless and in debt. He came here today to demand I give him our mother's jewels so that he could sell them."

"That can't be true. He wouldn't! I won't hear another word!" Sophia dashed up the stairs, sobbing dramatically.

Anne went from hoping the day wouldn't get worse to hoping it would end soon. Her mind played through the images of the old lady and the Fairy Steps. If magic existed, she'd gotten the most sadistic fairy of all. This was a nightmare.

Later, as Anne and Hannah finished preparing supper, Sophia came down, red nosed and puffy eyed. She said little through dinner, but then turned to Anne, malice twinkling in her eyes. "I have decided that if I cannot have Tony, I shall have Nathaniel. It is a more sensible choice, anyway. He is more mature and can provide for all of us. And since our father was a baronet and Nathaniel has no title, he should be pleased with the arrangement."

"Are you serious, Sophia? Can you change your feelings so quickly?" Juliet demanded.

Anne felt a pang of something she couldn't explain. The thought of Sophia and Nathaniel Matthews together just hurt. He had kissed *her*, not Sophia. He had held *her* hand. Could she step aside to allow her sister to marry him? The practical side of her brain kicked in. She had to admit that it was a better solution than borrowing money from Lady Danford. Nathaniel was wealthy enough to help them all. "Perhaps you are right, Sophia. If you truly can change your affections so easily, Mr. Nathaniel Matthews would make a better choice."

Sophia bounded up from her chair, almost tipping it over. "Don't worry, I can manage it. I'll begin my campaign at the supper at the Lodge." Pleased with her new plan, she bounded up the stairs.

"Where do you think she's going?" Juliet asked.

"Probably to work on the trims for the dress she'll wear to snag Mr. Matthews," Anne groused.

"Is it going to bother you when Sophia turns her charms to Mr. Nathaniel Matthews?" Juliet asked gently.

"What do you mean?"

"You like Nathaniel Matthews."

"Sophia may have him, if she is able."

"Do you mean that, Anne? I've seen the way you look at him."

"I do not look at him."

"Anne, do you want to give him up so quickly to Sophia? What if he's the one?"

Anne laughed bitterly. "There is no one, Juliet. Not for me."

Juliet covered Anne's hand with hers. "I wouldn't rule it out just yet, dear. I've seen the way he looks at you too. Sophia won't be able to win this battle."

Anne shook her head but couldn't explain. The wish had apparently affected three men. She had to find a way to break the spell before someone got hurt; before she got hurt.

"Thank you," she said simply and squeezed her sister's hand, feeling more alone than ever.

Chapter Four

Saturday morning, Anne walked through the woods in a daze. She had spent the night before reading the only book of fairy lore she'd found in Lady Danford's library. She had hoped there might be something in the book to counter the wish.

Birds twittered around her and acorns fell from the trees as she reached the kitchen door of the Lodge. She was sick of being hit by acorns every time she walked through the woods.

"Good afternoon, Miss Townsend," Mrs. Fellows said as Anne came into the kitchen.

"Good afternoon. Where is her ladyship?" Anne hung up her coat and bonnet. She removed her gloves and tucked them into the pocket of her coat.

"She's in her sitting room, miss. Shall I bring you tea in the parlor?"

"Yes, please." Anne made her way to the first floor and Lady Danford's parlor on the west side of the house. The late autumn sun lit the room brightly. Anne curtsied when she entered the parlor. "Lady Danford."

"Anne, dear. I had no idea you would be here today, but I'm glad you have come." Lady Danford smiled. She lifted the book in her lap. "Nathaniel has brought me a new novel from Town."

"What did he bring?" Anne looked at the cover. "*Persuasion*, by the author of *Pride and Prejudice*."

"It looks quite interesting. Will you read it to me?" Lady Danford asked.

Anne laughed. "Lady Danford, we should order you some spectacles from London. Then you'd be able to read it yourself."

"You read so well, and what else can I do with a companion?"

"My lady, if you don't wish for my company . . ."

"Nonsense, Anne. I look forward to your time here. You keep an old lady from being lonely."

Anne squeezed Lady Danford's hand and sat across from her. Even if she wasn't paid to attend to Lady Danford, Anne would still visit. It was nice to have a conversation without the other party whining or complaining.

Lady Danford shot her a side glance. "Did my grandsons call at the cottage?"

And yet, the lady had a knack for finding the one thing Anne didn't want to discuss. "Yes, ma'am, they did."

"What did you think of Nathaniel?"

Despite the casual way the question was asked, Anne knew that Lady Danford was fishing for information. "He seems very gentlemanly."

"He mentioned little of the visit, though I've asked him repeatedly. What did you do together?"

Anne played with the edges of the book's leather cover. "We walked together for a bit, but then I had to leave."

"He said you didn't stay long. I was wondering if you disliked him."

There was a loaded question. How *did* Anne feel about Nathaniel? He made her angry. He confused her. If she mentioned this to Lady Danford, the matchmaking would begin. "I don't know him well enough yet to decide if I like or dislike him." She opened the book to the first page. "Shall I start? I know how you loved Miss Austen's last book."

"If you aren't going to answer the question, then just read," Lady Danford grumbled.

Anne winced. She opened the book and began to read. Lady Danford settled in her chair and closed her eyes.

The story pulled Anne in quickly and she forgot her surroundings, as she always did when she was reading a good book. She paused at the end of chapter one and looked up.

Nathaniel Matthews stood in the doorway, watching her with those hooded eyes of his. He was dressed in a dark blue coat and buckskin breeches. His cravat was tied simply. His hair looked as if he had recently run his hands through it.

"Anne, why did you stop reading?" asked Lady Danford.

"I'm sorry, ma'am." Why couldn't Anne ignore him? She began reading again.

Nathaniel stared at her, his eyes warm, a slight smile on his lips. She stumbled again, then sighed. Damn him for making her so nervous.

"What is wrong with you, girl?" Lady Danford said. She then noticed Nathaniel in the doorway. "Nathaniel, what are you doing there?"

"Enjoying the story. Miss Townsend reads well." He strolled into the parlor and took the chair across from Anne. "Please continue."

"You're embarrassing the girl," Lady Danford said.

"I doubt that. Please continue, Miss Townsend."

Anne continued reading. She could feel the color wash into her face as Nathaniel watched her. She stumbled again and glared at him. He winked at her in return.

Lady Danford looked at Nathaniel and then at Anne. "What is going on between you two?"

"Nothing, ma'am," Anne said quickly. "Perhaps Mr. Matthews can enlighten you."

"I haven't had the chance to read this one yet. I picked it up right before I left Town," said Nathaniel.

"You are making her nervous. Go find something else to do," Lady Danford said. "This is my time."

"I want to hear the story," Nathaniel insisted.

"What story?" Tony said from the doorway. "Is Miss Townsend reading?" He came into the room and sat down next to Anne. She scooted over on the small sofa to make room for him.

"Now I will never hear the story," Lady Danford said, and threw up her hands.

"If you'd let me get you some new spectacles from Town, you'd be able to read it yourself," Nathaniel reminded her.

"I keep trying to tell her," said Anne.

"Miss Townsend, I was hoping to see you today," Tony gushed as he scooted closer to her.

Anne's eyebrows shot up at the odd tone in his voice. He was acting strange. There was an unnatural light in his eyes. "I can't read if you don't give me room to open the book, Mr. Matthews."

"Tony, give the girl room to breathe. Sit over there." Lady Danford pointed to a chair near the center of the room. Tony frowned but did as he was told. Anne breathed a sigh of relief.

"What are you reading?" Tony asked.

"She's reading *Persuasion*. I brought it from London," Nathaniel said.

"I didn't take you for a reader, Nathaniel. You never showed interest in my poetry," Tony said with a pout.

"That's because it's bad," Lady Danford said matter-of-factly. She looked over at Anne. "Really pathetic—maudlin even."

Anne covered her smile with her hand and looked back down at the book. Anne had to agree, but the hurt expression in Tony's face caused her to say, "It wasn't *that* bad."

"Thank you, Miss Townsend," Tony said with a smile. "I've written something new especially for you. Shall I read it to you?"

"That won't be necessary," Anne said quickly. She glared at Nathaniel, who was choking down laughter. "Shall I begin again?"

"No," Lady Danford said. "You won't do the voices with these two present."

"You do the voices?" Nathaniel said hopefully.

Anne felt her face flush. "I sometimes perform the voices."

"She's quite good," Lady Danford said. "But you've both ruined it. She won't do them now. You make her nervous."

"I am able to continue, my lady," Anne broke in.

"No point now, as the boys have ruined it for me."

"I had no idea Miss Townsend was so theatrical," Nathaniel said.

Tony again joined Anne on the couch, forcing her to squeeze into the side of the sofa in order to escape him. "I'm not theatrical."

"I'll read it to you instead, Miss Townsend," Tony said in a strange voice.

"Uh, no, thank you." Anne closed the book and placed it on the table. The two brothers were acting decidedly strange. With Tony pressing closer and Nathaniel watching her, she fought the urge to run screaming from the room. She glanced at the clock on the mantel. "Oh dear, is that the time? I really must get back to the cottage."

"Go, go. It's not like you'll be able to get anything done now." Lady Danford waved her hand toward the door.

Anne curtsied and made for the door as quickly as she could.

"Miss Townsend, I will see you home," Nathaniel said, rising quickly to his feet.

Anne caught the look of speculation in Lady Danford's eyes, which was the last thing she needed. "It's hardly necessary, sir." She kept moving toward the door. Her wish was making both men act strange, and there was no need to add more fuel to Lady Danford's suspicions either.

"I insist," Nathaniel said. He placed her hand on his arm, leading her out of the room and toward the front entrance.

"I must get my pelisse from the kitchen." Anne pulled away from him and moved to the back of the house.

"We've had this discussion, Miss Townsend. You should not be using the servants' entrance."

"It's appropriate, as I am in Lady Danford's employ." Anne continued toward the kitchen at a quick pace. She could hear Mr. Matthews behind her.

"Miss Townsend, I've a treat for you," Mrs. Fellows said as she entered, motioning to a basket on the kitchen table. "I thought you young ladies would enjoy a hank of pork. I've also added those ginger biscuits you like so much."

"Thank you," said Anne as she moved to the cupboard where she kept her pelisse and bonnet.

"Begging your pardon, sir. I didn't see you," Mrs. Fellows said to Nathaniel brightly.

Nathaniel picked up the basket meant for Anne and waited for her to finish putting on her bonnet. She grimaced at the intrigued look in Mrs. Fellows's eyes. *Wonderful, more gossip about me and Lady Danford's grandson.*

"Good day, Mrs. Fellows, and thank you again," Anne said as she led Nathaniel Matthews out the back door of the house.

Once they were both outside, Anne turned toward Nathaniel, allowing all her anger and frustration to bubble up. "I do not need your escort, nor do I want your company."

"Nevertheless, you shall have it, Miss Townsend." Nathaniel offered her his arm, but she ignored it and tried to take the basket from him. He moved it away from her reach, which was easy given how tall he was.

"Why must you be so obstinate?" Anne said.

"Me? Obstinate? You give new meaning to the word, ma'am." He led her around the house to the park. "You still insist on using the servants' entrance."

"Because it is proper."

"And you are excessively proper about all things?" Nathaniel teased.

"Of course."

"Miss Townsend, you have my permission to use the front entrance. Unless you prefer the servants' entrance."

Anne didn't answer, but picked up the pace.

"Are we running a race?"

She wanted to scream yes and run ahead, but didn't. Instead she slowed down to a stroll.

"I'm beginning to think you don't like to spend time in my company, Miss Townsend."

Anne looked up into his face quickly and saw the humor there. It was so hard to stay angry with him, which in itself was irritating. "It's not that," she said.

"Then what is it?"

"You don't approve of the match between Sophia and Tony."

"Only because they are young."

Anne arched a brow at him. She knew there was more to it than that.

"And your brother," Nathaniel added reluctantly. "He is a problem."

"We can't select our family. Believe me, I know."

"Tony was behaving oddly today, don't you think?"

Anne tripped on a root and Nathaniel grabbed her arm to keep her from falling. "I, uh, hadn't noticed."

"Seriously, Miss Townsend. He practically pushed you into the side of the sofa. He's never behaved like that before."

Anne refused to answer. She didn't want to encourage the conversation. Nathaniel Matthews didn't miss much.

"Did you see anyone lurking outside the cottage today?" he asked.

Anne almost stumbled again at the change of topic. "No. We've seen no one."

"Have your servants keep their eyes open. I didn't like the looks of the man I saw there last. He didn't fit here in Beetham."

"Honestly, Mr. Matthews, you see intrigues where there are none. I told you it was probably Mr. Worth."

"I checked with Mr. Worth yesterday. He was not the man I saw. While your brother doesn't seem concerned for your safety, as long as you reside on this estate, I am."

This was just too much. Anger burned in her. "Thank you for your concern, but it is misplaced. We are more than capable of handling any situation that should arise. We have for five years."

There was a tic in his cheek, as if he were grinding his teeth.

"Nevertheless, Anne Townsend, I will look into the matter. It is my responsibility to make sure those who live on the estate are safe." His words were clipped, cold. Gone was the teasing man from earlier.

This was outside of enough. Anne didn't need, nor want, his interference. But speaking those thoughts would do no good as she noted the tightening of his jaw. Arguing with the obstinate man was a waste of time.

As they turned the corner toward the cottage, Mr. Worth approached them with a smile.

"Miss Townsend, Mr. Matthews. I was just on my way up to the Lodge." He bowed and smiled down at Anne. "I was hoping to find you there, Miss Townsend."

"Mr. Matthews was seeing me home, but since you are here, perhaps you will escort me the rest of the way home, Mr. Worth?" Anne glanced up at Nathaniel. The tic in his jaw was even more pronounced.

"It is no problem, Miss Townsend," Nathaniel said. "I'm happy to accompany you."

"It's really not necessary with Mr. Worth here," she gushed.

Nathaniel's face flushed as he glared at Cecil Worth.

For Mr. Worth's part, he looked uncomfortable. Anne felt bad for almost a minute at Nathaniel's anger, but she was sick of his high-handed ways. "Thank you, Mr. Matthews." She held out her hand for the basket.

"Miss Townsend. Mr. Worth." He bowed and handed her the basket. It was heavier than expected and she almost dropped it. Mr. Worth took it from her.

"Mr. Matthews, please give my regards to Lady Danford. I look forward to seeing her in the service tomorrow," Mr. Worth said.

"Good afternoon, Mr. Matthews." Anne glanced at him. His jaw was tight, his eyes hooded.

"If you see anyone suspicious, you will tell me immediately, Miss Townsend."

"I will be cautious."

"Come, Miss Townsend, I will see you safely home." Mr. Worth led her away.

Anne looked behind them as Nathaniel walked quickly away, his head down. She felt a funny lurch in her chest.

"I hope you'll attend the service tomorrow, Miss Townsend," Mr. Worth said. "I have a special word for the Sunday service."

"I'm sure it will be very interesting," Anne said, distracted by the look on Nathaniel's face before he departed. He had been furious with her, but there was something else too.

"Why were you at Lady Danford's?"

Anne nodded absently. "I had promised to read her a new novel Mr. Matthews had brought from Town. Her vision isn't what it used to be."

"I don't approve of ladies reading novels," Mr. Worth said in a condescending tone.

"They can be very entertaining." Anne fought the urge to roll her eyes.

"Surely, you don't read them."

"Yes, when I get the chance." She smiled. "I delight in reading novels. It's such a lovely way to spend an afternoon. I highly recommend it."

"Perhaps I shall lend you a few books more appropriate for you and your sisters to read."

He really was full of himself. "That's very kind of you, sir," she said. They approached the small park in front of the cottage and she released his arm. "Thank you for accompanying me."

Mr. Worth tipped his hat and handed her the basket. "My pleasure, Miss Townsend."

Nathaniel stormed home. Anne Townsend was driving him crazy. He marched into the house and handed his hat and coat to the footman he had yelled at earlier. Damn, she had him yelling at the servants too. What the hell was wrong with him?

"You've already returned from seeing Anne home? That was a quick walk," Tony said, coming out of the parlor.

"We ran into Mr. Worth and he escorted her the rest of the way." Nathaniel stalked to the library and poured two drinks.

"Cecil Worth? He's interested in Anne?" Tony took a seat in front of the desk.

"Cecil Worth met us halfway and Miss Townsend jumped at the chance to have him accompany her home."

"The vicar? He's never shown an interest in Anne before. He's more interested in marrying a fortune. Likes to live beyond his means."

Nathaniel handed Tony a glass. "Why were you behaving so strangely with Miss Townsend today? You were practically sitting on her lap."

"I don't know. I had the uncontrollable urge to be near her. It was odd. The minute she left the room, it faded."

"Has it happened before?" Nathaniel took a seat behind the desk, in his father's chair.

"Yesterday." Tony scratched his head. "It is quite odd. After all, I'm in love with her sister."

Nathaniel frowned. Anne Townsend had been under his skin since he met her at the stone steps. "I imagine Miss Sophia was put out about your behavior."

Tony laughed. "Yes, she was. It was charming, actually. I didn't know she could get jealous."

Nathaniel wasn't sure he'd call either sister's anger charming. It seemed all three girls had tempers like their brother.

Nathaniel couldn't make sense of it. All of them were acting odd around Anne. It wasn't that she was something special. Yes, she was delicately made, barely reaching his shoulder. Her hair was more red than brown, with these curls that wouldn't be controlled, and she had a sprinkling of freckles across her nose. Her eyes were green, her skin was creamy. He'd seen more beautiful women in London. Hell, her sisters were more beautiful than she. Yet he could rattle off her attributes without a second thought. "Keep an eye open when you call at the cottage."

"Why?"

"I spotted a stranger lurking there. He wasn't from around here." Nathaniel toyed with the papers on his desk. "An older man with gray whiskers and a long scar on his face."

Tony set his glass down. "How do you know that?"

"I asked around the village. No one knew him."

"Why would he be watching the cottage? The ladies have nothing at all of value."

"I don't know, but I imagine it has something to do with Sir John being in Beetham."

"Townsend certainly didn't want to see you."

"He owes me a great deal of money. And he was caught cheating when he tried to win it back." Nathaniel tossed back his brandy.

"You in a gaming hell? I can't begin to imagine," Tony said sarcastically. "You were always telling me to avoid them. Aren't you afraid to get sucked into the same madness as Father?"

Nathaniel sighed. "It's not what you think. I went in with some friends from the club. We had a friendly game, then Sir John joined us. He won most of the games. The stakes got high. A good friend of mine bet and lost everything. I continued to play. I won. Sir John couldn't pay."

"Do you make a habit of this?"

Nathaniel shot a hard look at his brother. "No." Gambling had been his father's downfall. It wouldn't be his.

Tony set his glass down and faced Nathaniel. "Please tell me you didn't set Sir John up."

Nathaniel couldn't meet Tony's eyes. He got up and splashed more brandy into his glass. "I did what had to be done."

Tony cursed. He stood and slammed his glass on the table. Nathaniel winced as the crystal rattled. "What the hell were you thinking, Nathaniel?"

"After what his father did to our father and the family, what choice did I have? I saw an opportunity and I took it, especially after he ruined another man. He is just like his father." Nathaniel still couldn't meet his brother's eyes. Revenge was something they had both sworn to their grandmother that they would not pursue. "It was a mistake."

"Damn right, it was," Tony spat out. "You'd do this to the family I plan to marry into? How am I supposed to tell Sophia this? She idolizes her brother."

Nathaniel tossed back the last of his brandy. "What do you wish me to do?"

"Tell the Townsends what you've done," Tony said. "Stop this before it goes further. Make your peace with the past."

Nathaniel stared into the fire. Could he make peace with the past? It had driven him to accomplish so much.

"Does Grandmother know?" Tony asked.

"She knows most of it."

"I don't imagine she approves."

Nathaniel glared at his brother. "No. She does not."

"What about Anne?"

"What about her?" Nathaniel pretended indifference. Frankly, he wasn't sure he wanted Anne to know about the bet. It would lower her already poor opinion of him.

"I've seen the way you look at Anne, Nathaniel. I don't want to see her hurt."

"What do you mean?" Anne Townsend was the last thing he wished to discuss with his brother. He hadn't figured out his own feelings about her yet.

"Anne is different from her sisters."

"Different? How?"

"She's not used to dealing with men like you."

"You make it sound as if I'm some libertine determined to take advantage of Miss Townsend."

"I only meant that you have more experience than she. She's led a more quiet life, in the background. She's never even been to London."

"Matchmaking for her sister, I take it. You know my feelings on your relationship with Sophia Townsend."

Tony sat back in his chair with a huff. "You've made your feeling known perfectly well. I just choose to disagree with you."

"Tony, you're twenty-four years old. At that age, the last thing I wanted was to get married and settle down."

"I'm not you. I love Sophia and I will find a way to marry her."

"Fine." Nathaniel felt smug at changing Anthony's focus so easily.

"Now back to Anne. I don't want to see you hurt her."

Damn. "What are you talking about?"

"For some reason, she holds you in high regard."

Something near Nathaniel's heart quickened. "How do you know that?"

"I've seen the way she looks at you. You could break her heart."

Nathaniel laughed. "All that poetry has gone to your head. Anne Townsend would rather hit me over the head with a poker. Trust me, if anyone gets hurt, it will probably be me. I only seem to anger her."

"Anne, angry? That's unusual."

"The woman has a king-size temper." Nathaniel set his glass down and noticed Tony's astonishment. "You've never seen her angry?"

"No. Never. She's always been kind to me."

"Lucky man." Nathaniel stood and walked to the window. The sky was growing dark earlier and earlier of late. Winter was coming. He'd have to leave soon, before the snow came, or be stuck in Beetham for weeks. Funny, the idea didn't bother him as much as it had when he first arrived.

Anne sat in the pew of St. Michael's church beside her sisters. Lady Danford, Mr. Matthews, and his brother were across the aisle from her. She tried hard not to notice that Nathaniel Matthews was watching her. She tried, but failed. She fought the urge to squirm under his regard. She did her best to ignore him.

This fairy wish was going to be the death of her. Sophia was angry because Tony seemed to switch his attentions from Sophia to Anne, and because Nathaniel also appeared interested in Anne. Her snide remarks were growing more and more unbearable. Even Juliet was growing weary of trying to stop them.

Poor Sophia; it was probably the first time she'd had a dose of her own medicine. She wasn't taking it well. Juliet was just as puzzled. Two handsome men were clearly more interested in plain, dependable Anne than beautiful Sophia. Juliet watched her with questions in her eyes. Anne seriously hoped Juliet would keep her questions to herself.

Anne hated it. She could hear her mother's voice. *"Be careful what you wish for, you might get it."* The spell must be broken; otherwise her sisters would disown her. She didn't want Tony Matthews fawning over her any longer. She liked Nathaniel, more than was safe for her heart.

Juliet elbowed her in the side. "Anne, are you paying attention?"

"What?" she whispered back.

"The vicar, Mr. Worth. He's acting very strange."

Anne looked up at the pulpit and noticed Mr. Worth's eyes on her. She met his gaze and saw the change wash over his face. "Oh Lord."

"What?" Sophia whispered.

"We have a special biblical text today," Mr. Worth droned. "Song of Solomon, chapter seven. And I shall read:

"'How beautiful are thy feet with shoes, O prince's daughter! The joints of thy thighs are like jewels, the work of the hands of a cunning workman.'"

Gasps echoed around the church. Anne looked down at her hands, now knotted in her lap. Please God, don't let this be happening. Mr. Worth's high-pitched voice droned on.

"'Thy navel is like a round goblet, which wanteth not liquor: thy belly is like a heap of wheat set about with lilies.'"

"I didn't know there were texts like this in the Bible," Juliet whispered. "And here I've been wasting my time on novels."

Sophia giggled at Juliet's remark. "You have to admit, it's more interesting than his usual sermons."

Anne prayed that the ground would open up and swallow her. She glanced up at Mr. Worth and he smiled back at her. Could things get much worse?

"'Thy two breasts are like two young roes that are twins.'"

Oh heavens, he said *breast* in church! Some teenage boys laughed in the back. Anne risked a look around her. Many, including Lady Danford, were frowning. Mrs. Worth was glaring at her. She sank lower in her seat and tucked her head down. Please God, let it end soon.

"Anne, did he just compare your hair to a flock of goats?" Juliet whispered.

"Shh. You are mistaken." Anne glanced over at Nathaniel Matthews. His shoulders were shaking with laughter. Tony glared at the vicar. Nathaniel met her eyes and cocked one eyebrow. She turned away quickly. Hateful man, to laugh at her expense.

"Anne, is he talking about you?" Sophia whispered.

"No!" Anne whispered furiously. She felt her face heat up. She had no idea that they even used the word *breast* in that way in the

Bible. Cecil Worth kept looking at her as he read verse after verse. She slumped lower and kept her head down. For the first time in a long time she felt her eyes sting with tears.

"Anne, what is going on?" Sophia whispered. "Why is he reading this to you?"

"I have no idea," Anne shot back. She desperately wanted to leave, but if she got up now, it would confirm to everyone that Mr. Worth was reading to her. She cast another glance at Nathaniel. He winked at her and smiled.

Finally, Mr. Worth stopped reading and continued with his sermon. Anne forced a calm expression on her face and counted the minutes until she could escape the church. It was the longest service of her life. The congregation stood as the benediction was pronounced. Anne took an opportunity to escape during the closing prayer.

"Anne, where are you going?" Juliet asked.

"I'll meet you at home," Anne whispered, giving in to the urge to flee. As if there wasn't enough gossip about her family, Cecil Worth had just thrown fat into the fire. She escaped the church as quickly and quietly as she could. Anne couldn't face the congregation, make small talk, and pretend nothing had happened. She quickly crossed the yard toward the cottage, eating up as much distance between her and the church as she could without breaking into a run.

"Miss Townsend. A moment please," Nathaniel called out behind her.

Oh please God, not him. Nathaniel Matthews was the last person she wanted to see. She quickened her pace, but she couldn't outrun him.

He removed his hat as he caught up with her. "Miss Townsend, are you all right?"

The concern in his voice was her undoing. "I'm perfectly fine," she said, fighting back tears.

"You have another admirer," he said, chuckling. "Funny, I never thought reading the Bible could be so arousing."

Anne whirled on him. "Are you quite done? If so, I would appreciate it if you would just leave me alone."

"You didn't find that humorous?"

"What do you think?" She turned and continued toward the cottage, leaving Nathaniel behind. She could feel the tears welling up. She'd be damned if she'd cry in front of the likes of him.

"It does seem strange that you suddenly have so many suitors."

Anne stopped and whirled around. "Grant me one request and leave me alone. Please?"

He studied her face for a long minute. "Of course."

She walked quickly down the lane toward home. As she turned the corner to cross a pasture, she looked back and saw him regarding her from the distance.

Nathaniel stood in the lane until Anne disappeared around the corner of the next lane. *Stupid oaf.* Of course she wouldn't see the humor in the situation. She had been humiliated and embarrassed. He'd just made it that much worse by teasing her.

"I am an idiot," he mumbled. He had some unexplainable feelings for this woman and he kept mucking it up.

He turned back to the church just as the congregation was exiting. He moved toward them to meet Anne's sisters.

Tony was the first to reach him. He chuckled. "Well, you don't hear *that* text every day. Where is Anne?"

"She's on her way home," Nathaniel replied. He didn't like Tony's familiarity.

"I hope she's all right. Perhaps I should see her the rest of the way home."

Nathaniel stopped him with a hand on his shoulder. "She asked to be left alone."

Tony glared at him. "Did you upset her again?"

"No. Why don't you see Miss Sophia and Miss Juliet home? Miss Sophia is the girl you are planning to marry, correct?"

Juliet and Sophia joined them. "Mr. Matthews, where is Anne?" Juliet said.

"She's on her way home. She didn't want to face the congregation," Nathaniel said.

"That was the strangest thing I've ever seen," Lady Danford said as she joined the group. "Mrs. Worth is ready to kill her son for embarrassing her with that scandalous reading. I had no idea such things were even in the Bible."

"What possessed Mr. Worth to read such a text in church?" Tony asked.

"Mr. Worth has been calling on Anne recently," Sophia said. "I had no idea he was serious. He's not been in the past."

"Sophia! Do you have to put it that way?" Juliet chastised.

Nathaniel watched Tony frown over Sophia's comment.

"Allow me to see you home, Miss Juliet, Miss Sophia." Tony stepped forward and offered his arm.

Sophia took his arm and allowed him to assist her into Lady Danford's carriage. He then assisted Juliet.

Nathaniel offered his arm to Lady Danford. "Allow me to escort you to the carriage, Grandmother."

Lady Danford placed her hand on his arm. "Anne must have been very embarrassed. I'm worried about her."

"She was mortified. I tried to walk her home, but made a muck of it."

Lady Danford frowned at him. "She has enough worry on her shoulders without you adding to it."

He had to agree. "Unfortunately, I found this morning's performance rather funny."

"I imagine Anne did not."

"No."

"I don't like the idea of her walking home alone. It's nearly two miles. Well, at least supper tomorrow night will be entertaining."

Nathaniel chuckled. "We will have front row seats if Miss Townsend decides to retaliate."

His grandmother looked up at him. "I sincerely hope not! The girl has more manners than that."

"You can't blame her, can you?" Nathaniel said as he handed her into the carriage.

"I suppose not. Tony, did you talk to the vicar?"

"Yes. An odd conversation. He said it never occurred to him to read that particular text until he looked into Miss Townsend's eyes during the service, and then he couldn't help himself. It was never part of the sermon. He seemed embarrassed by it."

"He's never been interested in any of the Townsend girls," Lady Danford added. "No fortune."

"He has been calling on her of late. He met us on the way back to the cottage just yesterday. Still, it's a strange reaction." Nathaniel frowned. "You had the same reaction yesterday when Miss Townsend was reading."

"True, but it faded fairly quickly," Tony said. "What are you thinking?"

Nathaniel was thinking there was more to this than Anne Townsend was admitting. "I'm thinking that I shouldn't have let Miss Townsend walk home alone. See Grandmother home?"

"Of course."

Nathaniel took off down the lane after Anne. Something odd was going on and he needed to get to the bottom of it.

Anne walked as fast as she could without breaking into a run. She wiped at the tears on her face. Never in her life had she been so humiliated. To have Mr. Worth single her out was one thing, but to read that biblical text was another. Then to have Nathaniel Matthews make a joke of it. It was beyond the pale. The man had the manners of a goat. She sniffed. This stupid wish was more trouble than it was worth.

She slowed her stride as soon as the churchyard disappeared from view. The leaves were all but gone from the trees and the wind was turning cold. Anne shivered and pulled her pelisse closer around her for the long walk home.

This wish business had to end.

Somehow she would have to break the spell. It was causing all manner of nonsense. Tony Matthews fancied himself in love with her. Sophia was furious. Now Cecil Worth was bewitched. Lord only knew what his mother would say to Anne now. The woman was a shrew with very particular views on who was worthy of marrying her son. Dinner at Lady Danford's the next evening would be painful.

"Perhaps I'll have a headache," Anne said to no one in particular. It was a sound solution to the issue if her sisters would let her get away with it. As she was the only one who could play the piano and provide the music for dancing, it was doubtful. She sighed heavily. She was growing rather sick of her life of late, but didn't see any way out of it.

"Anne! Wait."

Anne groaned. Could her life get any worse? Her brother was running toward her. His face was red with effort. When he caught up, he could hardly catch his breath.

"Are you all right, John?"

"Just . . . give . . . a minute." He pulled in a deep breath.

"Exercise is very beneficial, John. You should do more of it." She continued her walk toward home. She wasn't in any mood to deal with John right now.

"Don't be snippy."

"You smell like a brewery," Anne said. To her dismay, John walked beside her. "What do you want, John?"

"You have to help me," he pleaded. "They are going to kill me."

"Who is going to kill you?" Anne wanted to care, but right now she just couldn't. Whatever this mess was, John had created it, so he could fix it for himself as well.

"The people I owe money to. I've gotten into debt rather deeply."

"In case you haven't noticed, I'm in no position to help you." Anne picked up her pace, wanting to get away from him, from everything.

"It's Nathaniel Matthews. He set me up, costing me five thousand pounds."

Anne stopped and turned to look at him. "Mr. Matthews? How?"

"We belong to the same club. It was supposed to be a friendly game, but he was out for revenge."

Anne frowned. "Revenge? For what?"

"I don't know. Something Father did. I don't remember much about it," John hedged.

He was hiding something, as usual. "Then pay him. It has nothing to do with me." Anne turned away.

"I can't. I owe others. They've already come and cleaned out the town house in London."

"What about the house in Kent?" She felt a pang at the potential loss of her mother's things in Kent. It was still home to her.

"The house itself is entailed and mortgaged. There's nothing left to sell there either."

She wanted to punch him. "Have you given thought to going to the Continent? You'd be doing us all a favor."

"This group would find me." John shot her a look. "They are here, in Beetham."

Anger wove its way through Anne, replacing the sense of humiliation. "You brought them here? And led them to your sisters? What is wrong with you?"

"I had no idea I was being followed," he mumbled.

"We have little to live on as it is. The cottage is leased and none of the contents belong to us," Anne said. "You cannot possibly think we have enough to resolve the debt."

"What about your mother's jewelry?"

"For the last time, I don't have Mother's jewelry. I've not seen any of it since her death."

John's eyes darted around. "You have to help me, Anne. You don't understand the pressure I'm under in Town." Emotion choked his voice.

She turned toward the cottage, unable to deal with one more thing. Unfortunately, her brother continued to follow her. "I've not had the opportunity to go to Town. Sophia and Juliet haven't had the opportunity of a Season. You ruined that, didn't you?"

"Not bitter, are we? Do we have to walk at such a quick pace?"

"You want to talk to me? Keep up. Why shouldn't I be bitter? You've ruined the lives of your sisters."

John stepped back from the anger in her voice.

She took a deep breath and let it out. "There is no use in rehashing history. John, please do us all a favor and leave us alone. Sophia and Juliet will get their hopes up of being a family. I honestly don't have the strength to deal with their disappointment again."

"Anne, I've nowhere else to go." His voice broke.

Anne looked down at the ground. Yes, things could get worse. "Why?"

"The inn threw me out. I couldn't pay for another night. Please, Anne. You're the only family I have."

"Unfortunate that we weren't important to you before now." Anne wanted to walk away. She really did. He could sleep out in the cold tonight, get a taste of what she and her sisters had to deal with. But she just couldn't do it. "Come with me."

"Thank you," John said. "You won't regret it."

"I'd better not." She turned to lead John toward the cottage when she spotted Nathaniel Matthews coming up the road. "Damn."

John went pale. "What?"

"Nathaniel Matthews." Anne straightened her spine and wiped at her face.

"We must leave now." John grabbed her arm and started down the path at a quick pace.

Anne jerked her arm from his grasp. "You will have to face him sooner or later. His grandmother is our nearest neighbor. I'm her companion." She was resolved, and turned to face the enemy. "Mr. Matthews."

"Miss Townsend. I was concerned." Nathaniel glared at Sir John, but otherwise didn't acknowledge him. Instead he turned to Anne and his eyes softened. "Are you all right?"

"As you can see, my sister is in good hands." Sir John threw his shoulders back and pulled at his waistcoat.

Nathaniel kicked up some dirt with the toe of his boot. "I owe you an apology, Miss Townsend. My comments were uncalled for."

"Apology accepted," Anne said sharply and then turned to leave.

"That's it?"

Anne turned back to Mr. Matthews. "Not unless you wish to discuss the card game that cost my brother a fortune?"

Mr. Matthews had the grace to look chagrined. "Now wouldn't be an appropriate time to discuss the matter."

"So genteel," Anne sneered.

Mr. Matthews winced and something like pain flashed in his eyes. "Since your brother is here to see you home, I'll leave you to his company. Good afternoon." Nathaniel bowed and then turned on his heel and left.

Anne felt a pang of guilt. Just because her brother had acted like an idiot didn't mean she had to stoop to his level. "Mr. Matthews!" she called out.

He stopped and turned toward her, hesitant, pain shadowing his eyes. Anne hurried to catch up with him. When she reached him she touched his arm. "I apologize. There are two sides to every story."

"Please don't judge me based on my behavior toward your brother—especially in this matter. It doesn't reflect well on either of us."

She glanced back at John, who was glaring at them both. "He is in dun territory and has nowhere else to go."

"He is your brother, Anne. No other explanation is necessary." Nathaniel pressed her hand with his and turned back toward the pasture at the edge of the Lodge's property.

Anne frowned as she watched him walk toward home. She should be angry with him. It was probably his doing that had brought John to their doorstep.

"Anne, I think he likes you." Sir John came up behind her, interrupting her thoughts.

"Don't be ridiculous."

"Think about it, Anne. If you could win him, then he'd have to forgive the debt." John warmed to his argument. "I had thought maybe Sophia would do the job, but he has clearly taken an interest in you."

Some things just didn't change.

"Enough!" Anne said sharply. "I will not be sold to a man to resolve your debts. And if I find you trying to manipulate Sophia or Juliet in such a manner, I will have you thrown out of the house. Do I make myself clear?"

"Perfectly," Sir John said in a small voice.

Anne resumed walking. Her heart had felt funny at John's comment about Mr. Matthews's feelings for her. It had to be the wish. Otherwise why would he ever pick her over Sophia?

Chapter Five

Nathaniel swirled the brandy in his glass in the gloom of the library. The humiliation he'd seen in Anne Townsend's face as she pushed past him on her way home this morning haunted him still. Whatever was going on, it wasn't something she wanted, but she had reacted with grace and dignity. He had acted like an ass.

His plans for Sir John were not going as he expected. Now Townsend was a burden to Anne. The brandy burned the back of his throat. If Townsend was so deep in dun territory that he needed to stay with Anne, things were truly bad. Unscrupulous creditors would stop at nothing to collect their money. He had brought even more trouble to Anne's door.

Lady Danford breezed into the room and took a seat across from the desk. "You remind me of my husband, sitting like that behind that great desk. It is too cumbersome for me, yet I can't seem to get rid of it."

He wished she had. He swirled the brandy and tossed back a healthy swallow. "The room could use a smaller desk."

Nathaniel ignored the pity in his grandmother's eyes.

"Heavens, I don't know what got into Cecil Worth this morning. To read such a text in service is unpardonable." She pulled her shawl around her. "Mrs. Worth was furious."

Nathaniel swirled the brandy in his glass. "Miss Townsend is the one who should be furious."

"You saw her before she left. How was she?"

Nathaniel felt a pang of guilt at his treatment of Anne. He shifted uncomfortably. "She was visibly upset."

"Poor girl. I regret inviting the Worths to dinner tomorrow night. Mrs. Worth is tiresome on a good day, but this will make her unbearable."

"Why did you invite them? It's clear the woman irritates you."

"Because we are the highest-ranked family in the county. It would not set a good example for the village if we snubbed the vicar and his witch of a mother. Still, given the events of today, I've a mind to cancel altogether."

He couldn't quite meet his grandmother's eyes. "I'm afraid I might have made things worse."

"Oh, Nathaniel, what did you do?"

He didn't like the censure in her expression. "You have to admit that the situation was humorous."

"You didn't laugh at her, surely," she chastised.

Nathaniel looked away. The pain in Anne's eyes when he had laughed still haunted him. The disappointment on his grandmother's face just made him feel lower than dirt.

"I thought I raised you with more sensibility than that, young man." Her voice was hard. "First this revenge scheme of yours, and now you laugh at Anne? How could you?"

Nathaniel swallowed the rest of his brandy. He'd been wondering the same thing. "I don't know. There's just something about her."

"Anne?"

He squirmed under her sharp eyes. "Yes. For one, why do Tony and now Cecil Worth act ridiculous in her presence, but not when she's away?"

She raised one thin eyebrow. "Except for Worth's behavior today, I hadn't noticed."

"Grandmother, Tony wrote poetry about Anne Townsend and wanted to read it to her yesterday."

"Oh, I had forgotten that." She watched him carefully. "Why your own sudden interest in Anne?"

"Just curious. Don't give me that look."

"What look? It's high time for you to find yourself a wife, Son, and frankly, you couldn't do better than Anne Townsend." She sat back in her chair, a smug expression on her face.

"I'm not particularly looking for a wife at the moment." He swirled his drink. "Even if I were, I wouldn't pursue Anne Townsend."

"For heaven's sake, why not?"

"Her father was instrumental in ruining this family."

"Pish. I'm surprised you'd blame the daughter for the father's sins. It's rather pot and kettle of you, isn't it?"

He sat straighter and tugged at his waistcoat. "It is not."

"Besides, you'd probably ruin things anyway with this unholy need for revenge."

"Sir John is the worst libertine. What am I supposed to do? Look away while he ruins another man, especially if that man is a friend of mine?"

"Be careful, Son, or you might lose something infinitely more precious."

"I guess it's too late to tell you to not get any ideas, isn't it?" Nathaniel said.

"I don't know what you mean." Lady Danford stood up and winked at him. "I'm glad Anne Townsend has caught your eye."

"I assure you, madam, that she's not caught my eye in that manner."

"We shall see, when everyone is here for supper and cards tomorrow night." Lady Danford stood. "I expect you to treat Anne with respect this time. In fact, you owe the lady an apology for treating her so shabbily."

Nathaniel grimaced. "I had already planned on calling on her to apologize."

"Good. Don't let it go until tomorrow. She'll only allow it to fester."

Nathaniel watched as his grandmother left, closing the door behind her. He tossed back the remainder of his brandy. He did owe Anne an apology—several, in fact. He looked at the paperwork in front of him and then closed the ledger. It was time for a walk down the lane to the cottage.

Anne led John into the parlor. She was daft for letting him stay. She didn't need creditors banging down the door.

"Hannah will have a light repast ready in about an hour," Anne said as she removed her pelisse and her bonnet. "One more thing, John—I would appreciate if you would keep your reasons for being here from Sophia and Juliet."

"Of course." John made himself comfortable in a chair by the fire, propping his feet up on a nearby stool. He looked *too* comfortable.

Anne's lips tightened. "I'd also appreciate you not getting their hopes up."

"What do you mean?" He attempted an innocent look.

"Do not make promises you have no intention of keeping. They've been through enough pain over the past five years."

John had the grace to look affronted. "I wouldn't dream of it. You wouldn't happen to have any brandy, would you?"

Anne snorted. "Not likely. We've a small amount for medicinal purposes. But you're not sick."

He burrowed deeper into the old chair and loosened his waistcoat. "Perhaps I'll order some for you."

"And pay with what?" Anne put her hands on her hips. "You are not here to run up more bills for me to try to pay."

John raised an eyebrow. "Surely you have credit in this small burgh."

"I prefer to live within my means. A lesson you should learn."

"Anne! Are you home?" Juliet's voice rang in the entryway.

"In here," Anne called out. She turned to John. "Remember what I said."

John laughed. "Or what?"

"I'll throw you to your creditors and let them deal with you." Anne paused in the doorway to greet Juliet and Sophia. "Our brother is here."

"Oh, how I've missed you!" Sophia squealed, and she ran to hug John, who stood up slowly.

Juliet held back at the door. "It's just temporary," Anne whispered to her.

"Come give your brother a proper greeting, Juliet," John said with a smile.

Sophia hung on to one side of him, looking happier than Anne had seen her in a long time. Juliet approached shyly and hugged him.

"I declare you are the prettiest girls in the kingdom," John boasted.

Sophia beamed up at him. "So are you here to take us to London?"

Anne frowned and shook her head. "John is just here for a short visit."

"You must give him your room, Anne," Sophia said quickly. "It is so much better than the guest bedroom."

"I'll take the guest room. I wouldn't want to put Anne out," John said.

"It doesn't matter, I'm just glad you're here. I've missed you so much," Sophia said and plopped down on the faded sofa.

"How long are you planning to stay, John?" Juliet asked.

"I'm not certain yet, but long enough to get to know my sisters again. You've all changed so much. Anne, fetch some tea so we can all have a nice chat."

Fury flowed through Anne. She was sick of being treated like a servant. "Sophia, please have Hannah bring tea in."

"But Anne, I'm visiting," Sophia whined.

"I'll do it," Juliet mumbled, rising from her seat with a frown.

Anne slowly made her way up the stairs, feeling old and tired. Between Mr. Worth and Mr. Matthews, she was done with men. What had possessed both men to humiliate her so? Mr. Worth was pompous, but he didn't seem to be cruel. Mr. Matthews already had a low opinion of her, but this seemed beneath even him.

She wiped her eyes and changed out of her Sunday clothes and into a warmer wool dress. Snow wouldn't be far behind. She looked at the grate in her room and shivered. She'd have to put more quilts on the beds to preserve the fuel. Lord, she hated to be cold.

Anne stared out the window. She could hear Sophia and John laughing downstairs. She heard Mr. Worth's name mentioned, followed by more peals of laughter. Tears smarted in her eyes. Here she was again, the butt of jokes.

Anne uncovered her face and controlled her emotions. Juliet opened the door and peeked in. "Anne, are you all right?"

Anne smiled. "Of course, Juliet. Thank you."

Juliet looked down the hall, then came in and closed the door. "Why is John really here?"

"He's come for a short visit to make amends." Anne kept her expression bland, her voice steady. "Perhaps he's had a change of heart."

"That doesn't seem likely." Juliet frowned. "There's something you aren't telling me."

"Juliet, enjoy this time to get to know him. As the youngest, you didn't get as much of a chance to know John as Sophia did."

"I'm not sure that I trust him. There is something insincere about him."

"He's still our brother. Try to give him a chance."

"If you say so, but I won't have the two of them treating you like a servant," Juliet said fiercely. "It's not right."

Anne smiled. "It will be fine." She infused as much persuasion into her voice as she could. Juliet was too perceptive. She'd catch on to the ruse very quickly.

"About this morning—was Mr. Worth talking about you?" Juliet said.

Anne groaned. "It would appear so."

"I had thought he would want a wife with money."

"He has been attentive of late for some reason." She couldn't tell Juliet about the wish, but she had no other explanation for Mr. Worth's strange behavior. "But I had thought the same, that he would marry a fortune."

"I'm sure Mrs. Worth is determined that he do so. Do you know why he behaved that way in church?" Juliet sat beside her on the bed and put her arm around her. "Mrs. Worth's face was priceless. I thought she'd have apoplexy right there on the spot."

"Now that would have been funny."

"Supper and cards should be very interesting tomorrow night."

"Good God, I forgot about that." Anne flopped back on the bed.

"Are you still going to go?"

"Not if I can help it," Anne mumbled. She had no desire to subject herself to more humiliation.

"Sophia will be livid. You are the only one who can play the piano well enough to dance to," Juliet said. "She's already furious that Tony is paying you more attention than her."

"Tony is in love with her. She has nothing to be angry about."

"Then explain why Tony couldn't stop talking about you on their visit here." There was an edge to her voice.

Anne propped herself up on her elbows. "Juliet, he's been here for several months. Why would he suddenly change his affections?"

"I don't know. He's acting different."

"He's trying to be friendly. That's all." Anne pulled herself up. "Come. Hannah will have luncheon ready."

Juliet stood and paused at the door. "Anne, do I *have* to spend much time with our brother while he's here?"

Anne frowned. "Don't you want to?"

"Not really."

"Has something happened?"

"No. No!" Juliet met her eyes. "He makes me uncomfortable."

Anne hugged her close. "Give it some time. You didn't know him well when we left. You might find that you have more in common than you think."

* * *

While Juliet changed and Sophia entertained John, Anne took the back stairs to the kitchen and put the kettle on. Hannah placed a platter of sandwiches on the table. "I see you've heard we have a guest, Hannah."

"Yes, ma'am. I'll have the tea ready in just a moment. His lordship demanded some sandwiches." Hannah slammed down the knife. "He'll be staying here, then?"

"Yes." Anne placed teacups on the tray. "For a while."

Hannah placed her hands on her hips. "It's not right for him to take advantage of your generosity, Miss Anne."

"I couldn't have him sleeping in a ditch somewhere." Though the thought had crossed her mind.

"There's talk all over town of how he skipped out of the inn without paying his bill," Hannah said. "If they find out he's staying here, they'll expect you to pay."

"That's the least of my worries." The little money she had put aside for fuel wouldn't cover John's debts. "We'll have to cross that bridge when we get there, Hannah. John is still family."

"My mother always said you can't pick your family like you pick your friends. You best be careful with that one. Once he and Miss Sophia get to scheming, there's no telling what will happen." Hannah placed another sandwich on the platter.

Anne nodded. "Were you in church this morning?"

"Lord, yes. What was wrong with the vicar? Embarrassing you like that." Hannah clasped Anne's hands in her work-roughened ones. "Your mother would have been proud of you this morning, miss. You showed a great deal of poise and grace."

"I wanted to throw the hymnbook at him." Anne studied Hannah for a moment. Hannah had always been superstitious, telling Anne many stories of fairies and witches. It was Hannah who had first told her of the legend of the Fairy Steps. "Hannah, you believe in fairies, don't you?"

She looked up from her task. "Aye, miss."

"I climbed the Fairy Steps the other day. Without touching the sides."

"Did you get your wish?"

Anne frowned. "I got *a* wish. I didn't believe, so I wished for the most outrageous thing I could. How could I be so stupid?"

Hannah chuckled. "Fairies are very mischievous, they are. What did you wish for?"

Anne felt her face heat up. She couldn't believe she was telling Hannah this, but she was desperate. "I think I wished for a husband," she mumbled. "One who was rich, handsome, and besotted with me."

Hannah laughed so hard she had to sit down.

"It's not funny," Anne muttered.

"That explains it. Mr. Worth was under your spell when he read that scandalous text," Hannah said with a smile. "Mr. Tony as well?"

Anne nodded. "Tony Matthews has written some poetry about me. And Nathaniel Matthews won't leave me alone."

"Mr. Nathaniel Matthews? Is he taking a fancy to you as well?"

Anne took a seat and played with the teacups on the tray. "No, he's too busy teasing me or questioning me about John."

"Doesn't sound like he's affected like the others." Hannah patted her hand. "Perhaps the spell doesn't work on him."

"Oh, it does. He hasn't given Sophia a second glance." Anne sat and propped her chin on her hands.

"Sophia is too shallow for his taste. He's very different from his brother."

Anne buried her face in her arms. "I need to find a way to break the spell, Hannah."

"A wish is different from a spell, miss. You've made the wish. I don't think it can be broken. You'll just have to let it run its course."

Wonderful. Something that can't be broken. How do I get into these messes? "How long can that take?"

"It takes as long as it takes, Miss Anne."

"I can't take much more of this." Anne drummed her fingers on the table. "I have to end it as soon as possible."

"Well, you could try to climb the steps again and wish to cancel your other wish," Hannah suggested.

"What a wonderful idea!" Hope surged inside her. "I've done it once, I can do it again."

"Be careful, Miss Anne," Hannah cautioned. "You don't want to anger the fairies. They can be very vindictive."

"Oh, I know. I was pelted with acorns on the way home for a comment that I made." Anne stood. "I'll climb them directly. We are at the Lodge for dinner tomorrow with Mr. Worth and his mother. I have no desire to be the subject of her wrath."

"That woman is a harpy. Everyone is too good for her son. Frankly, he'd be lucky to have you," Hannah said sharply.

Anne smiled. "You are biased, Hannah, but I don't want Cecil Worth."

"Nathaniel Matthews is right handsome."

Anne sniffed. "And well he knows it. I could have killed him after church today. He found the whole thing amusing."

"It was rather funny," Hannah said gently. "I saw that he went after you a bit later. Did he find you?"

"Yes, along with John. It didn't take long for him to disappear. He certainly doesn't like my brother."

"He seems to like you."

Anne felt her color rise. "His feelings will pass when the wish has ended."

"And what of your feelings?"

"My feelings are not important." Anne strove to keep her voice neutral.

"They are the *most* important," Hannah said. "Think on this. People react to how you act. While the fairies may have granted you a wish, you chose to believe."

How could that be? Anne stared up at Hannah. "I don't understand."

Hannah laughed. "That is precisely why you have a problem." She picked up the tea tray and walked out of the kitchen.

Anne shook her head. Impossible. She had no control. She hated it. Enough was enough. It was time to end this foolishness.

By late afternoon, the walls of the small cottage where closing in on Anne. Sophia and John were still talking in the parlor. Juliet was somewhere in the house, probably reading. Hannah was working in the kitchen. Anne slipped on her coat and pulled on her gloves, a scarf, and a sturdy bonnet. Stepping outside, she inhaled the crisp air, enjoying the smell of woods and smoke. The afternoon sun was low in the sky. She didn't have much time before dark.

It was a good fifteen-minute walk to the Fairy Steps. Once she reached her destination, she stood at the bottom and looked up. This was the source of all her trouble. She closed her eyes and remembered how she had climbed it the first time. She'd been distracted by her thoughts then. That shouldn't be a problem now. She placed her foot on the first step.

"Miss Townsend," Nathaniel Matthews said behind her.

Anne closed her eyes. *Brilliant.* He was the last man she wanted to see at the moment. She stepped down and faced him.

"Mr. Matthews."

He winced at her icy tone. "I wanted to apologize again for my behavior this morning."

She waited, saying nothing, fighting the urge to cross her arms and tap her foot. What was it about this man?

"I should not have found humor in the situation, at your expense," he continued.

"You weren't the only one." Anne looked away from his piercing eyes. The entire village had had a laugh at her expense.

"Yes, but you were visibly upset. I made light of your feelings. For that I'm truly sorry."

"Apology accepted." Anne turned to return to the house. There was no point trying to climb the steps in the growing dark, especially with Nathaniel Matthews watching.

"Perhaps I can accompany you back?" he said and fell in step beside her.

"No lectures on walking through the woods alone and I'll consider it." Anne accepted his arm. She felt the familiar tingle from touching him.

"I wouldn't dream of it, even though there have been strangers about of late."

His voice rumbled along her nerves. "Beetham is hardly a center for criminal activity. I think I'm safe to walk home alone."

"Pardon me for being cautious," he said sharply.

She could feel him getting angry. "Perhaps you are just accustomed to London. There are few strangers in Beetham."

"True. Which makes it all the more interesting that we've seen one." He helped her over a fallen log, placing her hand on his arm and holding it there.

Anne could feel the muscles work under her hand. His scent, masculine and reminiscent of bay rum, surrounded her. She shivered. "You don't travel here very often. Why come now?"

"My brother." He pushed aside a limb and allowed her to walk past. "I've been watching out for him since our mother died."

"He's been very kind to us because of his interest in Sophia."

"Good. Miss Townsend, may I call you Anne?"

Anne nodded. "Of course, sir."

"Nathaniel. I wanted to discuss my brother's interest in your sister without everyone around." He stopped and turned to her.

Anne crossed her arms and prepared herself.

"Tony is young, too young for marriage. He has yet to experience life after university. I wanted him to establish his living before marriage."

Anne felt her plans dissolve as she tightened her jaw. "I see."

Nathaniel touched her arm gently. "He falls in love so easily that I didn't take it seriously."

Anne had to concede that fact. It hadn't taken much for Tony to be captivated by Sophia.

"It's easy to see why he's attracted to your sister. She is very beautiful," Nathaniel continued.

"Yes, she is." Anne forced herself to drop her arms and relax. Of course he found Sophia beautiful. Everyone did.

Nathaniel took her hand once more. "I would like to suggest we give it some time. See what happens."

He rubbed his thumb against her gloved palm and she fought the urge to pull it out of his grip. His touch stirred inside her like butterflies. "If you wish," she croaked.

"Anne, will you still be at the Lodge for supper and cards tomorrow?" His voice dropped to a low rumble. "I hope so."

Anne looked down at their joined hands. "I had thought to stay home, given the circumstances. My brother is visiting."

Nathaniel frowned. "He isn't invited."

"I didn't expect him to be." She pulled her hand from his grasp.

"How long will he be staying with you?"

She frowned up at him. He was taking that stance of his. "I don't know."

"He left bills unpaid at the inn. I took care of them."

Her spine stiffened. "That was unnecessary, sir. I will repay you, of course. Please see that the bill is sent to me."

"Anne." He took her hand again and squeezed it until she met his eyes. "He will take advantage of you, if you let him."

"I can handle my brother. Please release me."

He raised her hand to his lips and kissed it before letting go. "I'm here if you need anything."

Just his touch had made her want more. More of what, she didn't know and didn't plan to dwell on. She could not let herself be drawn to him. Not now. "Thank you—uh—excuse me." She fled into the woods, headed for the cottage.

Nathaniel watched Anne depart. Just as he felt he was making headway with her, she ran away. At least he was able to apologize and have his apology accepted. He followed her through the woods, determined to make sure she got home safely.

Anne reached the back of her cottage quickly. She turned as if she knew he was watching. The sad look on her face cut him to the quick. She went inside.

He wanted her. He was tired of fighting against this uncontrollable urge to take care of her. Coddle her.

Despite her iron backbone and healthy dose of pride, she was fragile.

He wouldn't be acting on the attraction, despite how much he wanted to see if she would love as passionately as she did everything else.

His grandmother would box his ears for such carnal thoughts. He turned to make his way back to the Lodge.

"That's twice today I found you sniffing after my sister, Matthews." Sir John Townsend lounged against a tree just outside the cottage gate. He took a draw on his cheroot and blew smoke into the air. "I have to ask myself why. Why would a woman such as Anne tempt a man like you?"

"Leave it, Townsend. It's not your affair." Nathaniel curled his hands into fists.

Sir John straightened. He tossed his cheroot and ground it into the dirt. "I see the way you look at her. Frankly, I'm a bit surprised. She's nothing to her sister."

Nathaniel resisted the urge to wipe the smirk off of Townsend's face and forced himself to relax. "Not in beauty perhaps, but there are other qualities."

"You bastard!"

"So you do have feelings for your sisters. And here I thought you were just some bastard who threw them out on their own and walked away."

Nathaniel dodged Sir John as he rushed at him.

"I will not tolerate your insults to my family."

"Don't you think you're in enough trouble?" Nathaniel said. He turned to leave.

"This isn't finished, Matthews. And leave my sister alone."

"Not likely." Nathaniel touched his hat and walked toward the Lodge. It was a hell of a time for Townsend to start feeling protective of his sister.

Chapter Six

Anne looked in the mirror one more time and tried to smooth her hair into place. She was going to have to break down and sew some caps to hide her hair under. It just wouldn't cooperate, like everything else in her life at the moment.

She wanted this evening to be over. Better yet, to not have to go at all. Her stomach hurt and her head pounded, worrying over what the wish would make Mr. Worth do next. His antics during church were beyond the pale. She was afraid she'd punch him if she saw him. She hated being the center of attention, worse yet being laughed at. The village gossips must be having a field day with yesterday's debacle. She wouldn't be able to show her face in the village now without someone snickering.

The goal tonight was to be as invisible as possible, and this dark blue wool would help. She tucked a lace fichu into the low, curved neckline. She fastened her mother's gold cross around her neck and straightened the lace edging on her sleeves. She'd also have the piano to hide behind. No one would dance if she didn't play. If luck was with her, she might pass the entire evening without having to talk to either Mr. Worth or Mr. Matthews, except for the usual pleasantries.

Between Mr. Matthews and Mr. Worth, Anne didn't know whom she wanted to hit first. Mr. Matthews had found humor in her humiliation, but Mr. Worth was the cause of said humiliation.

It was enough to make Anne swear off men forever.

Sophia entered the room without a knock. "Here's a ribbon for your hair, Anne. Why is it pulled back so severely? What are you doing in that old dress?" Sophia threw the ribbon at Anne and stomped to the wardrobe. "You cannot go to Lady Danford's dressed that way. What will people say?"

Anne tossed the ribbon on her dressing table. "I couldn't care less, Sophia."

"You don't want to make it worse. It's bad enough that Mr. Worth singled you out at service yesterday with that scandalous sermon, but you must at least appear presentable. That old dress needs to be put into the rag bag."

"This dress is fine, Sophia." Anne's voice brooked no argument. "I'm not changing."

"You are impossible. How you look reflects on Juliet and myself—did you think about that?"

"Then I'll stay home." How she'd love to stay home with the book she brought back from Lady Danford's.

Sophia grabbed her arm. "You cannot! You must face down Mr. Worth and put the gossip to rest. The whole village is talking about his behavior yesterday."

Anne groaned. "All the more reason to stay home." She looked longingly at the book on her bedside table.

"Why can't John come? Who decided he should stay behind, anyway?" Sophia pulled a dress of pale green from the back of the closet. "It's a few years old, but it will do. And put this ribbon in your hair." She tossed the ribbon back at Anne.

"John can't just show up at Lady Danford's. He's not been issued an invitation." Anne picked up the green dress and hung it back in the wardrobe. "This is a ball gown. I'm not wearing it."

Sophia yanked the dress back out of the wardrobe and threw it on the bed. "I can't have Mr. Matthews thinking we are so poor that we can't properly dress for dinner."

Anne glared at her sister. "I don't care what Mr. Matthews thinks."

"Regardless, if you wish Tony to become a member of this family, you will appear respectable and not look like a poor relation." Sophia walked to the door. "I will see you downstairs in ten minutes." She slammed the door behind her.

Anne glanced at the dress on the bed. She remembered the last time she had worn it at a ball. She had actually danced that night. She put the dress back in the wardrobe. It was not a dress that encouraged invisibility. She wasn't changing.

There was another knock on the door. Juliet opened the door slightly and peeked through. "Sophia sent me up to help you dress."

She entered and closed the door gently behind her. "She's right that you can't wear that old thing."

"It's either wear this or not go," Anne said, sitting on the bed. "I'd rather stay home."

"You've never been one to hide from gossip, Anne. Why start now?" Juliet came over and toyed with Anne's hair. "This dress is old and faded."

"It's a reflection of my mood." Anne met Juliet's eyes in the mirror. "I really don't want to go."

"And miss Mrs. Worth's face when she sees you tonight? She's has been whining all over town about her son's behavior and how your allurements must have caused this breach in his good behavior."

Anne laughed but sat. "My allurements? That's a first." She looked down at her hands. "I don't think I can face them after what happened." Her voice broke and she blinked rapidly to fight back the tears.

"Anne, this isn't like you. You've faced everyone head-on with our circumstances, daring them to say anything. Why is this different?" Juliet pulled the pins from Anne's hair and picked up the brush.

The strokes of the brush soothed Anne. She wiped at her face. "I hate being laughed at."

"You should have seen Mrs. Worth's face. She was as purple as a plum." They both laughed. Juliet hugged Anne tightly. "Lady Danford was very upset on your account, Anne. She sent Mr. Matthews after you to make sure you were all right."

"He's part of the problem." Anne toyed with her fichu. She allowed Juliet to pull her hair back into a softer twist. Juliet pulled curls down around Anne's face and wove a ribbon through the tresses.

Juliet surveyed her handiwork. "Much better."

"Thank you, Juliet."

"Mr. Matthews seemed very concerned," Juliet said. "He was watching you quite a bit during church."

"You didn't see him laughing at me as I left."

"Did he try to apologize?"

"John was there. So Mr. Matthews didn't say much. He did apologize later."

"Later? When did you see him again?" Juliet had that curious look in her eye.

"I escaped the house yesterday afternoon for a ramble through the woods. He found me there." Anne kept her voice calm.

"You know Sophia will give you hell about not changing," Juliet said with a smile. "But if we remove the fichu, she might not say much." Juliet yanked the fichu from Anne's neckline. "There, that's so much better."

"Juliet, I'm too exposed!" Anne covered her chest with her hand. "It's not proper."

"It's no worse than what Sophia is wearing. In fact, it's less revealing. Trust me."

"If I must." Anne folded the lace and put it away in a drawer.

"Why isn't John invited?" Juliet played with the curls around Anne's face. "It seems strange for Lady Danford to not extend the invitation."

"John owes Mr. Matthews a good deal of money," Anne said. "He owes everyone a good deal of money."

"How long is he staying?"

"I don't know."

Juliet arranged a few more curls around Anne's face. "You look very pretty."

"I don't want to look pretty. I want to be invisible."

"I think Mr. Matthews likes you. You like him as well."

Anne whirled on Juliet. "I'm just a means of entertainment to Mr. Matthews."

"Anne, you are acting worse than Sophia. This is just supper and cards."

Anne grimaced. She *was* acting like Sophia. "You're right."

"Shall we go now?" Juliet said brightly.

"I guess so." Anne followed her sister out of the bedroom and down the stairs. John was sitting by the fire with a paper in his hands. There was a brandy glass next to him.

"John, where did you get the brandy?"

"I had Thomas pick some up from the village. It's not what I'm used to, but it will do." He turned back to his paper.

"How did you pay for it?" Anne demanded.

"Anne, must you always be the shrew?" Sophia said sharply. "If John needs something he should have it."

"John, how did you pay?" Anne repeated. He would not run bills up in her name.

"If you must know, I had a few coins and I paid on my own," John said with disgust. "Don't worry, Anne, I keep my promises. I won't run up any debt in your name."

"See that you keep it that way," she said, her voice sharp.

"So you ladies are all dressed for Lady Danford's, but who will escort you?" he said snidely.

"We usually go alone. It's but a short walk to the Lodge." Anne wrapped her old velvet cloak around her.

"It's pouring rain out there. I don't suppose you plan to arrive as drowned rats." John laughed.

"Didn't you bring your coach, John?" Sophia asked. "We could travel in that."

"Yes, John. Where is your coach? The one with the family crest?" Anne enjoyed the flush creeping through John's cheeks.

"It's being repaired in Town, I'm afraid, Sophia."

Anne glared at him. She hated when he lied to her sisters. Worse, he was making her look like a fool. Anne turned as she heard a carriage pull up to the house.

Juliet ran to look out the window. "It's the carriage from the Lodge."

"Tony must have sent it to us so we wouldn't get wet," Sophia said. "He's so thoughtful."

There was a knock on the door and Juliet opened it. Nathaniel Matthews stood in the doorway, his hat dripping. Anne could only stare at him as he ducked into the house. Nathaniel ignored John and instead bowed to her and her sisters.

"I hope you don't mind, but I took the liberty of coming to escort you tonight," he said smoothly. "I couldn't see you walking in this weather."

Sophia pushed past Juliet and Anne. "How kind of you, sir."

Juliet walked over to Anne. "This is your doing, Anne," she whispered. "Tony Matthews would never have thought of that."

"Hush, Juliet," Anne whispered back. She stepped forward. "Thank you for your kindness, Mr. Matthews."

"If we could be off, I believe dinner will be served shortly." He held out his arm to Anne. "If I may?"

Anne took his arm and glanced back to see the disappointment on Sophia's face as she trailed behind. Though Anne was the eldest, she rarely was escorted first. Most men only had eyes for Sophia, regardless of manners. Anne looked at Juliet, who mouthed "I told you so" and quickly turned away.

Anne allowed Mr. Matthews to help her into the carriage, then scooted over to allow her sisters to join her. Sophia came in and sat across from her. Juliet sat beside Sophia and winked at Anne. She sighed. The only place left for Nathaniel was by her side. He climbed in and sat next to her, filling up the space and pressing against her. He rapped on the ceiling to signal the driver to go.

Anne pressed herself against the wall of the carriage to avoid him, but he just moved closer. The smell of spice and masculinity filled her head. Why did he have to smell so good?

She pulled her cloak around her, willing herself to be invisible.

"Terrible rain tonight." His voice boomed in the small carriage. "And cold. Are you warm enough, Miss Townsend?"

"Yes," Anne whispered.

"Thank you for coming to get us, Mr. Matthews. We were dreading the walk in this weather." Sophia's voice was melodic and sweet.

Anne looked at Sophia. She was gazing up at Nathaniel, her eyes soft. How did she do that?

Anne chanced a glance at Nathaniel and found him staring down at her. She looked down at her hands and fought the urge to squirm.

"Are you thankful, Miss Townsend?" His voice was soft and low. Shivers ran through her.

"I was getting ready to send our regrets. You've saved us from disappointing Lady Danford," Anne said coldly. She looked away but not before she caught his wide grin.

"Anne!" Sophia exclaimed.

"I see I'm not forgiven yet," Nathaniel said.

"Forgiven for what, Mr. Matthews?" Sophia asked.

"I'm afraid I was rather callous to your sister, Miss Sophia. I have apologized, but I'm afraid that what I did is unforgivable."

"Nothing is unforgivable, sir," Anne said. "Some things just need more time than others."

"What have you done, Mr. Matthews?" Juliet asked.

"Nothing of consequence, Juliet," Anne said quickly. She felt Nathaniel chuckle beside her. Impertinent man. She fought the urge to punch him.

"I'm sure there's nothing Mr. Matthews has done that can't be forgiven, especially in the short time you've known each other," Sophia said.

She was fishing for information. She had that calculating look in her eye. Anne forced a serene mask and smiled slightly.

"You are correct, Miss Sophia," Nathaniel added. "Miss Townsend and I have not started out on the right foot, if you will. But I'm sure things will straighten themselves out to everyone's satisfaction."

What in the name of God did that mean? Given the warm look in his eyes, Anne didn't want to know. There was just something about the man that pulled on her like a magnet. She needed to be strong and resist.

Nathaniel had purposely picked the smaller of Lady Danford's carriages for the short trip to fetch the Townsend sisters. Anne pressed as far away from him as she could get in order to avoid touching him. Unfortunately for her, it did no good. Her scent of lavender and warm skin teased his senses the entire trip. It was worth the torture to have her near.

Upon entering the Lodge, his suffering became even more acute. When Anne's cloak was removed, he saw she was dressed in a plain, dark blue gown with a low neckline that made her skin glow. Her hair was swept up in such a way that curls teased the smooth flesh where her neck met her shoulder. She looked like a delicate flower.

Sophia Townsend placed herself in front of Anne in order to speak to him. "Thank you again for bringing us to the Lodge, Mr. Matthews."

"My pleasure, Miss Sophia," Nathaniel said. She smiled up at him warmly. He stepped back. "I think the rest of the party is waiting in the parlor." He offered his arm once more to Anne.

Anne took his arm. Miss Sophia pouted but followed behind them. Nathaniel led them into the parlor, where Lady Danford and Tony waited. Nathaniel watched as Anne released him and went to greet his grandmother.

"Thank you for inviting us, my lady," Anne said softly.

"Anne, come sit down," said Lady Danford.

Anne took a seat near her hostess. Juliet sat next to her. Nathaniel rested against the mantel. "When are the Worths expected? I thought they would be here by now."

"I imagine the weather might slow them up," Lady Danford replied. She turned to Anne. "I apologize, dear, for tonight. I had no idea—"

"Do not trouble yourself, my lady," Anne said. "We had no idea that Mr. Worth would do what he did yesterday."

"So we can speak of it?" Sophia asked.

"That depends," Tony said, moving to sit next to Sophia. "We mustn't embarrass Miss Townsend any further."

"Of course," Sophia acknowledged. "I just wondered if anyone knew why he read that awful text yesterday."

Nathaniel watched the color wash across Anne's skin. Her hands were clasped tightly in her lap. "I suggest we discuss something else, Miss Sophia. We wouldn't want to make your sister uncomfortable."

Anne met his eyes and smiled her thanks. Sophia looked angry.

"It is difficult to not discuss it, given all the gossip in the village," Anne said quietly.

"You shouldn't listen to that nonsense, Anne." Lady Danford patted her hand. "Best way to deal with gossips is with your head held high. You've done nothing wrong."

"The gossip will pass, Anne," Juliet added.

"Mrs. Worth and the vicar, Mr. Worth, ma'am," the footman announced.

Mrs. Worth and her son entered the room. Mrs. Worth was dressed in a gown that had to be several years old. A faded feather floated in her white hair. In contrast, Cecil Worth was dressed in the current fashion. The cut of his coat and the knot of his cravat spoke of a recent visit to Town.

"Welcome to our party, Mrs. Worth," Nathaniel said with a bow.

"The weather is so frightful, I was tempted to stay home by the fire," she complained.

"I'm glad you decided to join us," Lady Danford said.

"The truth is, Cecil wouldn't miss the party," Mrs. Worth said, taking a seat next to Lady Danford. She glared at Anne. "I can't imagine what would tempt him to drive in this weather. Except for your company, my lady."

"Now, Mother, don't insult all these young ladies," Cecil Worth said, moving across the room to take Anne's hand. She tried to pull her hand away before he pressed his lips to it. "Miss Townsend, I'm glad you're here tonight."

Anne finally freed her hand and returned it to her lap. She looked away and said nothing.

Nathaniel had a nearly uncontrollable urge to slam his fist into

Cecil Worth's face. He frowned at his protective feelings for Anne Townsend.

"Really, Mr. Worth, I think you've done enough to my sister without embarrassing her further," Juliet said.

Anne laid her hand on Juliet's. "Juliet, please. Not here."

"Shall we all go in for dinner?" Lady Danford said, and rose. "Mr. Worth, if you would be so kind to escort me to the dining room."

"Of course, my lady." Mr. Worth offered his arm and led her from the room.

Nathaniel wanted to offer his arm to Anne, but he offered it to Mrs. Worth instead. He didn't want to add to the gossip Mrs. Worth would likely spread after Anne had ignored her son. Tony led the rest of the ladies into the dining room. It was going to be a long night.

Anne pushed the peas around her plate, her appetite gone. She picked up her wineglass and forced herself to sip slowly rather than gulp it down for courage. Never again would she envy Sophia for all the attention men paid her. Sophia laughed and managed it easily. Anne wanted to run screaming for home. She hated the attention. She stabbed at a piece of meat on her plate.

Mr. Worth sat on her right. Nathaniel was to her left. Mrs. Worth was across from her. Each time Nathaniel spoke to her, Mr. Worth had to say something to pull her attention away.

Anne couldn't keep the two conversations straight, so she just nodded. As the meal went on, the two men were bent on gaining her complete attention to the point that she couldn't keep up with who said what.

Mrs. Worth seemed intent on making sure everyone knew that her son would not be marrying Anne. As if she wanted to marry him after his behavior in church yesterday! She could barely sit next to him. God was surely punishing her.

"Miss Townsend, is the meal to your liking? You don't appear to be eating." Mr. Worth moved in close to her.

Anne scooted closer to Nathaniel to avoid him. These chairs were much too close together.

"It's not good for a girl to not eat," Mrs. Worth added.

Anne choked on her food and grabbed her wine. Mr. Matthews made a noise something like a snort and she had an urge to pour her wine on his crisp white shirt. "I'm fine, Mrs. Worth, thank you."

"Perhaps it's just the peas," Nathaniel said under his breath.

"Perhaps it's the company, Mr. Matthews," Anne said under her own breath. She sipped a bit more of the wine.

"I didn't take you as a wine drinker, Miss Townsend," Mrs. Worth said. "One must be careful to present the right image to our parishioners. I've told Cecil that he must be very careful in his choice of wife so that the right image is preserved."

Anne gulped down the rest of her wine. "You are quite right, Mrs. Worth. A gentleman can't be too careful, especially when he represents God."

"Touché," Nathaniel whispered.

Anne crossed her legs under the table and kicked his shin. He grunted. She smiled for the first time that evening.

"Revenge is mine, saith the Lord," Nathaniel quoted. "Or shall I quote Song of Solomon again?"

His breath touched her ear. Anne stared at her plate and fought the urge to shiver. She could feel the heat in her face. "Quiet!" she hissed at him.

He chuckled and faced Mrs. Worth. "I don't think a bit of wine with dinner affects a woman's reputation, Mrs. Worth."

"She was gulping it down!" Mrs. Worth replied. "I daresay she might have a problem with spirits."

"I will, if this continues," Anne mumbled. Given Nathaniel's shaking shoulders, he must have heard her comment. She looked down the table to Sophia, who was in a private conversation with Tony Matthews. No help there. She looked over at Juliet, who rolled her eyes. Anne allowed the footman to refill her glass.

"Are you sure that's a good idea, Miss Townsend?" Nathaniel whispered as she sipped the dark red wine.

She set the glass down carefully, blaming the wine and not the man next to her for the unsteadiness of her hand. "Perhaps you are right," she answered. "But you've driven me to it."

"That's the first kind thing you've said to me this night."

She glared at him, wanting to kick him again. The room slightly tilted and she wished for a glass of water. Perhaps she *had* drunk too much wine.

"Miss Townsend, are you quite well?" Mr. Worth said on her right. "You look flushed."

"I'm fine, Mr. Worth," Anne said curtly.

"You are very out of sorts this evening, Miss Townsend," Mrs. Worth said coldly from across the table.

"My sister is fine," Juliet said a little too loudly.

Anne shook her head at Juliet. She must have drunk too much wine because suddenly everything was funny, including Mrs. Worth's pickled face. Anne pulled in a deep breath and returned to her food. Perhaps it would counter the wine.

"Juliet, dear, I have several new books for you to read," Lady Danford said from the other end of the table. "I have another one from Mrs. Radcliffe. I know how much you liked her last book."

"Thank you, ma'am," Juliet said and grinned widely. "I look forward to reading them."

"I think it's totally inappropriate for girls to read novels," Mrs. Worth said. "It gives them ideas."

"What a shame it would be for our girls to have ideas of their own, Mrs. Worth." Lady Danford smiled.

"My lady, you know that's not what I meant," Mrs. Worth said quickly. "It stirs false hope, these romantic novels."

"What an interesting view. Shall we discuss it over tea?" Lady Danford stood. "Gentlemen, I think we will leave you to your port."

Sophia grabbed Anne's arm as they left the dining room. "Anne, what is wrong with you?"

"I have no idea." Anne pulled her arm from Sophia's grasp. She felt herself weave and grasped her sister's arm.

"You're foxed!" Sophia accused. "How could you?"

"You try dealing with Cecil Worth and his mother and tell me you wouldn't be downing wine by the glass." Anne released Sophia's arm and pulled in a steadying breath. She could do this. Wine or not.

"Mr. Matthews seems to be paying a great deal of attention to you."

"He's not interested in anything but stirring up trouble," Anne said. "He spent the evening laughing at me." She moved to follow Lady Danford to the drawing room.

"Why did he grunt earlier?" Sophia asked.

"I kicked him." She wished she had worn her half boots instead of these foolish slippers. It would have hurt more.

"Anne, you didn't!" Sophia's eyes widened.

"Yes. I did."

"How do you expect to win Nathaniel Matthews's approval if you keep kicking him?" Sophia whispered furiously. "Are you deliberately trying to wreck this?"

Anne glared at Sophia. "I thought you were going to drop Tony and woo his brother with your feminine wiles."

Sophia stepped back from her, her eyebrows raised. "This is not to be borne. You're embarrassing us all. Perhaps you should claim illness and go home."

"When things are just getting interesting? I don't think so." She giggled.

"You're drunk—you can't continue this way. Perhaps Juliet can convince you." Sophia waved at Juliet before she took a seat next to the fire.

Lady Danford and Mrs. Worth had settled into chairs and were sipping tea. The room spun a bit more.

"Anne, are you well?" Juliet whispered, coming over to her quickly. "You look quite flushed."

"She's foxed," Sophia said sharply. "We have to get her home."

"Then who will play for your dancing, Sophia?" Anne said. "I'm not drunk—half sprung, perhaps."

"Take her home," Sophia whispered to Juliet.

"I will not."

"Shush," Sophia whispered. "She'll ruin everything if she continues."

"Oh please, Sophia," Anne said. "Enough."

"You'll just take all of Anthony's attention if you stay," Sophia sniped. "As soon as he hears you play, he'll be back to speaking nothing but your praises."

"Sophia, that's not true," Juliet said. "Tony only has eyes for you."

"Mr. Worth and Mr. Matthews seemed to monopolize all of Anne's time," Sophia whined.

"It's not what you think," Anne retorted.

"Between his impassioned speech at church and his attentions tonight, I've no doubt that Mr. Worth is smitten with you. Perhaps he'll propose tonight," Sophia said. "Wouldn't that be a fine thing for this family?"

Anne fought an uncontrollable urge to smack Sophia's face. "Perhaps he'll learn to live with rejection."

Sophia continued. "Then there is all the attention Mr. Matthews is paying you. What's that about?"

"Let's put this notion to bed. Mr. Matthews is not interested in me. He's interested in stirring up trouble and teasing me."

"Anne—" Juliet moved to hush their voices.

"Miss Townsend, what are you and Miss Sophia discussing over there so secretly?" Lady Danford said loudly.

"Nothing serious, my lady," Sophia said. She smiled serenely. "Anne was telling me she longed to play for us all."

"Perhaps later, Sophia," Anne said. Perhaps she would claim a headache and escape. It wasn't too far from the truth. The wine wasn't settling in her stomach.

"I must say, Miss Townsend, I didn't take you for the type to inspire Cecil's scandalous behavior in service yesterday," Mrs. Worth said. "I spent the afternoon defending him. You must have done something to bewitch him."

"Bewitch? Anne?" Sophia laughed.

Enough was enough. Anne turned on Mrs. Worth. "Your son humiliated me in front of the entire congregation and you have the audacity to blame me? If you will excuse me."

Anne forced herself to the door with as much dignity as she could muster and left the drawing room, closing the door behind her.

She all but ran to the empty library. Once inside she slipped off her shoes and curled into one of the large leather chairs, pressing her face into her knees. Tears pricked her eyes.

What is wrong with me?

Anne felt like a top spinning out of control.

She didn't like it. Not one bit.

Nathaniel sipped his brandy and watched Cecil Worth and Tony play billiards. Cecil was very different with his mother out of the room. He was quiet and somewhat shy around his shrew of a mother. Without her, he was the typical, full-of-himself gentleman Nathaniel had seen too many times in Town.

"What brings you so far north, Mr. Matthews?" Cecil asked as he lined up his shot.

"I'm visiting my grandmother and my brother." Nathaniel sipped his whiskey. "How long have you been in Beetham, sir?"

"Several years now. The vicarage was passed to me by my uncle. Not the living I wanted, but you know how these things are. Couldn't step into trade."

Tony cleared his throat. "Sir, is there a problem with being an investor in business?"

"No, not at all. I'd invest if I could. It's a grand time for investments."

"Indeed. We've been very lucky with ours." Nathaniel set his drink down. The vicar was an idiot but he had history in Beetham. "That was a very odd text for you to read during the service yesterday."

Worth took his shot, cursed, and then stood back to let Tony shoot. "It quite surprised even me, actually. It's not as if I did an in-depth study of that part of the Bible at university."

"What made you select it?" Tony asked as he lined up his shot.

"It was quite odd. I just opened to that passage and had this uncontrollable urge to read it." Cecil moved around the table as Tony lined up another shot. "One moment I was looking at Miss Anne Townsend, the next moment I was reading this salacious text in the Bible."

"Can you say salacious and Bible in the same sentence?" Tony quipped.

"I suppose Miss Townsend will expect a proposal now that you've declared your feelings so openly," Nathaniel said.

"Have you heard about the Townsend jewels?" Worth said, leaning on his cue stick. "They are said to be worth a fortune."

Nathaniel looked at Tony, who shook his head. "I would have thought the Townsend jewels would be with their brother." Nathaniel wondered what this had to do with Anne Townsend and the strange Bible text.

"Well, the rumor is that Miss Townsend took the jewels when she left Kent. I suspect that's why her brother is in the village." Cecil lined up his next shot.

"I would assume if the Townsend ladies had any jewels, they would have long ago sold them. Though with Sir John in the village, you may be right."

"Couldn't Sir John just want to visit his sisters?" Tony asked. "They are family."

Worth laughed. "Not from what I hear. He threw the girls out without a farthing. Perhaps Miss Townsend crossed a line. She kept house for the old baronet after her mother died. Maybe she took the jewels for revenge."

"Why would they live in such poverty if they had a fortune right under their noses?" Nathaniel asked. None of this made sense to him. Anne Townsend was practical to a fault.

"Now there's the question of the day," Cecil said with a laugh. He paused and tossed back his port.

"But why would Sir John throw his sisters out?" Nathaniel wondered.

"No one has ever spoken of it." Worth lined up his shot. "Mother thinks there was something inappropriate in their past. Sir John wouldn't have thrown them out, otherwise."

"Inappropriate? How so?" Nathaniel stood and splashed more port into Cecil's glass. He needed his tongue loosened a bit more.

"I'm not really certain."

"I'm sure, as a gentleman, you've not repeated the story given that it can't be proven." This made no sense. Anne Townsend didn't seem the type of woman who would behave in an inappropriate manner. She had passion in her, but it was tightly controlled and hidden behind that mask of hers. Was that all it was? A mask?

"Of course. Of course," Cecil said quickly. "I have to wonder about the existence of the jewels. The previous baronetess was French aristocracy. Rumor is, she brought the jewels with her from France."

"There is no evidence of wealth, at least from what I've seen," said Tony.

"The jewels would have gone to her husband," Nathaniel stated. "Perhaps they were sold?"

"That's just it—there is no evidence that they've been sold. Nor have they been found," Cecil continued.

Nathaniel turned toward Cecil. "How did you discover this?"

"Sir John himself told me."

Nathaniel found himself curious about the Townsend sisters. He tried to tell himself that it was just because of the debt that Sir John owed him, but he couldn't deny that Anne was getting under his skin. "Are you acquainted with Sir John Townsend?"

"We met in school. He was always going on and on about his mysterious stepmother." Cecil handed his cue stick to a footman. "My guess is that Miss Townsend has the jewels stashed away somewhere. How else could she and her sisters live without their brother's help?"

"It could be true," Tony mused. "Have you ever asked Miss Townsend directly?"

"Oh no. It would be impertinent. Miss Townsend doesn't like people meddling in her affairs."

"Sophia did tell me that Anne was counting on her marrying well," Tony said.

"Probably to take care of her sisters." Cecil tossed down more port. "Mother says that Lady Danford will provide for the girls, especially if you marry the younger one, Matthews."

"I'm fully aware of that, Worth," Tony said tersely.

Nathaniel exchanged another look with Tony. "Let's join the ladies, shall we?"

"Perhaps we can have Miss Townsend play. She is a superior performer," Tony said.

"Good idea," said Nathaniel. "A little music would defuse the tension." He kept his voice low as he watched Cecil Worth walk toward the parlor. "Don't say anything to anyone about this conversation, Tony."

Tony frowned. "Of course not. But why the sudden interest?"

"You know me. I like puzzles, and Miss Townsend is turning into a very complex puzzle."

"She's not like her sisters. She's much more vulnerable."

"I am capable of being a gentleman."

"You'd better be or I'll challenge you myself," Tony whispered harshly. "Those ladies have been through enough without you adding to their troubles."

Chapter Seven

Anne had no idea how long she sat staring at the fire in the library. The smell of books and leather wrapped around her like a warm blanket. The heat of the fire, combined with the wine she had drunk on a nearly empty stomach, was making her drowsy. She tilted her head back and closed her eyes, drifting into that place between sleep and awareness. The sound of the door opening startled her.

"Sophia, please just give me five more minutes before I have to face them again."

"If you think five minutes will be enough." Nathaniel Matthews's deep voice held a tinge of laughter as he closed the door and moved into the room.

Anne groaned. This was the last thing she needed. "Sir, with you I'd need weeks. Can you just leave me in peace."

He moved a chair to face hers and sat down. She couldn't look away from the earnest expression on his face.

"Is there anything I can do?" His voice was low and rumbled up her spine.

Anne sat up and slipped on her shoes. "No, I think you've done enough. I'm glad I could be so entertaining at dinner tonight."

"You don't like being laughed at."

"I prefer being laughed with."

"Point taken. We seem doomed to be at cross purposes."

Anne looked, really looked, at Nathaniel. The firelight played along his strong jaw. His eyes were kind. "Why aren't you in the drawing room, Mr. Matthews?"

"It's Nathaniel, and I'm here for the same reason as you, to escape. I'm sorry if you thought I was laughing at you earlier. Frankly, I thought you handled Mrs. Worth's rudeness very graciously."

"You missed the show in the drawing room," Anne muttered.

"That bad?"

Anne turned back to the fire. "Worse. I lost my temper. I never lose my temper."

"In that we are alike."

"What do you mean?"

"We both like to be in control. I would have had a difficult time handling the debacle yesterday, as well as Mrs. Worth's behavior today. I commend you on how well you dealt with both."

Anne laughed bitterly. "I'm not very proud of my behavior."

"Nor I. We tend to let people like Mrs. Worth get under our skin."

Anne chuckled. "I don't know whether to thank you or be offended."

"I meant it as a compliment. Mr. Worth was quite open while we drank our port."

"I don't care to know," Anne said sharply. She then sighed. "I'm sorry. The village gossip is rabid."

"I expect the matrons are expecting Mr. Worth to make an offer." His voice was gentle.

The thought of Mr. Worth proposing soured her stomach even further. Anne closed her eyes. Between the wish, Nathaniel Matthews's presence, and now this, she just wanted to crawl into her bed and pull the covers over her head.

"Would you—consider an offer from Mr. Worth?"

There was something uncertain in his voice that startled Anne. "It may be the only decent offer I get."

"Surely that's not true."

"Do you see a line of suitors lined up at the door?" His presence was disturbing. She could feel his eyes on her. "Why are you staring at me?"

Nathaniel smiled. "I like the way the firelight plays with the red in your hair."

Anne felt her face heat. "Please don't."

"I thought women liked compliments," Nathaniel teased.

"I prefer honesty." She kept her voice brisk. She was starting to like him a good deal too much.

"I am being honest. You deserve more than Mrs. Worth's insults. More than your sister's disdain as well."

"With all due respect, Mr. Matthews, you do not know of what you speak." Anne stood and brushed the wrinkles out of her dress. "I should return to the parlor."

Nathaniel stood and touched her arm. "Wait, Anne. I meant no offense."

"No offense taken, sir. You are entitled to your opinion. In this case, I'd appreciate it if you'd mind your own business."

Nathaniel moved closer to her, blocking out the light of the fire with his height. She looked up but couldn't see his face in the shadows. Awareness coursed through her and she fought the urge to step back. His scent, a mixture of wine and spice, surrounded her. It was a heady mix and she breathed it in deeply.

"I'd like to know you better, Anne." He lifted her chin so that he could see her face. His fingers were gentle against her skin and he rubbed his thumb along her jawline. "There's just something about you."

Anne shivered from his touch, so warm on her skin. "Sir, I don't think—"

He chuckled softly as he stroked her jaw. "You think a good deal too much, Miss Townsend. Sometimes you just need to feel."

He lowered his head to hers, his eyes on her mouth.

"Don't," Anne whispered.

"I can't help myself."

Nathaniel brushed his lips ever so gently against hers and she let her eyes close. She stood still, unable to move as his mouth brushed across hers several times. She gasped and he took the kiss deeper, settling his lips more firmly on hers. Anne put her hands on his chest to push him away, but as his tongue slipped into her mouth, she felt her knees go weak and she clung to him instead. He was ever so gentle, teasing her into a response she couldn't have hidden if she wanted to. Fire licked through her and she pushed her arms around his neck and her hands into his dark, curly hair. He lifted his head slightly and she stared up at him in a daze. He gently kissed her again and stepped back.

"We should return to the parlor." His voice was gravelly. He pulled her arms from around his neck and squeezed her hands gently. "Perhaps you will give me the pleasure of hearing you play. I've been told you are quite talented."

Anne pulled in a steady breath. Her face felt as if it were on fire.

There was no way she could face the group in the parlor now. Sophia would certainly know something had happened. "Perhaps you should go ahead, sir. We should not be seen entering together."

Nathaniel brushed a finger down her cheek before releasing her. "Always proper, aren't you, Anne?" He kissed her hand and left as quietly as he had arrived.

Anne sunk into a nearby chair. "Oh my." She touched her lips with her hand, sure that they'd be swollen from his kiss. Her heart thudded in her chest. How would she face him again? How would she face Lady Danford?

"The wish," Anne whispered aloud. It was the only explanation for Nathaniel's attentions. Fairy magic that made him attracted to her. Anne's shoulders slumped. She had been foolish to believe he really felt something for her. She would have to guard against any further interactions with Nathaniel. He could steal her heart before she had a chance to stop him. If her reaction to his kiss was any indication, it might be too late.

Anne stood outside the parlor door. Her hair was as tamed as it was going to get. Her lips were still swollen. She could still feel Nathaniel Matthews's mouth against hers.

Lord, will they be able to tell I've been kissed? She composed her face.

"Anne, where have you been?" Sophia rushed forward. "The gentlemen have been here for some time now."

Anne blushed as she caught Nathaniel watching her. "Sophia, keep your voice down and don't make a fuss."

Sophia frowned at her and looked closer. "What is wrong with you? You look flushed."

Anne resisted the urge to raise her hands to her cheeks. "I had a slight headache."

"I was just coming to ask if you could play for us. You don't have to bite my head off."

"Fine."

Anne made her way to the piano, not looking at anyone. She sorted through the music and picked a piece. Her fingers moved across the keys automatically. She let the music soothe her still-racing pulse. She looked up to find Nathaniel watching.

His clear blue eyes scorched her. She stumbled over the passage she was playing. She turned back to the music with a vengeance.

"Perhaps if you would play a jig, we could dance," Sophia said as she moved to replace the sheet music Anne was playing with another. "Please, Anne?"

"There aren't enough couples for a dance," Anne replied. "Besides, this piece suits my mood."

"Tony can dance with Juliet and I'll dance with Mr. Matthews," Sophia insisted. "I'm in the mood for a dance."

"Fine." Anne started playing the jig. Sophia scampered across the parlor and smiled at Nathaniel. Anne watched as they danced together. He was the perfect foil to Sophia's beauty despite the heated glances he shot her way. Anne quickly looked away toward Juliet, who was dancing with Tony. He was also watching Sophia and his brother. Meanwhile Juliet was staring up at Tony adoringly.

Anne looked back at the music as Sophia laughed at something Nathaniel said. She felt a pang of jealousy. He was probably thinking that he had kissed the wrong sister. He caught her looking at him. Anne hit a wrong key and winced.

"You usually play so well, Miss Townsend," Cecil said, peering over her shoulder.

"I'm sorry it's not up to your expectations, Mr. Worth." If she focused on the music perhaps he'd go away. He smelled of vinegar and wine. She wrinkled her nose.

He whispered in her ear. "Do you think I could call on you tomorrow?"

"I don't think I'll be available for a private audience tomorrow," Anne said, finishing the jig.

"Anne, play another," Sophia said loudly.

"Perhaps someone else can play so Miss Townsend can dance," Nathaniel said.

"No one plays as well as Anne," Sophia said. "She doesn't mind."

"No, I don't mind." Anne sorted through the music for another piece to play, watching Nathaniel bow to Sophia.

Mr. Worth peered over Anne's shoulder while she continued to play, even turning the pages of the music for her. It was just another typically disappointing evening.

The next morning, Nathaniel sat at the breakfast table rereading an old newspaper while waiting for Tony to come down. It took ten days to get any news from London, putting him behind on all the current business news. He wadded up the paper and threw it into the fire. He couldn't believe a woman was keeping him here, especially a woman like Anne Townsend.

She wasn't his type. She was short, much shorter than he. She was stubborn, bossy, and too practical for her own good.

Nathaniel smiled, remembering her with the fireplace poker, ready to wield it against her half brother. He liked her courage and her loyalty to her sisters. He was drawn to her like a bee to honey.

Kissing Anne had been a very bad idea. Very enjoyable, but bad. If they had been caught last night, he'd be engaged to her this morning.

Marriage to a Townsend was the last thing he needed. Nathaniel needed to accomplish his business and be done with Beetham before he was tempted any further.

"You're up disgustingly early," Tony said, coming into the breakfast room.

"I'm usually up early." Nathaniel watched as Tony poured.

Tony took a seat. "Did you enjoy dinner last night?"

"Of course."

"You've had the chance to see Sophia on several different occasions. Isn't she an angel?"

"She's nice enough." Nathaniel toyed with the food on his plate. "Are you still planning to marry this girl?"

"Of course. Where did you and her sister disappear to?"

Nathaniel looked up at his brother, surprised that he'd noticed. "I don't know where she was, but I stepped out for a bit of fresh air. Mrs. Worth was insufferable."

"Cecil is a bore, but his mother is worse. It was odd that he showed so much attention to Anne. He even said outright that he needed to marry for money."

Nathaniel was saved from commenting by Lady Danford as she breezed into the room. "Good morning. I see we are already starting on our day."

"Thank you for having Sophia and her sisters over last night, Grandmother," Tony said. "I'm off to call on Sophia. They have so little help around the cottage that I thought I'd chop some wood for them. The nights are getting cold."

"Who are you and what have you done with my brother?" Nathaniel said snidely. He'd never known Tony to do anything so exerting.

"Don't be an ass. I know how to use an axe." Tony quickly finished his tea and stood to leave.

"Just don't chop your leg off," Nathaniel yelled as Tony left the room.

"Well, last night was interesting," Lady Danford said. "Where did you disappear to and why did Anne come back to the parlor flushed?"

"I don't know what you mean, ma'am." Nathaniel kept his voice neutral. "I escaped for some fresh air."

"I saw you baiting Anne at dinner." Lady Danford's voice grew sharp. "I won't have you treating her disrespectfully. She's been through enough without you adding to it," she said as she helped herself to tea and toast.

"You are always defending her."

"I like Anne. She's not simpering like that middle sister of hers. I try to help when I can, but she just won't allow it. Very prideful she is. She reminds me of me at that age."

Nathaniel fought the urge to squirm. "What's the point of this conversation?"

Lady Danford nailed him with one of her looks. "I won't have you meddling with her. She doesn't need to have her heart broken by you."

Now he did squirm. "What makes you so sure I'd break her heart?"

"I know how you are. You'll push until you have her figured out, then leave, and I'll have to pick up the pieces."

"You don't stop Tony from seeing Sophia." Nathaniel winced at the defensiveness in his tone. Bloody hell, what was with this girl?

"In some ways Sophia is much wiser in the ways of the world than Anne is. Because her sisters garner most of the attention, Anne has not had the opportunity to know how to deal with men like you."

Nathaniel sat up in his chair. Even his grandmother couldn't talk to him like this. "What do you mean by 'men like me'?"

"Anne Townsend won't stand a chance against you if you set your mind to seduce her. I know you won't marry her."

He bristled under his grandmother's stare. "I have no intention of seducing Anne Townsend."

"Humph. You've watched her like a hawk watches its prey since you met her. Since that no-good brother of hers doesn't protect her, I will."

"Madam, you overstep your bounds," Nathaniel said coldly. "I have the highest respect for Anne Townsend."

"Of course you do. But I know how men's minds work. Hurt my Anne and you'll feel my wrath."

"*Your* Anne? When did she become *your* Anne?"

"When you started looking at her as if you want to devour every inch of her."

"Grandmother, I am a gentleman."

"Stay away from her."

"I'm not sure I can do that," Nathaniel said quietly to himself.

Lady Danford set down her teacup. He watched the gleam in her eye. "So that's the way of it," she said with a knowing smile.

"I'm simply curious about the family Tony wants to marry into." He needed to keep his grandmother from interfering until he had better control of the situation. He hadn't figured out where Anne fit into things yet. He didn't need others jumping to conclusions. "Leave it alone, Grandmother. Please."

Lady Danford sipped her tea, her eyes boring into him as if she could read his mind.

Chapter Eight

Anne woke up and scrubbed her face with her hands. Her head was pounding and her mouth tasted like bad cheese. She groaned as she threw back the covers. Late morning sun streamed through the one small window. She pulled back her hair with a ribbon, not wanting the added pressure on her head.

No more wine for her. Ever. Dressing quickly, she hurried downstairs to make tea, only to find the task already done. She poured herself a cup and added a bit of sugar.

"You've slept the morning away, miss," Hannah said, coming into the room.

Anne groaned. "Not so loud."

Hannah chuckled. "Bit too much to drink? That's not like you."

"Mrs. Worth was worse than her usual self last night." Anne sat at the table and nibbled on a piece of cold toast. "It was horrible. Where are Juliet and Sophia?"

"Gone into the village with your brother."

"Good." She didn't want to deal with their whining this morning. Nor did she want to talk about last night.

"Mr. Tony Matthews is out back chopping wood. Thomas tried to stop him, but he wouldn't hear of it." Hannah picked up the teacup and refilled it. "Drink."

"Bless you." Anne sipped the tea. "Why didn't he go with Sophia?"

"She's quite put out with him about his behavior last night, evidently." Hannah poured her own cup of tea and joined Anne at the table. "What happened last night?"

Anne didn't know where to start. "Besides Mrs. Worth's snide remarks and Mr. Worth making a cake of himself, I'm not sure."

"Did they fight?"

Anne shook her head. "They danced and seemed fine."

Hannah patted her hand. "Perhaps you should talk to him."

"You're right. If she doesn't marry Tony, we'll be in deep trouble." Anne straightened and gulped down the tea.

"A walk will clear the cobwebs and ease your headache," Hannah said.

"True." Anne fetched her pelisse and a bonnet. Leaves crunched beneath her boots as she made her way behind the cottage to the woodpile. Tony had removed his jacket and rolled up his sleeves. He split another log and paused to pull the axe out.

"Is the edge dull?" Anne said.

Tony looked up and smiled. He set the axe down and wiped his hands on his breeches. "Miss Townsend, I didn't see you there. The edge is a bit dull, but I'll manage."

"Why didn't you go to the village with Sophia?"

"She's rather angry with me at the moment." Tony picked up the axe again. He split another log with force.

"What happened?"

"I'm not really sure." He tossed aside the split wood and picked up another log.

"I'm sure it will pass. Sophia likes you a great deal."

"She was making eyes at my brother last night. She had nothing good to say about you either." He swung the axe with some force. "I don't know why I didn't notice this before."

Anne winced. He was starting to see the real Sophia. "She's been under a great deal of stress with Sir John here again."

"If you say so. I just wish she was more like you."

Her jaw dropped. "I'm sure you don't mean that, Mr. Matthews."

"Regardless, I'm happy to help your family. The closeness has meant a great deal to me."

"Thank you." Anne wrung her hands. "Please don't give up on Sophia. She really does care for you."

"I hope you're right. I best move this pile of wood closer to the house."

"Mr. Matthews, we do appreciate your help," Anne said. "It means a great deal to Sophia, to all of us. If you will excuse me." She moved to the path through the woods.

"You shouldn't be walking in the woods alone, Miss Townsend. Let me move this wood and I'll accompany you."

"That's not necessary, sir. I walk in the woods on my own quite often." She hurried down the path. Mr. Tony Matthews was getting too friendly with her at the expense of his relationship with Sophia. Anne needed them to marry, or else she wasn't sure how they'd get through the winter.

Anne made her way through the forest toward the Fairy Steps. She would cancel out this wish with another one. If it killed her, she was ending this craziness before it further ruined any possibility of Sophia marrying Mr. Matthews.

Her heart lurched. While she didn't want the attentions of Mr. Worth, Nathaniel Matthews was different. She liked him a great deal. But she'd rather have things back to normal than have his focus on her.

Anne stumbled over a root. Did she truly want things back to normal?

That kiss last night had been glorious.

Nathaniel was tall and strong and handsome. Anne's heart thumped at the memory of his mouth against hers.

He could break her heart into so many pieces she might not ever put it back together again. She had half a mind to let him.

She was so sick of being alone. She was ready to have someone else to lean on instead of everyone leaning on her.

But it was not to be.

Anne stopped at the foot of the Fairy Steps. This was it. Her one chance to break the spell. To return everyone back to normal. Still, she hesitated.

Traces of frost lingered on the steps, which were shaded from the sun. It would make climbing them difficult. She'd done it once; she could do it again. She placed one booted foot on the first step. Then another.

Her foot slipped on the icy steps. She caught herself on the wall. "Damn."

She climbed back down. How had she done it before?

At the time she'd been lost in thought about Sophia's marriage to Tony Matthews and all that it would do for Juliet. She tried to occupy her thoughts again like before.

It wasn't very hard to find a worry. Anne had so many of them.

What would they do if the marriage didn't take place? How would she find suitable husbands for her sisters if they couldn't get to London? It wasn't as though eligible men passed through Beetham on a daily basis.

Anne wrapped her arms around her and took one step, then another.

Money was going to be an issue. No marriage meant asking for charity from Lady Danford or the village. Anne hated taking charity, but she wouldn't let her sisters freeze or go hungry. She'd have to let Hannah and her husband go.

Then there was John to consider. She took another step, cautiously testing the iciness of the stone.

Men had so many more choices than women did. Women could marry well, marry poorly, or starve in the workhouse.

John could work. He could go to the Continent

It was clear he was waiting for Anne to solve his problems as well. She took another step. Then another.

Nathaniel walked quickly to the cottage but found it empty. The housekeeper hanging wash in the yard had directed him to the path leading into the woods. At the edge of the woods he found Tony, working away.

"What are you doing?"

"What does it look like?" Tony tossed a split log on the pile.

"Why?"

"They need the help and I need the work." He swung the axe with force and split another log. "What are you doing here?"

"I'm looking for Miss Townsend."

"She's walking."

Nathaniel fidgeted under his brother's gaze, but said nothing. He wasn't sure what was driving him to find Anne, and he didn't want to explain it to Tony. "Thanks." He turned to follow the path in the woods.

"Nathaniel, what are you up to?" Tony called out.

"Nothing."

"I feel as though I should ask your intentions for Miss Townsend, even though it's not my place." Tony set the axe down. "But damn it, I'm going to anyway."

"It's none of your concern."

"I'm making it my concern. Why Miss Townsend? She's not your usual type."

Why? Nathaniel wished he knew. "I like her."

"Are you contemplating marriage?"

"No," Nathaniel said quickly. He turned back and saw the frown on Tony's face. "It's not what you think."

"Really? How is it then?"

Nathaniel changed tacks. "Are *you* interested in Anne Townsend? Because you seem to run hot and cold with both of the Townsend girls."

"I just don't want to see Anne hurt. She's a friend," Tony said grudgingly. "She has no experience with dealing with men like you."

This was the second time today he'd heard that. "What in the hell are you talking about? Men like me?"

"You're easily bored. Anne is interesting for the moment. Do you still have that mistress in Town?"

"No."

Tony just shook his head. "You're bored."

"I'm not bored," Nathaniel growled. "What the hell is wrong with everyone?"

"Just don't hurt her."

"I have no intention of hurting her."

"Don't get lost!" Tony yelled after Nathaniel as he made his way into the woods.

Nathaniel cursed. He could follow a path like the rest of the population. This constant needling about his sense of direction was on his last nerve. He followed the path deeper into the woods.

"Surely she didn't walk this far." He stopped, listening for the sound of another person. Nothing. The woods were eerily silent. He pushed on. The path had to end up at the rock formation where he'd found Anne that first day.

What was her fascination with a pile of rocks? He knew the fable, but figured it was just a lot of nonsense. Surely Anne didn't believe in it. She was much too practical for that.

It was one of the things he liked most about her. A practical woman was hard to come by. She'd make a good wife, if he kept her.

Keep Anne? Where had that thought come from? He paused on the path. But now that he thought about it, she would make a good wife. She had all the traits required. He was also wildly attracted to her.

And she needed him. It was more than most marriages started with.

Of course, her brother would be an issue, but that could be dealt with easily enough.

Marriage? I?

The more he chewed on the thought, the more he liked it. It would burn Sir John's ass to know that Nathaniel was marrying his sister.

Nathaniel came around the corner of the stone wall that formed the Fairy Steps and found the woman who ruled his thoughts climbing the steps. His heart stopped as her foot slipped out from under and she started to tumble backwards.

"Anne!"

He raced up the steps to catch her, praying that he'd be able to stop her from bashing her head against the stones.

Anne landed on her bottom. She bent to rub her ankle, then turned on him. "You scared me to death!"

"Scared you? Christ, woman, you took years off my life. You could have fallen all the way down." Nathaniel sat down on the step below her. "What are you doing out here alone?"

She colored, not meeting his eyes. "Climbing the steps?"

Nathaniel frowned. She was hiding something. "Why?"

"It's beneficial exercise." She pulled her pelisse around her. The breeze teased strands of hair into her face and she brushed them away.

"I don't want you doing this again. I forbid it," he snarled. His heart was still pounding in his chest. What would have happened had she been alone and seriously hurt? How long would she have had to lie here waiting for someone to miss her?

Anne laughed. "You *forbid* it?"

"I know that's a foreign word in your vocabulary, but, yes, I forbid it. What if you fell and I wasn't here? You could have been seriously injured."

She sniffed and stared out at the woods in front of them. "And you would care?"

Nathaniel took his hand and gently turned Anne's face to his. He waited until she raised her eyes to his. "Yes. I would. I would care a great deal."

His mouth touched hers. Soft. Gentle. Cautious.

Anne turned her face away. "Stop."

He chuckled and cupped her face. "I don't want to."

"What if someone sees us?"

Nathaniel looked around. "We're in the middle of nowhere."

She pushed him gently away and stood. She winced from the pain in her ankle.

"Give me your hand, Anne."

She shook her head. "I'm fine."

"You give new meaning to the word stubborn." He clasped her hands to help her down. "Why are you really climbing the steps? I want the truth now."

Anne's face couldn't get any redder. "For exercise," she insisted

"Hmm. Why don't I believe you?"

Anne groaned as she put her weight on her ankle. "There's nothing wrong with exercise." She sank to the step and rubbed her ankle again.

"You're hurt." He bent down and raised her skirts without asking for permission.

She slapped at his hands. "What are you doing?"

"Checking your ankle." He tried again.

"No! It's unseemly." She pushed his hands away.

Nathaniel sighed. "Anne, I'm going to look at your ankle if we have to sit here all day."

"I didn't give you permission to use my first name," she snarled.

"I assumed I had permission after our kiss last night." He smiled at her blush. "Now let me look at that ankle."

"Mr. Matthews, it's not necessary. I'll just rest here for a few minutes and head home."

"Nathaniel."

"What?"

"My name is Nathaniel. Say it."

"Nathaniel," she forced through her teeth.

"Was that so hard?" He reached down and lifted her skirt to look at her ankle. Her half boots were worn, her stockings had been mended repeatedly. He pushed his fingers against her ankle, feeling for the bone.

"Ouch!" she cried.

"It's not broken." He released her ankle and Anne lowered her skirt. "Come. I'll help you home."

"I can make it fine on my own." She stood and held on to the wall as she slowly made her way down the remaining steps. He couldn't see her face because of her bonnet, but she flinched each time she put weight on her ankle.

"No wonder you and my grandmother get along." He took her arm, letting let her lean against him to make it the rest of the way down the uneven steps.

When she was on level ground again, Anne turned back to him. "Thank you for your assistance," she said crisply. "Good day."

"Anne, you can hardly walk."

"I'll be fine." She hobbled down the path.

"Enough." Nathaniel came up behind her and lifted her into his arms.

Anne squealed and grabbed at his shoulders. "What are you doing? Put me down!"

"No." He started walking down the path. Her face was a delightful pink.

"I'm too heavy."

"No."

"If someone sees us—"

"I'll explain that you are injured."

Anne tucked her head down, but held herself stiffly in his arms. "I'm sorry to be such an inconvenience."

"You are that," Nathaniel agreed.

She squirmed, trying to get him to release her. Nathaniel jiggled her in his arms until she clung to him.

"Be still."

"You're going the wrong way." Anne pointed to the other path. "The cottage is that way."

"Don't say another word," he growled.

"You have the worst sense of direction. How do you get anywhere?"

Nathaniel tightened his jaw but said nothing.

Anne snorted. "Seriously, how do you find your way? I'm curious."

He glared at her. "I'm not discussing this with you."

Anne laughed. He loosened his arms as if to drop her. "Stop!"

Nathaniel tightened his arms around her. "Stop laughing or I'll toss you over my shoulder for the rest of the way home."

Anne looped her arms around his neck, blessedly silent for a moment. Her hair fell in his face and she lifted a hand to push it out of his eyes. Finally, she rested her head on his shoulder and relaxed in his arms.

* * *

Anne had given up trying to fight being in Nathaniel's arms and decided to just savor it. She enjoyed his touch.

Every time she loosened her hold on his neck, he did something to cause her to tighten her hold again.

"You're doing that on purpose," she griped.

"What?"

"Threatening to drop me."

"You mean like this?" He moved as if to drop her and she squealed loudly. He laughed.

Anne laughed as well. "You're impossible."

Nathaniel was staring at her mouth, his dark eyes heating like they had the night before, just before he kissed her.

Anne licked her lips nervously. She wanted to kiss him again. This time really kiss him.

But she couldn't allow it. With each kiss, she felt as if he pulled a piece of her heart from her chest.

Nathaniel stopped walking, his eyes holding hers captive.

Anne's heart thumped so hard she was afraid he would hear it. She put her hands on his shoulders as if to stop him. But she knew she wouldn't. She couldn't stop something she wanted so desperately.

A sense of quiet waiting filled the woods, wrapping the two of them in a blanket of desire. Anne closed her eyes and felt Nathaniel's mouth touch hers.

His lips were firm, softly brushing hers, once, twice, a third time, leaving her hungry for a deeper taste. He pulled away.

Anne slowly opened her eyes. Nathaniel stared down at her with eyes so hot, so dark, she felt singed.

He released her, letting her slide down his hard body, his eyes never leaving hers. She was pushed against the tree behind her as he moved closer, pressing into her.

"What are you doing to me?" she whispered.

Nathaniel tossed her bonnet to the ground. He tucked her hair behind her ear as his knuckles brushed her cheek. "You have me bewitched."

His hands framed her face, gently brushing his thumb against her mouth, parting her lips and kissing her again.

Anne gripped the lapels of his coat, just holding on as her knees melted. His tongue touched hers, tasted hers. Never had she dreamed of a kiss like this.

Logic and propriety fled as a whole different fire coursed through her. Her blood thickened and she wrapped her arms around his neck and curled her fingers in his hair.

She gasped as his mouth trailed down her neck, causing her to shiver.

Nathaniel's hand reached down to cup her breast. He rubbed his thumb against her nipple.

She jumped. "Nathaniel—"

"Make me stop, Anne." He touched his forehead against hers. "Tell me to stop." He brushed his mouth against hers.

She cupped his face in her hands. "It's too cold."

He chuckled. "It's not too cold for what I want."

Anne wiggled until she was nestled in his arms.

He caught her hips. "Anne, stay still for a moment."

She breathed in his scent, memorizing it. When the wish was finally cancelled, she wouldn't get this chance again.

"We can't keep doing this," Anne whispered. "I can't risk—"

"Your reputation." Nathaniel retrieved her bonnet and placed it on her head. She put it on, tying the ribbons under her chin.

Anne squeaked as he picked her up again as if she weighed nothing. "I can make it home from here," she said.

"Not on that ankle." He continued down the path to the cottage.

"I don't want my sisters to see you carrying me," she said into his neck. She couldn't get enough of the way he smelled or the rough feel of his jaw.

"They might as well find out now."

Her head popped up. "What do you mean?"

"Anne, don't play dumb. It doesn't suit you."

"Put me down. Now." She pushed herself out of his arms until he had no choice but to release her. She put some space between them. "Explain."

"Anne . . ."

"Does this mean that we're courting?" She teetered on her one foot with her hands on her hips.

Nathaniel had the grace to blush. "I don't know."

He was playing fast and loose with her reputation. "Think about it and let me know. Until then, stay away from me."

"Anne, you can't walk on that ankle." Nathaniel tried to grab her arm. She jerked out of his grasp.

"I'd rather walk, thank you."

"Quit acting like a child."

She ground her teeth. "I'm not acting like a child."

Nathaniel just raised one eyebrow.

They walked the rest of the way to the cottage in silence. She refused to speak and he didn't, which was fine with her.

"Thank you for your assistance," she muttered.

Nathaniel looked at her as she fumbled with the door. "Good day." He bowed and turned to leave.

"Mr. Matthews," Anne called to him. "I have to ask that you— uh—that we no longer—"

"Message received, Miss Townsend."

A scream startled Anne as she opened the door. Nathaniel came running past her to the side of the cottage, and Anne followed slowly, cursing her ankle.

When Anne reached him, Juliet stood crying next to Nathaniel. John lay prone at their feet.

"Juliet! What is it?"

"It's John," Juliet cried. "I think he's dead." She threw herself into Anne's arms.

"He's not dead." Nathaniel turned John over. John groaned and curled further into a ball. "But he's been beaten pretty well, I'd say."

"Juliet, go to the house and have Hannah fetch the doctor." Anne pushed Juliet toward the cottage. She waited until her sister was out of hearing distance. "Who would do this?"

"I have no idea," Nathaniel said. "We need to get him into the house."

"What do you want me to do?"

"Get off that ankle." His voice was sharp. "I'll get him inside."

"Thomas can help you." Anne limped toward the cottage as quickly as her sore ankle would let her. She reached the door only to have it flung open by Sophia. "Sophia, where's Thomas?"

"Juliet told me about John." Sophia was wringing her hands. "What can I do?"

"Fetch Thomas. Nathaniel needs his help." Anne limped past Sophia.

"What happened to you?"

"I slipped and fell. Nathaniel brought me home."

"Nathaniel? When did you start addressing him by his first name?"

"Not now, Sophia. Please fetch Thomas. We need to get John inside."

Anne limped past Sophia and found her way up the stairs and to her room. She looked in the mirror, expecting to find something different about her. Her heart was racing, but her blood felt thick in her veins with a strange sort of excitement. She had never expected to be kissed like this. She touched her gloved hand to her mouth. Was this love? Lust?

"Anne!" Sophia shouted from downstairs.

"Coming." She removed her bonnet, gloves, and pelisse and put on her apron. She gathered rags and limped to the guest room to prepare for John.

Chapter Nine

Nathaniel and Thomas carried an unconscious John up the narrow steps of the cottage to his bedroom.

The man didn't wake as they moved slowly up the stairs. Anne was waiting in the bedroom with water and rags.

"Hannah has gone for the doctor," she said as she set a bowl of water down and soaked a rag in it.

"Good." Nathaniel removed the man's waistcoat. "He should have awoken by now." He glanced at Anne and noticed the stricken look on her face. "Do you have smelling salts?"

"Yes."

He saw her wince. "Send one of your sisters. You shouldn't be on that ankle."

She twisted one of the rags in her hands. "But I have to—"

"I'll take care of John. Go wait for the doctor downstairs. While he's here he can look at your ankle."

"But—"

The woman was beyond stubborn. "Anne, leave now." She jumped, and limped through the door, pulling it closed behind her.

Nathaniel glanced at the servant, Thomas, as he roughly loosened John's cravat. "Remove his boots as well."

"Yes, sir."

Never in Nathaniel's wildest dreams did he think he'd be in the position of offering aid to Sir John. "How long has Townsend been staying here?"

"Since Sunday, sir," Thomas said, a bit breathless from removing the boots. "Miss Anne couldn't turn him out."

"No, she wouldn't." Nathaniel jerked off John's jacket with enough force to cause him to groan. "Well, he's certainly not dead."

Townsend's face was bruised and starting to swell. Both his eyes were blackened. He was covered in blood.

"He's not that bad. Mostly bluster." Thomas wiped at some of the blood on John's face.

"Then why is he still unconscious? Perhaps he was hit on the head."

"Or drunk," Thomas added.

Nathaniel acknowledged the derision in the servant's voice. He walked to the washstand and picked up the pitcher. He carried it over to the bed and poured a bit of water onto Townsend's face.

"What?!" Sir John sat up, then groaned in pain and grasped his ribs. "Where am I?"

"The cottage," Nathaniel said.

John propped himself up and groaned. "What the hell are you doing here?"

"I'm the least of your problems," Nathaniel said. "Tell me what happened." He curled his hands into fists. The man disgusted him.

John glanced at the servant. "Leave us."

Thomas looked at Nathaniel, and he nodded. After Thomas departed, Nathaniel spoke again. "Continue."

John wiped his bleeding nose with his sleeve and puffed up his chest as much as he could. "I resent your tone."

"It's either me or the magistrate."

"Then call the magistrate." John dismissed Nathaniel with a wave of his hand.

"If that's what you wish—but are you sure you want the locals to find out the truth about why you're here?"

Townsend's jaw tightened. "I was set upon while walking from the public house. I was going for some ale. There is nothing to drink in this house but tea."

"Were you drunk?"

John shook his head. "I'd just finished a friendly game with the locals. I was walking through the woods to the cottage to be home before supper when two men approached me."

Nathaniel grew alert. Could one of these men be the same man who had been lurking around the cottage? "Did you recognize them? Did one of the men have a long ugly scar on his face?"

"I believe he did. I didn't recognize them. They were dressed too fine for locals. Their hats were pulled low, so I didn't see their faces.

As I passed, one hit me from behind and knocked me out. I don't remember much after that."

"Any idea why two men would target you?" Nathaniel had a pretty good idea why, but he wanted Townsend to admit it.

"Not really. I've been away from Town for a while now." John's eyes shifted away to stare out the window.

The man is lying, thought Nathaniel. "We've called a doctor who can confirm if your ribs are broken," Nathaniel said. "He should be here shortly."

"If you could find it, I could use a bit of whiskey."

Nathaniel stiffened at Townsend's tone. He'd be damned if he'd cater to the idiot. "I'll have Thomas fetch some from the Lodge." With that, he stepped into the hall and closed the door.

He found Thomas waiting in the hallway. "On Sunday, I noticed a man staring at the cottage. Have you seen anyone strange in the area?"

"No, sir. Beetham is a quiet village. If there are strangers about, I'd find out about it."

"Send word to the Lodge if you learn anything."

"Yes, sir. I'd best check on Sir John."

Nathaniel watched Thomas enter the bedroom again. He then went to find Anne. She couldn't help her unfortunate relations, but he'd not have Sir John putting her and her sisters in danger. Though Anne would deny it, this was out of her league. The men Townsend was involved with were vicious.

He found Anne and her sisters in the small parlor downstairs. Sophia paced the room and Anne worked on her mending as Juliet sat beside her.

"He's awake. He's sore and has a bloody nose, but he'll be all right. The doctor will confirm if his ribs are broken."

"Thank you," Anne said.

"Has the doctor arrived?" Nathaniel moved fully into the room and stood in front of the window.

"He should be here shortly. Hannah is back and has made tea. Would you like some?"

"Do not get up," Nathaniel barked. "Someone else can serve tea." He looked pointedly at Sophia, who was wringing her hands.

"Sophia, pour tea for our guest," Anne said.

Sophia moved forward, but Nathaniel waved her away. "I'll get it."

After the debacle in the woods and now this, a bit of brandy would be welcome.

"Miss Anne, Dr. Anderson is here," Hannah said from the doorway.

"Please show him in," Nathaniel said. "Anne, he'll look at your ankle first."

"I really don't think that's necessary. John is in much worse condition," said Anne.

"Anne is right—he should see John first," Sophia said tearfully.

Nathaniel ignored Sophia's comment as Dr. Anderson appeared in the doorway. He was a young man with an easy grin. He smiled at Anne and Nathaniel felt something primitive boil up inside him, especially when Anne easily returned the man's smile.

"Miss Townsend, how can I be of service?" Dr. Anderson came forward and offered his hand to Anne.

"Thank you for coming," Anne said and made to stand.

Nathaniel was beside her in an instant and placed a hand on her shoulder. "Sit down. Please. Doctor, Miss Townsend has fallen and injured her ankle. I wonder if you could look at it before we go upstairs to her brother." Nathaniel remained behind Anne's chair, his hand on her shoulder.

"Of course, sir." Dr. Anderson frowned at him but then smiled easily again at Anne.

"Dr. Anderson, may I present Mr. Nathaniel Matthews. He's Lady Danford's grandson, here from London. He was kind enough to assist me home after I was injured," explained Anne.

"If you will permit me to look at your ankle, Miss Townsend?" Dr. Anderson knelt down in front of Anne and she daintily lifted her skirt to show him her ankle. Nathaniel fought the urge to shove him away. He turned and found Juliet Townsend watching him thoughtfully. *Damn.*

"It's not broken, just a sprain. I think you should stay off of it for a few days, so no rambles through the woods," Dr. Anderson teased. "Wrap it with a cold cloth several times a day if the swelling gets bad."

Anne smiled down at him. "Thank you, Dr. Anderson."

"I'll take you upstairs to look at her brother now." Nathaniel winced at his tone, especially given how closely the sisters were watching him.

He just didn't like the way the doctor looked at Anne. Then again, he didn't like the way any men looked at her. This possessiveness was foreign to him. He squeezed Anne's shoulder gently and whispered, "Stay put."

Anne glared at him but picked up her mending.

"Follow me, Doctor," Nathaniel said, and led the man upstairs.

Anne frowned as Nathaniel led Dr. Anderson up the stairs. How dare he act so possessive! Dr. Anderson was a friend. Nathaniel Matthews was only here temporarily.

"Heavens, Anne. I thought Mr. Matthews was going to punch Dr. Anderson when he touched your ankle," Juliet said, handing Anne a cup of tea. "I think he likes you."

"Keep your voice down, Juliet," Anne said. "They'll hear you."

"How was it that Mr. Matthews found you?" Sophia asked suspiciously.

"I was walking at the Fairy Steps. He happened to pass just as I slipped and twisted my ankle. Naturally, he accompanied me home."

"Happened to pass?" Sophia mimicked. "Suddenly, Mr. Worth, Mr. Matthews, Tony, and now Dr. Anderson are fawning all over you. What's going on?"

Anne sipped her tea slowly. Honestly, this was getting harder to explain with each passing day. She was no good at secrets. "Nothing is going on."

Juliet also threw her a suspicious look. "There's something you're not telling us. You know how bad you are at lying."

"Yes, Anne. Tell us," Sophia urged. "Tell me why my soon-to-be fiancé sings your praises when you are near, but returns to normal when you aren't."

"Really?" Anne asked. "I hadn't noticed."

"I have a copy of the bad poetry to prove it," said Sophia.

"Ah! Even you agree that his poetry is bad," Anne teased.

"It's not so very bad," Juliet muttered into her teacup.

Anne looked at Sophia and grinned. "Yes, it is."

Sophia chuckled in return. "It really is."

"Did Mr. Matthews carry you all the way home, Anne?"

"He did." She could still feel his arms around her, his mouth on hers, hot and persistent. She squirmed in her seat. He simply had to stop kissing her. It was only a matter of time before they were caught and her reputation was ruined.

"How romantic," Juliet gushed.

"It wasn't romantic at all. He carted me home like a sack of potatoes," Anne said bluntly.

"Potatoes? I would hardly compare you to a sack of potatoes," Nathaniel said from the doorway. His eyes were twinkling. "You were wiggling too much."

Anne felt her face flush and set her cup down noisily. "How is John?"

"Broken ribs and bruises," Nathaniel replied. "Be thankful he has a hard head. I've also seen the doctor out. He'll check on Townsend tomorrow."

"So John's conscious?" Anne rose. "Perhaps I should ask him who did this."

"Stay off your ankle," Nathaniel ordered.

Anne sat back down with a huff and glared at him. "Did you at least question him?"

"He was hit from behind, so he has no idea who did it." Nathaniel sat down in one of the parlor chairs across from Anne.

"Who would do this?" Sophia asked.

"I'm not sure, Miss Sophia. The doctor has given him some laudanum for his pain."

"He'll be screaming for brandy," Juliet said. "Or worse."

"I'll have some sent from the Lodge," Nathaniel said. "It will help alleviate the pain."

"That isn't necessary," Anne said. "We can send to the village for some."

"I insist," Nathaniel said. "Should I assist you upstairs, Miss Townsend?"

Anne blanched. There would be no way she could hide her feelings from her sisters if he touched her. It would be all over her face, and the ridicule she'd have to put up with . . . well, she just couldn't. "I can manage on my own."

Nathaniel turned to Sophia and Juliet. "Have either of you seen any strangers in the area of late?"

"I haven't," Anne said. "I walk to the Lodge nearly every day."

"Not to mention your romps in the woods," Sophia added. "I have seen a few new people in town, but didn't think much of it."

"I ran across a man when leaving here Sunday," Nathaniel said.

"He was dressed rather roughly with a hat drawn over his eyes. His face was scarred."

"I'll ask Hannah and Thomas if they've noticed anyone," Anne said. "What do you suspect?"

"Your brother is deeply in debt," Nathaniel answered. "As you are well aware."

"In debt to you, I believe," Anne interjected.

"Not just to me," Nathaniel continued. "He's been playing deep in some of the more notorious gaming hells in Town."

"How do you know this?" Sophia demanded. "Why does he owe you money?"

"Yes, Mr. Matthews, please explain." Perhaps if Sophia heard it from someone else she would believe it.

"I caught your brother cheating at cards," Nathaniel stated baldy. "We were playing deep and I knew he had no money to back the bet. He cheated and was caught. I could have challenged him, but didn't."

"How much?" Sophia asked.

"Five thousand pounds."

Judging by the expression on Nathaniel's face, there was more. "What else does he owe?" Anne asked.

"My guess is that he tried to win what he owed me in the seedier hells and lost even more."

"I don't understand," Juliet said.

"It means John's debtors are looking to get the money from him any way they can," Anne said. *How dare John come here and bring his seedy friends with him?* If he didn't already have a head injury, she'd be tempted to strike him herself.

"So are we in danger as well?" Sophia asked finally.

"I don't know," Nathaniel replied. "I would keep the doors locked and be aware. No walking alone." He gave Anne a pointed look.

Anne glared back. What was he insinuating? "I'll be careful."

"You'll stay home." His voice brooked no argument.

How dare he order me about? "I'll have Thomas accompany me."

"I'll have the carriage come down for you."

"That's ridiculous. It's hardly a ten-minute walk." Anne had had enough of his high-handed ways.

"Nevertheless, the carriage will be here tomorrow." Nathaniel stood. "Now allow me to carry you upstairs before I leave." He removed the teacup from her hands.

"I can make it on my own. My sisters are here to help me."

"How do I know you won't do something stupid, Anne?" He stood back from her.

"I won't allow her," Juliet said quickly.

Anne was partly relieved and partly disappointed. She would have liked to be in his arms again, but didn't want to raise any more suspicions in her sisters. They were already catching on that Nathaniel was interested in her.

"Good. If she gives you trouble, let me know," Nathaniel said. "Anne, what time should I have the carriage here?"

"Nine tomorrow would be fine," Anne said reluctantly. Nathaniel was watching her mouth, his eyes hot. She fought the urge to squirm in her seat.

Nathaniel nodded. "If you see anyone about, send a message to the Lodge. Do you have a weapon here?"

"Just Anne and her fireplace poker," Sophia said snidely.

Nathaniel laughed. "Do you know how to handle a pistol, Anne?"

"Of course not!" Anne said.

"I'll bring one by and give you some lessons."

"No, thank you." Anne drew the line at guns. She didn't think she could shoot anyone. Hit them over the head with a poker, yes, but actually kill someone? No. "We will be fine, Mr. Matthews."

Nathaniel frowned at her. "I'll have one of the footmen keep an eye out for you."

Anne stood up. "That won't be necessary. We can handle things ourselves."

Nathaniel stepped closer but she held her ground. "How do you expect to do that with just a poker?"

"We'll manage. I'm sure Thomas has a pistol and he'll protect us."

Nathaniel shook his head, and Anne wanted to give in to the urge to kick him. Too bad her ankle hurt. "Thank you for your assistance, Mr. Matthews."

He looked surprised by her dismissal, but he stepped back toward the door. Anne allowed herself to breathe again.

"I will check on you tomorrow. Make sure you stay off that ankle." He glared at her before bowing and bidding them good day.

Sophia waited until the front door slammed before she looked at Anne. "He likes you."

"No, he doesn't." Anne collapsed back into the chair, picked up her tea and sipped. It was cold. She set it down.

"Yes, he does. I can tell," Sophia insisted.

"How?" Anne demanded.

Sophia sashayed over to Anne's chair, clearly enjoying her superiority. "It's how he looks at you. Like he wants to devour you."

"He's arrogant and overbearing."

"He's handsome and wealthy," Sophia said. "You should try for him. He could afford to send us to London for a Season."

"My lack of connections and fortune makes me unacceptable. Besides, he's just playing with me."

"How do you know, Anne?" Juliet moved to sit next to her. "Sophia's right. You should see how he looks at you."

"I've seen that look before. He'd have you in his bed before you could blink. It's that kind of look," Sophia said knowingly.

"How would you know that, Sophia?" Anne asked.

"Trust me. I know. You mark my words. He'll propose, and you better say yes."

"He won't propose and I don't have to say yes."

"Yes, you do, because, and I quote, 'he could save this family.' " Sophia smirked.

As much as Anne didn't want to admit it, Sophia was right. Regardless of the wish, marrying Nathaniel would save them. He'd make sure her sisters were taken care of and had the opportunities to marry well.

Anne just didn't know if she could cope with the heartache that would come when the wish wore off and he discovered what he was stuck with.

The next morning, Nathaniel settled Anne in the library at the Lodge to go over the invitations for the party his grandmother had insisted they have while he was here.

He hated balls. He wasn't good with small talk, and having to do it while dancing was worse. It was all he could do to concentrate on the steps. He'd much rather settle in the card room, but his grandmother would insist he dance.

Of course, he'd have Anne Townsend to dance with, if her ankle healed in time. For once he looked forward to the waltz and holding her close in his arms.

Certainly she came with baggage, such as her no-good brother, but she had spirit. He liked her independence. He liked kissing her. A great deal.

Nathaniel settled himself in the corner of the parlor by the window. Potted palms hid him from view and the morning sun provided light for reading. He tried to focus on one of the novels he'd brought from London, while he waited for Anne to finish what she needed to do for his grandmother.

His mind wasn't on the book. Anne's nervousness around him was just too much fun to watch. She had almost spilled ink on the desk, she got so flustered. He decided to let her get her work done on her own instead of torturing her, choosing to hide in the corner of the drawing room.

He reread a page of his book for the third time, but voices in the hall further interrupted his thoughts. His grandmother and another woman entered the room. From his chair the ladies wouldn't see him. He started to announce his presence, but hesitated when he found out who the guest was.

"Mrs. Worth, how kind of you to call," Lady Danford said.

"I had to call on you, Lady Danford, about your companion. She has bewitched my son." Nathaniel twisted in his seat to spy on the women through the palm fronds.

"Really, Mrs. Worth, I hardly think Miss Townsend is capable of bewitching anyone. Shall I call for tea?"

"I won't be staying long enough. I demand that you sack that girl." Mrs. Worth's face flushed red.

"And what good would that do?" Lady Danford kept her voice civil but cool. "Tell your son to ignore her. She has no fortune and it shouldn't be difficult for him to find someone who does."

"I'm not sure I like what you are implying, Lady Danford."

"I'm sure you don't. Now what is this really about, Mrs. Worth?"

"My son does nothing but talk about Anne Townsend. He embarrassed himself and me with his obscene reading on Sunday."

"Your son embarrassed Miss Townsend in front of the entire congregation. I think that warrants at least an apology," Lady Danford said.

"He wouldn't have done it if she hadn't bewitched him. He's never noticed her before, but now he looks at her and starts reading trash."

"You mean the Bible, dear. I wouldn't call it trash."

Nathaniel sat back. Mrs. Worth did have a point. Cecil had not noticed Anne until that Sunday. He knew Cecil Worth to be more interested in money than in Anne, or at least he appeared that way. Worth's conversations about the family were centered on non-existent jewels and Sir John's title.

Even Nathaniel's own connections might not have come up to scratch if her father were alive. The *ton* looked down on Nathaniel's investments for the most part, though they were interested in his wealth.

"You know what I mean," Mrs. Worth continued. "Please tell me you aren't including the Townsends on your invitation list for the ball next week. I don't think I can control what Cecil does."

"Mr. Worth is a grown man. He should be able to behave in an appropriate manner," Lady Danford said sharply.

"Those girls have no chaperone. Who knows what goes on in that cottage without any guidance from anyone?"

"What are you saying, Mrs. Worth?" His grandmother's voice was hard as stone.

"I'm saying those girls are not fit to attend the assembly. I insist they not be invited." Mrs. Worth's voice grew louder, more shrill.

A movement in the doorway caught Nathaniel's eyes. Anne.

Her face was pinched, white. She'd heard everything that harpy said.

"Lady Danford, Mrs. Worth. I hope I'm not interrupting anything important." Anne clasped her hands in front of her. She had her serene mask in place.

"Anne, dear. Come in. Mrs. Worth was just leaving." Lady Danford rose and pulled Anne beside her. "Mrs. Worth, you must excuse us as we have other engagements this afternoon."

"But what about—"

"Your opinions are duly noted. I would suggest if you can't keep your son under control, you take him to Bath, out of harm's way." Lady Danford turned to a footman who suddenly appeared in the room. "Please see Mrs. Worth out."

Mrs. Worth, her mouth set in a firm, thin line, left the room in a huff.

"Anne, how much did you hear?" Lady Danford took Anne's hands.

"Enough."

"Don't let that bitter old woman hurt you. You've done nothing wrong." Lady Danford turned to the corner where Nathaniel was hiding. "Nathaniel, you can come out now."

Nathaniel felt his face color as he rose from behind the plantings. "I wasn't hiding."

"You should have made yourself known the minute we came into the room," his grandmother said, taking her seat again. "We need tea."

"I shall fetch it," Anne said quickly.

"No, dear. Sit down. You look pale." Lady Danford pulled Anne next to her on the settee.

"The invitations are completed," Anne said, changing the subject.

"Good. Give me Mrs. Worth's. I want to burn it," Lady Danford said. "That woman just makes me angry."

"I don't know why Mr. Worth is acting the way he is," Anne said cautiously.

"You don't?"

"I've not encouraged his affections."

"What about Dr. Anderson?" Nathaniel asked. "How do you explain his reaction?"

"Dr. Anderson is a friend. We've danced twice in the five years he's been here. What are you suggesting, Mr. Matthews?"

"I'm suggesting that something funny is going on."

Anne stood. "Are you suggesting that I'm so unattractive that no one would dance with me unless—"

"You know that's not what I meant." Nathaniel began pacing. "Don't be silly."

"Now I'm silly? I've had enough of this."

"Sit down and get off that ankle," Nathaniel roared. Anne sat quickly and looked down at her hands. Nathaniel lowered his voice with a huff. "I'm sorry to yell, but I know it pains you."

"Children, would one of you like to tell me what's going on?" Lady Danford said gently. "Nathaniel, sit down."

"He is mistaken, my lady," Anne said. "Nothing is going on. Now if you will excuse me, I've work to do." She limped to the door and closed it quietly behind her.

Nathaniel watched her go, fuming.

"Son, what is wrong with you? You're acting like a jealous fool."

"I'm fine." He ran his hands through his hair. Why did he let her get to him? He knew something was amiss. Anne clearly had trouble dealing with the sudden attentions of the men around her. Yet she did nothing to stop it. He flopped into a nearby chair. Anne Townsend was making him crazy.

Chapter Ten

The smell of musty books and the quiet of the library soothed Anne's nerves as she finished the remainder of the work for the assembly. The menus and guest lists were ready for approval, and other lists ready for the cook and the housekeeper. She tried to block out Mrs. Worth's words but couldn't. The woman was a shrew, but she did have a point. Anne Townsend and her sisters were not fit for proper society.

She buried her face in her hands. No matter what she did, Anne failed. While her sisters were part of local society, their connections were insufficient for them to marry well. They were running out of money. Sir John was no help. He owed more money than Anne had ever seen in her life.

"Anne," Nathaniel said. She heard the door close behind him.

Anne's shoulders sagged. She just didn't have the energy to deal with him now. "Please leave me alone."

"I want to apologize for my behavior." He came closer. "I had no right to suggest you had anything to do with the behavior of Worth and the others."

If he only knew. "Mr. Matthews, I have to ask you to—"

He was so close she could smell his particular scent. She breathed it in.

"Don't ask me to stay away, because I can't." Nathaniel's voice was low, gravelly, and danced along her nerve endings.

Anne forced herself to be stern. Someone had to be the practical one. "People are going to talk. Lady Danford is already suspicious."

"Let them." He traced his finger delicately across the top of her hand.

Anne snatched her hands from his touch. "Why? For a bit of fun while you are here?"

"What's wrong with a bit of fun?" Nathaniel smiled a cat-and-cream sort of smile.

Lord, she was tempted. But he would ruin her, leave, and not look back. She'd be left to clean up the mess. "When do you return to London?"

"My plans are not firm yet. I'd like to stay for the assembly." His voice was soft. "If you want me to, that is."

"Do as you wish." She kept her voice crisp.

"One word from you is all it will take."

Anne pushed herself back into the chair to avoid him. He pulled at her with his warm eyes and smiled, but she shook her head. "I can't."

Nathaniel moved around the desk and pulled her up and into his arms. She wanted to fight him, but couldn't. His warmth wrapped around her, comforted her. She closed her eyes and let him envelop her.

Nathaniel lifted her chin so that she met his eyes. His thumb feathered gently across her bottom lip. "I don't want to leave."

"I can't risk—"

"For once in your life, Anne, just take it as it comes." He bent down and kissed her gently.

Something inside her snapped. He was right. Why shouldn't she take what she wanted?

Anne raised her hands and cupped his face. The roughness of his whiskers rubbed against her fingertips. She pulled him down for a deeper kiss, her lips parting and her tongue seeking his. She needed him at this moment to blind her to what was going on around her.

She needed to take the reins, to have control of something at this time when everything was out of control. Her hands trailed into his hair as Nathaniel groaned and returned her kiss.

She molded her body to his, wanting to be closer. He was leaning on the desk. She pressed her hips to his, could feel him growing hard. She ran her hands down his chest to his waist, feeling his strength. She wanted to feel his skin, to taste it with her tongue.

Anne was hungry for more of him. For something she couldn't even put a name to. Never had she felt so reckless, so wild. Her lips clung to his. She pressed her body closer.

Nathaniel came up for air. "Anne, we have to stop, sweetheart."

Anne took his mouth again, unwilling to let go of this sense of power, of reducing this man to a puddle as he'd done to her so many times before.

His hands traced her back and cupped her bottom, melding his body with hers.

"Pardon me."

Anne felt as if ice water had been dumped on her. Nathaniel acted faster. He quickly turned her to hide her from the maid.

"What do you need?" His voice was gruff.

"Her ladyship needs Miss Townsend in the drawing room, sir."

"She'll be there directly."

As soon as the door closed Anne pushed herself out of his arms. This was why she always remained in control. She should never have given in to the passion. "It will be all over Beetham tomorrow that you and I were—" She moved to the door. "I need to go."

"Anne, wait. I didn't mean—"

"No. The best thing you can do for me is to stay away." She opened the door and looked back at him. He had a puzzled look on his face. "Please."

"I'm not sure I can, Anne. But it will be as you wish."

Anne closed the door behind her and covered her face in her hands, feeling tears pricking her eyes.

"Are you all right, miss?"

Anne had forgotten the maid. She wiped her face and smiled. "Just a sudden headache. Would you give Lady Danford my regrets? I fear I need to lie down."

"Are you well enough to go home? Should I call for the carriage?"

"No, thank you. The walk will do me good." She smiled to reassure the maid.

Thankfully, the kitchen was empty when Anne went to collect her cloak and bonnet. She quickly made her way out the back of the house and into the crisp air. Her ankle was sore but not terribly so. She'd have to put compresses on when she returned home.

She was such a fool.

She'd let things get way out of control. It had felt so good to be touched, kissed, loved.

But it wasn't love. It was desire. Passion. It would burn hot and fast but die quickly.

Nathaniel Matthews was only interested in a bit of fun, not marriage.

Anne would be no man's mistress.

Anne found Sophia in the kitchen nursing a cup of tea. "What are you doing in here?"

Sophia looked up from her teacup. "John has the front parlor. If I had to hear him whine one more time about the brandy being upstairs, I was going to scream."

"Who are you and what have you done with my sister?"

"Seriously, Anne, all he does is complain." Sophia sipped her tea. "I thought you'd be at the Lodge all day."

Anne kept silent as she removed her pelisse and hat and hung them on the hook by the door. "I came home early. Mrs. Worth called on Lady Danford and had some really scathing things to say about me."

"That sow!"

"Sophia!" Anne laughed. She was thinking the same thing. She retrieved a cup from the cupboard. "Any more tea?"

Sophia poured her a cup. "Doesn't she realize her son is a total idiot? Honestly, to read that passage in church. It was totally uncalled for."

Anne sipped slowly, letting the warmth chase the cold away. "True."

"What's going on between you and Nathaniel Matthews? The man won't even look my way if you are in the room."

Anne sputtered. "Nothing. Really, it's nothing."

"John swears that Mr. Matthews is going to offer for you."

"Why would he say that?"

Sophia looked smug. "I think it's more hope than anything else. If Mr. Matthews marries you, then he'll have to forgive John's debt."

"You cannot be serious." Anne set the cup down with a clatter.

"He also said Mr. Matthews had you pressed against a tree. He thought the man was attacking you but soon realized you had your arms wrapped around him. A tree, Anne? Really?"

"Oh God."

"If that's the case, you will have to marry Mr. Matthews."

It'd be a cold day in hell before that happened. The man desired her, for sure, but he wouldn't want his family connected to hers. "John has hinted as much, but I doubt very seriously Mr. Matthews wants to attach his family to ours, especially given the amount of debt that John has incurred."

"The sum is that much?"

Anne nodded. "John is in a great deal of trouble. The fact is, I think he's put us all in danger."

Sophia looked alarmed. "Surely not."

"Creditors want to be paid. Who knows what they'll do to get their money? Even come after us for it."

"But we don't have it!"

"I know. I'm at a loss as to what to do."

"John made this mess—he should fix it." Sophia pushed her teacup away.

Anne snorted. "That's not likely, is it?"

"Perhaps you should encourage Nathaniel Matthews," Sophia said. "He is very rich and he likes you well enough to kiss you. He's not likely to approve of my match with Tony."

"I don't expect to marry," Anne said shortly.

"I know we've disparaged your looks, but you aren't ugly."

"It doesn't matter."

"I think it does." Sophia paused. "There is something else going on. You've been acting strangely for a week now. I thought it was because you were jealous, but that's not it."

"Jealous? I doubt that." Anne watched her sister for a moment. Perhaps Sophia would have a clue how to fix this. "I will tell you, but you cannot laugh and you cannot tell another soul. Swear."

Sophia laughed. "Honestly, Anne, you're being melodramatic."

Anne whispered, "I climbed the Fairy Steps."

"So? You walk them all the time."

"I climbed them without touching the walls." She stared at Sophia, willing her to understand.

"But that's just a fable . . ." Sophia's eyes met hers. "Did you see a real fairy?"

"I don't know about the fairy, but I did get a wish." Anne felt the heat creep up in her face.

"What did you wish for?"

Anne frowned at her. "I was thinking about our situation and this old woman kept hounding me to come up with a wish."

"There was an old woman? Not a fairy?"

"Yes. It was all quite odd. I thought it was just a joke, so I wished for a rich, handsome man to fall passionately in love with me."

"So that's why Mr. Matthews cannot leave you alone. I knew it had to be something!"

Anne glared at her sister. "Thank you for that."

Sophia had the grace to look chagrined. "That's not what I meant. You know he'd never have noticed you if we were in Town."

Anne agreed but didn't want to belabor the point. "Now I'm trying to undo the wish before anyone gets hurt. But nothing is working."

"Let me get this straight. You think Mr. Matthews's attentions are related to the wish?"

Anne nodded.

"Mr. Worth and Tony as well?"

"Yes. They are all affected by the wish." Anne slumped in her chair. "None of it is real."

Sophia shook her head. "I don't believe it. Mr. Matthews has real feelings for you. I've seen the way he acts around you. The way he looks at you. It's different from the others."

"It's all because of the wish," Anne said. "Sophia, I have to do something."

"Fine. I'll help," Sophia said. "What do you want me to do?"

"I need you to climb the Fairy Steps to get a wish. You will then use that wish to cancel out my wish."

"But what if I want to wish for something else?"

"Sophia, please," Anne begged. "I have to put an end to it."

"Why, Anne? A rich, handsome man likes you a great deal. You like him back or else you wouldn't kiss him in public."

"It was not public! It was the woods."

"What's the harm in letting things go as they are?"

Anne sighed heavily. "I can't stand the thought of him waking up and suddenly finding himself married to me and then hating me for it. I can't face him, knowing that it was all fairy magic. I can't trap him like that."

"I'll climb the steps for you, if I must," Sophia said. "But I think you're wrong about Nathaniel Matthews."

Anne sighed and picked up her teacup. If only.

The next day Anne hurried away from the Lodge, her head down to try to block the cold wind. She pulled her cloak closer around her.

She'd managed to escape before Nathaniel found her. The man practically stalked her while she was in the house. Now the servants were teasing her about him being sweet on her.

Then there were the cravings. She wanted to see him. She wanted to kiss him. She needed his touch on her skin like she needed to breathe. She couldn't turn it off. Even while she was avoiding Nathaniel, she was secretly hoping to see him. Just once more.

"Miss Townsend, I've been waiting for you."

Anne looked up, startled to see Cecil Worth leaning against a tree near the road. *The arrogant toad.* "Why would you wait for me?" She brushed by him, intent on ignoring him.

"Surely you know my feelings for you. I thought I had made them clear." He held out his hands in supplication.

Was he serious? "Make your feelings known to someone else. After the debacle in church, I want nothing more to do with you."

Mr. Worth grabbed her arm. "At least give me the chance to apologize, Miss Townsend. Anne, please."

His voice grated on her ears. "Apology accepted. Now please leave me be."

He clasped her hand in his. Anne tried to pull away. "Let me go."

"My dear, I want to marry you."

Anne's eyebrows rose. "Perhaps you should discuss this with your mother before going further." She yanked her hand from his.

"What has Mother to do with us?"

Anne raised her chin. "She has accused me of bewitching you."

Mr. Worth laughed. "She is mad."

"Mad or not, I have no wish to cross paths with her again. I've heard quite enough already." She turned to leave him. The hour was growing late. The last thing Anne's reputation needed was to be caught alone with Cecil Worth, the idiot.

"Mother was here at the Lodge?" Cecil's face flushed with anger. "I specifically told her not to meddle in my affairs."

A tremor of fear went through Anne. "She is trying to keep you from an imprudent match. In this case I agree with her."

Cecil grabbed her arms and pulled her close. "You don't mean that, Anne."

Anger warred with fear and the anger won. Anne shoved Cecil hard, forcing him to release her. "Get your hands off of me."

"Anne, Mother won't interfere."

"There is nothing to interfere with, Mr. Worth."

"I want to marry you."

"I do not want to marry you." Anne moved past him, hoping if she ignored him, he'd take the hint. He didn't. He followed her.

"You won't get a better offer."

She gasped and whirled. "I'd rather be a spinster, thank you."

"If you are holding out for Nathaniel Matthews, you will remain an old maid. He would never marry for so little a temptation."

A sharp pain seared through Anne. Hearing the truth from a third party was a great deal more painful, even from a worm like Cecil Worth. "I'm not holding out for anyone, Mr. Worth, including you."

She turned on her heel and walked toward the house before she gave in to the urge to slap the smile from his face.

"You should consider my offer, Miss Townsend," Worth shouted at her.

"I would rather die, Mr. Worth, than marry you!" she shouted back. She walked faster, anger churning inside her. *Stupid man. How dare he?*

"Who's going to protect you from the trouble your brother is in?"

Anne turned and found him close behind her. She clenched her hands into fists. "What do you know about John?"

"Only that he's in deep with some very nasty people. It could ruin your family's good reputation."

"We've managed before. We will again."

Cecil just glared at her. Lord, he was short. They almost met eye to eye. "Get to the point."

"Those men will come after you. They won't rest until they have their money—or blood."

Anne was afraid that might be true. "We have nothing. Surely they will see the reason in that."

He chuckled. "You are so naïve. These men don't see reason."

"We will manage."

"My offer stands, Anne. I can take care of you."

"And my sisters?"

Cecil remained silent. Anne pushed past him. Did he expect her to just walk away from her sisters? After a few steps she turned and looked back. "Mr. Worth, nothing could tempt me to marry a man who would leave my sisters alone to fend for themselves."

Chapter Eleven

The house was quiet the following Sunday afternoon. There was no repeat of the past Sunday's special Bible reading, for which Anne was thankful. Sophia was napping on the couch. Juliet was curled up with a book. Anne sat close to the fire, mending. A cold November wind blew, causing the old cottage to creak. The fire provided little warmth.

"Where is John?" Sophia said, covering her mouth for a yawn.

"He needed to get out." Anne pulled hard on a stitch and then had to smooth out the gathers in the fabric.

John was always disappearing now. Anne suspected he was in town getting into some sort of trouble.

"He's never around. I'm not sure why he's even still here," Juliet complained.

Anne looked up from her work. "Where else would he go?"

"You'd think he'd have to check with his steward or something," Sophia said. "Surely he shouldn't be away from his estate so long."

"He's sold everything that wasn't nailed down. The estate is entailed, so he can't sell that. Frankly, I don't think he cares what happens to the place," replied Anne.

"I didn't think things were that bad," said Sophia.

Anne nodded and went back to her work. It was time Sophia faced the truth about their brother and the situation he'd involved them in.

"Miss Anne. There is someone at the door for you," Hannah said quietly from hall.

"Who is calling?" Sophia stood and straightened her dress.

Hannah looked uncomfortable.

"Hannah, what is it?" asked Anne.

"It's a man who was looking for Sir John, but asked for you instead."

"Should we alert Thomas?"

"I already have, miss." Hannah twisted her hands in her apron. "I tried to tell him you weren't home, but he insisted."

Anne stood. She might as well get it over with. "Juliet, please go upstairs to your room."

"Why am I always the one who has to leave when things get interesting?"

"Juliet, please. Hannah, give us a few minutes and show him in."

"Are you sure, Anne? He might be dangerous," Sophia said.

"Please have Thomas come join us after the man has been here a few minutes. I don't want to be left with him very long. Also, should Sir John come in, have him avoid the parlor."

"Yes, miss," Hannah said as she returned to the front door.

Anne figured it was only a matter of time before the creditors came calling here. She had no idea how she was going to deal with them.

"Should I get your shawl?" Sophia said nervously.

"We won't be long." Anne wiped her hands on her skirts. "Stay close to me and don't say anything. Let me do all the talking."

Sophia nodded. Her eyes were wide with fear and her hands were clasped so tightly her knuckles were white. Anne wanted to soothe her but there was no time.

"Miss Townsend, Mr. Jones is here to see you," Hannah said from the doorway.

Mr. Jones was short, squat, and mean looking. He removed his hat as he stepped into the room and looked around. He had a long scar on his face. It was the same man who had been lurking around the cottage.

"Good afternoon, Mr. Jones. It's rather late for visiting."

Mr. Jones glanced at Hannah, who left the room, leaving the door open. "I've come on a matter of business with your brother, ma'am."

"My brother isn't here." Anne kept her voice calm despite the burn of fear in her stomach.

Mr. Jones moved into the room. "Aren't you going to ask me to sit down? Perhaps share tea? Isn't that what you ladies do?"

"Please state your business."

He chuckled. "Your brother owes my partner a great deal of money. I'm here to collect."

"I'm afraid you've come on a fool's errand, Mr. Jones." Anne forced a smile. "What Sir John does is none of my concern."

"Strange for a man to leave his sisters alone and unprotected." Threat was heavy in his tone. "If you get my meaning."

Anne raised one eyebrow. "Why don't you explain yourself, Mr. Jones?"

"You're a calm one. My client is wantin' his money. Plain and simple."

"I don't owe your client money, nor am I responsible for Sir John's debts."

"You be his sister, and that's good enough. I'm here to warn ye that if we don't get our money, well, let's just say you won't be likin' the consequences."

A movement from the hallway caught Anne's eye. It was Thomas. Anne turned back to Mr. Jones. "Your client condones threatening women? Perhaps I should call the magistrate to deal with this."

Mr. Jones started to speak, but Anne held up her hand. "We have nothing further to say. Thomas, please see Mr. Jones out."

"Yes, miss," said Thomas, stepping into the room and taking the man by the arm.

Mr. Jones yanked his arm away from Thomas and pulled his hat on his head. "You just be careful, Miss High-and-Mighty. You've been warned. I'll have them jewels as payment."

"Thomas, hold. What jewels?"

Mr. Jones snarled at her. "You be hiding jewels from your brother. Don't deny it."

Anne laughed. "Someone has been telling you Banbury tales, sir. There are no jewels."

"My source is good," he said.

"Do you honestly think we would be living like this if we had access to the funds jewels would bring?" She could see the indecision on his face. "I suggest you go back to your 'good' source and ask a few more questions."

The next morning, Anne sat with Lady Danford in the sunny parlor at the Lodge. The wind that had blown cold through the cracks in the cottage yesterday had died down. In its place a weak sun flooded the room with light.

A cheerful fire warmed the room. Anne sat close, needing the warmth. Since the unexpected visit from Mr. Jones, she'd hardly slept, afraid he would come back in the night. She now wished that she'd allowed Nathaniel to teach her to shoot.

Anne looked at Lady Danford snoozing in her chair. God, how she longed to tell her about the trouble they were in. But Lady Danford would just pay the debt. Anne couldn't take charity to save John's hide.

All this trouble over some jewels she'd not seen since her mother's death! No one wanted to believe the truth. Anne pulled her shawl tightly around her. She hadn't wanted to leave Sophia and Juliet at the house, even with John sleeping off the drunken stupor he'd come home in.

"What the hell is going on, Anne?" Nathaniel said as he burst into the room.

Anne jumped. "Good Lord, you scared me."

"Someone needs to." He was angry. His nostrils flared and his eyes were hard.

Anne fought for calm. She smiled at Lady Danford, who had awakened, but the lady simply stood and quietly left the room. *Damn, I was hoping for the lady's support.*

"What has you so angry?"

"You had a visitor. Don't deny it. Thomas told me this morning."

Now he has my servants spying on me? "We can't have a caller on a Sunday?"

"Don't insult my intelligence." Nathaniel pulled up a chair beside her. "Tell me everything."

"Honestly, Nathaniel, there isn't much to tell. John owes his client money. We don't have it."

"Did he threaten you?"

She looked away.

"He did, didn't he? What did he say?"

"I can handle it."

He raised an eyebrow. "Really?"

She fought the urge to throw something. "I have it under control."

Nathaniel looked as though he wanted to shake her. For one moment, Anne thought she'd pushed him too far.

"Bloody hell, Anne. This is serious." He pulled in a deep breath. "What did he want?"

Anne studied his face for a long moment before continuing. "He wanted jewels."

"Jewels? What jewels?"

Anne sagged against the back of the chair. "My mother evidently had some very expensive jewels that she brought with her when she married."

"I take it you don't have them," Nathaniel said.

"If I did, I'd have sold them. We really could have used the money." She hated admitting that, especially to Nathaniel, though there was a part of her that was relieved to tell someone what was going on.

Nathaniel nodded in understanding.

"I was frightened," she admitted in a small voice.

"Perhaps you and your sisters should move here into the Lodge."

Anne shook her head. "I couldn't take advantage of Lady Danford like that. She does so much for us as it is."

"I need you safe, Anne."

The concern on Nathaniel's face wrapped around her like a warm blanket. It felt good for someone else to worry about her for a change. She hadn't felt that in a very long time. "Mr. Jones is gone. He must realize that we can give him nothing."

"You think that will matter to him?" Nathaniel stood and started pacing. "He'll take what he wants. It's what he does."

"But we have nothing."

"As long as Sir John is living there, you aren't safe. I need to know you'll be safe, Anne."

The soft tone of his voice, the concern on his face, stirred something deep inside Anne. "I appreciate your concern, but we will be fine."

"Sweetheart, these men are dangerous. Do you want me to talk to Sir John?"

"No."

Nathaniel's mouth grew tight. "Why? Don't forget that he owes me money as well. A conversation might solve a lot of these issues."

"What good would it do? He has no funds."

"Where is your brother, Anne?"

Anne frowned at him. "I'm not sure. He's been missing since yesterday."

"Did he leave the village?"

Anne stared up at him. "How? He has no funds. Where would he go? London? They hound him worse there than here."

"The Continent?"

Anne shook her head. "No money."

"Anne, is anything missing at the cottage?"

"Not that I know of, but we have nothing of enough value to get him far. Do you think he's in trouble?"

Nathaniel laughed. "Yes."

Anne shook her head. "No, I mean, do you think Mr. Jones has hurt John? Perhaps we should look for him. He could be hurt somewhere."

"I didn't think you cared."

"He is my brother. I can't desert him despite what he's done." She needed him to understand. It just wasn't in her to give up on John.

"He's left you to deal with his debts. These men won't leave you alone."

She blinked away the sting of tears. She didn't want to break down in front of Nathaniel. "I don't know what to do."

"Move in here. I can talk to Grandmother. If she knew you girls were in trouble, she wouldn't hesitate to help."

Anne looked down at her hands, clasped together so tightly. She searched for the right words. "We can't. I can't. Lady Danford has already done so much for us."

"Damn it, Anne, it's dangerous."

Anne jumped at the anger in his voice. "We will be fine, Nathaniel. Thomas will stay with us."

He pulled her into his arms. "Sweetheart, trust me with this. Come stay at the Lodge where I can protect you."

Anne wanted to relax in his arms. It felt good to be held. "If things get worse, I promise that my sisters and I will come stay here—if Lady Danford permits it. All right?"

Nathaniel released her. "You are a stubborn woman."

Anne smiled for the first time. "Are you just discovering that, sir?"

"Now you are flirting with me. It makes me question whether you are taking this seriously enough."

"I am taking the threats seriously, but there is nothing I can do."

"What if I offered to pay his debts?"

"No. Absolutely not. It's not right. What would people say?"

"They would see that I'm helping the family of the woman I'm courting."

"But you aren't."

He shook his head. "You are the strangest woman. Even your sisters recognize that I—care for you."

Anne's mouth fell open. *He is serious. Dear Lord, he is serious.* She turned her back on him and moved to stare out the window. The gardens were barren, like she'd feel when he finally woke up from this dream.

Nathaniel came up behind her and wrapped his arms around her. He nuzzled her neck and she shivered. "Anne, you must realize how much I regard you. I can't seem to keep my hands off of you. I thought you felt the same."

Anne remained silent, closing her eyes to seal off her emotions. He couldn't know how his touch affected her. He couldn't know how tempted she was to lean back into his arms and give herself up to the emotions churning inside her. She didn't feel the same as he. She was in love and he could never know.

Nathaniel released her and stepped back when she didn't respond. "Anne?"

She held herself still, silent. She couldn't deny how she felt, but she could keep herself from declaring it if she didn't look at him.

"I see." He spoke softly, but there was an edge of something in his voice. Disappointment? "If you'll excuse me, then, Miss Townsend, I'll leave you to your thoughts."

Anne waited until the door closed behind Nathaniel. Then she wrapped her arms around herself, around the pain, tears streaming down her face. Why did doing the right thing have to hurt so?

"I think you are completely mad, Anne," Sophia said breathlessly as they walked quickly toward the Fairy Steps. "I can't believe you walk this nearly every day."

"It is beneficial exercise." Anne pulled her cloak around her and winced. Her ankle was still just a bit tender. The low-hanging clouds reflected her mood, but this had to end today. She couldn't take another confrontation with Nathaniel.

"It looks like snow. Are you sure we should do this today?" Sophia paused at the base of the Fairy Steps to catch her breath.

"It's not going to snow," Anne said.

"Why are we doing this again? Oh, yes. Now I remember—my foolish sister believes in fairy stories."

"This was a bad idea." Anne would never hear the end of this from her sister.

"Anne, instead of us breaking our necks trying to climb these insane steps, why not just accept the fact that Mr. Matthews cares for you?"

"Mr. Worth also finds me attractive. You're comparing the two?"

"Please don't make me spell it out for you. You are capable and competent."

"Capable? Competent? Why not add *plain* and *boring* to the list." Anne laughed harshly.

"You know what I mean. It's not as if you had warts on your face and scales for skin."

"Thanks for that." Anne sat down beside Sophia. "I just don't see what he sees."

"I do." Sophia's voice was derisive.

Anne looked at Sophia. *What did that mean?*

Sophia pulled in a deep breath and let it out. "I've been jealous of you for a long time."

"Jealous? Please." Anne laughed.

"You can do anything, Anne. You made sure we had a place to stay, food, clothing. I don't think I could have done it. You work for Lady Danford. You forgive Mrs. Worth for the awful things she says. You are a saint."

"I'm no saint."

Sophia pinned her with a hard look. "You're also dimwitted if you can't see that perhaps Mr. Matthews sees the same things Juliet and I see."

Anne hadn't thought of it this way. Hope sprang up deep within her. She wanted so badly to have Nathaniel's feelings be real. "I don't know."

"I don't understand you." Sophia took her hand and clasped it in hers. "You're afraid of nothing. You faced everyone after the humiliation at church with grace and dignity. You stood up to John and Mr. Jones. You are the most courageous person I know. Yet you push real feelings away."

Anne could feel the tears welling up again. "What if he wakes up one day and looks at me with disdain or feels trapped? I couldn't survive the pain, Sophia. I don't know if I can risk it."

"He won't." Sophia looked up at the stone steps, then back at

Anne. "I've had men fawn all over me. I've had them claim to be in love with me. Write poetry and music. But I've never had a man look at me the way Nathaniel Matthews looks at you."

Anne let herself embrace the hope building inside of her. "Really?"

"See? Dimwitted. You are going to force me to climb these steps and prove it to you." Sophia released Anne's hand and stood. "This is going to take a while."

Anne laughed and wiped the tears from her cheeks. "I don't even know how many times I did it before finally getting the wish. I was so lost in thought that day, I didn't even realize it."

"I cannot believe I'm doing this. You better appreciate it." Sophia lifted her skirt and started up. "Stay behind me—I don't want to fall. I'm not letting anything interfere with the assembly next week. I plan on dancing every dance."

"I forgot about that."

"Anne, you handled the invitations for Lady Danford."

"I've had a lot on my mind of late."

"Really, Anne, most women handle this sort of thing all the time. You've only got two suitors. This should be easy."

Sophia tottered on the uneven stones. Anne caught her by the waist. "Steady. Mr. Worth is another one under the spell. He keeps mumbling something about Mother's jewels."

"I would seriously have to question your sense if you chose to marry *him*. He's creepy, and his mother is so hateful."

"That she is." Anne placed her hand on Sophia's back to further steady her. "Careful through here, this passage is very narrow and steep."

"This is ridiculous." Sophia was breathing heavily. "I barely fit through it."

"I had no trouble with it."

"You are thinner than I." Sophia took the next step gingerly. "I hope you appreciate this."

"I do. Just keep going."

"Sophia? What are you doing up there?" Tony's voice echoed through the narrow stone pass.

Sophia tripped and grabbed the wall to keep from falling. Anne caught her waist again. She turned and found Tony and Nathaniel below them. *Damn.* Nathaniel frowned at her.

"Stay calm, Anne. I'll handle this," Sophia whispered. Then, in a louder voice, she addressed the brothers. "Gentlemen, what brings you to this section of the woods?"

Tony put a foot on the first step. "Sophia, come down before you fall."

"Actually, it's easier to just keep going up," Sophia said.

"Then I'll meet you at the top." Tony disappeared with Nathaniel behind him.

"Where are they going?" Sophia whispered.

"There's another path to the top," Anne said and pushed her forward. "Just hold on to the wall. You've already touched it, so it doesn't matter. I'm right behind you."

"You could have told me about the other path."

"It doesn't get you a wish, and besides, it's a much longer way around." They climbed as quickly as they could and soon reached the top.

"I can see why you like it here. The view is amazing," Sophia said. "You can see all the way into Beetham."

Anne heard a twittering around her. *Fairies?* "Do you hear anything?"

Sophia cocked her head and listened. "No. Do you?"

Anne nodded and heard the faint sound of fairy laughter. *Will they ever leave me alone?* "I think I'm going crazy."

Sophia took Anne's hand and squeezed. They heard the men approaching. "Stay calm and let me do the talking."

The last thing Anne wanted was to face Nathaniel after the scene in the drawing room yesterday. The more time she spent around him, the less she was able to hide what she felt.

"Gentlemen, what brings you so far from the Lodge?" Sophia said brightly when the men appeared at the top of the rocks.

"I was just going to ask you the same thing, Sophia," said Tony.

"Anne told me of the fabulous view from this point and I had to see it," Sophia said. "You have to admit, it's spectacular."

Nathaniel and Tony looked out. "It is nice," Tony admitted. "But you should have taken the easy way like we did."

"Anne insisted," Sophia said. "Besides, its beneficial exercise—isn't that right, Anne?"

"Uh, yes. It is." Anne looked up and smiled at Tony. Her smile faded when she looked at Nathaniel. His brow lifted as if he were questioning the truth of their story.

He didn't believe her.

"Allow us to escort you ladies home," Nathaniel said. "Given the events of the past few days, you really shouldn't be out here unaccompanied."

Sophia shot Anne a look that said *behave* and took Tony's arm. Anne had no choice but to walk beside Nathaniel. He didn't offer his arm, and for that she was thankful. She wasn't sure she could hide her reaction to his touch. If he caught on, he'd know that everything she said to him the day before had been a lie.

Chapter Twelve

Nathaniel glanced at Anne walking quietly beside him. He'd give anything to know what was going through her mind. Hell, he'd settle just for knowing what her fascination was with the Fairy Steps.

Anne walked slowly. He had thought perhaps her ankle was still bothering her, but as the distance grew between her and the couple ahead of them, he became more suspicious.

Miss Sophia kept looking back at them every few minutes. Nathaniel couldn't tell if it was to see if they were talking to each other or if they were doing something else.

Frankly, he'd love to be doing something else with Anne Townsend.

"What brings you all the way out here, Nathaniel?" Anne asked.

He loved how she said his name.

"Just walking. What brings you here?"

"Sophia wanted to see the steps."

Anne kept her eyes focused on the uneven ground. Nathaniel ground his teeth, then forced himself to relax. "Odd, given that you've lived here for five years. I would have thought she would know about the place."

Anne stumbled, but caught herself quickly. "Oh, well, uh. She usually walks to the village rather than up here."

"It seems as though you've made peace with your sister."

Anne smiled. "We are progressing. I think John's coming here has helped a great deal. Now she sees what I've had to deal with."

Nathaniel stopped and caught her arm. He waited until she looked up at him. "You know, Anne, you don't have to take things upon yourself so much. There are . . . friends who would help."

"I know."

Want and need filled him. Despite her denial, or rather her lack of response yesterday, he still wanted her. She had more honor than most men he knew. "Any more visits from Mr. Jones?"

Anne frowned. "It's odd, but no. I can't imagine he would just arrive, threaten us, and then leave."

"Men like him are like snakes. They lie in wait for the right moment to strike. Has Sir John been giving you any more trouble?"

"We don't see much of him. He sleeps most of the day away and is out somewhere most of the night." Anne paused. "I don't think he's staying in Beetham, but I'm not quite sure how he'd get to Milnthorpe."

"Do you want me to say something?" He found himself hoping she'd say yes. Anything to quench this uncontrollable urge to fix things for her.

She shook her head. "I can handle John."

"Did you tell him about Mr. Jones?"

"What would be the point? He's likely more terrified of Mr. Jones than I am."

Nathaniel saw red. He grabbed Anne's arm. "I can't believe you let Sir John hide behind your skirts. Damn coward! Does he not even care that he's put his sisters in danger?"

"I don't have a great deal of choice in the matter at the moment."

"Just promise me you'll be careful." Nathaniel released her.

Anne moved away as if she were afraid of him. *Damn.* The last thing he wanted was for her to be afraid of him.

"I'm sorry I was so abrupt," Nathaniel muttered.

"It's fine." She gave him a slight smile. "It's been nice to have someone else to lean on right now." She looked at her sister, walking with Tony. "I think you were right about those two."

"Are you sorry you pushed so hard?"

"For Sophia's sake, yes. They both have some growing up to do."

Nathaniel nodded but stayed silent. She obviously didn't want to discuss consequences of the marriage not taking place. She had to be worried.

He glanced back at the Fairy Steps. Her fascination with the place bordered on obsessive.

Nathaniel thought back to the first time he'd seen Anne. He'd been watching her from a distance as he approached.

"Anne, why are you trying to climb the steps again?"

"I'm not," she said quickly.

"Why did you have Sophia climb them?" He watched Anne carefully. Emotions flitted across her face and then he knew. It was the damned fable. Surely Anne didn't believe in that nonsense.

Nathaniel stopped and touched Anne's arm. He waited to let Tony and Sophia move farther away. "Have you climbed the Fairy Steps before?"

Anne glanced around her before nodding. "I've climbed them for years. This was just the first time I climbed without touching the sides."

"You think you've been granted a wish?"

Anne blushed and looked away from him. "Yes."

"You saw a fairy?"

"I saw an old woman."

"What did you wish for, Anne?" He pulled on her arm to coax her closer. She didn't push him away. Her eyes were wide and a bit frightened. "Did you wish for a husband?"

"No! Of course not!"

"What did you wish for?" He knew that desperation colored the tone of his voice but he couldn't stop it.

Anne looked at the ground and pulled in a deep breath. "May I ask you a question?"

The change in subject startled him. Her face was serious. "Certainly."

It took her a long time to finally speak. "If you had seen me in Town at a ball or assembly, would you have asked me to dance?"

He frowned. It felt like a trick question, but he had to answer honestly. "I don't know."

Anne pushed away from him. "I thought so."

She seemed to shrink into herself. Nathaniel felt a moment of panic. What answer was she expecting? "Anne, what's going on in that head of yours?"

"I can't." Her voice cracked. "I have to go." She pulled from his grasp and ran into the woods.

"Anne, wait!" Nathaniel started after her.

"Let her go."

"What did you say to her?" Sophia asked, her hands on her hips.

"I asked her about her wish!" Nathaniel almost shouted.

"Oh no! I need to find her." Sophia turned to leave, then whirled back. "Is that all?"

Nathaniel rubbed his hands over his face but said nothing.

"Out with it. What else did you say?" she demanded.

"She asked me if I would have asked her to dance if we were in Town."

"And how did you answer?"

"I told her that I didn't know."

"You are an idiot, Nathaniel Matthews." Sophia turned and followed Anne into the woods.

Nathaniel could hear her muttering something like "stupid men" as she left.

She is right.

"Stupid answer," Tony said as they watched Sophia chase after Anne. "I thought you'd figured out all the trick questions women ask."

"I was honest. I probably wouldn't have noticed her," Nathaniel said angrily. "She is driving me crazy."

"I know the feeling," Tony said with a laugh. "Come on. Let's find the ladies. I don't think they should be wandering these woods alone."

Anne ran until she couldn't breathe. She stopped to rest against a tree. The stitch in her side was nothing to the pain she'd felt at Nathaniel's words.

He was only being honest with her. She'd give him that.

"Anne?" Sophia shouted.

Anne wiped at the tears on her face. She had to quit letting Nathaniel hurt her so.

"There you are." Sophia was breathing hard. "Don't make me do that again."

"Sorry," Anne muttered.

"Are you all right?"

"I will be," Anne whispered. She let Sophia hug her close. She closed her eyes and fought the urge to cry harder.

"I leave you alone to talk with a man who likes you and you ask him a trick question," Sophia said.

"I don't know what you're referring to." Anne was confused.

"You asked Nathaniel Matthews if he'd have noticed you in Town. You never ask men questions like that. They will never be able to answer in a satisfactory way. If he says no, you get hurt. If he says yes, you don't believe him."

Anne had no clue what Sophia was talking about. "You're not making sense."

"It's a rule, Anne. You have to abide by it."

"There are no rules like that," Anne scoffed.

"What do you know? You've never had a man court you." Sophia gave her a superior smile. "In this area, I am the expert."

"Fine."

Sophia started walking toward home. "So why did you ask him that question anyway?"

Anne fell into step beside her. "I can't help but feel if circumstances were different he wouldn't have noticed me, much less danced with me."

Sophia turned toward her. "Good Lord, Anne, be realistic. In Town, you'd be competing with so many other women. It would take a miracle for a man to notice any of us. We lack a fortune or a title. This has nothing to do with your looks and everything to do with a lack of competition."

Anne frowned as she thought. "I don't know. Mother and Father always raved about how pretty you and Juliet were."

"Didn't they tell you the same?"

"I honestly don't remember."

"Anne, you are pretty. Despite every effort you make to downplay your appearance, I can see why Nathaniel likes you so much."

"It's not real, Sophia."

"I don't know. He's not acting as crazy as Mr. Worth is." Sophia clasped Anne's hands. "He sees in you what Juliet and I have always depended on but never acknowledged."

"I don't believe it. I can't believe it." Anne pulled her hands free and dabbed at her tears with a handkerchief. "Why did I let it get this far?"

"How far has it gone? Have you and he—?"

"No!" She blushed. She couldn't admit how much farther she'd let him go, given the chance. "He's kissed me a couple of times."

Sophia gave her a curious look. "Really? What was it like?"

"Sophia!"

"Seriously, all Tony has done is a quick press of his lips. There has to be more to it than that."

Anne felt her face heat up. "I'm not saying anything more."

"Anne, you're blushing! You have to tell me now."

"Let's go home." Anne grasped Sophia's hand. "Thank you."

"Don't get used to it."

Nathaniel was frantic to find Anne. He couldn't believe she had turned the tables on him like that and twisted his words.

He was glad he hadn't met her in London. He would have missed her completely in the crowds. It had taken coming to Beetham to open his eyes. She had completely misunderstood.

He found the sisters walking quietly back to the cottage, arm in arm. He stopped and watched them for a moment. Sophia was comforting Anne. It was about time those two were talking.

"Anne," he said behind them. Sophia whispered something to her as they stopped. Anne didn't turn but Sophia glared back at him. "May I speak with you?"

"I'll stay if you want me to," Sophia said to her sister.

"No. I'm fine."

Nathaniel waited until Sophia was out of hearing range before he approached Anne. Her eyes were red rimmed. He felt pain in his chest for hurting her. "Anne, I'm sorry."

"For what? Being honest?" Her voice was tight.

"You misunderstood."

"You are allowed to be honest."

Nathaniel took hold of her shoulders and turned her to face him. When she didn't lift her eyes to his, he tilted her chin with his hand. "Anne, look at me."

She finally lifted her lashes.

"I'm glad I didn't meet you in London. The crowds in the ballroom would have kept me away."

"You don't like crowds?"

"No. They scare me to death." Nathaniel smiled at her.

She smiled shyly. "I don't think many men would admit to being afraid."

"Especially to a pretty girl." He tucked a piece of hair behind her ear. "You are pretty, Anne. Not in a flashy way like your sister, but in a quiet way."

"Thank you for that." She moved slightly away from him. "I should get home before it's dark."

"Of course, but allow me to escort you."

She nodded and led the way back to the path to the cottage. They walked in silence. Nathaniel hated the polite coldness between them. Somehow he had to convince her that, wish or no wish, he was here to stay. He was serious and intended to make her his wife.

As they came up to the cottage, he spotted Tony and Sophia talking outside. They both looked up as he and Anne approached.

Anne immediately went into the cottage as if she couldn't wait to get away from him. *More mixed messages.* Nathaniel kicked up some gravel with his boot, then heaved a heavy sigh. One step forward, two steps back. This was some crazy dance. He turned to walk back to the Lodge.

Tony fell into step beside him. "Did you fix things?"

"No," Nathaniel said. "Not yet."

"Perhaps the assembly will help."

Nathaniel felt that familiar knot in his stomach. When he told Anne he hated crowds, he wasn't kidding. The thought of so many bodies being crowded in the small ballroom at the Lodge made his pulse jump. "That's in a few days?"

"Yes." Tony laughed. "I have to say I'm enjoying the shoe being on the other foot."

Nathaniel felt his face grow hot. "You know how I hate crowds."

"You won't get out of this one, Brother. Grandmother's invited half the county. Besides, you'll get the chance to dance with Anne. Do you want to pass that up? Grandmother will insist."

"I can handle Grandmother," Nathaniel said.

"Are you sure about that? It appears you are losing your touch with women."

Nathaniel shot him a nasty look and cursed under his breath. He *was* losing his touch, but no more. He'd figure out how to convince her his intentions were honorable. First he had to dispel her belief in this fairy nonsense.

He needed to get out of the Lodge. Between Tony's teasing and Grandmother's knowing looks, Nathaniel was ready to explode.

He was only going to the Sheep and Crow for a pint, not to spy on Sir John. At least that was the story he was sticking with. The Sheep and Crow was rumored to serve a great ale. From the looks of the crowds as the carriage pulled in front of the old, rambling pub, Nathaniel had to agree.

He stepped out of the carriage, into the frigid night. It wouldn't be long before the first snow fell in the Lake District.

He should be working. Piles of letters needing responses had finally found their way to him via the post. He was getting farther and farther behind, thanks to a certain lady with haunting green eyes.

A gust of cold air caught him from behind, pushing Nathaniel toward the entrance and away from his thoughts.

Tonight was about Sir John and his lack of responsibility to his sisters. The man was gambling again; Nathaniel was sure of it.

He was also sure Sir John was avoiding him. They were going to deal with each other sooner rather than later. Until Sir John was taken care of, Anne would be reluctant to accept his suit.

Nathaniel stepped into the pub. Just about every chair was occupied. The air was filled with the smell of food, smoke from the fires, and ale. Sir John was in the corner by the fire, holding court with a deck of cards in his hands. He was chatting up some of the locals.

Nathaniel made his way to the bar and asked for a pint. He threw down coin and made his way to Sir John, where he settled down with his pint to watch the card game Sir John had evidently convinced one of the men to play. It didn't take long for Sir John to cheat. Nathaniel finished his drink and made his way to the table.

"Sir John. A word, please." He kept his voice low. He glanced around the table. "Gentlemen."

"Matthews. Sit down, sit down." Sir John gathered his winnings and stuffed the coins in his pockets. "Do you wish to play a game?"

"I'd rather not." Nathaniel looked around. "Have a pint on me, gentlemen, while I talk to Sir John." He waited until the few men surrounding the table shuffled their way to the bar. Then he spoke to Sir John. "I'd suggest you stop cheating."

Sir John's nostrils flared. "I could call you out for that!"

"But you won't."

"Why are you here? Did Anne put you up to this?" John sneered.

Nathaniel tightened his fists. "Don't you think you're in enough trouble?"

John laughed. "What trouble? I'm winning."

"By cheating. I'll not have you digging yourself into a hole and then expecting your sister to dig you out."

"Is Anne telling that old lie again? She is such a prude. No imagination at all."

Nathaniel controlled his anger. "Did you know that a Mr. Jones called at the cottage?"

John's hands stilled. "I don't think Anne mentioned it, but then I've not been around much of late." His hands shook as he gathered up the cards. "Is she all right?"

Nathaniel sipped his ale. "For now. Do you happen to know why Mr. Jones is looking for jewels?"

Sir John had the grace to look guilty. Nathaniel had thought he wasn't capable of feeling that particular emotion.

"I may have mentioned that my sisters might have my step-mother's jewels. I was stalling."

"He thinks Anne is hiding them for you."

Sir John glanced around him nervously. "Anne can take care of herself. She's tough."

Nathaniel glared at Sir John as he squirmed. The man disgusted him. "Tough enough to deal with Jones?"

"What do you want me to do about it? I can't pay him." He tossed down the rest of the ale in his glass.

The urge to slam his fist into the man's face was almost overwhelming. Nathaniel curled his fingers into a fist. The only thing stopping him was Anne. She'd have to clean up the mess. He tossed back the last of the ale and stood. "Let's go. You're done for the night."

John pouted. "I'll have to listen to Anne complain."

"You stay and I tell every man in this place you've been cheating them for the last few nights."

"You wouldn't!"

"Try me."

"I can't believe I'm letting someone like you treat me thus." Sir John tossed a few coins on the table and shuffled to his feet. "Please tell me you brought the carriage."

Nathaniel closed his eyes and prayed for patience. "It's outside."

Nathaniel led him out to the carriage and opened the door. "Get in." Nathaniel spoke to the driver. "Take the long way to the cottage."

"Yes, sir."

Nathaniel climbed in after Sir John and closed the door behind him. He pounded on the ceiling to signal the driver before turning his attention back to John. "Now we'll talk."

Sir John sniffed. "I have nothing more to discuss with you."

Nathaniel gave in to his anger and grabbed the man by the throat.

"Fine. I'll talk and you'll listen." He shoved the man back into the corner of the carriage. "You've brought trouble here. You are going to put a stop to things before someone gets hurt."

"Who are you to tell me what I should do?" Sir John sneered. "I'm a baronet."

"I'm the man you owe a great deal of money to. Now I've been happy to hold your vowels, but that could change."

"Why are you so interested? Is it Anne?"

Nathaniel said nothing for a long moment. "Let's just say I have an interest in keeping your sisters safe."

"You mean Anne?" Sir John cackled. "You're courting the mouse? What exactly are your intentions toward my sister?"

Nathaniel ground his teeth at the comment. He itched to beat the man to a pulp. "Why do you care?"

"I did abandon them. I wasn't ready to be the head of the family."

"But to leave them with nothing?" Nathaniel just couldn't understand why a man would leave his family destitute.

"She has done well. They aren't starving, probably thanks to her mother's jewels."

"According to Anne, they were sold by your father."

"The agreement was for my stepmother to retain the jewels she brought from France when she married my father. The housekeeper seems to think that the jewels were taken from the house by Anne, that her mother gave them to her for safekeeping. My stepmother knew she was dying."

Nathaniel pondered this. Anne had no knowledge of where the jewels could be. He believed her. "You must complete one task or I'll have you thrown into the poorhouse: Take care of Mr. Jones."

The carriage pulled to a stop and they exited the carriage together. From the inside of the cottage they could hear shouts.

Nathaniel's heart stopped. Anne was in trouble.

Chapter Thirteen

Anne set her book on the side table and blew out the candle. Ordinarily she couldn't afford to burn the candle this late at night, but she couldn't sleep.

Thoughts of Nathaniel kept her awake. Even the novel she borrowed from Lady Danford didn't occupy her. She closed her eyes and listened to the noises around the old house.

It was getting more and more difficult to avoid Nathaniel. She loved him. She had to admit that much to herself. She had tried pushing him away and was miserable as a result.

Would it be better to give in to the passion he stirred and treasure the memory for the rest of her life? She was beginning to think so. No man had made her feel like this. It was doubtful another man would come along after Nathaniel.

Anne stared at the ceiling, pulling the blankets up to her chin to ward off the cold. She didn't think she could keep treating him so coolly. She couldn't control her reaction to his touch. She was making them both unhappy.

A noise startled her from her thoughts.

Could it be John? He had been avoiding her. Probably with good reason. Still, he didn't usually bang around unless he was drunk and was fumbling with the key.

Anne got out of bed and put on a robe, pulling it tight against the cold night air. She opened the door, silently waiting to hear John's footsteps on the stairs.

There it was again. A soft thump, like the closing of a drawer. Whoever it was, he was in the parlor.

Anne crept back into her room and picked up the fireplace poker. The wood floor creaked under her feet and she cringed.

Anne crept down the stairs, avoiding the ones that made any noise. Luck was with her and she found herself outside the library door without having made any noise. She could hear shuffling inside, and then another drawer was opened. Someone was searching for something. It had to be Mr. Jones.

Anger burned inside Anne. She was sick of this whole mess and the fact that the man broke into their house was beyond the pale.

She gripped the poker like a cricket bat and pushed the door open. It squeaked, and Jones looked up from his position behind the desk.

"What are you doing?" she demanded.

"Bloody meddling bitch," he mumbled and headed toward her. Anne swung the poker and hit the man on the side of his head as hard as she could. He went down, blood gushing from the wound.

"Bloody hell," Anne whispered, almost dropping the poker.

"Anne, what is going on?" Sophia said, coming into the room behind her. "Oh God. It's Mr. Jones!"

"He broke into the house." Anne looked down at the man. "I think I killed him."

Juliet peeked from behind Sophia and screamed. "He's dead?"

"Good God, Juliet, you don't have to scream so," Sophia said. "Anne, how hard did you hit him?"

"I don't know. Do you think he might wake and grab one of us?" Juliet screamed again.

"Juliet! Enough!" Sophia shouted. "If you can't stop screaming, go upstairs. What are we going to do with him?"

"I guess we should tie him up."

"There's no point if he'd dead," Sophia said.

Anne suddenly felt ill. "He can't be dead."

"Where's John?" Sophia said angrily.

"Out," said Anne.

"Can we drag him outside?" Sophia said. "He's bleeding all over the carpet."

"What if someone finds him?" Juliet cried. "Anne, you could hang!"

Anne lowered the poker. "Juliet, this is not useful."

Mr. Jones groaned and tried to sit up. His jacket fell open, revealing a pistol in his pocket. Before she could give it another thought, Anne hit him again, then looked bleakly at her sisters as he fell to the ground once more. "He might be dead now."

"How can you just hit him like that?" Juliet cried. "What has happened to you?"

"Juliet, go back to bed. Anne and I can handle this." Sophia pushed Juliet from the room.

"Why do you always shoo me away when things get interesting?" Juliet said as she stomped her way up the stairs and slammed the door so hard the windows rattled.

Anne stared at Mr. Jones. "He isn't moving."

"No. Is he breathing?" Sophia leaned over him. "I can't tell."

"I'm not touching him to find out." Anne put down the poker.

Sophia nudged Jones with her slippered foot. "We need some help. I don't think we can move him."

"Why is it that John is never around when these things happen?"

Sophia looked at the mess in the small room. "What do you think he was looking for?"

"The jewels, I suppose." Anne walked around the prostrate man, keeping her distance. She gingerly removed his pistol, but he still didn't move. "If he's not dead, he will be very angry when he awakes."

Sir John and Nathaniel Matthews barreled into the house, slamming the door behind them. "What has happened? Are you all right?" John said breathlessly.

"Mr. Jones has paid us another call," Anne said as she handed John the pistol she had taken. "I hit him. Twice."

"With what?" John said.

"The poker."

"We think he's dead, but we didn't want to get close enough to tell," Sophia added.

"Step aside and let me check." Nathaniel knelt down beside Mr. Jones and felt for a pulse. "He's not dead. Did he see you hit him?"

Anne glared at Nathaniel. "As he was charging toward me when I hit him, I think so."

"We need the magistrate," John said. "He should be locked up for breaking into the house."

"I'm not sure that will help keep Anne safe," Nathaniel said. "What was he doing here?"

"Looking for jewels." Sophia added, "Should I put the kettle on?"

"Does anyone want tea?" Anne asked. "I could really use a cup."

Nathaniel looked at her strangely. "Are you all right?"

"Of course," Anne said more brightly than she felt. It wasn't every day she bashed in the head of a burglar.

Nathaniel was still watching her as if she was going to break into hysterics. She hid her shaking hands behind her. "I'm fine, really."

Nathaniel shook his head. "Sir John, we need to tie him up before he comes to. He's going to be angry as hell when he wakes."

"I'll go get rope," John said and turned to leave.

"Do you even know where it is?" Sophia said, following after him. "I had best help him find it."

Anne was suddenly so cold. She couldn't stop shaking. She wrapped her arms around herself. "What are you doing here?" she asked.

"I brought your brother home from the public house. He was cheating at cards. You're trembling."

Anne stepped away from his touch. If she gave in, she'd end up bawling her eyes out. "What will you do with Mr. Jones?"

"Keep him locked up until we can get him out of town. He's going to want revenge once he awakes."

Anne glared at Nathaniel. "He broke into my house."

"He doesn't see it that way. You are just a means to getting the money that Sir John owes him." Nathaniel stepped back, letting his hands fall to his sides.

Sir John came into the room with a good length of rope. "We found it. I also have something we can gag him with." He held up a rag.

"You found the rope? You couldn't find your way out of a sack," Sophia said, following him in. "*I* found the rope."

Anne stepped back into the corner of the room as the men tied up and gagged Mr. Jones. They then carried him out to the carriage. Anne couldn't stop shaking.

"I'm freezing. Let's go upstairs and let the men handle this," Sophia said, rubbing her hands up and down her arms.

"Yes. Good idea," replied Anne.

"Do you want to say good night to Mr. Matthews?"

"No. I'm sure I'll see him at Lady Danford's tomorrow." Anne couldn't let him touch her now or she'd fall apart. And once she started falling, there would be no stopping her descent.

Sleep had eluded Anne. She was haunted by images of Mr. Jones's face and the poker.

She'd been an idiot, thinking she could protect her sisters with just a fireplace poker and sheer force of will. Things could have gone horribly wrong.

The day hadn't gotten any better, either. Hannah was complaining of the mess in the parlor. Her sisters were bickering over their usual nonsense before they left for the village. Lord only knew what John was up to. He still hadn't risen from bed when Anne entered the library to clean up the mess.

She replaced the discarded books, smoothing pages that had been wrinkled in the man's haste to find the nonexistent jewels. She moved to the desk and straightened it up, putting away parchment and righting the inkwell. Luckily it had been pretty empty or she'd have an even bigger mess to clean up.

"Miss, the vicar is here," Hannah said in the doorway.

The man couldn't take a hint. "I don't have time for this."

"I know, miss, but he is the vicar."

Anne dusted her hands on her apron, then removed it and handed it to Hannah. "No tea. It will be a quick visit."

"You shouldn't anger a man of God," Hannah whispered.

"Please just do as I ask. And show him in." Anne was beyond frustrated. She knew why he was here. The assembly that Lady Danford was planning was a week away.

She had tried pretending to not care about the assembly, but Lady Danford had seen to it that she was involved every step of the way. Next week they would begin decorating the Lodge's ballroom for the event.

Anne was not looking forward to standing in the back of the room in her old green dress and watching everyone else waltz by her. She'd either be forced to dance with Mr. Worth or not dance with anyone at all, as she was avoiding Nathaniel's touch.

She put on her best Sunday smile as he stepped into the room. "Good afternoon, Mr. Worth. To what do we owe the pleasure?"

"Miss Townsend, I was hoping to find you at home. You've been gone a great deal." He bowed to her.

Anne took a seat in a nearby chair, ignoring the sofa he had risen from. "I've been needed at Lady Danford's. You know I'm her companion."

"Ah, yes. I forgot. She is planning the assembly next week."

"Yes. She is."

Mr. Worth paced back and forth for a few minutes before sitting on the couch. He rubbed the palms of his hands on his breeches.

"Miss Townsend, may I have the first dance on the night of the ball?"

Anne almost groaned. "Sir, I thought it was your preference to not dance at these occasions."

"Well, there is nothing wrong with a country dance. I'm sure Mother will approve."

I'm sure not. Anne tried to think of a reason to not dance. "I may be engaged with Lady Danford during the assembly, so I will have to let you know."

Why couldn't she make herself be rude to this man? Oh yes, he was a man of the cloth. It was almost worth angering God to avoid having to deal with Mr. Worth's sweaty palms.

"Then I ask that you reserve one dance for me, my dear. I hope you realize how much I admire you, Miss Townsend."

"Thank you, Mr. Worth," Anne said woodenly. Heavens, she was so sick of this. She was never going to complain about Sophia and all her beaus ever again.

"I've been speaking to Mother about you. She is really sorry about the harsh words she spoke when we were last together."

"I appreciate you telling me, sir." Mrs. Worth wouldn't take those words back if her life depended on it.

"I've also spoken with her about our marriage."

"What?" *Dear God, he is serious.* "There is no understanding, sir," Anne sputtered.

"I want you to know that my intentions are honorable. Unlike some gentlemen in the neighborhood."

"Whomever do you mean, Mr. Worth?" Nathaniel said from the doorway. "I'm sorry, Miss Townsend, Hannah let me in."

"Mr. Matthews, good afternoon." Anne rose and Mr. Worth followed suit.

"It appears I've come at a bad time," Nathaniel said with a smile.

"You do have a habit of doing so." Anne smiled back at him, relieved he was here. "Mr. Worth was just leaving. I believe you have the poor to visit?"

"Uh—yes." Mr. Worth's face was flushed as he walked to the door and glared at Nathaniel. "Good day, Miss Townsend. Please remember what we discussed."

"Good day, Mr. Worth."

Nathaniel stared at her, waiting. She sat again and smoothed her dress over her knees. "Nathaniel, please sit down."

Nathaniel took the chair by the fire. "Why was he here?"

"He is courting me. He practically proposed before you interrupted."

Nathaniel's jaw grew tight. "Did you answer him?"

"There was no time. Shall I call for tea?"

"How will you answer him?" His voice sounded calm but there was a vulnerable look in his eyes.

"I must consider my future carefully. What did you do with Mr. Jones?"

"He's with the magistrate."

"Good."

"Is Miss Sophia here?"

Anne's eyebrows rose. "Sophia? I think they just got back from the village. Let me fetch her."

"Thank you."

Anne left the room, frowning. Why did he express displeasure at her comment about marriage, then promptly ask for Sophia? She climbed the stairs and knocked on Sophia and Juliet's door. Sophia opened the door.

"Mr. Matthews is here to see you, Sophia."

Sophia stood and straightened her dress. "Me? Why?"

"I have no idea," Anne said flatly.

Sophia chuckled. "You don't sound happy about it."

"What do you mean?"

"You should see your face, Anne." Sophia giggled. "You're jealous."

"I'm just curious."

"For someone who isn't in love with him, you certainly act like it."

"Sophia! Just let me know why he wishes to see you."

"Maybe." Sophia smiled as she left the room, closing the door behind her.

Anne sat down on Sophia's bed. Perhaps the wish was over? Was there a time limit? Did Nathaniel wake up today and decide not to bother with her any longer?

"Are you all right, Anne?" Juliet asked, looking up from the book she was reading over on her bed.

"I'm fine. What are you reading?"

"A new book from Lady Danford. It's very scary, but I can't put it down." Juliet marked her place and closed the book. "Do you love Mr. Matthews, Anne?"

"I'm afraid so," Anne said and smiled sadly. "But it will pass." *When I'm dead, maybe.*

"Could it be possible he loves you as well? I see the way he watches you all the time," Juliet said.

"I don't know."

"I think he does." Juliet moved to sit beside Anne and took her hand. "I think he might marry you."

Anne laughed. "I'm not getting my hopes up, Juliet."

"You just wait and see. I'm right."

Anne patted Juliet's hand. She secretly hoped her sister was right.

Nathaniel waited in the small parlor for Sophia. He had seen the confusion in Anne's eyes when he asked for Sophia, but he needed Sophia's help for the ball.

He wanted to show Anne that she was worthy of the attentions she was getting, especially from him. He'd never met a woman so insecure.

She had bashed a thief over the head with a poker. Surely she could see the real woman in the mirror, but evidently it didn't work that way.

"Mr. Matthews, to what do I owe the pleasure?" Sophia said, coming into the room.

"Where is Anne? I don't want her to overhear."

Sophia frowned. "She's upstairs."

"Is there somewhere we can talk privately without being overheard?"

"Perhaps we should walk for a bit?"

Outside the sky was heavy with rain and a slight breeze was picking up. It wouldn't be long before weather would chase them inside again.

"You wished to speak about Anne?" Sophia said after they had walked away from the house.

"Yes." Nathaniel searched for the right words.

"Perhaps if you got to the point?"

"Anne is acting strangely. One moment she seems interested in me, the next she's not. Then she has this sense that she doesn't deserve the attention of men."

"It's complicated," Sophia said. She studied him closely. "What are your intentions toward Anne?"

"They are honorable." That was all she needed to know.

"Maybe too honorable?" she said with a smile.

"What's that supposed to mean?"

"Anne has this idea that she's been granted a wish that has men acting crazy for her. Frankly, I think it's all nonsense. She had me climbing those inane steps the other day when you happened upon us. Something about breaking the wish."

Nathaniel chuckled. "She must have just finished climbing the steps when we first met. She was a little rattled."

"Anne's not in company much. She's a bit awkward, so prefers to remain in the background. I thought she'd remain a spinster forever."

Nathaniel shot her a look. "Funny, I never got that impression from her."

"Mr. Matthews, what do you see when you look at Anne?"

Nathaniel thought for a long moment. "She's courageous, loyal, and funny."

"She doesn't look like Juliet or myself," Sophia said. "Does that bother you?"

"She looks just fine. I like her looks. And she's not vain about them."

Sophia had the grace to blush.

"She doesn't like how she looks?" Nathaniel continued.

Sophia paused before she spoke. "Our father was a shallow man. Anne could never meet his standards, so she found another way to be noticed: She made herself indispensable to Father after Mother's death."

"Why did Sir John throw you out after your father died?"

"Jealousy. Father was so dependent on Anne that he ignored John. John was always in Town, gambling and such. Father was furious with the way John was going through money. He constantly threw Anne's accomplishments in John's face."

Nathaniel nodded. It all made sense. Anne made herself into whatever everyone around her needed. "Thank you for telling me this. So that act at the stone steps was about ending the wish?"

"Yes." Sophia laughed. "I don't know how she climbed them without clinging to the sides, except that she walks there nearly every day. It's her way of dealing with upheaval. Living with us cannot be easy."

"Please don't share this conversation with her," Nathaniel said.

"Fine, but I will tell you this—if you hurt her, I will come after you with a poker. Anne and I have had our differences, but I won't allow her to be hurt. She feels things too deeply."

"And you are shallower?"

"I am my father's daughter," Sophia said dryly.

"One more question. Tony."

"Tony is a good man, but just not the one for me. I was interested in him mostly to escape our situation. I've decided that that's not the right reason to marry someone."

Nathaniel nodded. "I'll walk you back to the cottage." Sophia's insight had surprised him. He'd sworn that he'd never let Tony be sucked into marriage by a woman like her, but now, he wasn't sure. Sure she was vain, but he didn't doubt that she loved Anne. She just wasn't as shallow as she thought she was.

Chapter Fourteen

Finally the day of the ball had arrived. Dodging Nathaniel and Mr. Worth while trying to plan the party for Lady Danford had been exhausting for Anne. All she wanted to do was collapse into a heap and sleep for days.

Anne had enlisted Juliet and Sophia to help decorate the Lodge with the hothouse flowers that Lady Danford had picked out. Invitations were sent. Cook had things under control in the kitchen and Lady Danford was resting before the party.

Anne had finally sat down, for the first time all day, when Sophia and Juliet burst into the library carrying three boxes.

"Anne, look what has just arrived!"

They looked suspiciously like dress boxes. "Where did those come from?"

"It's from the dressmaker in the village," Sophia said, setting the boxes down. She picked up the note. "There's one for each of us. Did you order them, Anne?"

"No." She pushed down the pang of guilt she felt. They had no money for new dresses. "Perhaps John did it."

"He'd not waste his money on us," Juliet said sharply.

"That's unfair, Juliet," Anne said. "He's getting better at that sort of thing." She noticed the look of doubt on Sophia's face. "It could happen, Sophia."

"Not bloody likely," Sophia said. She took the top box off the stack. "This one is for you, Juliet. Open it!"

Juliet opened the box and lifted a white muslin dress from the tissue. Her face lit up with such pleasure that Anne had to smile. "It's lovely."

"I've never had one like this." Juliet touched the fabric with awe. "Look at the ribbons and the edging. It's not a girl's dress."

"You aren't a girl any longer, but a young woman." Anne wished her mother were here to see this.

"Let me look at mine," Sophia said quickly. She lifted the lid of her own box and pulled out another white muslin, but this one was edged with dark green. The hem also had dark green embroidery on it. "This is beautiful! Now, Anne, look at yours."

"This must be Lady Danford's doing. I wish she hadn't." Anne pulled the top off of the final box. She moved the tissue aside and gasped. Her gown wasn't white, but a pale, buttery yellow. She pulled the dress out and held it up. The underskirt was a deeper yellow. The bodice was low and curved, with puffed sleeves. It was the prettiest dress she had ever owned.

"Oh, Anne, it's beautiful," Juliet said. "It's the perfect color with your hair and skin."

"It is pretty," Sophia said. "But we are going to have to do something with your hair. You can't walk into the ball wearing that dress and your usual hairstyle."

"Curls," Juliet said to Sophia. "She needs some curls framing her face."

"Yes! And I have ribbons at the cottage we can weave into her hair."

"I don't want a fuss made," Anne grumbled as she replaced the dress in the box. It was so soft against her hand.

"For once, we aren't going to listen to you, Anne," Sophia said, replacing her dress in its box. "Just leave it to us."

"Now I'm worried." *Lord, I've become a project.* The last thing she needed was to be made more visible. This evening was about staying out of the way of bewitched suitors.

"Perhaps you should be," Juliet said as she tied the string on her dress box. "We had better go. The ball is in just a few hours!"

"I love dancing," Sophia said, and twirled as they left the library. "Do you think they will play a waltz?"

"Oh, I hope so," Juliet said. "I would love to waltz just once."

Anne laughed and shook her head at her sisters. She couldn't believe Lady Danford's generosity. The dresses were beautiful. She would never have been able to provide them for Sophia and Juliet.

* * *

Nathaniel exited the carriage in front of Anne's cottage. He pulled up his collar against the cold rain as he ran to the door. It was a dismal night for a ball.

He couldn't wait to see Anne in her new finery. He wanted everyone tonight to see her as the pretty sister, not a spinster nor a wallflower. He wanted Beetham to see Anne Townsend as he saw her.

Hannah closed the door behind him. "I'll get Miss Anne."

"Thank you, Hannah." He wandered into the parlor and found Sir John slumped in a chair.

"Good evening."

"I take it you've come to escort my sisters to the Lodge."

"Is there a problem?"

"I don't appreciate you buying dresses for my sisters," Sir John sneered. "It's unseemly."

"My grandmother did it. She thought it a fitting gift for your sisters given how hard they worked to make this ball a success." Never would he let it be known that it was his money that had paid for them.

Sir John stood. "Stay away from my sister, Matthews."

Nathaniel raised an eyebrow. "Bit late for that, I think."

"Have you compromised her?"

"No." It wasn't for lack of trying, but Townsend didn't need to know that. "I have more respect for Anne than to treat her that way."

"John, what are you doing?" Anne said from the doorway.

Nathaniel felt his breath escape him. She was beautiful. Her curls tumbled effortlessly around her pixie face and teased the bare skin of her shoulder. The dress was sinful, dipping low on her chest, giving him a hint of the curve of her breasts. She looked ethereal. Sophia had done her job well.

"Good God, Anne. Are you showing your bosom to the entire world?" John said. "Get something to cover up."

"She will not," Sophia said, coming into the room. "John, since when do you get to act like this?"

"I'm your brother, damn it!" John glared at Sophia.

"Fine time to discover that now, isn't it?" Sophia spat the words out.

"Enough!" Anne said loudly. "We are going to be late and I promised Lady Danford I'd help greet the guests."

Nathaniel snapped out of his trance to find Sophia smiling at him. "We should go. The carriage is out front."

"That's not necessary," Anne said.

"It's raining," Nathaniel replied. "I didn't want you walking to the house in the rain."

"Thank you, Mr. Matthews," Sophia said quickly. "John, are you coming?"

"What else is there to do in this godforsaken place?" John shuffled to his feet and pulled on his coat.

"Have you been drinking?" Juliet asked with a frown.

"There's nothing to drink here, either," John mumbled. "Damned country."

Anne looked like she was praying for divine intervention. Nathaniel caught her eye and winked at her. "Shall we?"

She smiled at him and took his arm. Nathaniel had arranged the carriage so that Anne could sit next to him, but with Sir John joining them, it would be tight. She would practically have to sit on his lap.

In the carriage, Anne was pressed closely up against Nathaniel. Her cloak parted and he had a clear view down her dress. He looked up to find Sir John watching him. Nathaniel cursed silently. He'd need all his control tonight just to keep from embarrassing himself.

At the Lodge, Nathaniel first helped Anne down from the carriage, then her sisters. Sir John mumbled something about finding brandy.

Nathaniel watched as Sir John made his way to the nearest footman and demanded a drink. He was going to have to do something about the man when he married Anne.

And he would marry her.

She came with responsibilities, but her loyalty to her family was one of her most appealing qualities.

The servants were scurrying around with last-minute errands. Nathaniel handed his coat and Anne's cloak to a passing footman.

"Anne."

She looked up at him, her eyes sparkling, her curls dancing around her face.

"You look lovely tonight."

He watched the blush color her cheeks. "Lady Danford gave us these dresses. This is the prettiest one I've owned."

"Before your card is filled, may I have the first dance?"

"I'd like that."

He stepped closer. "And then perhaps another?"

"I rarely dance at these things."

"Oh, I think tonight will be different." Nathaniel took her gloveless hand in his. Her skin was so soft. "Until then." He turned her hand over and kissed her wrist. "Grandmother is looking for you."

"Oh dear—I must go." She was flustered, looking around her, reluctantly pulling her hand from his.

Nathaniel watched her leave.

"Good heavens, you do have it bad," Sophia said, coming up beside him. "Please tell me you aren't writing any poetry like your brother does."

Nathaniel chuckled. "No poetry, I promise."

Sophia shot him a side glance. "Thank you for the dresses, by the way."

"How did you know?"

"Lady Danford was a good cover, but the style of the dress was specific to Anne's coloring and shape. I knew you had picked it out."

"Don't tell."

"I won't, but only because you purchased one for Juliet and me." She smiled and left his side to enter the ballroom, dragging Juliet with her.

Nathaniel watched as immediately heads turned to look at Sophia, including his brother's. Tony seemed to be losing interest in Sophia, as his eyes quickly moved to Juliet.

With her hair up and her new dress, Juliet looked less like a girl and more like a woman. The way Tony's jaw dropped spoke volumes. Nathaniel chuckled. It was going to be an interesting evening.

Anne moved into the ballroom. Lady Danford's ball was a success. Most of the neighbors had arrived. Even a few gentry from the nearby villages had come. The musicians were tuning up. Anne moved quietly through the crowds toward the wall where the rest of the spinsters gathered.

"Miss Townsend?"

Anne turned and found Mr. Worth behind her. She dipped a curtsy. "Mr. Worth, I didn't think you'd be attending without your mother."

"Mother is here. Lady Danford showed great Christian charity by sending an invitation late yesterday," he said pompously.

Anne had seen the invitation go out. "Are you enjoying yourself?"

"What have you done with yourself?" he sputtered.

"Pardon?"

"You look completely different."

"Thank you?" Anne turned to leave when he caught her arm. She looked back at him and pulled away. He was acting even stranger than normal.

"Perhaps we can have that dance now?"

"I'm sorry, the lady is spoken for." Nathaniel came up behind her and placed a hand on her shoulder.

Mr. Worth backed away, his cheeks red with anger. "My mistake."

As he disappeared into the crowd, Anne shook off Nathaniel's hand. This territorialism was on her last nerve. "Was that really necessary?"

"Yes. I don't like him." He looked down at her. "Don't tell me you welcome his attentions."

"No, but I'm more than capable of taking care of him myself. Your behavior will only make the gossip worse."

The musicians started playing a waltz.

"Come, I believe this is our dance," said Nathaniel.

"I haven't danced the waltz in so long."

He grinned at her as he pulled her close. His hand was warm about her waist, reminding her how thin the dress was. "It will come back to you."

Nathaniel whirled her around one turn and pulled her indecently close. Anne saw nothing of the other couples moving around them. She only saw Nathaniel, his eyes filled with an emotion that made her tremble inside. His scent of bay rum and crisp linen surrounded her. The music wove them into a deeper spell. Her lips parted and he swept her through another turn, her skirts brushing against his dress trousers. She could dance like this for days.

Nathaniel took in the look on Anne's face as he moved her through the dance. Her eyes were slumberous and his gut clenched, the urge to kiss her overwhelming his good sense. He wanted her. Now.

He'd never known this urgent need, but the minute he was with her, there it was, in the quickening of his pulse. She was the beat of his heart.

He danced Anne toward the edge of the dance floor, then whirled her into one of the rooms sealed off from guests. He closed the door, locking it.

Anne was breathless, her eyes wide. "What are you doing?"

Nathaniel trailed a finger down her warm skin to her neck, then played with the lace edge at the top of her breasts, then back to her mouth. "Do you know how much I want you?"

The curls around her face danced as she shook her head.

"You're so damn beautiful," he whispered as he brushed his thumb across her bottom lip.

"It's the dress—"

He touched his forehead to hers. "It's not the dress. It's you." His mouth found hers in a deep kiss. She sighed into his kiss. Her hands gripped the lapels of his jacket.

He explored her mouth, savoring the taste of her. He framed her face with his hands and tilted her head to deepen the kiss.

Anne responded by tangling her tongue with his. His blood headed south, taking his good sense with it. He let one hand trace her slender shape through the thin dress, cupping one of her small breasts. She gasped.

"God, Anne. I need you." His voice was rough and harsh to his ears, but she responded by leaning into his hand so he could cup her breast more fully. He trailed his mouth along her neck to dip his tongue at the indention at the base of her neck, then looked at her. Her eyes were closed, her breathing labored.

He could hear the music just outside the door. It was insanity to take this further, but he couldn't stop himself. She felt like home in his arms.

"Anne, sweetheart, we need to stop, before I can't."

Her eyelids slowly lifted. She looked dazed, her mouth moist from his kisses. "More." She cupped his face with her hands and raised her mouth to his.

Nathaniel lost the war. The party be damned. He needed her so badly he ached with it.

He traced the edge of the bodice of her dress, grasped the dress and chemise, and yanked it down to free her breasts. "You are perfect."

She gasped as he cupped her with his hand and teased her nipple.

"Perfect and lovely." His mouth found her breast and sucked. She jerked in his arms, gasping. He moved to the other breast and raised her skirts, letting his hand caress her thighs as he inched his way to the slit in her drawers.

He captured her gasp with his mouth as he parted her folds and touched her. She was wet, and he felt his control slip a notch. He teased her with his thumb, then inserted one finger in her heat. She was tight, so tight. He felt himself harden further. He moved within her, then inserted another finger, stretching her.

Anne gasped as his mouth released hers. Her blood felt sluggish, as if she were drugged. She couldn't stop herself from moving against his hand as Nathaniel pumped his fingers in her. Never had she felt anything like this. The tension was building. She needed something. Something just out of reach.

"It's all right, sweetheart. Let go. I've got you." Nathaniel's voice was harsh. He was breathing hard as well. He bent and took her breast into his mouth again.

"Oh God!"

His mouth moved over hers. "Quiet, love." He kissed her, capturing the rest of her cries as she tipped over the edge.

Pleasure shattered her into a million tiny pieces. Anne collapsed in his arms, her eyes closed, her breathing rough. She was so relaxed she didn't want to move.

Nathaniel eased his hand from between her legs and adjusted her dress. "You all right?"

"Oh my," she whispered.

"Indeed." He kissed her gently and stepped back. Anne saw the pain on his face. "You didn't . . ."

"No, but I won't ravish you here with the ballroom just a doorway away." His voice was rough, husky.

Anne covered her face with her hands. Embarrassment coursed through her. What must he think of her?

Nathaniel pulled her hands from her face. "Never be embarrassed by what we do together, Anne. It's too precious."

"You can't go back to the ballroom like that."

Nathaniel grimaced as he adjusted himself. "I'm going to need a few minutes."

She adjusted her bodice and touched her hair. "Is there something I can do to help?"

He laughed harshly. "Oh yes, my love, but now is not the time or place." He kissed her again. "I'll get my turn soon enough."

"What do you mean?"

"Later, love." He pulled her away from the door and to a mirror in the room. "Touch up your hair. There's nothing I can do about your swollen mouth. With luck no one will notice."

Anne looked in the mirror. *Will people notice?*

"Come, love, we need to get back." Nathaniel opened the door and looked around. "No one is coming—let's go."

Anne let him lead her to the ballroom. They blended into the crush easily. She strove to put an indifferent expression on her face as she approached Sophia and Tony. It was difficult to chase away the giddy smile on her face.

Sophia frowned, looking between Nathaniel and Anne. "Where have you been?"

Anne felt the heat creep up her face. "I had to check something."

"Hmm. Interesting."

"Leave it, Sophia," Nathaniel said. He turned to Anne and kissed her hand. "I'll see you later for our next dance, Miss Townsend."

Anne smiled at him and watched him head into the crowd. She loved him. She wasn't going to fight it any longer. Nathaniel Matthews was addicting, and she couldn't get enough. If it ended, it ended, and she'd deal with it then. Right now she just wanted to embrace this feeling.

Chapter Fifteen

The ball was a whirlwind for Anne. She danced every dance and Nathaniel had the supper dance. She had never felt so happy. Finally, Mr. Worth came to collect his dance. She couldn't avoid him any longer.

"Miss Townsend." He bowed and offered his hand. Anne took it and let him lead them to the dance floor for a country dance with the other couples. The music began with a flourish.

"Are you enjoying the ball, Mr. Worth?"

"Not as much as you are, I hear," Mr. Worth said snidely. "If I weren't a gentleman I would have passed on this dance. It doesn't do for a vicar to dance with one such as you."

Anne's steps faltered. She looked around to see who had overheard and noticed the pairs of eyes looking away. *Damn.* "I don't know what you mean."

"Don't be coy, Anne, it doesn't suit you. Mother caught you sneaking off with Nathaniel Matthews."

"We've done nothing wrong."

"Not according to Mother." He took her hands for the next turn. "She heard you. Shameful, it was."

Anne's cheeks burned as all the joy she'd felt earlier drained out of her. *Mrs. Worth, of all people. Why did it have to be that old cow?*

"You have nothing to say in your defense?" said Mr. Worth.

Anne released his hands and stopped dancing. She opened her mouth to say something to wipe the smirk off the man's face, but no words sputtered out. So she did what she could manage—she raised her chin and slapped him so hard his head turned.

Anne stomped away from the dance floor, shaking the sting from her hand. *Odious man.*

What an idiot she was for letting things go so far with Nathaniel. Anne would have to deal with that later. Now she wanted Mrs. Worth and all her poison tossed out into the cold. How dare she ruin the best night of Anne's life? Hateful woman.

Anne searched for the old bat, determined to give her a piece of her mind. She was sick and tired of being the woman's target.

"Anne, dear, you look ready to do harm," Lady Danford said, stopping her in the hall. "Come away before you do something you'll regret."

Anne closed her eyes and tried to calm herself. "You are right."

"Come with me." Lady Danford led her to the back parlor. "I had this room prepared so I could rest before supper." She moved to the table and poured out a small amount of brandy, which she handed to Anne. "Drink it."

Anne did as she was told, grimacing as the brandy burned its way down her throat. "That is awful," she said between coughs.

"Yes, but it does settle the nerves. Take another sip. It goes down easier when you drink more." Lady Danford sat in a chair by the fire and Anne followed suit. "I heard some very interesting gossip about you and my grandson."

Anne flushed. "We didn't do anything wrong."

"Anne, you know it's all about perception. Everyone in that ballroom now perceives that Nathaniel has compromised you."

Anne covered her cheeks with her hands. It was worse than she'd thought. She'd let Lady Danford down. "I'm so sorry, ma'am."

"Nathaniel should have known better."

How will my sisters and I recover from my idiocy? "I don't know what came over me."

Lady Danford chuckled. "I do. Now don't worry about anything. I'm sure we can resolve this quickly."

"But Mrs. Worth—"

"I should never have relented and sent that invitation. The woman is a menace."

Anne knew why the lady was so unconcerned. This would force Nathaniel to marry her.

If he didn't, she would be ruined and she'd take her sisters with her. Anne wiped at the tears burning her eyes.

This is all my fault.

Anne peeked around her chair cautiously as John and Sophia entered the room. Sophia gathered Anne's hands in her own.

"How bad is it?" Anne whispered.

"What the hell were you thinking, Anne?" John exploded.

Sophia shot John a quelling glance. "It's bad. You know Mrs. Worth. She's painting it as dark as she can."

Lady Danford stood. "You've things to discuss with your family, dear. I'll go see if I can quiet the gossip."

"Sophia, I'm so sorry," Anne whispered as tears welled up.

John paced the room. "You should have been more careful. But through this whole affair you've thrown caution out the window. With no thought of what this would do to the rest of us."

"Good Lord, John, you sound ready for the stage," Sophia said. "Things can't be that dire, surely."

"I spotted her and Matthews kissing in the woods. He had her up against a tree!"

"Oh dear God." Anne buried her face in her hands. "It's the wish, Sophia. It makes him want me and I can't resist. I don't know how to make it stop."

Sophia shook her. "Stop! Do you love him?"

Anne nodded her head miserably. She felt tired and used.

Sophia handed her a handkerchief. "Wipe your face before you blotch."

"You will have to marry him, Anne," John said, coming to a stop in front of her.

"Really, John? Now you've become the protective brother?" said Sophia.

"She has been compromised."

"I've not been compromised. I've just been kissed," Anne said sharply. "There's a very big difference."

"Still," said John.

"You don't care about us, John. Why the sudden interest in marrying Anne to Mr. Matthews?" said Sophia.

John had the grace to look sheepish. His cheeks colored. "If she marries Matthews, he'll have to forgive the debt," he mumbled.

Sophia threw her hands up in the air. "Ooh! I don't believe you."

Anne stood to face her brother. If he thought she was going to force Nathaniel to pay his debts, he was mad. "He doesn't have to do anything, John. *You* ran up the debts. *You* cheated at cards."

"You take his side already. Because he ruined you," said John.

"I wasn't ruined!" Anne cried. Sophia smirked at her. "Fine. I was a little ruined."

"Isn't that like being a little bit enceinte?" Sophia said.

"Remember the night Mr. Jones came to the house?" Anne said to John. "Nathaniel brought you home because you were cheating at the pub."

"I was trying to get us some money."

"Right."

"This is not the discussion we should be having," Sophia interjected. "What are we going to do?"

"She's going to have to marry him," John said. "I'll negotiate it."

"Oh no, you won't!" Anne started pacing the room. The last thing she needed was John acting on her behalf. She'd end up married to the blacksmith's son, or worse.

"Marrying Nathaniel solves all of our problems," Sophia added.

"What?" Anne whirled on her.

"Nathaniel can give Juliet and me a Season in Town. He can help our worthless brother as well. What difference does it make if you marry Nathaniel rather than I marry Tony?"

"I thought you wanted to marry Tony."

Sophia tossed her head. "I've decided we won't suit. We'd kill each other after two months. You know this. Marry Nathaniel."

Anne stopped pacing. "I don't want him forced to marry me. It was only a kiss. Well, a lot of kisses. Still—"

Sophia took her hands. "He likes you. And he told me himself he had honorable intentions."

Anne couldn't keep the spark of hope from burning in her chest. "He did? When?"

"That's not important. What is important is that he does like you. How can that be bad?"

Anne plopped into a nearby chair. "One day he will wake up married to me and regret it. He'll get a mistress, leave me in the country, and I'll die of loneliness."

"And I thought John was ready for the stage! The man cannot keep his hands off of you. Doesn't that count for something?"

Anne paused to think. "I don't know."

"You will marry him, Anne. He ruined you, he can marry you," John said loudly.

"No one is ruined, Sir John." Nathaniel came into the room and closed the door behind him. "I won't have you berating Anne for something that isn't her fault."

"So you will marry her?" John said hopefully.

"Lord, John, could you be any more obvious?" Sophia said. She took her brother's arm. "Let's leave these two alone to work it out."

"Thank you, Sophia," Nathaniel said.

"Remember what I said about hurting her."

Anne looked between the two of them, bewildered, as the door closed behind them. "Why is she threatening you?"

"She loves you." Nathaniel came close and tried to take her into his arms.

Anne resisted. She needed to think. She couldn't think if he touched her. Her head was teetering between despair and hope. Could he love her? Did she want to take a chance?

"Anne, sit down."

"The gossip is all over the ballroom."

"I know." He sat across from her.

She wiped her eyes. "Don't be nice to me, Nathaniel. It will just make me cry more."

"Love, it breaks my heart to see you cry." He took her hands in his, rubbing his thumb against her skin. She shivered from the slight touch of his roughened skin against hers.

"Marry me, Anne." He stared into her eyes.

Anne pulled her hand from his. "Why?"

Nathaniel sat back in his chair in shock. "What do you mean, why?"

"Why do you want to marry me?"

"Have you heard the gossip out there, Anne? You won't be able to show your face in the village. Do you want that?"

"No, I don't want that, but what choice do I have?"

"You have the choice to marry me!" *What does she want from me?*

Anne met his gaze. Her look was steady, serious. "Then answer the question, Nathaniel. Why do you want to marry me?"

The question brought him up short. He stalled. "The gossip will only get worse, Anne. With each telling of the tale, the embellishments will grow."

"The gossip that Mrs. Worth is spewing will pass." Anne felt calmer for saying it, but still hurt. Even after all of this, she still wanted to be loved.

"Do you know what she's saying?"

Anne shook her head.

"She heard you."

Anne's eyes grew big.

"When you climaxed against my hand, she heard you cry out."

"Oh God." She felt her face flush again. "She thinks we . . ."

"Yes." Nathaniel straightened and began pacing again. "You see now why it's imperative we marry."

"She doesn't know what she heard."

"Anne, she has one child. She obviously has had sex at least once."

"Don't be crude."

"I'll be whatever it takes to get you to accept the inevitable. We will marry." Nathaniel felt as if his whole world were collapsing around him. He wanted to shout at her to tell him what she wanted, but he was afraid she'd want to know his feelings.

He couldn't say the words because he wasn't sure what he felt. He put little stock in love.

Anne stood up. "I can't marry you, Nathaniel."

He felt like shaking her. "You don't have a choice!"

"I have a choice."

Nathaniel retreated, the pain in his chest overwhelming him. "It doesn't get any clearer than that."

"That's not what I meant."

Nathaniel studied the fire. "Then tell me what you want, Anne."

She was quiet for so long he had to check to see if she was still in the room.

"I don't want to trap you," she finally said.

"If anyone is trapped, it's you." Nathaniel stared back into the fire. "I couldn't keep my hands off you."

"Nathaniel, there's something I have to tell you. Remember that day at the Fairy Steps when you first arrived?"

"You said you were granted a wish."

She twisted her hands. "I wished for a way out of the mess we were in. I was thinking about money, about marriage to a rich, handsome man—"

"I don't understand."

"It's because of the wish. You are feeling these things because of fairy magic."

Nathaniel raised is eyebrows in surprise. *She doesn't really believe this fairy nonsense, does she?* "And you believe this?"

Anne nodded, staring down at her hands. "When the magic wears off, you'll be stuck with me."

Nathaniel didn't know how to convince her his feelings had nothing to do with magic.

"I want you. Not Sophia. Not Juliet. *You.* This insecurity you have about your looks, this continuous comparison to your sisters, it's not good, Anne. I don't know how to fix it."

"I'm not asking you to fix it. You can walk out right now and never deal with it again. I am what I am."

"Bloody hell, Anne. You really believe that what I feel for you isn't real?"

"Yes. The spell will break. I know it."

"And you won't marry me because of some fairy magic nonsense."

She nodded.

Nathaniel stood, pulled Anne out of her seat, into his arms and kissed her. Hard at first, but then he gentled, gently teasing a response out of her.

Anne sighed, clutching his lapels to keep from falling. His tongue teased her mouth, tasted her. He poured all the feelings he couldn't put a name to into the kiss, molding her body against his hard one.

He pulled away and looked at her. "This isn't any bloody magic, Anne. I just hope that you realize it soon."

He left her standing by the fireplace, stunned. It was the hardest damn thing he'd ever had to do.

Anne jumped when Nathaniel slammed the door behind him. She sank into a chair, shaken. She pressed her hand to her mouth, still able to feel his mouth against hers. She closed her eyes, committing the kiss to memory. It was probably the last time she'd feel Nathaniel's lips. What had she done?

She couldn't face going back into the ballroom and seeing all those people. She wanted to go home.

She rose and peeked out the door. The hallway was deserted, and it sounded as though everyone was at supper. She made her way down the hall to find her cloak.

"Anne," Sophia said from the doorway to the cloak room. "Where are you going?"

"Home." Tears filled her eyes again. "I can't go back in there."

"Let me ask them to bring the carriage around."

"No, that will take too long. I'll walk." Anne took her cloak from the footman.

"Don't be a fool. It's raining."

"I'll be fine."

"Let me come with you." Sophia motioned to the footman.

"No, don't, please. I just need to be alone."

Sophia moved close and hugged her. Anne clung to her, needing some comfort. "Go have fun, Sophia."

"Are you sure?"

"Yes."

"What happened with Nathaniel?"

"He proposed, of course."

"And?"

"I declined."

Sophia glared at her.

"Not you too. Please understand. What he feels isn't real. I need to stop pretending it is."

"What he feels is real, Anne. Don't throw away a beautiful future with a man who cares for you over some silly wish."

Anne laughed harshly. "He's even got you fooled."

"Anne—"

"Please give my regrets to Lady Danford." She pressed Sophia's hand and then crept out the door into the rain.

The night was damp and cold. Anne shivered and pulled her cloak closer. The rain was more of a mist rather than drops, but it didn't take long for her to feel wet and cold to the bone.

It was fair punishment. She had allowed Nathaniel to go too far, but she didn't regret it. She'd treasure what few moments they'd had together. She'd have precious memories of his touch, his kisses.

She trudged the short distance to the cottage with her head down. Hannah and Thomas would be home now. She could see a light burning in the window. For once, Anne was glad for the extravagance. Coming into a cold, dark house would be a sad ending to an even sadder day.

She stepped inside the cottage and removed her cloak. The house was quiet and cold, despite the lit candles. She hung her cloak and made her way to the kitchen. She needed tea.

The kettle was already on the stove, so she coaxed the fire to warm up. A noise startled her and she whirled around to see the angry face of Mr. Jones.

Then all went black.

Chapter Sixteen

Nathaniel walked from the back parlor into the library and poured himself a liberal amount of brandy. The crowds were dying down as people left for the evening. He glanced at the clock on the mantel, not realizing how late it really was.

God, he wanted to shake some sense into Anne. She actually believed that drivel about magic. *This isn't magic, damn it! This is real.* Though he couldn't put into words what he felt, he did care about her. He was going to marry her.

None of it made sense. She'd come in his arms. She'd loved it. He tossed back more brandy. He wanted to throw the glass or punch something.

The door opened and Sir John came in. Nathaniel balled his hands into fists. "What are you doing in here?"

"I thought we'd discuss the settlement for Anne." Sir John sat in a chair in front of the desk and looked expectantly at the brandy.

Nathaniel laughed bitterly. "No need. She's refused me."

"Don't worry about that. I can get her to change her mind."

"What do you want, Townsend?"

"I propose that we agree to forgive the debts I owe you in exchange for Anne's hand in marriage."

"You disgust me." Nathaniel tossed down the rest of his brandy and stood.

"I don't suppose I could have one of those?"

Nathaniel ignored his comment and poured himself another drink. "You would sell your own sister to pay off your debts. That's low, Townsend."

"Word has it you ruined her, so I thought it appropriate."

"Get out!"

"But what about Anne?" Sir John whined.

"This is none of your business."

"She's my sister!"

Nathaniel wanted to punch him hard, but tossed down another brandy instead. He looked up as Tony came into the room. *Now what?*

"Nathaniel, did you know that Anne left?"

Nathaniel set his glass down. He wasn't surprised. She probably wanted to escape him. "Was the carriage called for her?"

Sophia pushed her way past Tony and into the room. "Nathaniel Matthews, you are an idiot!"

Bloody hell. Is the whole Townsend family against me now? "What was I supposed to do?"

"You shouldn't have touched her in the first place," John said. He got up and helped himself to brandy.

"Sophia, please tell me she didn't walk home in the rain," Nathaniel said, ignoring Sir John.

"Of course she did. She couldn't face everyone from the village looking at her. Mrs. Worth has done her job well." Sophia's voice was sharp. "What did you say to her?"

"I told her we were getting married," Nathaniel mumbled.

"Told her? Do you know her at all?"

Nathaniel felt heat crawl up his neck. "I might have been a bit heavy-handed."

Sophia laughed. "Really? John, see if you can stop Cecil Worth from writing a sermon about this for Sunday. Tony, find Juliet for me. I need to speak to Nathaniel. Alone."

"Of course," said Tony, and he quickly left the room. John remained, intent on finishing his brandy.

"Now, John," Sophia said.

"Damn bossy woman," John groused. "I'm surrounded by them." He closed the door behind him.

"Tell me everything," said Sophia.

"It's bloody magic again. She really believes this drivel. I can't fix her insecurities."

Sophia sighed. "You aren't going to fix them overnight. She's felt this way for years."

"This isn't going to blow over, Sophia."

"No, it's not. But if you care anything about her, you'll tell her how you feel."

It was the one thing he couldn't articulate. She needed the words—but he couldn't say them.

"Nathaniel, come quick!" Tony ran into the room, dragging Juliet behind him. Her face was flushed.

Nathaniel looked between the two. "What's going on?"

"The cottage is on fire," Juliet gasped.

"God, Anne!" Nathaniel ran for the door.

Tony raced after him. "They are bringing a horse around. I have the footmen gathering as many people as they can to man the buckets."

Nathaniel rode as fast as his horse would go. He prayed Anne was all right. He prayed she got out. His gut was telling him there were darker forces at work. He urged the horse even faster, leaning forward in the saddle.

At the cottage, he could see the flames in the front windows. He leapt off the horse and ran to the front door. He turned the door handle but then released it quickly. It was hot to the touch. He ran around the back of the cottage and tried the back door. The handle of the door was cool, but the door was locked. Nathaniel shoved on the door but it wouldn't budge.

Frustration and anger flared up. He stepped back and kicked at the door until it gave. He rushed in and almost tripped over Anne. She lay unconscious on the kitchen floor. Smoke filled the room and fire licked at the doorway from the hall. He didn't hesitate and scooped her up in his arms and carried her outside. Away from the house, he sat with her in his lap and started looking for injuries. He felt the back of her head and his hand came away bloody.

"You found her?" Tony said, running toward them. "The servants weren't in the house. I sent someone to check on them."

Nathaniel brushed the hair away from Anne's face. "Good."

"Is she all right?"

"I found her on the floor in the kitchen." He removed his cravat and wiped her face clean.

"Where's the blood coming from?"

"She's been hit in the head with something." Nathaniel pressed the cloth to the wound. He looked up at his brother, feeling more afraid than he'd ever felt in his life. "She won't wake up."

"Give her a few minutes. She's breathing."

"Yes." Nathaniel looked at the cottage that was now engulfed in flames. He shook with fear for Anne. *Damn, I almost lost her. If Tony hadn't seen the glow—*

"Dr. Anderson is still at the Lodge," Tony said. "Come on, Nathaniel. We need to get her some help."

Nathaniel didn't want to let her go. He held her close, his eyes pricking with tears.

"Nathaniel—"

"I know." His hands were shaking so badly that he was afraid he was going to drop her. "Take her."

Tony took Anne into his arms. Nathaniel stood and led Tony quickly to his horse.

A crowd had gathered outside the cottage. Everyone was mesmerized by the fire. Nathaniel spotted Sir John staring up at the house.

"There was nothing left to save. We were too late to stop it," Tony said as he looked over at Sir John. "They'll all have to stay at the Lodge tonight."

"Can you make sure they get settled?" Nathaniel asked his brother.

"Of course. I'll have some men stand guard to make sure the fire doesn't flare up again."

Nathaniel mounted his horse and held his arms out for Anne. "I'll be back at the house."

Tony nodded. "I'll stay with Sir John and see what we can salvage. I don't think it will be much."

"No." Nathaniel looked back at the house. "See if you can find out if anyone saw anything. I want the person who did this found." Nathaniel turned the horse and headed back to the Lodge. Anne groaned in his arms in pain. "Sorry, sweetheart," he whispered into her hair.

"Nathaniel?" Her voice was rough. She started coughing.

"I'm here, love."

"Where am I?"

"I'm taking you back to the Lodge."

Nathaniel ached for her. She had already borne so much, and now this. One thing he was sure of: He bloody well wasn't letting her out of his sight again.

Nathaniel stopped in front of the Lodge, where a footman waited. Anne struggled in his arms. "I can stand."

"Not a chance. You have a nasty lump on the back of your head."
He handed her down to the footman. He then dismounted and took
her back into his arms before carrying her into the house.

Lady Danford had sent the last of the guests home. Anne's sisters
waited in the entry.

"Is Anne injured?" Sophia asked.

"She's been hit on the head," Nathaniel said.

"I'm fine, really. You can put me down."

"Not a chance, love." Nathaniel looked at his grandmother. "Is Dr.
Anderson still here?"

"Yes. I have a room ready for Anne." Lady Danford led the way
upstairs to one of the guest rooms. "Set her here."

Nathaniel set her gently down on the bed, but was reluctant to release her.

"Nathaniel, I'm all right," Anne whispered. "Thank you."

He had an overwhelming urge to kiss her, hold her, cherish her,
but with his grandmother and the doctor in the room, he couldn't.

"Nathaniel, release the girl," Lady Danford said.

Anne gripped his hand. "Stay?"

"Of course." He stepped to the other side of the bed and glanced
at the doctor. "She had a large knot on the back of her head. It was
bleeding pretty heavily."

Dr. Anderson touched the back of Anne's head and she winced. "That
is a nasty blow. Do you remember what happened, Miss Townsend?"

"It was Mr. Jones. He hit me in the head with something. He must
have set the fire. The next thing I knew, Nathaniel had carried me
outside." Anne started coughing again.

Nathaniel and Lady Danford exchanged worried glances.

"You should be fine, Miss Townsend," Dr. Anderson said. "I would
recommend someone check on you throughout the night because of
the knot on your head. Chances are you will just have a bad headache."

"Thank you, Doctor," Anne said hoarsely.

"No talking, and take a bit of honey for the throat." Dr. Anderson
turned to Lady Danford. "If you need me, send a footman."

"Thank you for staying, Doctor," Lady Danford said. "Perhaps a
brandy before you leave?"

Dr. Anderson smiled. "Thank you, my lady."

Anne watched Lady Danford lead the doctor out of the room and close the door. She looked over at Nathaniel, who sat next to her. "Nothing could be saved?"

"No, love. It's gone."

"I smell like smoke."

"As do I. Want a bath?"

"Where are my sisters?"

"Probably just outside the door, waiting to talk to you."

"And John?"

"I suspect he is helping Tony tie up loose ends at the house. They needed to make sure the fire didn't spread. Do you want to tell me why you ran away?"

She looked away, wincing again when she moved her head. "Not yet."

"You are the most stubborn female I've ever met."

"Let's leave the girl alone, Nathaniel," Lady Danford said as she came back into the room. Sophia and Juliet followed her.

Nathaniel squeezed Anne's hand one last time and kissed her on the mouth. "I'll be back later."

Anne watched him leave and then tried to sit up. The room spun around her and she collapsed back to the bed. "My head hurts."

"I'll have a bath prepared for you, and I've brought you one of my own night rails. Give that dress to the maid and she'll see about getting the smoke out of it," said Lady Danford.

"Thank you, my lady," Anne murmured.

"Sophia and Juliet are settled in the room across the hall, so you can sleep undisturbed tonight. I'll have some laudanum prepared for the pain." She left the room again.

Sophia waited until the door closed before asking, "What happened?"

Anne hesitated, unsure how much she should tell her sisters. "I don't know. I was making tea. Someone hit me on the back of the head and the next thing I know, Nathaniel is there."

"How romantic—he saved your life," Juliet said.

"He did, Anne," Sophia reminded her.

"I know."

"Have we lost everything, Anne?" Juliet looked lost.

Anne nodded and tears filled her eyes again. "I don't know what we'll do now."

"Don't worry about it now." Juliet stepped forward to gently remove the pins from Anne's hair. "We'll deal with it tomorrow."

Anne nodded and drew in a deep breath. She didn't think she could deal with one more thing this evening.

"You should have seen Nathaniel's face. What did you argue about?"

"It's not important, Sophia."

"Sophia told me about the wish. You are crazy, Anne, to let such a handsome man go," Juliet said. "Everyone knows that magic can't create true love."

"You've been reading too many books," Anne said.

"It is rather farfetched," Sophia said. "Nathaniel isn't acting like someone under a spell."

"I know," Anne said quietly.

"You are a coward, Anne Townsend," Sophia said sharply. "You are the last person I expected to be afraid to take a chance. You've been taking chances for five years to provide for us."

"Can we discuss this later?" Anne asked wearily. There was a knock on the door as a tub was brought in and filled with hot water. Anne waited until the servants left before saying, "Help me out of this dress, Sophia. Is it ruined?"

"I don't think so." Sophia laid the dress out on the bed. She helped Anne with her stays. Finally Anne could step into the steaming water and lean back.

"If you are all right, we'll leave you and check on you later," Sophia said.

"Thank you both." Anne closed her eyes and sank into the warm water. It felt so good. A bath like this was such a luxury. She quickly washed her hair. She didn't know how long she'd be alone nor how long the water would stay warm. She wanted to soak in it as long as possible.

A knock at the door interrupted her peace. "Yes?"

"It's Nathaniel."

"Don't come in." Anne sat up, looking for something to wrap around herself.

"Still in the bath?"

"Yes."

He rattled the doorknob and Anne squealed and ducked into the water. "Don't!"

He laughed. "Don't stay in there too long."

"Thank you." Anne stood and wrapped the toweling around her.

She dried her hair and slipped on the night rail Lady Danford had left on the bed. Her last thought before she slipped into sleep was that she hoped the maid could remove the smell of smoke from the dress she loved so much.

Nathaniel sat by Anne's bed, watching her breathe. He never imagined he'd be one of those lovesick fools like Tony, yet here he was. Watching the woman he wanted to marry, the woman he almost lost, as her chest rose and fell in sleep.

Anne looked so painfully young. The coming days would be difficult as she decided what they would do next. He brushed the curls from her face.

"Nathaniel, let the poor girl sleep." Lady Danford came in and closed the door quietly.

"Is the rest of the family settled?"

"Yes." Lady Danford stood by the bed. "You shouldn't be here, especially after tonight."

"Does it really matter? I almost lost her."

His grandmother gave him a knowing look. "You love her. I knew it. I knew you wouldn't be able to help yourself."

"She refused my suit."

"Impossible. The girl loves you as well."

"I never knew anyone so stubborn."

"Are you sure about that?" Lady Danford chuckled. "She's afraid."

"Of what?"

"I don't know. I've tried to figure that out for years. Anne is one of the strongest women I've met. Much stronger than her mother."

Nathaniel realized he knew nothing about Anne's mother. She never talked about her. "What was her mother like?"

"She was beautiful, but so fragile. She was French and had come to England to escape the revolution. I introduced her to Anne's father."

"How did she die?"

"I was never sure, and Anne never mentioned it. I suspect consumption."

"What was Anne's father like?"

"Very much like his son. He saw his wife's beauty but not her fragility."

"Did you see them much once they were married?"

"No. Mary rarely went to London," Lady Danford said. "Anne could tell you more."

"She doesn't talk about it."

Lady Danford was silent for a few seconds before speaking again. "What are you going to do?"

"Marry her."

"Because of what Mrs. Worth said?"

Nathaniel shook his head. "I had always intended to marry her. Mrs. Worth and the gossip just forced me to ask her sooner."

"Don't let anyone see you leave this room. We need to protect what's left of the girl's reputation."

Nathaniel nodded. He followed Lady Danford to the door and locked it behind her. He wasn't leaving Anne alone. He stirred the fire in the grate to add warmth to the room.

After getting more comfortable, he climbed into the bed beside Anne and pulled her into his arms, tucking the blankets around them for warmth.

She smelled of roses from his grandmother's soap. He'd bathed earlier, unable to bear the smell of smoke on his skin. Still asleep, Anne snuggled closer to him. It would be a long night, but worth it. He wouldn't let her go again. Nathaniel brushed his lips against her cheek and closed his eyes.

Chapter Seventeen

A nne woke to a feeling of warmth and the sound of snoring. She tried to move, only to find Nathaniel's arm and leg pinning her down. *Oh dear Lord, is he naked?*

She slowly moved her foot back until her toes brushed the fabric of his trousers. He was clothed. A part of her was a bit disappointed.

Nathaniel tightened his arm around her and nuzzled her neck. "Good morning," he said.

"What are you doing here?"

"Keeping an eye on you." He flipped over on his back, his arm over his eyes. "You gave us a scare."

She clutched the blankets to her chest. "Where is John? And my sisters?"

"They were given guest rooms last night."

Anne had to ask, even though she knew the answer. "The cottage?"

"Is gone."

Anne turned her back to him as tears stung her eyes. *It's gone. Just gone, along with everything we own.* There was no way they could recover from this.

"I'm sorry, love." Nathaniel wrapped his arms around her.

She fought the tears, hating her weakness.

She was tired, so tired.

Nathaniel turned her into his shoulder and held her. He brushed her hair back tenderly. The gentleness of his warm touch against her skin was all she needed for the floodgates to open. She wept.

She wept until his shirt was wet beneath her cheek and she was hiccupping from crying so hard.

Finally she pushed back from him and wiped her face with her hands. She was tired and her head hurt still, but it was better than the alternative. "Thank you for saving me, Nathaniel."

"I'm sorry you lost the cottage."

"At least no one was hurt."

"Except for you. You shouldn't have gone off by yourself."

"I was acting like an idiot."

"I won't disagree, but more on that later. I'll send for the magistrate to deal with Mr. Jones. Though I suspect he's long gone now." Nathaniel got up and went to the fireplace. He poked at the grate, trying to stir the fire. Finally he gave up, crawled back into bed, and pulled her into his arms.

Anne snuggled deeper into his arms. "Aren't you afraid the maids will find you in here?"

"I locked the door." He rubbed his hands up and down her back as he cuddled her close. "I could get used to this."

"What about your grandmother?"

"She knows I'm here."

"She approved?"

"I was supposed to be gone hours ago, but I couldn't leave."

Anne's heart thumped hard in her chest. While she knew she should push him away and demand he leave her alone, she couldn't. She toyed with the tie strings of his shirt, then touched the skin revealed at his throat. She could feel him catch his breath.

"You are playing with fire, love." His voice was gruff in her ear. "I can't finish what we start here."

"I want you," she said and lifted herself up to look into his face. Her hand cupped his cheek, rough with the growth of his beard. "I almost died. Without ever knowing passion. Without knowing you."

He groaned and pulled her closer. "You're killing me." He brushed his mouth softly against hers.

She wrapped her arms around his neck and pressed her mouth harder to his. She kissed him with all of the crazy emotion coursing through her. He groaned, and her tongue touched his with an urgency she couldn't have controlled if she tried.

Suddenly, Nathaniel's hands were everywhere. He made quick work of removing the night rail and she was naked in his arms. She needed to feel his skin against hers. She tugged at his shirt until he pulled it off and tossed it on the floor.

They were skin to skin. The hair on his chest teased her nipples.

Anne gasped. Heat pooled low and grew moist. She knew what to expect, that glorious release she'd experienced the night before. She needed to feel it again.

She pressed her mouth to his neck and licked his skin. She raked her hands across his chest and circled his nipples, hungry to experience more, to experience all of it.

Nathaniel took her mouth, kissing her deeply. He turned her so that she was on her back and then moved his mouth down her neck and nipped the delicate skin at the joining of her neck and shoulder. She gasped as he moved lower and pulled her nipple into his mouth.

He sucked first one breast, then the other, before blowing lightly on her skin. She arched against him.

"Nathaniel," she whispered.

He raised himself up on his arms, looking down at her. "If I don't stop now, I won't be able to," he whispered against her mouth.

Anne brushed her hands down his sides to the edge of his breeches. His skin was so warm. She dipped her fingertips into the waistband, rubbing against his skin. "Then don't stop, Nathaniel."

He groaned as he took her breast into his mouth. She slipped her fingertips beneath the edge of his breeches.

"Anne, you aren't making this easy."

She reached up and tried to pull him down. "Make me yours."

"Damn." He pushed himself away, rolling onto his back. "I can't."

Anne felt her skin flush. She pulled the blankets up over her shoulders as Nathaniel sat up on the bed, his back to her. He was breathing heavily.

"Perhaps I should get dressed," Anne said quietly.

"Oh, you're not getting out of bed today, love." Nathaniel stood and pulled on his shirt. "Not after last night."

"I'm fine." She winced at the raspy sound of her own voice.

He tossed the night rail to her. "Put this on, or otherwise I'll be tempted to change my mind."

She pulled it on and snuggled back under the blankets, some of her embarrassment easing. "I don't see a reason why I can't get up."

"You almost died last night. I think that warrants a day of rest."

"I have too much to do. I have nothing to wear. I need to find us a new place to live and see what we can salvage."

Nathaniel bent down and kissed her, hard. "Nothing that won't wait for a day or so."

"But—"

"Seriously, Anne, I don't want you to leave this house until Jones is captured. I won't take any more chances with you."

"If you insist, but can I at least have some books to read?"

"I'll send Juliet up with some selections for you." He kissed her again. "Now I must go before you tempt me to crawl back into that bed. Get some rest."

Anne smiled and watched him unlock the door then check the hall before he turned back to her and winked. He pulled the door closed behind him. She threw herself back against the pillows, then groaned as she knocked the lump on her head.

Heavens, I love this man.

Dressed for the cold weather, Nathaniel made his way to the stables. He needed to check on the cottage. The magistrate had been alerted to Jones, but so far there was no word of his whereabouts.

Anne wouldn't be safe until Jones was locked up.

"Matthews!" Sir John shouted behind him.

Nathaniel sighed. Townsend was the last thing he needed this morning. "Sir John."

Sir John was gasping for air. "Were you riding out to the cottage this morning?"

"Yes."

"I thought I'd join you."

Nathaniel looked down at his feet. He didn't have time for this. "Of course."

"Is Anne all right?"

There was actual concern in Sir John's face. Nathaniel could almost believe he cared about his sister. "I don't know."

"I saw you leaving her room this morning."

"She's fine." *This is damned uncomfortable.* "She's to stay in bed today."

Sir John chuckled. "Good luck keeping her there. Anne never made a good patient."

Nathaniel led Sir John to the stables where two horses were saddled. Once they were riding, Sir John spoke again. "Has she accepted your proposal?"

"No." The fact that she hadn't, galled him. Each night Nathaniel spent with her put them at greater risk of the scandal getting out of hand, more so than it already was. "She will."

"She'd better," Sir John said. "Frankly, I'm surprised by her behavior. She's never been one to cross the line."

"I've not seen that side of her." Nathaniel pulled up to the cottage. The roof was gone; the stone shell of the house was all that was left. Hannah and Thomas were standing in front of the ruins. Thomas stepped forward to take the horse's reins as Nathaniel dismounted.

"Good morning, sir."

"Thomas. Did you just arrive?"

"The missus came early but found the house gone. Where are the young ladies?"

"At the Lodge. You and your wife should come by. I'm sure Anne will want to make arrangements for your pay."

"Yes, sir."

"Was anyone hurt?" Hannah asked.

"Everyone is fine."

"I left the candle lit so the young ladies didn't have to come home to an empty house. It's my fault." Tears welled up in the older woman's eyes.

"Now, Hannah," Thomas said.

"You aren't at fault, Hannah," Nathaniel said.

Sir John stepped forward. "Have you seen anyone snooping around this morning?"

"Are you thinking that someone set the fire, sir?" Thomas gripped his wife's hand.

Nathaniel shot Townsend a look. *Idiot.* "Thomas, take Hannah up to the Lodge. You can see for yourself that all is well."

"Thank you, sir," Thomas said.

Nathaniel waited until they disappeared around the bend before turning to Sir John. "Did you know the fire was set?"

Townsend looked surprised. "It was? By whom?"

"Jones. He was released just days ago." Nathaniel stepped closer to the ruins of the cottage. "He was told to leave the village and return to London." Nathaniel glanced back at Sir John. "How much did you owe?"

"Two thousand pounds."

Nathaniel glared at Sir John. "You told them your sister had that kind of money? Do you have any idea what you've done?"

Sir John hung his head. "All I cared about was getting away with my life. I figured this far north, no one would follow me. I had no idea they would go after my sisters."

"You knew they were here? Living on next to nothing?"

"Sophia wrote me, begging me to come take her to London. I couldn't afford their upkeep, give them a Season. By the time my father died, I was in so deep, it took all his money just to get me barely out of debt."

"Gambling?"

"I can't stop."

Nathaniel nodded his head. "There is no shame in work, Townsend."

"I know."

"Let's check the house. I want to know how this fire was set." Nathaniel picked up a stick and moved through the doorway. The fire still smoked in places. The second floor had fallen through. "I think the fire started in this room," Nathaniel said, stopping in what had once been the parlor.

"How do you know?"

"It's more damaged than the other side of the house." Nathaniel moved through a burned-out doorway. He used the stick to move more charred remains around.

He picked out a miniature from the rubble. The edges were scorched but he could make out the face. He slipped it into his pocket for Anne.

Sir John glanced around, being careful not to touch anything. "What are you looking for?"

"This," Nathaniel said and lifted up a lamp with the stick. "This was probably used to start the fire." He tried to control his temper. "You sent him here."

"I was desperate," Sir John cried.

"Bloody hell, man. What were you thinking? Three defenseless women against a man like Jones?" Nathaniel fought the urge to wring Townsend's neck.

Sir John grew pale as he glanced around at the mess. "I have much to make up for."

Nathaniel studied him for a few moments. "If you want help, ask."

"I thought I was."

"You may not like the answer."

"I can't keep doing what I'm doing."

"Let's get back to the Lodge and we can discuss your debts." Nathaniel led them back to the horses. There was little left to do here.

"You don't have to do this because of my sister."

"I might not like you, but you're going to be family." If he was going to connect his family to the Townsends, there would need to be some changes.

"A comforting thought," Sir John said wryly. "I have a feeling I should be cautious."

"Probably." Nathaniel mounted his horse and turned toward the Lodge.

"I'm still not sure you'll be able to convince Anne to marry you, ruined or not," John said as he mounted his horse. "She can be damned stubborn when she wants."

Nathaniel shot him a look. "She's not ruined. At least not quite."

"I'm not sure I want to hear more of this."

Nathaniel snarled. "Mrs. Worth has stirred up a hornet's nest."

"She can be an old witch where her son is concerned. But what do you care? She's played directly into your plans."

"My plan did not include forcing Anne to marry me. I had hoped to persuade her."

"You may still get the chance."

Nathaniel doubted it. Sir John didn't know Anne any better than Nathaniel did. She was stubborn to a fault and she believed this nonsense about fairy magic. How was he to fight that? His feelings weren't caused by some bloody fairy magic. He wanted Anne now, forever. She was his and nothing was going to change that.

Chapter Eighteen

Anne stretched out on the chaise, sick of lying around. Her mind was whirling with all there was to do. They had to find a place to live. There were clothes to purchase. She'd asked for pen and paper and had been refused. She couldn't even make a list of things to do.

Even more galling was letting Lady Danford and Nathaniel take care of everything, including the clothes on their backs. She hated taking charity from anyone, but what choice did she have? She'd just have to pay them back, somehow.

Juliet was sitting in the parlor with her, her nose stuck in another book from Lady Danford's library. *So much for Juliet being good company.* Anne had tried to read, but she couldn't focus on the words. Her head still hurt.

"Juliet, dear, it's too dark in that corner to read. At least come by the window," Anne said.

"If I must," Juliet mumbled, not looking up from her book.

"Now would be a good time. You'll ruin your eyes."

Juliet slammed the book shut and pulled herself out of the chair with a huff. She stomped over to the window seat and plopped down. "Better?"

"Don't be smart."

"Are you going to marry Mr. Matthews?" Juliet asked suddenly.

"No." Anne was adamant about that. She still didn't trust his feelings for her.

"But everyone says you are ruined. Shouldn't you marry him?"

"Mrs. Worth is not everyone." Anne had managed to avoid this discussion with her sisters for two days. She guessed her time was up.

Sophia burst through the door. "Mrs. Worth has told everyone that you are fast. It's all anyone can talk about." She removed her bonnet and sat down on a nearby chair. "When you make a mistake, you certainly do it wholeheartedly."

"We're going to have to move, now, aren't we?" Juliet muttered. "I liked it here."

"You like Lady Danford's generosity with her library."

"Perhaps we can go with John to London or return to Kent," Sophia said. "How are you today, Anne?"

"Sick of having to lie here. I have to find us another place to live. John can't afford the house in Kent. London would be out of the question. The creditors are after him."

"Then you have to marry Mr. Matthews," Juliet said. "He does like you and he's rich."

Anne shot a nasty glance at Sophia. She should have kept her mouth shut.

Sophia laughed. "Don't give me that look, Anne. He does like you."

"He comes out of your room often enough," Juliet added.

Anne felt the heat flood her face. She couldn't deny it. The last two nights, Nathaniel had insisted on sleeping, just sleeping, beside her. She rather liked it.

"This is ridiculous. We must find another place to live." Anne swung her legs to the side of the chaise. "I can't lie here any longer."

"I wouldn't get up if I were you," Nathaniel said from the doorway. He was still dressed for riding and hadn't yet removed his greatcoat. "You're supposed to be resting."

"I feel fine."

Nathaniel looked at Sophia. "Please tell me she didn't come down the stairs by herself."

"Of course I did. How else would I get down?" Anne said.

Sophia smiled. "She's never been a good patient, sir."

"I'm perfectly well." Anne stood too quickly and grabbed the back of the chaise to keep from falling. "I just can't get up very quickly." Her sisters smothered another round of giggles.

"I came to ask if you'd like to take a stroll around the garden. I suspected you would need to escape your imprisonment." There was a twinkle in Nathaniel's eyes.

"I would like that."

"Here's the cloak you requested, sir," a maid said as she stepped into the room. Nathaniel took the cloak and placed it around Anne's shoulders. He put up the hood around her hair. "This is rather thin, so we can't stay out long, but I know how you miss your walks."

He took her arm and led her out of the parlor, down the stairs, and outside. Anne breathed in the crisp air, which held a hint of wood smoke. The bare trees stood in stark contrast against the blue sky. It felt good to be outdoors again.

Nathaniel led her to the side garden. The hard frost had withered the remaining roses and the garden had the look of winter to it. He waited until they were away from the house before asking, "You are feeling better?"

"I'm fine. It was just a bump on the head."

"And smoke inhalation," he reminded her.

"Very little of that, thanks to you. Have you found Mr. Jones?"

"The magistrate and some men are still looking for him. He's probably long gone by now. "

Anne nodded. "He must have been searching for anything of value."

Nathaniel shook his head. "The parlor furniture was overturned. There was more damage than what a fire would cause."

A bleak feeling washed over Anne. "What about the rest of the house?"

"There might be something we can salvage." Nathaniel pulled the miniature from his pocket. "I found this."

Anne took the small picture from his hand and clasped it to her chest. Tears welled in her eyes. "Thank you."

"Is it your mother?"

Anne nodded, too emotional to speak. She gently brushed the soot from the picture.

Nathaniel pulled her into his arms and pressed his lips to her hair. Anne snuggled into him, shivering in reaction to his touch.

"We need to talk. Juliet saw you leaving my room in the morning," she said.

He trailed a gloved finger across her cheek. "Then you'll have to marry me."

"Nathaniel, we've been through this."

"I'll not have my future decided on the whim of fairy magic."

"You don't believe me. Why am I not surprised?"

"Anne, the talk in town is serious. We have to marry."

"No. We don't." She turned to walk around the edge of the garden. "I need to send out some inquiries for a place to live."

"Feel free to use the library for your correspondence," Nathaniel said. "Though I'm not sure how you'll pay for a place to live."

Anne shot him a hard look. "That's not your concern."

"Anne, Sir John can't take care of you."

"Lord no, he has no money."

"And you do?"

"We'll manage." She still had some of her mother's small inheritance. They had lived on less. "I think I'd like to return to the house now."

Nathaniel took her arm and led her back to the Lodge.

Nathaniel had been in bed for over an hour, unable to sleep. He was starting to hate this wish of Anne's and her belief in fairy magic. Worse still was her lack of confidence. How did one go about making someone believe they were worthy? He had no idea.

He needed Anne. As painful as it was, as sexually frustrating as it was, he wanted to hold her, breath in her scent, feel her curves against him. He flipped the covers back and pulled on his clothes. *Society be damned.* Anne was his and he would sleep with her, marriage or no marriage.

He crept down the hall in bare feet. Easing open the door of her bedroom, he slipped in and closed it. He turned the lock as quietly as he could.

Anne lay in bed with the blankets tucked under her chin, her dark braid curved around her neck. Nathaniel shivered in the cold room and moved to stir the embers in the fireplace before removing his robe and slipping into the bed. He curled his body around Anne's, letting her warmth sink into his skin. Her scent wrapped around him. He loosened her braid and then ran his fingers through the softness of her hair.

"Nathaniel?" she said, turning to him. She was sleepy and warm. "You shouldn't be here."

"I sleep where you sleep." He spread her hair on the pillow, smoothing it from her face. It curled on the linen as if it had a life of its own.

"It won't change things."

Nathaniel nuzzled her neck, moving her nightgown down from her shoulder. "I hate this thing. It looks like something my grandmother would wear."

"It probably is."

"Go back to sleep before I forget myself."

"Not without a kiss."

Nathaniel groaned. "You don't understand, Anne."

She kissed him. "I understand that you want me. I want you too, Nathaniel." She pressed her mouth to his as she ran her hands across his chest. She teased her tongue across the seam of his lips.

"You are a quick learner," Nathaniel growled as he took her mouth in a deep kiss. She tasted like mint. She tangled her tongue with his and he caught his breath. "You are tempting me."

"Good," she whispered.

He gasped as she played with his nipples. He had no idea he was so sensitive there. "If we do this, we will be married before the week is out. I'll not risk our baby being born out of wedlock."

Anne studied him through lowered eyelashes. "Aren't there ways to prevent it?"

"How would you know that?"

"I live in the country. We talk about everything." Anne kissed him again, winding her arms around his neck. "Isn't there a way?"

"It's not foolproof. I won't risk it."

"And you say I'm stubborn."

"There are other ways to make love." He started unbuttoning her night rail. His mouth found her breast and pulled the nipple into his mouth. She arched beneath him. Her hands caressed his back.

He loved how she responded to him. With each new introduction to passion, she embraced it. He longed to sink himself into her warmth, feel her tight around him. But not without marriage.

Anne relished his warm skin against hers. She couldn't control the desire coursing through her as he pulled on one breast then the other. He pulled the nightgown over her head and tossed it aside. His chest hair teased her sensitive breasts.

"Oh God," she gasped as his hands caressed her stomach. His hand found his way to her curls and she arched up against him. "Nathaniel?"

"Easy, sweetheart." He kissed her briefly. "I need to taste you." His lips teased her breasts, then trailed down her stomach before settling between her thighs.

She tried to push him away. "No! It's not proper."

"Trust me," he said as he nuzzled her. "You taste delicious." He settled in to the task.

Anne arched against him and cried out, unable to stop herself.

Dear God, the things he is doing are unseemly. His mouth, hot and moist, drove her ever closer to the edge.

"Easy, sweetheart. You don't want to wake the entire house."

Anne felt like she was coming out of her skin. His mouth teased at the throbbing between her legs. She wanted more. He entered her with his fingers, stretching her, pumping her as she pressed against him.

Finally, she arched against his hand and gasped. Her body shivered with release. She collapsed back against the linens.

Nathaniel looked at the sated woman beneath him. He ached to sink himself within her. She smiled up at him as her hand trailed down his chest. He sucked in his breath as her hand followed the trail of hair down his abdomen. "Anne—"

"Let me." She pushed him over onto his back. He was powerless to prevent her. She took his cock in her hand and caressed him gently.

"Like this, sweetheart." He showed her how to stroke him, how much pressure to use. Soon he found himself arching into her hand and gasping. A bead of moisture on the head of his cock was licked away and he looked down. "What are you doing?"

"You did it to me." She swirled her tongue around the rim, then took him into her mouth.

"Anne, don't." His voice was hoarse. Never in a million years did he expect this. She had no clue what she was doing, but it didn't matter.

Nathaniel gently brushed her hair back so he could watch as she pleasured him. His heart raced. He couldn't hold on for long; her naïve enthusiasm was driving him insane. He pulled her head gently away, then took her hand and placed it on him until he was finished.

He collapsed back against the pillows, too spent to move. After a few moments he threw back the covers, quickly moved through the cold room to the wash table. He cleaned up and rushed back to bed, shivering. He bent down and retrieved Anne's nightgown.

"Here, put this back on before I'm further tempted." He climbed back under the covers and pulled her into his arms. "Love, you didn't have to do that."

Anne snuggled into his side. "I wanted to."

He brushed his lips against her forehead. "Go to sleep, my love."

Anne stood in front of the library door, pulling in deep breaths. It wasn't calming her down. She had just finished a conversation with John, who was giddy at the prospect of Nathaniel paying off his debts.

The gall! Now she suspected Nathaniel would expect her to agree to marry him in gratitude for saving them all. He could bloody go to hell.

Anne entered the library silently, resisting the urge to slam the door hard enough to rattle the windows in the hall. She cleared her throat.

"Anne." Nathaniel got to his feet. "Are you all right?"

"What do you think?" She walked to the front of the desk. "John tells me you've paid his debts."

"Of course. Once we are married, we'll be family."

"You presume a great deal."

"Anne, the gossip is already flying."

Anne placed a hand on her stomach. While he never said how he felt, she thought he felt something. Now she wasn't so sure. "So you are just doing your duty."

"That's not what I meant. It's my responsibility—"

"I see."

"I don't know why you are upset. This solves all your problems."

"Let me save you the sacrifice of ruining both our lives, and decline any offer of marriage you choose to offer."

Anne winced at the pain in Nathaniel's eyes.

"I see." He clasped his hands behind his back and turned toward the window. "Forgive my intrusion, then, Miss Townsend."

"I'll see that John returns the money to you."

"That won't be necessary. While you do not wish to be my wife, I still feel responsible for Sir John's predicament."

Anne gazed at him, feeling as if she was letting something precious slip away. "Thank you for that."

If John wanted to stay involved with Nathaniel, she'd deal with it. John would go back to London and she'd stay here. She'd only have to see Nathaniel when he visited Lady Danford. The silence bore down on her. She turned to leave.

"This is because of the goddamn wish, isn't it?" His voice was hard as stone.

Anne turned back to Nathaniel. Her heart cracked open at the pain on his face. Tears stung her eyes. She couldn't speak.

"You think what I feel is all because of some silly fairy magic. You're afraid that I'll wake up and suddenly see you as you see yourself. I'm right, aren't I?"

"I—uh—" Her mind was blank.

"How did you see this ending when you lay in my arms last night, Anne? You screamed out in the pleasure I gave you." He crossed the room and stood in front of her. He grasped her chin, forcing her to meet his eyes. "You think this is magic?"

"Why else would you look at me? You'd have never noticed me otherwise." She yanked her face from his grip.

"There is no magic."

"How do you know? All my life, no one has noticed me because of my sisters. Why would you be any different?"

"You refuse me because you doubt I could be attracted to you?"

"You have to admit it's coincidental."

"What I feel is not because of some damn fairy magic."

"You can't know that, Nathaniel. And I can't risk it." She turned to leave, but he grabbed her arm.

"Well, since you won't marry me, I'll be happy to set you up in London as my mistress. I can assure you I'll be very generous and we can continue your—education."

Anne slapped him, hard. She stared at Nathaniel for a moment, then whirled away, slamming the door so hard she heard the crystal jangle in the foyer.

She raced down the stairs, needing to put as much space between them as possible. *How dare he?* She barreled into Tony, who grabbed her arms to keep her from falling down the stairs.

"Anne, slow down," he said. "Good heavens, what's wrong?"

"Nothing." Anne fought for calm. "I was . . ." She glanced at the top of the stairs, where Nathaniel was staring down at her, his face full of anger and pain. "I'm going for a walk. I was just getting my cloak."

Tony looked between the two of them. "But it's not safe. Nathaniel, tell her."

"Miss Townsend knows her own mind, Tony. She's made that clear enough." He turned and went back into the library, closing the door behind him.

"See, it's safe enough," Anne said as she brushed past Tony. "I won't be long."

She closed her eyes as the front door shut behind her. She was hurt. Nathaniel was hurt. All because of her foolishness.

He deserved so much better, someone pretty on his arm. Someone without so much baggage. Her brother was broke. Her sisters needed a Season. They needed a place to live and clothes to wear.

The last thing Anne wanted was to burden Nathaniel so badly that he'd be forced into poverty again. He'd get over the pain soon enough once he was in London.

She, however, was going to have to live with this for the rest of her life.

Chapter Nineteen

Gravel crunched under her feet as Anne walked quickly through the park to the lane. She glanced back at the Lodge.

Nathaniel stood at the window, watching her as left the park. Even when angry, the wish drew him to her. *Blasted magic.*

Anne turned toward the cottage. She had to see for herself if there was anything to salvage. She needed something to start with, something to give her hope.

She shivered from the cold wind blowing in from the north. A bank of gray clouds edged the horizon. Snow was on the way. She kept her head down and walked briskly, wondering if Nathaniel would follow her. Part of her hoped he would, but another hoped he wouldn't. She couldn't take another confrontation.

Nathaniel would leave for London soon. Probably sooner, now that she'd rejected him. The wish would wear off and Anne would watch from a distance as he moved on. He would find someone he really loved, and be happy.

She would spoil the children that Sophia and Juliet would eventually have with their husbands, and retire to the country as Lady Danford's companion.

Anne approached the cottage and gasped at the burned-out shell. Gone. All of it.

She stared up at the ruins of the stone cottage. Somehow, knowing she'd have to start over and seeing the proof of it in front of her were completely different.

Tears welled in her eyes. How was she to start over here? John couldn't afford to bring out two young ladies in London. Perhaps Anne could make something of the house in Kent now that John's debts were paid. At least they wouldn't be so far from London.

She felt better with some sort of plan, even if it was just in the beginning stages. She entered the ruins of the house and looked around. The smell of smoke overwhelmed her, so she pulled her scarf up over her nose.

Anne pushed the debris out of her way as she moved to the back of the house. Books with scorched pages lay crumbled on the floor in what used to be the parlor.

Anne picked up some of the books, brushing off the soot. They were like old friends. She looked around and noticed other things of hers. She was moving several of the more damaged books when her foot hit something metallic.

A small metal box lay underneath some burned fabric. Anne picked it up and brushed away the soot. The box was unfamiliar.

She lifted the tiny latch and looked inside to find an old velvet pouch. It was oddly heavy. She tucked the metal box under her arm and started to open the pouch when she heard voices.

"Jones, what are you doing here?"

Anne stilled. *Dear God, Mr. Jones is here? And is that Mr. Worth?* Slowly she put the pouch in her pocket and moved farther into the parlor, afraid to make a sound. Her heart raced. She needed a weapon. The voices continued.

"I've been looking for you for some while, Worth. You owe my boss a great deal of money. More than Townsend, even."

More rustling. Anne looked around. She had to find something to protect herself with. Where was a poker when you needed one?

"You have me confused with someone else," Mr. Worth said.

Anne moved carefully out of the doorway, closer to the wall. Burnt wood planks dangled from the ceiling from the floor above. She shifted slightly to avoid brushing against them. The old floor squeaked under her feet. She held herself perfectly still.

"What was that?" Worth said.

Anne held her breath, afraid to move.

"Damn house is about to fall down," Mr. Jones said. "I have to give you credit for picking some place so far from Town, we'd never look. And in the disguise of a vicar. Takes bollocks to pull that off."

"I think you're mistaken," Mr. Worth said.

The other man laughed roughly. "From what I hear in this damned village, Townsend cleaned you out. Still got that taste for the games."

"He was cheating!" Worth shouted.

"You shouldn't play if you can't afford it."

Anne heard a rustling of fabric.

"There's no need to bring a pistol to the party," Mr. Jones said.

Anne heard Mr. Worth pull back the hammer of the pistol. She pressed a hand to her mouth to cover the sound of her breathing.

"Give me the jewels now," Mr. Worth demanded.

"I've not found them," Jones shouted back.

How was Mr. Worth involved in all of this? Anne had to get back to the Lodge before she was seen. With the walls between the dining room and the parlor burned away it would be difficult.

"Enough!" Worth's voice was panicky. She could hear movement as if the two men were wrestling. Gunshots were fired. *But who was shot?*

Anne wasn't sticking around to find out. She crossed the room quickly, not caring if anyone heard her.

"Miss Townsend!" Worth called out. "Stop right there."

Anne froze in the burned-out entry and turned around slowly. Why hadn't she learned more curse words? *Bloody hell* just didn't seem strong enough for this moment.

"What are you doing?" Anne winced at the high pitch of fear in her voice. She cleared her throat.

Worth pointed the pistol at her. "How much did you hear?"

"Nothing." Her voice shook. She gulped in air. "Nothing at all." Anne inched away from Mr. Worth back into the house and nearly tripped over the boot of the very dead Mr. Jones, who lay on the ground beneath her. "Oh God."

"That's far enough, Miss Townsend. How long were you standing there?"

"I just got here."

"Don't lie to me!"

"I won't say anything, I promise!"

Worth laughed. "You expect me to believe you won't go running to your lover and tell him everything?"

"Excuse me?"

"You've become Matthews's mistress. Everyone in Beetham knows it."

Anne didn't deny it. There was no point. It was the truth. "What are you doing in my house?"

Cecil Worth looked around. "Your brother told everyone about your mother's jewels."

Anne felt anger surge through her. Enough was enough. "If there were jewels, do you honestly think I would live like this?"

"You were supposed to marry me," Worth said snidely.

"Marry you? Your mother would never approve."

"What choice do you have? You are nothing compared to your sisters."

She flinched. "Since there are no jewels, you should let me go."

"Stupid girl. If there are no jewels, then we'll have to figure out something. It won't be long before someone else like Jones will be along to collect on my debts."

Anne shook inside. "You can't be serious. I'm worth nothing."

"Except to Nathaniel Matthews." Worth moved forward and grabbed her arm.

"No!" Anne fought, twisting and turning to loosen his bruising grip. She kicked at Worth, shoving and pushing to get free.

"Enough of this!" Worth yelled. He raised the pistol.

Anne cringed, waiting for the shot. Then everything went black.

Nathaniel had his head in his hands. *What an ass I've been!* The harsh words he'd uttered to Anne whirled in his head. His mistress? He wanted to go after her, seduce her until she was so boneless from pleasure she'd have no choice but to marry him. But he couldn't make himself do it. She had to choose to be with him, and she'd made her choice—fairy tales over reality.

The door opened and he looked up, hoping to see her.

"Well, you mucked that up," Tony said.

"That woman is infuriating."

"I warned you that she'd react this way." Tony poured a brandy and handed it to Nathaniel. "She's very stubborn and headstrong."

"And proud, too damn proud." Nathaniel swirled the brandy in his glass. He loved when Anne got her back up. His Anne was strong.

"You love her," Tony said with a smile.

Nathaniel shot his brother an irritated look. *This love business is damned nonsense.* "Yes."

"Did you tell her?"

Nathaniel shook his head. "No."

"Why the hell not?"

"I offered to marry her—what more could she want? She was ruined. What was I supposed to do?"

Tony laughed. "How romantic. I take it she didn't say yes?"

Nathaniel glared at his brother. "I don't know how much more rejection I can take."

Tony was quiet for a moment. "She's frightened."

"Of me?" This surprised him. Nathaniel couldn't imagine Anne ever being afraid of anything.

"No, of her feelings. She's had to hide them for a long time. She's been alone for so long."

"She thinks that it's fairy magic and will wear off."

Tony laughed. "Seriously?"

"How do I make her understand that this is the real world? How do I fight this?"

Tony shrugged. "I don't know."

Sir John stepped into the library and made his way to the brandy. He poured himself a healthy portion. "Anne is on her way out. Are we supposed to let her walk alone?"

"Give her time to cool off," Tony said.

"Townsend, what possessed you to tell Anne that your debts were paid?" said Nathaniel.

Sir John blushed. "I thought she'd be happy. She's not happy?"

"No, she's bloody angry. Thanks to you." Nathaniel stood and paced the room. He wanted to punch something, and Townsend's face made for a temptingly good target for his anger. "How am I supposed to fix this?"

"She'll calm down and see reason," said Sir John, settling in a chair. "Let her walk it off."

Nathaniel plopped back into his desk chair. It would take more than a walk to calm Anne down. It would take a damn miracle. He rubbed his chest, feeling heartache for the first time. He didn't like it. Worse, he had no idea how he was going to live without her.

Several hours later, Nathaniel had thrown himself into work. He'd let it pile up over the last few days and was now getting letters from his solicitor in London begging for him to make decisions on the factories in Lancashire. One decision he had definitely made: Nathaniel wanted Anne with him when he left. If he left without her, he'd not see her again. That thought alone kept him in Beetham. He just wasn't ready to let her go, even though she wanted nothing to do with him.

There was a tap on the door. Nathaniel looked up, hoping it was Anne, but Sophia stood in the doorway.

"Mr. Matthews, have you seen Anne?"

"Isn't she walking? Check her precious stone steps." He set his quill down and went to the window to look out. It was growing dark.

"You don't think she'd go to the cottage, do you?"

"She hasn't seen the damage yet." The woman had no sense of self-preservation. She'd probably walked to the cottage to survey the damage. "I'll get my coat and go fetch her."

Just then a maid came into the room with a note. "This was just delivered, sir."

"Thank you." Nathaniel broke the seal and quickly read the note. "Damn!"

"What? Is it Anne?" Sophia asked.

"Where's your brother?" *What an idiot I've been! Why did I let her go outside by herself?*

"He's in the parlor with Juliet. Why?" Sophia said anxiously. "Tell me what's wrong!"

"Anne has been taken."

"By whom? Mr. Jones?"

Nathaniel could kick himself. He should have protected her better. "I don't know, but there's a ransom demand." He thrust the note into Sophia's hands as he went out to find Sir John.

Anne regained consciousness slowly, realizing that she couldn't move her arms. She twisted her hands against the bindings. The coach she was in bounced along the road, battering her against the cracked leather of the squabs. Her head throbbed.

She slowly eased her way up to a sitting position, closing her eyes to ease the dizziness. Nausea washed over her in waves at the dank, dirty smell of the coach. She fought the urge to gag. When she opened her eyes again, Mr. Worth's visage greeted her.

"Where are we?"

"Heading south to Lancaster." Cecil Worth glanced up from his book. "Not that it matters to you."

Lancaster? "How long have I been out?" Anne needed to figure out how far from Beetham they'd traveled.

"About an hour, I think. I was afraid I hit you too hard. Can't have the goods damaged for Matthews. Although it's too late for that, isn't it, Miss Townsend? You're already damaged goods."

She glared at him while trying to keep her head from bouncing off the back wall of the coach. "You couldn't find a coach that is better sprung?"

"Beggars can't be choosers."

Anne stared out the window. Snow fell in big, fat flakes. She shivered. The temperature was dropping. She was trying to remember the roads leading out of Beetham and which one they might be on. If she escaped, she'd need to know how to get home. "Can you at least unbind my hands?"

"We have several hours of travel left, so I don't think it will hurt. Turn around."

Anne turned to let Worth untie the rope. Once freed, she stretched her arms, wincing against the pain. "Have you notified my family?"

"No more questions, Miss Townsend."

Anne stared out the window, searching for anything familiar. The snow was making everything look the same. Escaping without knowing where she was would be a death wish in this weather. She was hardly dressed for it.

But she had to escape. She'd rather die than wait to discover what Worth was going to do to her. They were moving fast, too fast for this type of weather. She could feel the wheels of the coach slip on the ice. There would be no escape unless the coach stopped.

"I can see the wheels turning in that brain of yours. You won't escape, you know," said Mr. Worth.

"I don't know what you mean."

"Only an idiot would try to escape in this weather. And you don't strike me as an idiot."

Anne said nothing. She turned back to the window, wrapping her cloak closer around her.

Worth moved the curtain to cover the window, and shot her a considering look. "It would, however, save me the trouble of killing you. You'd not last an hour in this weather."

"Why take me?"

"Matthews will pay to get his lover back."

Anne laughed bitterly. "You've planned poorly. Mr. Matthews and I are not involved."

"Mother heard—"

"Yes, tell me what your mother heard. After all, she's ruined my reputation with her accusations."

"That's not the point. Matthews is in love with you."

"You don't know the truth. I made a wish . . ."

"Anne, my dear, how naïve you are. There is no wish. The whole fairy thing is a joke. I can't believe you fell for it."

"What do you mean?" Anne thought back to the old lady she'd seen that day back at the steps. The woman she hadn't been able to find in the village. "The old woman—where did you find her?"

"The old woman was some traveler passing through. I added the rattling leaves." Worth cackled with glee. "It always amazes me how gullible people are."

Anne looked away. She was so stubborn. She had thrown away love. Real love. She blinked away the tears in her eyes. "You've known all along?"

"Of course." He was clearly pleased with himself.

"And that stunt in the church?"

"Matthews was showing too much interest. I knew you'd pick him over me unless I did something that would discourage him. You should have seen your face. It was priceless."

Anger burned through her. "I was humiliated. How could you?"

Worth tsk-tsked. "Anne, do you think anyone cares? The minute your sister walks in the room, you are forgotten."

"What else have you done?"

"I didn't have to do anything, my dear. Because you believe in fairy magic, you did it all to yourself. I just had to sit back and enjoy the show."

Things started to click in Anne's head. "And you think that Mr. Matthews is so in love with me that he'll part with whatever amount you are requesting?"

"Five thousand pounds," Worth said confidently. "He'll pay up."

Anne gasped. Nathaniel had just paid John's debts. How would he be able to come up with such a sum so soon?

"You have no idea how wealthy your lover is, do you?"

Anne was suddenly so tired. "This isn't going to end well for me, I take it."

"I'm afraid not, my dear."

"What are you going to do?"

"Do you really want to know?"

Anne nodded and prepared herself.

"I'm torn between shooting you or just handing you over to a brothel. I'm leaning toward the brothel. Much less messy."

Anne turned and looked back out the window. She refused to give up hope. Nathaniel would come. He was an honorable man, despite their argument. Despite her turning him down. Despite denying his feelings were real. *God, I don't have a chance.*

"Miss Townsend, are you crying?" Worth's voice had a singsong tone to it. The man was insane.

"No." Her voice trembled.

The snow was worsening and they were slowing down. This might be her only opportunity to escape. She'd rather die in the cold than be shot, or worse. "I think I'm going to be sick." She covered her mouth and forced herself to gag.

"What?" Mr. Worth went pale.

"I think I'm going to vomit. I can't sit in this position in the carriage. It makes me ill." She coughed into her palm.

Cecil Worth scooted out of the way and signaled for the driver to stop. "Stay near the carriage," he said to Anne.

Anne gagged again and pushed her way out of the carriage. Mr. Worth followed her. "Get it done."

Anne clutched her stomach. "I need a bit of privacy."

"Fine. But don't go farther than those trees."

Anne forced her limbs to move as her head spun. She wasn't going to have to try hard in order to vomit. Just being upright and trudging through the snow was making her more nauseous.

Snow was falling steadily now. Anne stepped behind a few bushes and stuck her finger down her throat. She coughed and wiped her mouth, all the while moving deeper into the woods, trying to blend into the shadows. Her skirts brushed a trail in the snow behind her.

"Anne. Come out!" Mr. Worth shouted.

She crept deeper into the woods and the cover of some evergreens. Mr. Worth called her name again.

"Anne! This is foolish. You aren't dressed for this weather!"

As if he cares; he's going to kill me. Anne kneeled in the shadows of the trees, barely daring to breathe as Worth moved to the edge of the forest. He peered into the woods.

Anne held perfectly still, willing him to leave.

"We need to go, sir. The weather is turning bad," the carriage driver said in a gruff voice. "As it is now, the roads will become impassable quickly."

"Well, we didn't need her anyway," Worth said. "Let the elements take care of her."

"Will her lover still pay?"

"Matthews will never know. By the time he discovers it, we'll be gone. Let's go."

Anne heard the carriage leave. She stayed where she was for just a few minutes more. Then she stood and brushed the leaves from her dress. She walked through the woods back toward the road and headed for the village.

She would stick to the woods and remain out of sight in case Worth doubled back, trying to find her. Hopefully, she'd come upon an inn or a farmhouse—even a barn would be welcome at this rate.

The wind picked up, pulling at Anne's cloak as she held it around her. The snow fell harder as she trudged through the drifts trying to follow the road as closely as she could. It reflected the little bit of light remaining, allowing her to see where she was going.

Anne was so damned cold her teeth were chattering. She trudged on, afraid to give in to the exhaustion that was dogging her. If she sat down, she'd sleep. If she slept, she'd die. She didn't want to die.

She had to see Nathaniel again. Tell him she loved him. Beg his forgiveness for her foolishness. And, if God was kind, Nathaniel would still love her. Still want her.

Please God, let me see Nathaniel again, she chanted in her head. *Please give me a chance to tell him that I love him.*

Chapter Twenty

Nathaniel felt a fear so intense he could barely focus. They had found the body of Mr. Jones at the cottage. In his pocket were Cecil Worth's vowels. It appeared that Worth owed even more than Sir John did. He saw the evidence of Anne's struggle and his fear grew. Desperate men sometimes did desperate things.

Tony had stayed behind to deal with the magistrate. Sir John had chosen to ride with Nathaniel.

Carriage tracks led from the cottage through Beetham to the main road south. If Worth kept to the main roads, Nathaniel stood a chance of catching them.

"Who do you think did this?" John asked.

"Cecil Worth." Nathaniel walked out of the house and mounted his horse. "I found his vowels in Jones's pocket."

"Where do you think he's heading?" John said, reining in the horse.

"Not sure. Lancaster, I suppose." He'd either leave or face prosecution, if Nathaniel didn't kill him first.

"I can't believe he was hiding among us all this time," Sir John said. "Did you know he owes me a tidy sum? He's a worse gambler than I."

"Cecil Worth? The vicar?"

"He plays deep and doesn't know when to quit," Sir John said.

Nathaniel thought of Anne. Was she hurt? Frightened? "We need to move faster, before the snow gets worse." He nudged his horse into a gallop. He hoped Anne stayed with Worth and didn't try to escape on her own. In this weather, she'd have no chance at all.

They rode for several miles more, Nathaniel yelling her name. He stopped his horse on the road when he saw footprints, still fresh in the snow, leading into the woods. He dismounted and looped the reins over a bush.

John reined in nearby and dismounted. "See something?"

"Yes. There are footprints leading into the woods." Nathaniel followed them and found the traces of where Anne had been sick. "Does she get sick in carriages?"

"She used to as a child. It made for miserable trips." John wrinkled his nose in distaste. "That's disgusting."

"She was here. Anne!" Nathaniel shouted as he followed the footprints farther into the woods.

"Worth is heading south. Do you think she escaped him?" John said.

"Yes. I'll backtrack and check the woods. We must have passed her." The footprints were still visible, but they were filling up with snow quickly. If Anne had escaped, she'd be poorly prepared for the weather. *God, please let me find her in time.*

Nathaniel and Sir John made their way back to the horses.

"They can't be that far ahead of us. Want me to pursue?" Sir John said.

Nathaniel nodded. "If I don't find her, I'll catch up with you. I suspect he'll contact us once he's in Lancaster. He'll want his money." He mounted his own horse.

"When do you want to meet up?"

Nathaniel turned his horse toward home. "Find a place to spend the night. We'll catch up tomorrow."

"All right. Good luck," Sir John said.

"You too. Be careful. We know Worth is armed."

Nathaniel shook with fear. She could be anywhere out in the snow. She could be disoriented or already dead from cold. Fear gripped him as he urged his horse down the road. He shouted Anne's name over and over until his voice was hoarse.

He stayed to the main road, afraid that if he veered off it, he'd be lost. *Damn lack of direction.* Nathaniel couldn't fail Anne now. He had to find her.

About twenty minutes later, he spotted her on the side of the road. He pulled the horse to a stop and dismounted.

"Anne!" Relief had him trembling. "Anne!"

Her lips were blue and her teeth were chattering. "Nathaniel."

"We need to get you warm." He removed his greatcoat and wrapped it around her. "Anne, sweetheart, I need your help to get you up on the horse."

"So cold. So tired."

"I know, love, but you have to get on the horse. Can you do that?" She could barely keep her eyes open.

"Nathaniel? You came?"

"Yes, love." He kissed her. Her lips were like ice. "Where else would I be?" She was so cold. He rubbed his hands up and down her arms, trying to warm her up.

"I knew you would come."

"I'm going to put you on the horse. You'll need to hold on while I mount behind you. Can you do that?" She nodded. He lifted her into the saddle and she grabbed the horn. He mounted behind her and took the reins. "Where's your bonnet?"

"In the carriage." Her words were slurred. "So sleepy."

"No sleeping, Anne. Fight it. You'll be warm soon. We are almost at the inn." He nudged the horse into a gallop, holding Anne tight. They pulled to a stop at a small inn just minutes later.

"I was so close," Anne murmured.

"Yes, you were." Nathaniel motioned to a groom at the inn. "Can you help my wife?" He handed her down to him, then dismounted. He took Anne from the man's arms. "Thank you."

"I can walk," she protested.

Nathaniel set her down but didn't release her. He could feel her shivering. He quickly got a room and ordered a bath and food. All the while she shivered against him. Her hair was wet under his chin.

He ushered her into the room and closed the door. "We need to get you out of these wet clothes."

She tried to unbutton her cloak, but couldn't make her fingers do anything. "I can't."

"I know, love." He removed his coat and her wet cloak. Next was her spencer. He tossed it into a wet pile.

"I have to wear that tomorrow."

"I'll deal with it after we get you beneath the blankets." He bent and removed her half boots. He reached under her skirts and pulled off her stockings. He turned her and unlaced her dress. She was still shivering violently.

"My feet hurt."

"Good. It means the feeling is coming back." A knock sounded on the door. He wrapped Anne in a blanket and answered. A tub was brought in, along with buckets of steaming water. Food and hot tea followed. Nathaniel thanked the staff and then closed and locked the door. He turned back to Anne and found her staring at him with wide eyes. "What?"

She blushed.

"Anne, don't tell me you are embarrassed. We've been together before."

"But not in the light."

He looked down at his feet, fighting a laugh. She must be feeling better to be feeling so bashful. "I'm not leaving you alone."

"Turn your back?"

"Fine. Let me finish unlacing you first." She turned and allowed him to unlace her dress and then her stays.

"What am I to put on?"

He hadn't thought of that. "Is your chemise dry? Wrap up in the blanket. When did you last eat?"

She shook her head. "I can't eat anything."

Nathaniel gently cupped her face. He didn't want to ask the question, but he needed to know. If Worth had abused her, the man was dead. "Did he hurt you?"

"Another knock on the head."

"Show me."

She motioned behind her ear. He gently touched the area and she winced. There was no blood, just a knot. "Time for your bath."

He turned his back and listened as she got into the tub. She groaned as the hot water hit her cold limbs. "It hurts?"

"Yes."

Nathaniel turned his back on Anne while she was in the tub. He moved to the small table where the food had been placed. He poured a cup of tea and added sugar, trying to take his mind off the sounds she was making in the tub.

He was never letting her go. She could protest all she wanted, refuse his proposals for the next year. He didn't care. She was his. Finally he heard the rustling of fabric behind him. "Do you need any help?"

"No. Thank you." Her voice was soft. "You can turn around now."

He turned and found her in her chemise and a blanket that she struggled to keep around her.

"Come sit by the fire," he said.

Anne took the seat nearest the fire and he handed her a cup of extra-sweet tea. She sipped it, then closed her eyes and sighed.

"This is delicious."

"Anne, it's time to tell me what happened."

Anne let the warmth of the fire soak into her bones. It felt so good to be warm and dry. She couldn't take her eyes off of Nathaniel. He'd saved her again.

"Try to eat something." Nathaniel placed some bread and cheese on a plate and pushed it toward her.

She set down her cup and nibbled at the food. The warmth of the fire and the bath were working their magic. Her eyes were growing heavy. "Thank you for coming for me, Nathaniel."

"What happened?"

She shook her head, feeling foolish. "I was an idiot about all of it. Mr. Worth was behind the whole thing. He arranged it all as if it were some big joke."

"How would he know you'd be there at that particular time?"

"I walk there every afternoon to escape the house. If he was following me, he'd have known that."

Nathaniel studied her face. "Your brother said Worth was playing deep in Town."

"Mr. Worth wanted the jewels."

"You said Jones hit you."

She frowned. "It was Mr. Jones who hit me at the cottage. Everyone wants some nonexistent jewels."

"If Worth was behind the wish, why make a fool of himself at church?"

"He did it on purpose to embarrass me and to make me believe in the wish. I feel so foolish for not believing you."

"Then you believe me when I tell you I want to marry you. No hiding behind the wish now." He stood up and pulled her into his arms.

"Yes. I believe you, Nathaniel." Anne snuggled into his embrace. She slipped her hands beneath the fabric of his shirt to run them against the smooth skin of his back. She suddenly felt free to love him, to marry him.

Nathaniel stiffened as her fingers grazed his skin. "Don't start something you don't want to finish."

"It's time to finish it. I want you."

He stood perfectly still. "I won't be able to stop this time, Anne. If you'd rather wait until we are wed—"

Anne stood on the tips of her toes and kissed him. She traced his lips with her tongue, begging him to deepen the kiss. Her heart thumped hard in her chest. She felt weightless, relieved of the stress caused by her belief in the wish.

Nathaniel pulled her tightly against him. The blanket dropped to the floor as he lifted her and carried her to the bed. He tossed her down on the bed and pulled his shirt off. "You'd better be sure. Because I've been waiting a long time for this."

"No more waiting." Anne looped her arms around his shoulders as his mouth trailed down her neck. She felt his hands pull her chemise down her body. She ran her hands through the hair on his chest and circled his nipples with her fingers.

The feel of her breasts against his chest had him gasping. Nathaniel took her mouth in a deep, tongue-swirling kiss. Never in his life did he think he'd have trouble holding on to his control, but Anne was pulling him closer to the edge with the arching of her back and her restless legs.

He needed to slow things down. She was a virgin. She would be his wife, and while they'd done a great deal already, he wanted this first moment together to be perfect.

Nathaniel caught her hands to still their wandering before he completely lost control. He sucked her nipple into his mouth before giving it a light nip.

Anne gasped. She couldn't control her movements as she pressed against his warm skin. His mouth trailed down her stomach and tongued her navel. She giggled and pulled away from him.

"Ticklish? That's good to know," he growled.

Anne wrapped her hands in his hair as he kissed her mound tenderly. Her body bowed to meet his mouth.

"No more," she begged.

"Yes, more." He grinned up at her. "Sweetheart, there is so much more." Her skin was like satin, sweet and smooth. He wanted to taste her everywhere. Her scent filled his head as he bent down to kiss her sex, and licked.

He grasped her hips to hold her still while he delved deeper. He slipped one finger inside her. *Damn, she is tight.* He slipped in another finger and teased the nub of nerves until she quivered.

"Nathaniel?"

"Take your pleasure, Anne." He fingered her and kissed her until she came against his mouth.

Nathaniel inched his lips up her body again, gently caressing her damp skin, then her breasts, pulling on each one until she roused again. Her skin was dewy and flushed, her eyes slumberous.

"More?" he asked.

She smiled and pulled his mouth to hers. She kissed him deeply, rubbing her tongue against his, until he groaned and ravished her mouth.

"All," Anne whispered against Nathaniel's mouth. Her hands found the buttons at his waist and released him. "But without these."

Nathaniel stood and removed his breeches. He blew out the candle, letting the firelight fill the room with shadows. He eased into the bed and pulled Anne into his arms.

He groaned as her soft skin touched his. He buried his face in her neck, kissing the skin behind her ear gently. Her scent filled his senses and overwhelmed him.

Nathaniel was in unknown territory. All he knew about virgins was that it would hurt. Hurting Anne was the last thing he wanted to do. He moved his mouth slowly down to the base of her neck. He could feel her pulse racing.

His hand moved between her legs. She was so wet, so ready for him that he almost lost it right there. He lifted himself over her, his cock positioned at her entrance. "Anne, love, this might hurt."

She responded with a deep kiss. When she nipped his bottom lip with her teeth, he nearly lost his mind. He captured her mouth as he slowly sank into her, inch by inch. She was so damn tight. It was heaven.

Discomfort and pain pulled Anne out of her daze of passion. She squirmed against Nathaniel, trying to pull away.

"Sweetheart, don't move," he whispered against her neck.

"I don't think this is right, Nathaniel." Tears filled her eyes as he pushed deeper. "It hurts."

"Love, I'm sorry." He kissed the tears from her face. "Give it a few minutes." He trailed his lips down her neck, savoring her skin before finding her mouth again.

Anne felt full, stretched beyond comfort. "Is it over?"

"Not yet, love."

Anne let him kiss her, and she kissed him back. Slowly she started to feel a bit of the desire she'd felt earlier. She felt his hand touch her where they were joined and a jolt went through her.

Nathaniel groaned as she tightened around him. He slowly pulled back and thrust again, watching her face for signs of pain. She was so tight he wasn't sure he could hold on much longer. He kissed the tips of her breasts.

Anne felt as if she were flying apart. She had no choice but to move in tandem with Nathaniel. The more she moved, the more she felt. She gasped as he nipped at her breast. She wrapped her legs around him and held on, letting the passion carry her where it would. Nathaniel plunged deep and she cried out.

Nathaniel gave a shout as Anne climaxed around him, squeezing him tighter. He collapsed against her, drained. She pushed against him and he rolled off her and pulled her into his arms. "Are you all right?"

She smiled and kissed his chest. "Yes."

Nathaniel rose from the bed to get a wet cloth. He came back and tenderly took care of Anne.

"Don't," she said and tried to sneak under the covers.

"This will ease the pain, Anne." He tossed the cloth on the floor and climbed into the bed, pulling her into his arms. He felt sated to his toes, and tired as well.

"Sleep. We have a long day ahead of us tomorrow."

It was late in the day when Anne woke. She was alone in the bed, but the linens still bore Nathaniel's imprint. The sheets were still warm. She stretched and groaned due to the various aches in places that had never ached before. She sat up in bed.

Nathaniel was gone. He had probably gone to get tea. She threw back the covers and quickly pulled on her chemise. She moved across the room to where her clothes were laid out to dry. She shook out her dress; it was wrinkled beyond repair, but still wearable. She shook it again and heard a clanging noise.

Frowning, she checked the pockets and pulled out a pouch. She'd completely forgotten about finding it among the rubble of the cottage.

She moved back to the bed and crawled under the covers for warmth. She opened the pouch and dumped the contents on the bed. Rubies and diamonds twinkled in the early morning light. "Bloody hell."

"Such language so early in the morning," Nathaniel said, coming into the room. "The snow is melted and I've made arrangements for a carriage home. John has arrived here as well. I've spoken to him."

"John is here?"

"Apparently, John found Worth just a few miles from us. He spent the night here in the inn."

"Mr. Worth?"

"Trussed up in one of the private rooms."

"It couldn't have been that easy. Worth wanted his money," Anne said.

"John found the carriage in a ditch. The coachman ran off. Worth waved his gun around but apparently your brother is a better shot than I thought."

"My brother? John? Did he kill him?"

"No, Worth is facing a worse fate. John wants him turned over to Worth's creditors. Worth will face the magistrate first, for taking you." Nathaniel kissed her. "You won't have to worry about Mr. Worth again."

"Look what I found at the cottage!" she said, holding up the ruby necklace.

"Where did you get that?"

"I found it in the rubble in a metal box. I'd never seen it before. It was in the bottom of my trunk, underneath some old books. Mama was always putting things away for my wedding. There were some bits of embroidery and lace she made while she was ill. She must have wrapped them around the box and tucked it into the trunk."

"Are they your mother's jewels?"

"Yes." Anne felt lighter than air. "This means no more scrimping. I can give Sophia and Juliet a Season. I can rent something nice in Bath."

Nathaniel was quiet. He picked up a bracelet and earrings and held them up in the light. "These are beautiful. Why haven't you found them before now?"

"I couldn't bear to look at them. She made those pretty things right before she died. I just buried them deep." All of their problems were solved, thanks to her mother. "Here's another necklace with sapphires and diamonds. And another with emeralds."

"You have a fortune there."

"Isn't it wonderful?" She placed the jewels back into the pouch and tied it closed.

"I can't wait to tell my sisters!" She pulled on her petticoats and stockings. She turned her back to Nathaniel. "Can you help me with my stays?"

"Of course." He quickly laced her up, then helped her on with her dress.

"Should we get John?" she asked.

Nathaniel nodded and pulled on his coat.

Anne studied him. "Are you all right? You're very quiet."

"I'm fine." He held the door for her and then led the way downstairs.

They met John in the front room and had breakfast together. Anne felt better than she had in months. It was as if a weight was lifted from her shoulders.

"I can't believe how free I feel," she said as they finished their meal.

John looked over at Nathaniel, who shook his head.

"That's wonderful, Anne. I'm glad capturing Worth put such a smile on your face," John teased.

Anne felt the color heat her face. "It's not that. John, you were right. Mother *did* give me the jewels."

"What?"

"I found them at the cottage in the rubble. I would never have found them if it hadn't been for the fire."

"Them? There's more than the ruby necklace?" John said.

"It's all the jewels Mother brought from France. There are rubies, emeralds, and diamonds." Anne turned to Nathaniel. "Perhaps we should take the jewels to London. I want to get the best price for them."

"I can help you with that," Nathaniel said. "If you want."

"Thank you." She gave him a sunny smile.

John set his cup down. "You intend to sell them?"

"Yes, of course. We need the money, John. This can give us a place to live, and clothes. What would you have me do? It's the answer to our prayers."

John shrugged. "If you say so, but I think you're making a mistake."

Anne laughed. "What mistake? Nathaniel, tell him I'm right to do this."

Nathaniel felt his life getting more and more desolate with each of Anne's smiles. The jewels were exquisite. They would fetch a large sum. Anne wouldn't have to scrimp any longer. Her worries were over. "You should sell them, if you wish."

She didn't need him.

He didn't doubt she still had feelings for him. She wasn't the type of woman who would fall into bed with a man without the benefit of marriage unless her heart was involved. She just hadn't said the words.

Of course, he hadn't either, but he'd shown her by his actions. She couldn't doubt his feelings now.

Nathaniel threw down his napkin and tossed back the last of his tea. "If you're ready, we should leave as soon as possible. I've leased a carriage to take you back to the Lodge."

"I'm ready, but what of Mr. Worth?" Anne said.

"He's with the local magistrate until he can be brought before a judge." Nathaniel led them to the carriage and seated her and John inside.

"I'm going to ride," Nathaniel said, giving Anne a long look. He shut the carriage door with a snap.

Anne leaned back against the squabs with a frown. "What's wrong with him?"

"I don't know. Perhaps you are more excited about finding your mother's jewels than you are about marrying Nathaniel."

"He hasn't asked."

"Anne, how many times has he asked you over the course of the last few weeks?"

"But that was the spell. The fairy wish." *But wait—Mr. Worth said there had been no wish, that it had all been in her head.* She stared out the window and watched Nathaniel on his horse, looking so alone.

"Was it really? I always thought he was beneath you in social standing. You are the daughter of a baronet. He's the grandson of a knight. Now I'm not so sure *you* are worthy of *him*."

Pain zinged through her. "John!" Her emotions were a jumble. So much had happened over the last twenty-four hours. She'd gone from total despair to hope.

Nathaniel had been a huge part of that. He'd been tender, caring. He'd stirred feelings inside her she hadn't known she was capable of.

He had been happy this morning until he saw the jewels. Until she went on and on about what she and her sisters would do with the money. "Oh."

John raised an eyebrow. "He has gone above and beyond what is called for in a suitor, Anne. And I don't deserve the help he's providing me."

"I know about the debts."

"It's not just that." John looked out the window. "I'm leaving for India in a few weeks. I'm going to look into investments for him there, to work off my debt."

"India? So far away?"

"Yes. I need to get away from London, from the temptation of gambling. This is a great opportunity for me, Anne. I had hoped that with you marrying Nathaniel, you girls would be taken care of. Men don't always say how they feel, Anne. You have to weigh a man's feelings by his actions."

"You think he loves me?"

John nodded. "When you were taken, he went still. He was icy calm. But his eyes burned. It was clear that someone he cared deeply about was in danger."

Anne didn't know what to say. She looked out the carriage window at Nathaniel.

"Anne, why do always question me? Marry him. If you don't you'll be ruined and so will both your sisters."

"John, I won't force him."

"I don't think you'll have to force him, but you might have to convince him that you *want* to marry him. He would let you go if he thought it was what you wanted."

"He loves me," she whispered, then smiled. "He loves me!"

"It certainly looks that way to me."

Chapter Twenty-One

The carriage arrived at the Lodge just hours later. The sun had melted most of the light snowfall; only those patches in the shade remained. Anne stepped out of the carriage and was suddenly surrounded by her sisters. She spotted Nathaniel watching the reunion, his face shuttered.

Juliet hugged her close. "Anne! Are you all right?"

"What happened to Mr. Worth?" Sophia asked.

"He's with the magistrate. And I'm fine. Nathaniel got there in time." Anne smiled over at him. He dismounted and led his horse to the stables, ignoring her. Her shoulders slumped.

"Anne, what's happened?" Sophia whispered. "I thought you would have made up by now."

"Come inside and I'll tell you. I have great news," Anne said in a low voice. She led Sophia and Juliet into the house.

Lady Danford was waiting in the entrance hall. "Anne! You've come back to us." She enveloped Anne in her arms. "I was so worried."

"I'm fine, thanks to Nathaniel and John."

"Well, upstairs with you. Change your clothes and rest. You've earned it."

"Thank you, ma'am." Anne led her sisters to her room. Once the door was closed she reached for the pouch in her pocket. "Look what I found at the cottage." She opened the bag and dumped the contents on the bed.

"It's Mother's jewelry!" Sophia whispered. "Where did you find it?"

"In the rubble of the cottage, right before Mr. Worth kidnapped me." Anne spread the jewels out on the bed. "I hid the pouch in my pocket."

"There's a fortune here," Juliet said with awe.

"We can go to Bath or London. You can both have a Season in Town if that's what you want. No more scrimping and saving. No more being a companion. We are free." Anne tried to put as much enthusiasm in her voice as she could without it sounding false. The truth was that she didn't want Bath or London anymore. Not without Nathaniel.

Sophia set the ruby necklace down. "Is this what you want, Anne? That we all go away together?"

Anne looked away from the question in Sophia's eyes. "It's the opportunity we've wanted."

"What about Nathaniel?" Juliet asked. "I rather thought you'd marry him."

Anne was quiet as she gathered up the jewels and placed them back into the velvet pouch. "He hasn't asked again." *And isn't likely to.* She wished he'd talk to her. Tell her what was going through his head. Everything had been fine until she showed him the jewels.

"What happened last night?" Sophia asked. "You didn't reject him again, did you?"

Anne gave Sophia a pointed look, but said nothing.

"Juliet, time to go," Sophia said, grabbing her arm to help her to the door.

"Why do you get to stay?" Juliet protested.

"Because I'm older."

Juliet stood and stomped her way to the door. "It's not fair!"

"Life's not fair," Sophia said as she tried to push Juliet out the door.

"Juliet can stay," Anne said. "She's going to hear most of it anyway when the gossips get hold of it."

Juliet stuck her tongue out at her sister and perched on the bed. "Tell all, Anne. Don't leave a single thing out."

Anne blushed. "There isn't much to tell. I escaped Mr. Worth. Nathaniel found me on the side of the road. It was snowing and so cold."

Sophia looked at her expectantly. "And?"

"He took me to an inn for the night."

"And?" Juliet said, waggling her eyebrows.

"Juliet!" Anne felt the color creep into her face. "And nothing"

"I'm young, not mad, Anne."

"Perhaps you should check those books she's always got her face buried in," Sophia said. "So did he propose? Again?"

Anne's face fell. "No. I think I've ruined everything."

Sophia squeezed Anne's hand. "He loves you."

"I've hurt him, continuously. I was so excited about finding the jewels and what it would mean for you and Juliet, I didn't think about how it would make him feel."

"But you let him, uh, I mean, he was with you all night, yes?" Sophia said.

"Yes."

"What was it like? Did it hurt?" Juliet asked.

Anne's face flamed. "It was—I don't know how to express it. He was . . . tender."

Sophia hugged her. "He'll come around. You'll see. He just needs time."

"I hope so."

"Perhaps you should prod him. Show a little initiative. Propose to him," Juliet added.

"I don't know," Anne said. She'd never be brave enough to do that.

"What if you are with child, Anne? You'll have to tell Nathaniel."

Part of her hoped for a baby, but the other part of her dreaded having to tell Nathaniel. What if he went back to London and had no intention of asking her to marry him? Anne rubbed her forehead. Things were such a mess.

"He loves you, Anne. I know it. I've seen how he looks at you. Just give it time," Sophia said.

Anne nodded but looked away. She had ruined it.

Her constant refusals because of the dratted wish and her selfish response to finding the jewels had driven him away.

Nathaniel threw himself into his work. Another packet from London needing his immediate attention had arrived. He barely left the library, even taking trays there instead of eating with the family.

He didn't go to her room either. He wasn't sleeping. He just lay in his bed, staring at the ceiling, wishing she were with him, wrapped around him.

He added another letter to the growing stack on the desk. A half-eaten sandwich sat on a plate beside him. Empty brandy glasses littered the desk.

"Good Lord, it smells in here," Lady Danford said, coming into the room and closing the door behind her. "Has the maid been in to clean?"

"I'm working," Nathaniel said, not looking up. The last thing he wanted was his grandmother's interference.

"Well, then I guess I should leave you alone, except that you need to get out of this room. It has been three days." Lady Danford opened the curtains, bathing the room in light. "That's better." She turned back to him. "You look like hell. When was the last time you slept? Bathed? Had a decent meal like a decent person?"

Nathaniel refused to look up at her. He scanned the letter in front of him. "I have a great deal of work to do."

"Son, just ask her to marry you."

He carefully set down the quill, blotted the page before him and set it aside. Finally, he looked up. "For the first time in Anne Townsend's life, she has the freedom she desires. She doesn't have to marry for money. She can give her sisters what they all want—a Season. She deserves this freedom."

"That is bloody nonsense. You love her and she you."

"She's never said that."

"Have you?"

"Have I what?"

"Told her you loved her."

He set his jaw, refusing to answer.

"I never took you for an idiot." Lady Danford turned to leave the room. "If you let this one get away, you'll regret it for the rest of your life."

"Thank you, Grandmother."

"Just do me a favor and bathe. And I expect you at dinner tonight. No more hiding in this cave."

"I'm not hiding."

"Aren't you?" she said as she closed the door.

Nathaniel started back on his paperwork only to be interrupted again, this time by Sir John. "Now what?"

"I want to know what you plan to do with my sister," Sir John said. "She's moping around and you are testy."

"This is none of your concern," Nathaniel growled.

"She's my sister. What are your intentions?"

"Sir John, I've already proposed and she has refused."

"But that was before."

"Before?"

"Before she discovered the jewels. Surely, you plan on proposing again."

"I've not decided."

"Look, Matthews, everyone knows how you feel about her. She's obviously in love with you."

How can everyone be so certain she loves me? "How do you know that?"

"You are being a fool, Matthews. She's spent the night in your bed. Do you really think she'd do that without love? She's just not that kind of woman."

"I suggest you drop the subject, Townsend." Nathaniel pulled the papers back in front of him. "Leave now."

"Fine. I'm done, for now, but you'd better decide what you are going to do. The gossip has hit the town in the worst way."

Sir John slammed the door hard enough to rattle the windows. Nathaniel picked up the next letter and his pen, determined to focus on something else. Anything else, but Anne Townsend.

Five minutes later he threw the pen and paper down in disgust and cradled his head in his hands. What was he going to do to fix this? There weren't enough pieces of his heart left after the last three rejections. He just didn't know if he could survive another one, but he didn't think he could live without her, either.

Anne had spent the same three days pacing in front of the library doors while Nathaniel was holed up inside. She missed him. He hadn't come to her room once since they'd returned from her adventure. He wasn't at dinner. He wasn't at lunch.

He never left the bloody library.

Laborers had started to tear down what was left of the cottage. She had walked out to watch, hoping to find something of value to save, but she found nothing.

Nathaniel hadn't come to watch. He didn't come to comfort her. She had stood there all by herself as they carted away her past.

It had been a long five years, but good ones. She and her sisters had survived and now they wouldn't have to scrimp and save.

Fine. We'll all be fine.

She was going to have to find a new way to feel fine now that Nathaniel was avoiding her. The thought of him moving on, of seeing each other only as acquaintances at parties in Town, tore at her heart. Being fine meant coping with the pain of losing him.

"Anne, what are you doing here?" Sophia said, coming upon her in front of the ruins of the cottage.

"I wanted to see if there was anything further to salvage," she said. "There wasn't."

"It's like a piece of our lives is now gone, isn't it?"

"Yes, but think of it. We'll have ball gowns and day dresses," Anne said with a smile that she hoped passed for genuine excitement.

"You don't care about all that nonsense. That doesn't make you happy."

I'll learn to care, damn it. I'll be happy again.

"I think you should go into that library and demand that he make things right," Sophia said.

"I can't do that! What if he said no?"

"What if he said yes? Take a chance on something, Anne."

Anne shook her head. "Has he said when he will leave for London?"

"Neither John nor Tony has mentioned it. He seems to be throwing himself into his work. He needs to make this right! If you're with child, he'll have to make it right."

"If I am, I'll deal with it. I had always planned to live quietly in the country after you and Juliet married."

"You never planned to marry?"

"I really didn't expect to be asked."

"He's asked you several times and you've refused him. He may not ask again."

"I wouldn't blame him. I have treated him terribly, and all because of that stupid wish. Who knew Cecil Worth had orchestrated the whole thing."

"What does it matter, Anne?" Sophia took her arm and led her toward the woods. "I cannot believe you would throw love away as if it were rubbish." Sophia picked up a stick and toyed with it. She looked up at the sky. "We'll have snow again before long. Nathaniel will have to leave soon. Do you really want that?"

Anne's time was running out. "No."

Sophia glared at her sister. "Think hard, Anne, about what you really want. Nathaniel Matthews loves you. He was frantic when he found you gone."

"He's never said that."

"You are an idiot. A man may spout poetry, sing the praises of your beauty, and yet have as little feeling for you as this twig."

Anne laughed. "You are talking about Tony."

"Such a grand passion that turned out to be. I thought he was my ticket out of Beetham. Thank God you found the jewels."

"I imagine Juliet is relieved. She's rather fond of him. So you've spoken with Tony?"

"Yes. We both agreed that we are ill suited to each other. I miss his attentions, but I'm glad for it."

"There is someone out there for you, I'm sure of it."

"I plan on cutting a swath through London before I settle. I'm so looking forward to our time in society. I'm sick of the country," Sophia said with a smile.

"Lady Danford insists we stay with her in Town."

"She will know best how to present us to society."

Anne felt her eyes well. "I wish he'd talk to me. Tell me."

"I suggest you take your walk up to the Fairy Steps and see what the fairies tell you. Perhaps you can get a wish to bring him up to scratch."

"Magic doesn't exist, but some time to myself would be welcome. It's been so hectic of late."

"Go. I'll make excuses for you at tea."

Anne found herself following the old path through the woods to the steps. At the base she looked up. The sky and stone were the same gray color. Autumn was gone, along with its bright colors. Winter, with its heavy skies and snow, tinted the landscape like a charcoal drawing.

She loved these woods so much. They had listened to her hopes and dreams for five years now.

The bare trees waved in the cold breeze that cut through the heavy wool of her cloak. She climbed the steps carefully, holding on to the sides. There was no point now risking life and limb to climb them.

Reaching the top, she sat on a stone, wrapping her cloak around her. The village of Beetham lay before her. Smoke rose from the chimneys and scented the air.

Fairies and magic were the stuff of children. Anne had thought herself so mature, but she had to admit to being romantic, a part of her nature she hadn't known existed.

She closed her eyes, remembering Nathaniel's face as he lay sleeping beside her. She could watch him sleep for hours, and had, afraid he would suddenly wake up and decide that he didn't want her.

She had wasted an opportunity for love because she couldn't believe that someone like him would want her. Why shouldn't he? There wasn't anything wrong with her.

As she thought of their time together, she realized that Nathaniel was trying to make her see the person he saw. Anne had gotten so comfortable with being the plain sister.

But that was changing. He had changed her. Nathaniel had shown her that she was worth so much more, that she deserved to be loved. She squeezed her eyes shut.

She'd thrown it all away.

She wished the damn fairy would show up again. This time she'd wish for a proposal and would be ready with a different answer when it came.

Nathaniel stared out the window. He had watched Anne walk to the cottage alone, then saw Sophia follow. The cottage was being torn down that afternoon. He had expected her to be there, to watch the end of this phase of her life.

He spotted Sophia coming back from the woods alone. She waved at him. He raised a hand and hurriedly unlatched the library door to let her in.

"Where is Anne?" He tried to keep emotion from his voice, but it crept in anyway.

"At the Fairy Steps, I suspect."

"They have finished at the cottage?" When Sophia nodded, he hesitated, then continued. "How did Anne handle it?"

"She is excited that we are to have a Season and for the change that is occurring. She is a bit sad to lose the cottage. Of all of us, she loved the country the most."

"So she would prefer to stay here?" He had always wondered if that were the case with Anne. *If she hates London, how would we get along?*

"You'll have to ask her that question yourself. Go to her, Nathaniel. Ask her again."

"I couldn't survive another negative response," Nathaniel said. "If she doesn't love me—"

"You two are a pair, both of you whining that the other one doesn't love you. Good Lord, man! Open your eyes. Anne loves you. She just lacks the confidence to believe that you love her. A woman needs to hear the words."

Nathaniel hesitated still. Could he subject himself to that pain again?

"Just go. Climb the steps for her and see if magic is in the air." Sophia pushed him out the door.

He clasped Sophia's hand. "Thank you."

"Don't come back without a fiancée this time," Sophia said as he left.

Nathaniel grabbed a coat, his hat, and gloves and walked with purpose through the woods. *No more taking no for an answer. The woman is going to marry me, or else.*

He stopped at the edge of the woods, right before the steps. Anne sat at the top, looking out at Beetham, lost in thought. She looked lovely, yet sad. Dark circles under her eyes told him she hadn't been sleeping well either. They were both fools to let an argument get in the way of their feelings.

He stepped to the edge of the stone steps.

"Excuse me, miss—I seem to have lost my way."

Anne looked down at him in shock. "Where are you going, sir?"

"I heard a fable about these steps." He climbed the first few steps toward her, hat in hand. "If I climb them I will be granted a wish."

Anne's eyes filled with tears. "It's just a fable, sir. There is no magic."

A breeze caught Nathaniel by surprise, pushing against his back and urging him forward. It danced around the skirts of Anne's dark blue dress. "I don't know. It seems a magical place." He climbed a few more steps.

"And you believe in magic?" she asked.

"I didn't until I met a girl several weeks ago who took my breath away. She was dressed in an old wool dress but had stars in her eyes. She believed."

"She's not sure she can believe any longer."

He moved closer to her. "Why doubt now?"

"Cecil Worth said—"

"Worth was a fool, Anne. Don't let him take away the magic of what we have." He had almost reached her, was almost close enough to pull her into his arms and kiss the tears from her face.

Hope welled up in him.

Anne stood as he approached. "If you were granted a wish, what would you wish for?"

"I'd wish for a way to ask you to marry me so that you wouldn't refuse." He reached the top step and smiled down at her. He took her hand and pressed his lips to her cold fingers. "To ask in such a way as to fully convey how much I love you."

Anne smiled at him. "You love me?"

"More than my life. Marry me?"

"Yes."

A strange voice spoke from somewhere below them.

"Foolish human. You can't dabble with magic and love."

Nathaniel looked at Anne. "Did you hear that?"

"Hear what?" She wrapped her arms around his neck and pressed herself against him.

"That voice. It's an odd little voice." He looked around them and saw no one.

"You did climb the steps without touching. You get a wish."

Nathaniel hugged her close. "I only want you, Anne, with me forever. Nothing else matters."

"But the wish—"

"I'm thankful for the wish. It broke through your shell and allowed the world to see the real you. For me to see the real you. I love you, Anne."

She closed her eyes, savoring his words.

"Please tell me how you feel."

She opened her eyes, eyes filled with love. "I love you, Nathaniel. I don't know how I managed to get so very lucky, but I don't care."

"I'm the lucky one." He bent his head and kissed her.

"Foolish human—make a wish and be gone."

Nathaniel lifted his head. "I wish us to be happy forever."

"Nathaniel, no one can wish for that!"

"Done!" said the voice.

The wind picked up and whirled around Anne and Nathaniel, bringing with it leaves and twigs and pushing them closer together.

"See," said Nathaniel, "even the fairies agree. We belong together."

Epilogue

It was another cold winter's day. Mrs. Anne Matthews stood at the top of the Fairy Steps looking down at Beetham. She placed a hand over her stomach where her and Nathaniel's child grew. They had married not long after that magical day at the Fairy Steps.

Lady Danford had been delighted and invited the whole village to the wedding breakfast. Anne had worn the beautiful ball gown that she'd first worn at Lady Danford's assembly. The maids were able to restore it to its original beauty.

Juliet and Sophia had taken London by storm, just as Anne had predicted. It was clear that Juliet was in love with Tony. Sophia had yet to meet anyone who caught her fancy. John was off to India to make his fortune, with support from Nathaniel.

Anne hadn't told Nathaniel of the baby yet. She wanted to wait until they were in Beetham again, surrounded by family at the Lodge.

"I knew you couldn't resist coming out here," Nathaniel said, quickly coming up the steps behind Anne. He wrapped his arms around her and pulled her close. "Are you cold, love?"

"No." She smiled. "I just needed to stretch my legs."

"It is a long carriage ride from London. You were so sick. Are you sure you should be rambling through the woods instead of resting?"

"I'm fine. Very fine." She turned in his arms and stood on tiptoe to kiss him. "I have something to tell you. A surprise."

He frowned. "I don't really care for surprises, Anne."

"You'll like this one." She whispered, "I'm expecting your child."

He whooped and whirled her around, then pulled her away from the steps. "You shouldn't stand so close to the edge."

"Then you are happy?"

"Anne, no one could make me happier." He kissed her deeply. "I love you so much."

"I love you more." She laughed and snuggled back into his arms. "I wish Juliet and Sophia could have this."

"They will get their chance, love. It just takes time."

"Or magic."

The romantic trials and tribulations of the Townsend sisters
continue in Eileen Richards's

AN HONORABLE WISH

Keep reading for a special sneak preview.

A Lyrical e-book on sale November 2015!

Chapter One

He had finally lived up to his brother Nathaniel's low expectations of him.

Tony Matthews stared through the veil of newly budded leaves at the village of Beetham below. The cold stone of the Fairy Steps seeped into his bones from his perch at the top. Spring fought against the winter chill in the air and in the faint green of the grass were the blooms of early flowers. New life.

God, how he wanted a new life, a different direction.

What had seemed like a good idea at the time, in hindsight was now a nightmare.

Usually, the rolling hills of the southern portion of this part of England soothed Tony's soul unlike any other place. The restlessness inside him eased with each breath of the fresh, clean air.

Not this time. This time he was trapped in his own stupid arrogance. This time he'd matched his father's unfortunate legacy.

He'd taken a man's estate in a card game. A game he wasn't even planning to play except for too much alcohol-fueled bluster and a dare from a friend. He'd played and lost a fortune, then played again and won an estate.

The man, Chelsworth, ended up being a neighbor of his brother's. Honor and pride wouldn't let Chelsworth back away from the bet. No, the man signed away his estate and his livelihood to Tony.

Tony hadn't wanted to take it. The alcoholic stupor had started to wear off with the realization that he'd stepped into his father's shoes. Only this time he was on the winning side. Tony had sunk to the lowest depths of vile.

Tony's brother, Nathaniel, was never going to forgive him. Hell, he'd probably be thrown out of the family and left to his own devices.

At least he had money. He also had the reputation of a rake and a gambler, which were well deserved at this point.

But it wasn't who Tony really was. His entire life was an act. One he didn't want to maintain any longer.

The fact that it took no effort to become this vile man scared the hell out of Tony. When he looked in the mirror, he didn't know whom he saw anymore.

He wanted the house, but not this way. The estate must be in a bad way already, given that its previous owner was willing to wager it in a card game. If it was making any living at all, Chelsworth would not have been at the tables.

Unless Chelsworth was sick with gambling. Tony knew that sickness existed. Hell, even his sister-in-law's brother was addicted to gambling, always pushing for that next win.

Tony felt he could walk away from the games and not look back. He was sure of it. At least on most days. His problem was infinitely more difficult. He needed a way to repair the mistakes he'd made without alerting his brother. Tony could not disappoint him again.

Nathaniel was a man of high regard in Beetham and in Town. His business prowess was legendary. Nathaniel had a lovely wife, a child, a house, and the respect of his peers. He had everything that Tony wanted but hadn't been able to achieve.

And now Tony had lived up to his brother's greatest fear: that he'd become their father.

Hence the trip to Beetham. Tony needed to convince Chelsworth that he meant to tear up the vowels. He would not take a man's livelihood. He would not allow gambling to define him as a man.

Chelsworth had to be desperate. Tony could offer to buy the estate. He had wanted to invest in property. He wanted to do something with his life other than what he was doing, which was drinking and gambling.

Tony pulled in a breath of the clean, fresh country air. He'd forgotten what clean air smelled like. He'd forgotten what the wild space of the Lake District felt like. Unconstrained. Open.

No more choking on the London air. No more buildings closing in on him as he walked narrow streets. No more gaming hells. No more lies. No more hiding.

Tony wanted what Nathaniel had: a life of honor and respect. Honor had been missing from his life for a very long time, if it had ever existed. The only respect Tony had gained was winning more than losing in the hells of London. He wanted more. He wanted Nathaniel's respect.

Leaves danced as a cold wind whirled around him. Suddenly, a woman cackled in the distance. Tony frowned and looked around for the origin of the voice. No one was there. The cackling grew louder as the leaves spiraled up around him, pulling at his coat, knocking his hat to the ground. He moved to catch it before it blew down the steps.

"What the hell?"

A twig snapped behind him. Tony turned and saw Juliet Townsend, his sister-in-law's sister, tiptoeing past him at the edge of the woods.

She was dressed as a boy.

"Miss Juliet, up to your hoyden ways again, I see," Tony said.

She huffed indignantly and kicked at the weeds beneath her feet. Her boots were so scuffed that they seemed to flop about on her feet. She was covered in dirt. Her dark brown hair was tucked under an old hat that had been pulled down low over her face.

Tony raised one eyebrow. "Hiding from someone?"

Juliet turned and finally faced him, resigned. "You weren't supposed to see me or recognize me."

"Why?" Tony moved closer to her. She was dressed in brown breeches that were a tad too tight around her hips and a rough linen shirt and waistcoat. "Whom have you stolen that outfit from? One of the groomsmen?"

She pushed her spectacles back on her face. No one could do stubborn like Juliet Townsend. "Aren't you supposed to be in London?"

"I asked you first."

She flounced toward him and plopped down at the edge of the steps. "If you must know, I'm helping a friend."

"Dressed as a boy? Have you lost your senses?"

Juliet was different from her sisters. She wasn't afraid to take up a cause and see it through. Tony sat down next to her on the stone steps. "Who is this friend?"

She glowered at him. "You must swear to not tell a soul."

"If your sister Anne disapproves, it must be bad."

"What would be the point of it, if it weren't?"

"One day, Miss Juliet, your wild ways are going to get you into trouble."

Juliet looked out across the trees. "You are probably right. My friend, Penelope Williams, and her family are tenants of the Horneswood estate nearby. Her father was in a serious accident that has left him disfigured."

"She is far beneath you, Miss Juliet."

She glared at him. "I don't care about that. Penelope is a dear, and I have found that I enjoy helping them work the land."

"What do you know of farming?"

"A great deal more than you, I'd wager. I've read at least three books on the subject."

"You have me there. The last time I read a tome on agriculture, I was having trouble falling asleep."

"You are too wicked, Mr. Matthews." Juliet rested her arms on her knees. "Horneswood's land steward is threatening to have them evicted. They have nowhere else to go. Penelope and her brother may end up working in a factory in Lancaster, or worse."

"There's nothing wrong with factory work, Miss Juliet. It puts a roof over one's head. It might be a better fate than the workhouse."

"I knew you wouldn't understand." She stood and dusted off her pants, drawing Tony's attention to her nicely rounded bottom.

Tony had no idea that breeches would look this good on a woman. Perhaps they should become fashion. He pulled himself up and started down the stairs. "Allow me to escort you home."

Juliet stared at his horse, tethered at the bottom of the steps. "Thank you, no. I prefer to walk. I'm inappropriately dressed. If my sister sees me, I'll not be allowed to call on Penelope again." Juliet skirted around Tony toward the path through the woods.

"How do you plan on avoiding her? Sneak in through the kitchens?"

Juliet smiled widely. "That's a splendid idea."

"Miss Juliet, there is no way I'm letting you go through those woods unaccompanied."

"I walk through these woods daily. I'm safe enough."

"And if you're seen? Word would reach Anne before you could even reach the kitchen door. Enough nonsense. I'll see you home."

She looked at the horse and shook her head. "He's huge."

"He's a horse," Tony said. "You've been around horses all your life."

"If I must." She stomped down the narrow stairs. He followed her down, enjoying the view of her swinging hips.

"If we are seen together, I'll be in great peril of ruining my reputation," said Juliet.

"If we are seen, you'll be chastised for being so inappropriately attired," he retorted. "And not because you are in my company. We are practically brother and sister."

Tony almost ran into her as she abruptly turned around.

"Your brother is married to my sister. That does not make us family."

Tony gripped Juliet's arms to keep her from falling backwards down the stairs. Her eyes were pools of dark chocolate as she stared up at him through the lenses of her glasses.

"Please, sir, release me."

"I wouldn't want to have you take a tumble down the stairs. How shall I explain it to your sister?" He cleared his throat and released her.

Juliet continued down the steps, her hands finding purchase in the stone walls. She stumbled to a stop at the bottom. "I will not get on that horse."

"Why not?"

Juliet didn't answer, but rather started walking down the lane toward the Lodge.

Stubborn woman.

He grabbed the reins of the horse and rushed to catch up with her. "It's just about tea time and the horse can get us to the house faster."

"The house is barely a mile away. Hardly worth troubling the horse, if you ask me."

"You are afraid of him? I didn't think you were afraid of anything."

"Don't be silly, everyone has fears." Juliet picked up her pace, the loose boots making a clumping sound with each step. "We had no notice that you were coming home, Mr. Matthews."

Tony shrugged. "The Season was over. I thought it time."

"Beetham is a quiet village. Will you be able to bear being away from the gaming tables while you are here?" There was a sneer in her voice.

"You'd be surprised," he mumbled.

Juliet looked up at him, a questioning look on her face. "Excuse me?"

"It's of little matter."

"We heard about your exploits in Town."

"What have you heard?"

"That you prefer to spend more time in your clubs than you do at home."

He slowed and his horse butted him with his head. "Easy, boy." He rubbed the horse's muzzle. "Juliet, you know better than to listen to gossip."

She started walking again. "Take care that you don't end up penniless like my brother."

Tony winced. If the truth were made known, he would probably lose Juliet's friendship as well.

Juliet's face grew solemn. "Do you think there will come a time, Mr. Matthews, when you'll grow tired of cards?"

"One never knows. It might be sooner than you think."

Juliet glared at Tony. "What do you mean?"

"It's of little consequence." He looked back at his horse, a strange expression on his face.

In the three years Juliet had known Tony Matthews, she sensed that all wasn't what it seemed. Certainly on the surface he was affable, fun, and carefree. But there were hidden depths hinted at in quiet moments like these.

She was never able to crack the façade and see what really lay beneath. She suspected there was a great deal more to the man than the pieces he allowed others to see.

They rounded the bend and approached the park of the Lodge.

Juliet touched his arm. "Mr. Matthews, the only expectations you need to live up to are your own. You do know this."

Tony glanced down at her hand. Juliet felt an odd kind of warmth radiate up her arm.

"Miss Juliet, thank you." His voice was gruff.

"I shall see you at tea."

Juliet sprinted around the house and snuck into the kitchen. She slipped off the too-large boots, leaving them by the door, and crept up the stairs in her stocking feet, avoiding the stairs that she knew creaked.

The clock in the hallway chimed the hour. Juliet moved more quickly down the darkened hallway to her room. She closed the door behind her and changed into a suitable day dress, stashing the breeches and shirt in the bottom of her cupboard.

She looked down at her hands, caked in dirt. Pouring water into a basin, she scrubbed, trying to remove most of the dirt from her nails.

There was a rap on her door. "Juliet? It's time for tea."

"Coming!" She scrubbed faster. Foolish of her to not wear gloves while digging in the dirt. She was going to have to get a proper pair if this kept up.

Juliet's sister Sophia stepped into the room and closed the door behind her. "Did you know that Tony is here? Good heavens, what have you been up to? You are in no state for company."

"Really, Sophia. It is not that bad."

"Very well, but do something with your hair. It is a mess. And come down as quick as you can." Sophia left and closed the door behind her.

Juliet fussed with her hair, looking in the mirror. Tony Matthews never came home unless he had to, usually when he needed money from Nathaniel.

In the three years that Nathaniel and Anne had been married, she worried for Tony. Juliet was well over her infatuation with him, though they remained friends. Gambling was a sickness that ruined men greater than Tony would ever be. It had ruined her brother. It had ruined Tony and Nathaniel's father. It was only a matter of time before it ruined Tony as well.

Eileen Richards's stories are filled with what she loves: snarky humor, love, laughter, and lots of village gossip. She lives in North Carolina with her husband, a greyhound named Honey, and a bunch of exotic fish. Eileen has two grown sons, a fabulous daughter-in-law, and the most beautiful granddaughter. Of course, she is a bit biased.

Visit her on the Web at eileenrichards.wordpress.com.